Sin & Lightning

Also by K.F. Breene

Sin & Lightning

By K.F. Breene

Contact info:
www.kfbreene.com
books@kfbreene.com

Chapter 1

ALEXIS

B RIA WIPED HER mouth and leaned toward me over the small, round café table. "Quit stalling. Finish your wine and let's go. If we leave now, we can get to that psycho rock wielder's lair and back by dark."

"What? No!" Jack pointed at Bria, though she didn't notice because he was dead, a spirit, and unlike me, she couldn't see or hear him. "No way. Nuh-uh. Kieran will go apeshit if you go without him."

I swallowed the last of my tart wine and wiped my mouth with a napkin before leaving it on my finished lunch plate. Bria was right—we needed to get moving. We were in this small town in Montana for one purpose only: to meet the level-five, rock-wielding giant who plagued the nearby mountains. A giant who had killed a Demigod a handful of years ago and then sectioned himself off from society. A giant who wouldn't be swayed by Kieran's considerable charm.

Or so Bria kept telling me. She was convinced I was the one for the job, and Red, Kieran's former assistant and my current bodyguard, agreed with her. In fact, they'd convinced me to participate in their plan to recruit him behind Kieran's back.

"Even if Kieran was the best one to go, he won't be able to get away," I said to Jack, standing. "The leader of this place is on Kieran like stink on a pig. He's only a level five of…" I squinted, trying to remember.

"It doesn't even matter," Bria said, standing with me. "His territory is tiny, he's not a Demigod, he's got no money, and he has to know Kieran's only here to try his hand at that giant. The guy's getting all the face time in while he can. He probably hopes Kieran will lift him out of the slums like a professional Cinderella. It's great for us, because it takes Kieran out of the equation. Come on, walk and talk. Let's go."

I'd told Kieran the advice Harding had given me six months back—bulk up the collection of magical people around you. Fill your new, larger team with the best and brightest you can find, equipped with all different types of magic.

Since Kieran had to stand up to my biological father, Magnus, a powerful and well-connected Demigod who had a history of killing his children, he had taken the advice to heart. He needed the best, and he needed them soon, because the next Magical Summit, the government leadership conference for magical people, was drawing ever nearer. Which was why he'd been traveling around the country under the guise of meeting other leaders in order to woo select magical workers from their territories. Poaching magical workers was fair game, apparently, so long as they hadn't taken a blood oath. It was like recruiting employees from a business: offer the person more perks than they had, and they might just take you up on it. Many of the people he'd pursued were diamonds in the rough— people who had attitude problems, lacked social skills, or just didn't have the gloss and *je ne sais quoi* that Demigods typically sought out for their inner circle of employees.

In every single case so far, the strongly powered misfits had taken him up on his offer, in part because he *was* giving them something more—a place in his inner circle and a blood oath. In exchange for the increased strength, speed, and healing ability bestowed by the blood oath, the recipient would be magically compelled to protect him. They'd decided it was a fair trade.

The new members of the team had made the trek to San Francisco and were in the process of setting up a new life. I hadn't interacted much with any of them. They didn't hang around our house like Kieran's Six, the original oath-holding crew, did. The Six were family; the new people were part of the job.

This situation wasn't like the others. This guy had literally barricaded himself inside a mountain after claiming vengeance on the Demigod who'd killed his fiancée. Anyone who'd had a mind to punish him had died trying to reach him. Many trespassers had gone the same way. But because magical folk weren't very good at taking a hint, more than a few Demigods had sent their people up that mountain to gain the giant's favor. Fewer had come back down, and yet people still tried.

That was the magical world for you—brutal to a fault, and if you were powerful enough to get away with it, good for you. Well done.

Kieran was determined to recruit him before the Magical Summit.

"Kieran should be heading up to that nutter in the mountains, not you gals," Jack said, still talking to Bria as though she could hear him. "You're going to get yourselves killed."

As we left the café, I repeated what Jack said to Bria, because it was a fair point.

"How many times do I have to say it? He has a soft spot for women," Bria said, climbing into the passenger seat of the black SUV parked by the curb. Red was waiting in the driver's seat.

"Did you get it?" Bria asked as she settled in.

Red nodded.

"Get what?" I shoved Jack back from the door before closing it. I didn't need him crawling over me. It was gross. A moment later, he drifted in through the other side with a disgruntled expression.

"He doesn't have a soft spot for women," Jack said, reaching for the seatbelt to strap himself in. "The nutter has been known to rape and murder women."

His hand passed through the belt, and his face fell. He faced forward with a hardened expression, and my heart broke a little more for him. I'd always had a soft spot for Jack, and it was hard watching him adjust to his new life. It was hard not to dwell on what I could have done differently if I'd known my magic better. It was a stark reminder of how much work I had left to do. I wouldn't lose anyone else. Which made the current situation all the dicier.

"I've never heard of any raping," Red said after I'd repeated Jack's warning. "There have been a couple escapees, so something like that would've gotten out. He's murdered plenty of people, though. Women, men, shifters in animal form—he eats them, too."

She said this with a straight face, steering the car through town as calmly as if we were discussing the weather.

"He…" I scrunched up my nose. "Okay, let's take a moment here. I wasn't told that."

"A good hunter eats what he kills," Bria said. "Who cares? Dead is dead, no matter what happens after. Which won't matter for us, because he won't kill us. Lexi will rip his soul out before he can."

"You guys told me he only killed *some* of the people that went up on the mountain," I said, leaning forward to try to see their faces. The angle made it impossible.

"Some, all, it doesn't matter. We've got you," Bria replied.

"It matters. Honestly, even if he doesn't kill us, which I'm suddenly not so sure about, because I'm not as awesome as you seem to think, do we really want someone like that around? He's not interested in job offers, clearly. I doubt he's going to be real keen on a blood oath."

"Look, like I said before…" Bria turned in her seat so she could see me. "The reason he went nuts is because Demigod Sarges killed his fiancée. That's understandable, right? You'd rip the soul out of the world if someone killed Kieran—don't say you wouldn't. Then, because he killed a Demigod, he had to go off-grid to a place he could defend with his magic. That's all logic. The rest is just grief. It has to be. Grief makes us do strange things. But he's had enough time to wade through his feelings, and he's sequestered himself long enough that he *has* to be lonely by now. Or at least incredibly bored. He got his revenge, he's had time to grieve, and now he'll be ready for action, just you watch. Level-five magical people—sorry, *normal* level-five magical people—have trained their whole lives to use their magic. We aren't built for solitude. He'll be ready;

all he needs is a pretty girl who's a little nuts herself to sweet-talk him. *Voilá*, out he comes."

I waited a moment, willing Red to say something. Because while I'd been given the broad strokes of this plan, suddenly it seemed hopelessly simple. Like…foolishly simple. Like…we were morons.

When Red didn't offer any convincing arguments, I said as much.

"You are in a unique position," Red said as we headed out of town. Beautiful, rolling hillsides filled in around us. "Your magic is feared the world over, but you're a dunce regarding the magical world. It makes no sense. You're this superpower who can create puppets out of living people, and you're hopelessly clueless about almost all things. It's endearing." I frowned at her. "Then there is the fact that Magnus is your father, Demigod Aaron wants to rule you and will kidnap you to do it, and everyone is desperate to get their hands on you…" She glanced back at me. "See the connection?"

"No, I just see a whole lot of backhanded compliments…"

"He'll identify with your story," Bria said. "He's basically in the same boat. Add in the fact that you went to see him behind Kieran's back, and we have a winner."

I rubbed my head as we wound our way into the mountains. "Was I drunk when I agreed to this?"

"Drunk on fear, yeah. Remember? You caught the

spirit of Demigod Lydia lurking in your flower garden," Bria said. "You would've agreed to just about any sort of bulked-up defense at that point."

That night came rushing back to me. At that point we'd already been attacked by two of the Demigods of Hades, my father and Aaron, so I hadn't been pleased to see the curvy shadow figure standing in my zinnias. I'd known from the exaggerated bust that it had to be Demigod Lydia, the only female Demigod of Hades's line. She was checking me out, just as the others had, likely not expecting the extravagant team of spirit sentinels that loitered around my house twenty-four seven. They'd sounded the alarm, and Kieran and I had chased her away.

The very next day, Demigod Lydia had called Kieran's office to apologize and ask for a meeting. A meeting Kieran had not agreed to yet, wanting Henry, one of his Six, to compile a list of all her allies to make sure it wasn't a setup.

I knew Kieran was hopeful Lydia would become an ally against the other Hades Demigods, but shortly after Lydia showed up, a few of my spirit sentinels disappeared, Mia among them. Just vanished, without a trace. John said there had been a lot of talk lately of spirits heading to their final resting place, but I'd tried to pull one or two of them toward me, just to make sure (and to get a proper goodbye!), and they hadn't shown up. Sure, they could've gone beyond my reach, but the timing was too close to be a coincidence. Lydia might be playing nice right now, but I worried something sinister waited underneath the cooperative exterior.

Either that, or another of the Hades Demigods was messing with my spirits without my knowing. It was entirely possible. Aaron and Magnus had both been unnaturally quiet. It didn't bode well. I was terrified when they'd pop up next, and what they would do.

Bria was right, though. The incident with shadow Lydia had freaked me out. The Demigods of Hades could waltz through my neighborhood at any time. Even in their shadowy spirit form, they were more powerful than I was. So far, the Demigods had all "visited" in the dead of night, when Kieran was home. Someday they'd show up when he wasn't.

Adding a giant to our arsenal, especially one with power known across the globe, would greatly help our chances. Or so I'd thought. Now I wondered if it would help escort me into the spirit realm.

"We probably should've told Kieran," I said as we wound our way higher, the hillside becoming increasingly rocky. "What if this goes badly?"

"It won't. Or not any worse than if Kieran had come. Hopefully it'll be better, though. Much better. I don't want to end up like Jack any more than you do."

"Oh yeah, real nice," Jack mumbled, looking out the

window. "If I had a body, I'd turn this car around so fast…"

"Don't worry, though," Bria went on. I didn't bother to tell her what Jack was muttering. "I left him a message. On paper. He'll get it when he gets back to the Airbnb. By then, we'll have recruited a new member of his entourage without having lied about anything."

Jack stuck a hand out Bria's way, looking incredulous. "Does her absolute conviction against the odds not set off warning bells? Lexi, come on—she's always been crazy, but this time she's just turned off reason altogether."

I passed that one on.

"Demigod Kieran won't admit it," Red said as she slowed the car to a crawl. The SUV rocked badly, a tire going over a large rock on the road. The bottom scraped against another. "But if he wants to turn heads in a major way at the Magical Summit next spring, he'll need some wow factor. He's got you, and you wear his mark—that's a good step in the right direction. The people he's picked up recently are powerful. Another step. But he needs more key players, the kind of people no one else could get. And not by accident, this time, like he did with you. If he can get even a few of the talents on the list Henry, Bria, and I compiled, he'll be in prime shape to show up at the Summit in six months with guns blazing."

"They compiled a list?" Jack asked, leaning forward a little as though Bria held that list right now. "Why didn't I know?"

I had the same question. This was news to me.

"Because Demigod Kieran hasn't seen it yet. He doesn't have a chance at recruiting the people on that list," Red replied. "He does great with magical workers who care about earning a place of prominence in the magical world. Those people *like* being charmed, and beneath his flattery and manipulation, they can tell he's a fair and just leader, as well as a good man. But it's different with the people who have flipped the bird to the magical world. They will hear his candied words, and they'll want to kill him for it. He'll remind them of the people they were desperate to escape. Henry agrees, Lexi—Kieran is no good for guys like this giant. He needs help, and thankfully, he's got an ace in the hole."

"Who...me?" I asked.

"Yeah," Bria answered. "Kieran needs your help, and you're going to prove it to him by winning over the giant. You're perfect for this role, Lexi. You're the snake charmer of weirdos. You are not even remotely part of the normal magical society, even when you try. It's pretty clear to anyone who meets you."

"Neither are you," Red told Bria.

"There's a difference. I know the rules—I just don't care to follow them. She blindly stumbles along, willy-nilly. She might get herself killed at the Magical Summit because of it, but when dealing with other nutters, she's going to shine, just you watch."

"I already said her quirks were endearing," Red said dryly.

I shook my head and looked out the window, anxiety coiling tightly within me. I didn't want to think about my ignorance or how things would go at the Magical Summit. I couldn't, or acid would eat through my guts. I needed to focus on the here and now. On the moment. And in this moment, we were going after a dangerous giant who might kill and then eat us.

Was it too late for a redo of the past year?

Chapter 2

ALEXIS

THE HIGHER WE climbed, the more the landscape changed. The slope on the right side of the car shot up steeply, and on the left the land dropped away to limitless blue sky. The narrow road wound upward, and our speed continued to drop as we hugged the side of the mountain. The SUV pitched and rolled, shaking us as it lumbered over rocks or dipped into craters.

Finally, Red stopped the SUV in the middle of the small road. Looking forward, I widened my eyes.

Another black Cadillac SUV, just like ours, was parked in front of us, hugging the mountain as closely as it could. In front of it, the road was blocked by a large boulder sitting in a pool of earth of its own making, having clearly fallen or rolled from farther up the mountain. Red and Bria climbed from the SUV.

I pushed my spirit sense as far out as I could, looking for souls. I found two, Donovan and Thane, stationary, ahead of us but clearly waiting. The lack of any other souls in the area indicated we'd be hiking the rest of the way.

Jack stared at me.

"Don't lecture me," I said into the sudden hush.

"Kieran doesn't need a wow factor at the Summit," he said, not at all what I thought he'd say. "He does need more people guarding his back, but they don't have to be exceptional. They just have to be good. Once he gets into the politics of everything, he'll bring the wow factor himself. He's as good as his father ever was—maybe better."

I shook my head slowly, my stomach churning. "Maybe if I wasn't in the picture, sure. Maybe if I wasn't marked. But I change things, Jack. You must see that. My magic, the fact that all of the Demigods of Hades want me—hell, anyone who needs an assassin wants me—puts more pressure on Kieran. Strip me away and he can slowly build up his empire. Who would bother to stop him? Keep me in the picture and he's basically at war with two, maybe three established Demigods and a plethora of treasure seekers. He doesn't just need wow, like the ladies said—he needs an incredibly potent, somewhat rare arsenal to keep his growing list of enemies at bay. Or he needs to get rid of me."

"He'd never *get rid* of you. Don't even talk like that."

"Exactly. So I need to help where I can, and apparently I'm a weirdo charmer. Worst case, I can drop this giant sonuvabitch before he kills and eats us."

"Not if he drops a rock on your head."

"Donovan is up ahead. Surely he can use his magic to hold the rock up so we can scramble away. If we get desperate, Thane can go Berserk on him."

Jack started, looking ahead. "Has everyone lost their minds?"

"No." I swung the door open and accidentally slammed it on the rockface at our side. Hopefully Kieran got the full insurance, because that was going to leave a mark. "They just want to help where they can. Kieran would never ask for something like this. He wouldn't admit he needs the help. But that won't stop us from trying."

"His ability to inspire loyalty is unequalled," Red said as I met her and Bria at the back of the SUV. The tailgate was down and Red was strapping weapons onto her person as Bria dragged dead bodies out of the back. So this was what Red had "needed" to do instead of joining us for lunch: she'd been on cadaver collection duty.

I hoped I never got used to that.

"The level-five fire elemental in Sydney has to be a close second," Bria said. "What's Dara's story, anyway?" She pulled out her backpack and took incense from the side pocket, preparing to call spirits to shove into the cadavers. "She helped take down Valens, so you'd think

15

she'd be in Kieran's camp, and yet she's keeping her distance."

"I can do it," I said in annoyance. "I'm faster. Who are you calling?"

Bria replaced the incense, pulled out a locket, and handed it to me without missing a beat.

"Valens was a thorn in Dara's side," Red said. "It behooved her to usher him out of his office. But she doesn't know what direction Kieran is going to take politically. Until she does, it's smart to keep her distance."

"True," Bria said, motioning me on. "That's Chad's locket. Remember him? The powerhouse with the eighties name?"

Of course I remembered. He was back at the house in magical San Francisco, watching over things and leading the spirit sentinels in shifts with John, a spirit that had been with us since we'd freed him from Valens.

I handed back the locket. "You could've just said. All I have to do is think of them when they're on this side of the Line and they sail toward me, remember?"

Five minutes later, four spirits were strapped into fairly fresh bodies and learning the ropes—John, Chad, and a couple of others from their squad. Jack stood a few paces away, pouting because he couldn't understand why he didn't get to participate. Given he'd never been in a cadaver, I didn't want this to be the first time.

It would be distracting as he tried to learn how it worked, something he didn't much like hearing.

"These falling rocks weren't an accident," Red said, looking at the steep road ahead. Beyond the huge boulder, small and medium-sized rocks littered the way, clustered together or solitary, all too large and plentiful for a car or SUV to navigate around. "Our guy is trying to head off visitors."

"That's nice, at least. It's like posting a warning." I chanced a look over the edge, immediately dizzied by the drop. "He can't be all bad if he's at least warning people away."

"Both his parents were giants, right?" Bria said, making it around the boulder and hiking her backpack a little higher on her shoulders.

"Yes," Red answered. "He was born of two immortal Demigods of Athos, but he didn't get the Demigod magic. Both of his parents are dead, but I couldn't figure out how they died. It was before modern-day recordkeeping."

I knew that mortal Demigods still lasted five hundred years or more, but I hadn't heard of a non-Demigod living that long. I said as much.

"It usually only happens to those with two Demigod parents, though it's not common," Red said, glancing back to make sure the animated cadavers—which I called zombies, given how they lurched and jolted when they moved—made it around the large barrier rock. "Sometimes the kid of two Demigods gets the long life without getting the power. Magical genetics can be unpredictable."

"Why didn't those nut sacks wait in the car?" Bria mumbled as we went around the bend, finding more rocks littering the road. "Where are they, Lexi?"

"Hundred feet as the crow flies, give or take. Probably a few turns to go."

A shape manifested next to me, and I jumped back with a start. Bria grabbed my arm, probably worried I'd trip and pull a Superman over the edge of the road.

Harding, the Spirit Walker of old, grinned at me. His tousled blond hair, dark brows, and the slight bags under his eyes made him look like a wild child, worn out from too much fun. His sparkling blue eyes said he knew I was in danger and wanted a front-row seat.

"What are you doing here?" I asked him, crossing to the mountain side of the road. I didn't trust my clumsiness.

"What?" Bria asked as Red looked back in confusion.

"Harding," I answered.

"What's he doing here?" Bria asked, her eyebrows pinched. "Did you bring the pocket watch?"

Harding was tied to the pocket watch he'd had when he was living, which was buried in a safe in deep waters beneath a particularly turbulent part of the ocean. Kieran was the only person who knew exactly where it was hidden.

"No, I didn't," I said, waiting for Harding to explain his sudden appearance.

He shrugged, his grin growing. "You complete me."

I gave him a flat stare. "But seriously, how'd you find me? Or…why, I guess. Without your pocket watch, I'm not your home base."

He shrugged again. "You *weren't* my home base. Maybe you are now. You've grown on me. I like watching you…go about your day."

Shivers racked my body at the change in his tone. At the unwelcome sexy glimmer in his eyes. That pause spoke of twisted sheets and writhing bodies, and the words he'd uttered did nothing to conceal his true meaning.

I could feel my expression closing down into a scowl. He knew his flirtation annoyed me—I was pretty sure that was why he did it. "Look, we're about to enter a hairy situation here. I don't need any distractions. If you're here to help, great. If not, shove off."

"What are ya up to?" he asked, looking up at the mountain. "Looking for giants?"

"A particular giant, yes. A level five with a bad attitude, I guess."

"A very bad attitude," Red murmured.

"And I see you brought my favorite Necromancer. We're going to have beautiful babies, her and I. Tell her I said so."

"You're dreaming of days gone by," I said dryly.

"Tell her."

I did as he said without really thinking about it, looking hard at a half crater punched into the side of the road. An enormous boulder had clearly fallen, too big to stay on this small shelf of a road. It had smashed its way through and kept going.

"No fucking way," Bria muttered. "A Demigod is plenty bad enough."

"She's fooling herself," Harding said with that handsome, devilish smirk.

"I don't think she's the fool, and also, this is getting gross. Knock it off." I edged around another boulder, three feet across and two feet high. "Where are these coming from?"

"The top, I'd imagine," Red said.

Even the spirits in the bodies tipped back their heads to look up the mountain.

"But there is no evidence of these things rolling down this slope," I pushed.

"They probably weren't rolled. He's a giant—he can make it rain rocks, if he wants to," Bria said. "A Demigod could shake this whole mountain. This guy can probably only shake a portion of it. What do you bet that's the portion he lives on?"

"Well, this just got interesting," Harding said, and slipped his hands into his pockets. "You and your friends do entertain, I'll say that much."

A rust-red splotch on one of the rocks caught my eye, and I wondered if it was dried blood. If so, was it from a human or an animal? Either way, the source had probably been eaten.

I swallowed down a lump in my throat. My stomach turned a little faster.

"There they are." Red pointed as we went around another bend. The road leveled off for a brief period with a small grouping of trees stuck in a little ravine at the side. Donovan leaned against a large boulder, not unlike the one that had blocked the SUVs. Thane stood with his hands on his hips, looking up through the trees.

"Hey, guys," Bria said as we drew near, both of them turning to face us. "Why did you walk this far in?"

Thane nodded at me in hello before glancing back at the cadavers following us. "We wanted to see if he'd throw any rocks or whatever it is he does." It didn't sound like he was worried about the possibility. "It's been quiet."

"Too quiet," Donovan said, his subdued voice raising the small hairs along my arms and neck.

"What do you think about the size of these boulders?" Red asked, sweeping her gaze across the road.

Donovan shrugged. "Individually, not a problem." He was a level-five Telekinetic and would hopefully keep us from getting smooshed. "If he creates an avalanche, it'll get hairy."

"What about you?" Red turned to Thane.

"I can bust through a decent-sized avalanche, I think. I can catch and relaunch rocks. But once I go Berserk, you'll have to run."

As a level-five Berserker, Thane was incredibly strong and powerful. He was also incredibly unpredictable and dangerous. After the change, he stopped distinguishing friend from foe. He saw red and attacked.

An attack on his spirit box, if continued for long enough, would force him to shift back into his human form, but that wouldn't help if rocks were being thrown at us.

"Right. So we're essentially trapped up here with very few options should this giant want to kill us," I summed up, feeling the urgency for action. I was very close to losing my nerve.

"We got this," Donovan said, moving around to massage my shoulders. "It's universally believed that this giant likes to play games with his prey. He'll want to meet us. Feel us out. Then he'll try to kill us in a clever way. He's probably bored—he'll want a little sport. All we need to do is get an audience with him. That's it. I can lob rocks away to get us there."

"What if I can't talk him into joining us?" I said, shrugging him off.

"Then you kill him before he kills us." Donovan motioned me forward. "Let's get to it. Kieran thinks we're escorting you to the outlets. As soon as he has a second to think about the direction we've gone, he'll know something is off. Time is ticking."

"It's not going to take him long. He's not a stupid man," Red said.

"He's got that useless magical mayor in his hair all day long," Donovan replied. "We've got Daisy monitoring the situation, ready to step in and run interference if need be. We're good for a while."

"Like I said back at the Airbnb, Mordecai is going to give us away," I said.

"Daisy figured out a way around that. She locked Mordecai in the basement. That little gremlin doesn't play." Thane laughed as we got underway, not taking the road, as I had thought we might, but heading through the trees and onto a small path that wound along a natural spring cutting through the mountainside.

"Oh, and Lexi, we'll absolutely be blaming all of this on you, just so you know," Donovan said. A huge boulder loomed in our path, and although Thane easily launched onto it, Donovan stood to the side and gave me his hand. I allowed him to help me up, following Thane along the path. "He won't kill you."

"Oh yeah, I meant to mention that bit." Bria took the help as well, then curtsied once she'd made it onto the rock. Red gave Donovan a confused look and hopped up after us as though on springs.

"What am I supposed to do, float up?" Jack said, looking perplexed.

I yanked him up behind us, dragging his spirit like an old tire on a rope.

"That doesn't feel nice," he bleated.

Harding didn't need the boost. He just floated up with a smug look on his face.

Despite everyone's fitness level and all-around athletic ability, we were all breathing hard in another fifteen minutes. The zombies had fallen back, unable to keep the pace but still coming along slowly. The frigid air, getting colder the higher we climbed, didn't stop sweat from trickling down my temples and wetting my back and chest. My runners, great for actually running, weren't as great for the rocky terrain, and I nearly rolled my ankles several times.

The trees thinned, as did the grasses, until we were cutting along a tiny path on the side of the mountain, winding upward. Coarse rock scraped along my left side, and the ground dropped away on my right, revealing the steepest incline I'd seen yet. A puffy white cloud almost looked eyelevel as it slowly glided by.

A soul bleeped onto my radar, higher still, and pushed back a ways, indicating we needed to cut back into the center of the mountain at some point. It sat idle, a gorgeous, sparkling thing that reminded me of a sunburst on a cloudy day.

"There *is* goodness in him," I murmured, trying to ignore Harding as he floated up next to me. And kept floating, hanging out over nothingness as the mountain fell away beside the tiny path.

"Is that right?" Harding said, making me miss whatever Bria had muttered behind me. "And you feel that in a soul, do you?"

"Are you mocking me?"

"Not at all." Harding once again drowned Bria out. "I'm just trying to get more information."

"It sounds like you're mocking me, but yes, I can get that from a soul. A person's soul doesn't lie. When their soul is bright and shining and beautiful, there is goodness in them. But if it's somewhat dull or tarnished, or feels like it needs a good polish, the person is probably a weasel. At least, that's been my takeaway so far."

"Interesting." Harding pursed his lips. "But even good people can do bad things. For example, a good person might think it's fair to just kill a bunch of trespassers who have ignored the *many* warnings. He might even decide to eat them."

"Good and bad are sometimes opposite sides of the same coin, yes. To save yourself or your family, sometimes you have to rip someone's soul out of their body, stuff it back in, and control them before they have a chance to realize they're dead, which I have done. War and battle get messy, and so does life after loss. It's the people that cause this crap that need to get their intestines dragged through their buttholes. Like Demigod Aaron, that lowlife dipshit. I bet his soul is turd brown, but I wouldn't know, would I, since he is a coward and hides in spirit whenever he comes around."

"Yikes. That's an…image," Harding said with a little grin. "I'm not offended, by the way, in case you were wondering—that lowlife dipshit being my biological father."

"That just proves my point, the cheating jerk."

Thane slowed then stopped, looking at the rockface. He took a couple of steps forward before turning to face me, his eyes tight.

It was then I noticed the tall opening in the rock, like two doors stacked on top of each other. Each side of the opening was a clean slice through the solid rock, the edges polished-looking and nearly sharp enough to cut, similar to onyx but dull gray in color. Darkness pooled in the opening, but when I stepped past Thane to get a better look, I saw that the gap acted as a tunnel to the horror show beyond. Adrenaline pooled in my gut, and if we hadn't been standing precariously on the side of a mountain, I would've turned around and sprinted in the opposite direction.

"Been nice knowing ya," Harding said behind me.

Chapter 3

ALEXIS

"WHAT IS IT?" Donovan called up as Bria pushed into the opening beside me, careful not to bump me lest I go careening off the side.

The short tunnel led to a light-filled, somewhat narrow crevasse in the mountain. The sides were perfectly parallel up until about head height, at which point they gradually flared outward for fifty or so feet. That was where the first shelf was built into the crevasse, a line of large rocks sitting on top like predators waiting to pounce. The walls kept flaring, leading up to another shelf about fifty feet above that, and another beyond it, the last one holding massive boulders that didn't seem like they would fit into the bottom area. On their way down they would, however, scatter all the smaller rocks beneath them, killing whoever was stupid enough to wait at the bottom.

All the small hairs stood up along my body. I could barely speak, looking at the walkway below certain death. The giant was not trying to hide the obvious danger. In fact, he was putting it clearly on display. Once those rocks came barreling down, they'd hit the ground, bounce around together, and then gush out the tunnel and over the side of the mountain, taking any trespassers with them.

"Good…heavens," Bria whispered, looking in from behind me. "This is…well thought out. Our giant is a smart man."

The area beyond the hell walk was masked in shadow, but I could feel the giant's soul blazing amidst the darkness.

"Can giants feel through the rock?" I asked, trailing my fingers along the cool, smooth stone to either side.

"Level fives can," Thane replied. "Lexi, that canal in there is a death sentence for you if I change. You'd be trapped in there with me."

"A canal is an artificial waterway to allow for boats, ships, or irrigation, but we get what you mean," Jack muttered beyond Bria.

"So that giant doesn't need to actually have eyes on us to know where we are," I said to myself. "Can Donovan handle all those rocks without you?" I asked Thane. I stepped aside, moving Bria with me so Thane could get a better look.

"Let me up to see," Donovan called.

"You try to step around me, chances are you'll go on a wild ride," Red said to Donovan. "This path is precarious at best."

Thane ducked so he could look higher, but after the third shelf of rock, there was nothing but brilliant blue sky. It looked like the giant had lopped off the top crust of mountain. "No, not all that," he answered. "He can probably handle the first shelf, and after that, it's smoosh-ville."

I took a steadying breath, goosebumps now coating my skin, looking beyond him at the path that wound around the edge of the mountain, then back to the path cutting through the stone, a very clear display of the giant's awesome power. Either way was precarious, and I wasn't a fool to think one was rigged and the other wasn't. Hell, if he could cleave a slice down the middle of this beast, he could surely shake things a bit and knock anyone on the sides off. Bria had already indicated as much. If we didn't want him on our side and in a good mood, I could just grab his spirit box now.

"Okay, so we play by his rules." I stepped farther into the tunnel. "We're on his land, after all. That seems fair."

Thane's large hand covered my shoulder. "Or we go home and tell Kieran this is suicide. Bria and Red put together a list of people to recruit. If we don't get this one, we can get another."

"Bria, be honest," I said, "do you suspect anyone on your list is going to be easier to get to than this guy?"

"I have absolutely no idea," she said.

"Educated guess," I pushed.

She blew out a breath. "There is a reason the people we've discussed haven't been snatched up. Danger is definitely one of those reasons, but I'm not sure any of the others would be this...calculated. I pictured some pretty intense scenarios, even for a giant, but I have to be honest, this guy has cemented himself as the king of this mountain, without question. Maybe Thane is right. The giant has the upper hand and he knows it. Everyone seems to agree that he'll use it. This doesn't look good for us. It's a risk that we probably shouldn't take without Kieran's say-so."

"Fat lot of good logic does you now," Jack said, obviously pissed. "The guy likes to play with his food, and you've already climbed up onto his plate. He's not just going to let you wander away now—you're on his bloody doorstep."

"Yeah." I chewed my lip, stepped into the mouth of Death Alley, and squatted down, thinking. On the other side, the giant's soul glowed and sparked, vibrant and alive. He hadn't killed us yet, so that probably meant my crew had gotten one thing right. He liked to meet his prey. Maybe he even wanted a little sport—a momentary distraction from what *had* to be a boring existence.

I turned, looking at the view stretching out beyond Bria. It sure was beautiful up here. Breathtaking, really.

The crystalline sky dusted a sparkling river far below. Green stretched out in a natural haven, lush and gorgeous. In the winter it would be blanketed in white, I knew. Cold and crisp. Silent as the grave.

But there had to be more to him than sitting up here, all alone, watching the world turn. Like Kieran, this giant had gotten revenge for past wrongs, but unlike Kieran, he didn't have the loyalty and support of the Six. He didn't have anyone to lean on. He'd been cut off, set adrift, with nothing but pain and sorrow to keep him company. Revenge was a shallow victory, I knew. I still felt it through Kieran.

This giant was hurting, he had to be. He was hurting, and he was misunderstood. My mother had taught me to help people who were suffering. Usually that translated into helping spirits, but now (hopefully) it would mean I helped a giant at the top of the world.

Otherwise, I was about to get a rock facial.

"Whelp. Let's see if he's ready for a chat. Bring up Chad and John, please," I said to Thane, straightening up.

"Wait, wait, wait." Thane reached in and grabbed my arm.

Normally I would punch him in the spirit box to make him let go, but he was still close to the entrance. I didn't want him to startle backward and pitch off the mountain.

"Best let go, Thane," I said softly, my tone holding a warning.

"Thane is just reacting to a situation none of us expected," Bria said. "None of the survivors got close enough for a look inside, and I haven't heard of any other non-Demigod giant with a setup like this. It's…startling."

Annoyance flared through me. "Bring up the zombies. You wanted me here, and I'm here. I might as well try to help somehow. There's clearly no chance of us just wandering back, although it might've been wise to mention the bit about none of the survivors making it this far *before* we made the trek, huh? A little less faith in me would be wise going forward."

Bria shrugged and signaled for Thane to pass the message along.

Shoes scraped against rock behind her. A strange sort of shuffle reverberated through the short tunnel. A scream tore through the air.

"Oops. There goes one of the cadavers," Donovan called up. "Wasn't one of the ones you wanted, though—"

Bria spun around. "Catch it with your magic! That's a good body."

"Oh." Donovan paused. "Should I have? Too late now. Its head popped off on the landing. I'll catch the next one."

"Don't worry about the cadavers," Thane said, peering in at me with a frustrated expression. "Donovan, save your energy for those rocks. Lexi is going to need backup."

Harding appeared by my side, standing in the open below the shelves of rocks lining both sides.

"Must be nice not to be corporeal at this moment," I muttered as John and then Chad jerked and shuffled in, moving past Thane and Bria. Donovan had probably ignored Thane and lifted them around the others on the treacherous path.

"Let me take a look at the setup." Chad shoved in around John, my being able to hear his spirit through the cadaver even though the body had no vocal cords. The space was a little larger in the short tunnel than it had been along that ledge.

I flattened against the wall to let Chad pass. An advisor to Valens in life, he was extremely adept at strategy and warfare. He stared up at the rock shelves, analyzing the setup.

"Get the Necromancer to use a rat on that mountain pass to see what lies ahead," Chad said. "Let's not engage here unless we have to. This is a death trap."

"Death Alley, actually," I mumbled before passing that along.

"Good idea," Bria said, shaking her head. She unslung her backpack to grab the rats. "I'm off my game."

"Do you know where he is?" John asked.

I watched Harding float up along the right side, looking at the first shelf of rocks. I pointed at the dark end of the alley.

"They're all just sitting here," Harding said, bending down to look at a rock's base. "Nothing is holding them here."

"Gravity is holding them there," I said, and my voice ricocheted around the walls before spilling out of the open top and fading.

"Let me out of here, and I'll go check it out," John said, wiggling in his body.

I nodded, bent back the casings I'd fastened on his soul to keep him in the body, and ripped him out. He tumbled across the ground.

"Sorry," I said before staring at that pool of darkness, wondering if the giant was lurking within, watching my every move. To him, it would look like I was talking to myself. Or the teetering corpses.

"What a strange life I lead," I mused as John made his way across Death Alley, the perfect spy because he couldn't be seen or heard by anyone but me.

"It could be stranger," Bria said. "You could be a giant who sections himself off from society at the top of a mountain and eats his visitors."

"Bria!" Thane hissed, his voice echoing around the walls. "He might be able to hear you."

"He can definitely hear you," John called from the darkness. "He's got a cave back here, and he's sitting in a Barcalounger watching and listening to all of you. You don't have any secrets from this guy. Nice little setup, though. Homey. If you like that sorta thing. You're sitting on his front stoop."

The situation solidified in my mind. I cut off the murmuring behind me with a violent hand gesture and edged forward as Harding touched back down onto the ground. His smile had left his face and he stood in my way.

"Think this through, Alexis," he said softly, his tone sending shivers of warning through me. "I cannot help you here. The man in that cave has been here a long time. He has killed many. You mean nothing to him, and while you can surely kill him, he'll easily take you and all your friends with him. You're the best of us. Don't let today be the day you return to spirit."

"The only reason he kills people is because they want something from him, and he clearly wants to be left alone," I said, stepping into the open. Two rocks wiggled on their perches, a pretty clear warning.

My heart sped up and I put up my hands, danger pressing on me and making it hard to breathe.

"I know you can see and hear me," I said, then motioned for Chad to get out of the way. We'd put him in a huge body, and he was blocking my view. "Sit down or something, Chad."

"What do you think your death puppets can do for you?" The booming voice bounced off the walls, surrounding me, beating against me, before flying out of Death Alley. "They cannot protect you here."

"Big pile of bones over here," John hollered, sounding like he was deep within the recesses of the mountain. His voice barely echoed out.

Swallowing became a little harder.

"They aren't my death puppets," I said with an elevated voice so he'd be sure to catch all my words. Fear swirled in my gut at the thought of the large rocks arranged above me, but I took another step forward. "Seriously, Chad, sit or something. I can't see past you."

A rock the size of my upper body rolled off the first ledge on the right and picked up speed faster than was natural, thundering down the side. I didn't get a chance to say, "Look out!" before it slammed into Chad's upper body, smashing it against the rock wall. Bones splintered and his jaw crunched. A rib popped out of his dead flesh. The rock hit the ground and thudded against the other side before rolling a little farther and settling.

Bile rose in my throat. Chad stayed standing, clearly fucking amazing at working his spirit within a dead body.

"You are strong for a Necromancer," the voice boomed. "You have great control."

I wiped my mouth with the back of my hand, needing a second before I looked in Chad's direction. "I'm not a Necromancer and I have no control over Chad—he's the one in that body. He withstood that all on his own." I braced a hand on my stomach. "That is not a good look, Chad. It really isn't. You can take that body off if you want."

"Or I could run in there and gut that giant," Chad responded, his anger seething.

"He'd bring this whole place down on top of us, Chad. Think it through."

The ground shivered below my feet. The rocks shook in their perches. My heart choked me.

I threw up my hands again. "I just want to talk to you, sir. That's it. I mean you no harm."

His laugh had no humor in it. "Yet you talk about killing me. You speak of using me."

"I don't think we said anything about using him," Jack said, having drifted in at some stage.

I put up a finger. "If you try to kill us, I will take you down with us, yes. That's just the truth. But there's no reason for it to come to that."

"And how would you do that? With your dolls?" Another rock plummeted from its perch, barreling down at Chad.

Above me, movement caught my eye. A rock the size of my head barreled down, faster than thought, propelled by some unseen hand. I dodged out of the way, adrenaline coursing through me. The rock crashed into the side. Amazingly, it hadn't put a single dent in the stone walls.

"That was incredibly rude. We are your guests!" I grabbed the giant's spirit box in an unyielding grip before squeezing with everything I had. It wouldn't kill him or jeopardize his soul, but it would hurt like hell and probably scare the daylights out of him. No one was prepared for magic like mine.

Rocks shook on their shelves. The ground heaved under our feet.

"Get in, get in, get in!" Thane yelled to those still out on the ledge. The mouth of Death Alley had become the only safe place to be.

Red and the guys squeezed into the tunnel. Boulders rained down on the outside of the mountain, slamming off the small path before careening away. Another rock loosed above Death Alley. It sped down, aiming for my face.

I jumped over the rock that had previously fallen and dove into the bodies pressed into the tunnel. A monstrous thud echoed behind me.

"I will bring them all down," the giant thundered.

The mountain heaved. More boulders tumbled down outside. The rocks on the shelves shook, three breaking free and tearing down to Death Alley. One bounced off the lower wall and shot toward us, only stopped by Donovan's fast thinking. A crack grew along the top of the tunnel, slight at first but enlarging quickly. We had no escape, and he was working on bringing down our safe haven.

I did the only thing I could think to do. I stood up and spoke the truth.

"I will rip your soul out of your body, shove it back in, and make you dance to my tune. Try me, asshole!"

Chapter 4

ALEXIS

A HUSH FELL across Death Alley. A small dribble of dirt dusted us from the crack above. Chad, in spirit form, sat on top of the stone that had finally taken his body to the ground.

"The giant looks ashen," John called from across the way. "Guess that means you're still alive. You've still got a hold on his soul."

"Le—let go." The voice was no longer booming.

"I think you freaked him out," John said.

"I'll let go if you agree to give the rocks a rest for a while," I said, my voice tight.

"They aren't moving, are they?" the giant yelled.

I released my grip on his soul casing. Everyone breathed heavily around me, still crammed in the small tunnel with no desire to leave.

"You could've really hurt us." I stood on shaky legs and stepped around the rock Donovan had kept from ramming into us. Adrenaline filled my body again, thankfully standing in for my wavering courage.

"You're trespassing," the giant said.

"This mountain is not owned by you. It is state property. *You're* trespassing."

"Please do not pick a fight with the incredibly powerful giant on his home turf," Jack said. "I do not want you all to join me in this fucked-up plane of existence."

"It's not that bad after a decade or two," Chad said. "Better than the beyond. At least here we have some purpose."

"You're not helping, brother," Jack replied.

"Squatter's rights," the giant said, and there was no trace of humor in his words.

I chuckled anyway. "You got me there. Fine, we trespassed, and you really could've hurt us but didn't. Are we square?"

"What are you?" the giant asked.

"He's gripping his chair pretty hard," John said. "Don't let his tone fool you; he's still freaked out."

"I'm a Spirit Walker. Your people call it a Soul Stealer. I'm sure you've heard the stories about what I can do."

"My people?"

"Yeah. Magical people. Our people, I guess. I don't know. I didn't grow up in the magical world."

"You are lying."

"Nope. I might look rich and polished now, but it wasn't always the case."

"You don't look rich or polished right now," Bria mumbled. "Without Aubri on the trip to help style you, you keep making weird clothing choices and don't know how to do your hair."

I had the feeling she was trying to be helpful.

"You wear the Demigod's mark," the giant said.

"Yeah. Kieran Drusus, Valens's son, found me, and… Well, it's a long story. I love him, and I willingly wear his mark."

"Valens…"

The viciousness in his tone was unmistakable. The ground tremored under our feet. Everyone had known Valens by reputation. He had not been a nice man, to put it mildly.

"Whoa, whoa." I put up my hands. "I helped Demigod Kieran take Valens down. Kieran is in charge of magical San Francisco now, and he's a fair and just leader. He wasn't even going to take the job, but the people pushed it on him. His goal was to claim vengeance for his mother, that's it. The rest has been like a snowball rolling downhill."

"What do you want?"

I took a deep breath and leaned against the side of the wall. "I'm not going to lie to you: we came looking for help." I gave him a quick recap of my situation and my parentage, finishing, "So unless I want to be kidnapped or worse, I need to help Kieran find some backup. We heard you were the best. I was hoping you would help."

Silence descended, into which John said, "He's rubbing his chin. Looks indecisive. I'd get ready to yank out his spirit, because it could go either way at this point."

I held my breath. I'd trespassed and forced myself on a stranger who was just trying to protect his home. For that, I might need to rip out his soul to save myself and my friends. I was pretty sure I was the bad guy in this scenario—I'd started it.

The sweat on my brow turned chill, and a deep, thick silence filled Death Alley as we awaited the giant's decision. I felt the Line pulsing power through my blood, preparing me to grab his soul at a moment's notice. If this went tits up, it would come down to who was faster working with their magic. Could he pull the mountain down on top of us before I gained control of him?

The seconds ticked by. Minutes followed. Thane rolled his neck and then his big shoulders. He was preparing to change. He suspected this wouldn't go our way.

Donovan, too, had braced himself, his eyes tight.

The pressure pressed down on me. Fear compelled me to talk.

"What kind of a life is this?" I asked, feeling the question in every fiber of my being. "It's a beautiful view, but if you don't have anyone to share it with, what's the point? Would she want you to be living like this?"

"What did you say?" His voice was low and rough. Rocks wiggled in their spots. I'd struck a nerve. A very dangerous, possibly explosive nerve.

"He just stood up, and he's pissed," John yelled. "Watch yourself."

The words tumbled out a lot faster now, my pulse racing. "You lost the love of your life. I can't even begin to know what that would be like. But if someone took me from Kieran—which might happen, let's be honest—I wouldn't want him to hide away. I wouldn't be able to stand it. I'd want him to kill the miserable sonuvabitch who killed me, that's a given, but after that, I'd want him to live his life. I'd want him to be happy. Seeing you like this would probably kill her."

A huge rock on the highest shelf rolled toward the edge, poised to shoot down and scatter all the rocks beneath it. If that thing let loose, all of us would go tumbling over the edge like bowling pins by the time I had his soul. He'd die, but so would we.

"I can ask her," I said quickly, stepping forward into the sunlight. "I can call her to you and ask her."

"What, and put her in one of those rotting corpses?" His voice boomed around us again, pinging off the walls. Fracturing. Coming together. Blasting me.

It had a physical force that made me step back.

"You are currently standing," I yelled above the thunder rolling beneath my feet. "You have a homey little setup in there and a pile of bones deep inside, which is definitely the first sign of madness."

"His fists are clenched," John supplied.

"Your fists are clenched," I repeated. "One of my spirit associates is in there with you right now. Has been for a while. Hold up two fingers, if you want."

"It's just one, and you can probably guess which one," John said.

"Well, that's not very nice. I can call her. Ask her whatever you want, and I'll act as the go-between."

"You'll feed me lies."

"Most people probably would, that's true. But I have had this magic all my life, even if I didn't always under-stand it. I'm used to doing this, to being a go-between. I can summon her. You'll see for yourself. And if you don't believe what I have to say, well then…we're no better off than when we started."

A great swell of fear and anger ripped through my middle. Kieran's emotions drowned me, changing so fast that I couldn't keep up—shock, surprise, love, rage, worry, rage—around and around they went, speeding up my heart.

"But we need to do this now," I said, stepping for-ward again. "Kieran has just realized where I am, and he is not happy. We're going to have a rage-filled Demigod on our hands in an hour or so."

"He's walking out," John said.

I repeated his warning, and everyone behind me stepped forward, Thane and Donovan at my shoulders.

A man emerged, probably about six feet six, with broad shoulders, thick arms, and fists still balled at his sides. The sun shone on his shiny bald head, naturally tanned. His pecs pushed at his tattered and stained shirt, and his ripped and torn jeans were too desecrated to be stylish.

"I thought you'd be taller," I blurted, then scrunched up my face and wished I could pull that comment back in. "Sorry. I just meant...everyone called you a giant. I was thinking...you know..." I lifted my hand, indicating someone incredibly enormous. "You're just the usual tall, you know? Not *giant*."

"Stop babbling," Thane whispered. "You are on a very thin line. Watch your words."

That was easy for him to say—he didn't get nervous babbles.

"This Demigod you speak of...he doesn't know you're here?" the man asked.

"No. We figured you'd probably seen enough Demigods for a while. We didn't want to show up with him and immediately sully the waters."

"So you show up and grab the middle of my..." He

brushed at his chest.

"Yes, well…desperate times, as they say."

"You're part of his first ring?" The man flexed, his cut muscles showing through the tears in his clothes.

"Is that like an inner circle?" I asked the area at large.

"Yes," Donovan murmured.

"Oh. Well, the guys are." I hooked a thumb at each of them. "I have a blood link with Kieran but didn't do an oath. He offered me the link so I could be stronger, that's all. A love token, kinda. Like the mark. Anyway, one of the spirits here is a past member of the inner circle who died in battle and now helps out in spirit form. The girls are just his employees. Oh, and the other spirits are kinda…along for the ride. They want to help."

The man stared at me for a moment, silence stretching between us. I couldn't read his flat expression.

"Are you thinking of her?" I asked. "If you are, then she hasn't come. She might be across the Line, in which case I'll need a memento of hers to call her back."

"You are either an incredibly good actress, or wholly unprepared for the magical world," he said.

"I…" I furrowed my brow, feeling like I was missing something. "Be that as it may, ahm…" I brushed the hair out of my face. "I can call her if you have something of hers."

"I do." The man turned, but before he could reach the dark area in the mountain, a petite figure in a limp, pale purple dress glided toward me, her expression filled with sorrow.

"I think she's here," I said, watching her flit around the rocks and fall in at his side.

He stopped and turned, not looking around for her spirit, as many would have. He was looking for the truth or lie in my face.

"Spirits are able to change their appearance," I cautioned him, watching her stare up at his face with longing. "They often choose younger, better versions of themselves." I described her appearance, including the nail polish that perfectly matched the sundress, which seemed dissonant on this cold mountaintop.

"Try again," he barked.

"Well...I can't, because that's what she's wearing. Hey, lady there. Chad, do me a favor and get her attention, would ya?"

Chad moved from his rock and waved his hand in front of her face. She blinked a few times before she finally glanced around her, seeing everyone as though for the first time.

"She's been across the Line," I said, stepping forward again to see her better. "That's the look of someone at rest." I narrowed my eyes at the man. "Bria, have you ever heard of a regular person capable of pulling someone from across the Line?"

"Yes. It's very rare, but if the connection is strong enough, usually intense love, it can be done, usually by accident."

The man continued to stare at me, but I could see the question in his eyes.

"First we'll make sure that is her, and then we'll talk about the situation at hand, yes?" I waved at the woman, attracting her gaze to me. "I can see you."

She looked back, as if convinced I had to be talking to someone else. John nodded and pointed my way. "She can see us."

"You can see me?" she asked, taking a longing step toward me. I grimaced.

"What?" the man asked, clearly unable to help himself.

"Oh, nothing," I answered. "Don't watch my expressions. I have a lot of bad habits. Usually when spirits realize I can see them, they are all over me. Then I feel obligated to help, and it's a whole big thing. Anyway, lady, do you know this man?"

"You can hear me?" she asked.

"Yes, I can hear you. Do you know this man?"

"Of course I know him. Jerry Twindlebaumb. We were set to be married when..." Her face screwed up into a look of rage.

"Jerry Twindlebaumb?" I asked incredulously.

"What kind of a giant's name is Jerry Twindlebaumb?"

Donovan elbowed me.

"Sorry," I said at the man's glower.

"Anyone could find out my name and what she was wearing when she died," he growled. "You're not even good at the ruse, and now you will see what it is like to fly."

The rumble deep beneath my feet was terrifying. His mask of cold rage was infinitely worse.

"Wait. Wait, my knight." The woman stepped in front of Jerry, her hand out. "We must not haste today, for we'll have nothing to occupy us tomorrow."

Thane ripped off his shirt, his body enlarging, his breathing speeding up, his muscles popping out like on some exaggerated bodybuilder.

"Go," he said, stepping forward to shield me. "Run. Now! I'll keep him busy."

"You'll never get off this mountain," I yelled as the lower rocks rolled free from their shelves.

Donovan flung up his hands, lifting the rocks into the air and shoving them toward the giant.

"At least Jack will have a friend to talk to besides you," Thane said.

The rocks stopped in midair, hovering just before the giant as Jerry and Donovan waged a silent battle.

Bria ducked around me, then Thane, and flung a knife. It dug into Jerry's shoulder. He didn't even take a step back. If he felt it, it didn't show through his emotionless mask.

Above the increasing roar of the mountain, and the thick grunting of Thane, I could hear the woman's voice. Begging. Pleading.

"She says that you are so infinitely powerful, Jerry. She called you *my love*. But she urges you to take some time for reflection. For cool tranquility." I readied my magic to grab his soul but lost focus when Red yanked me back, trying to get me moving.

"If I don't talk him around, we all die," I yelled, punching her in the spirit box to make her let go. "His woman is trying to get through to him. Keep the faith!" Red released her hand. "Jerry, earlier she told you to wait," I yelled, trying to be heard above the noise. "She called you her knight. She said that we shouldn't haste today because we'll have nothing to occupy us tomorrow. Please, give me a chance. Let me ask her something—"

The rumble under my feet quieted. Jerry could turn his magic on and off at the drop of a hat.

Thane couldn't.

A growl sliced through my body. Little spiders of fear skittered across my skin. The Berserker was coming, and his sole purpose had always been to destroy everything in his path, friends be damned.

"I'll give you a chance," Jerry said, but I was backing

away.

His height now double mine, his body as wide as Death Alley, his muscles so enormous they were grotesque, Thane finished transitioning into his other form.

"A little late, *Jerry*." Bria said his name like an accusation. "Thane is about to rip through your whole world." She darted behind me. Donovan backed up, knowing that Thane in close quarters was no match for even him.

The rocks sailed back toward their respective shelves, Jerry's peace offering. If only it hadn't come too late. Thane reached up and slapped one at Jerry, sending him hurtling backward. The rocks that hadn't yet made it back to the shelves fell, knocking into the sloping walls and starting to roll.

"Get out, get out, get out," Donovan shouted, stepping in front of me.

Thane grabbed a rock in an enormous hand, palming it like a basketball. He threw it at the mouth of Death Alley with such force that it slammed into the top of the tunnel and made a large crater. Cracks spiderwebbed out. The rock exploded on impact.

"Damn it, Thane, calm down. He wants to talk," I yelled, grabbing Thane's spirit box.

Rocks fell into the canal, as Donovan had called it, bouncing as they hit the ground. Some hit off the others, propelling them in Thane's direction.

He roared, the sound pinging within Death Alley, growing as it did so. The might of it slammed into me, nearly buckling my knees in fear. He kicked a rock, sending it careening at Jerry. He kicked another, sending it sailing into the side of the mountain, absolutely no aim. Others hit him, doing no damage.

"Fight back, Jerry, just don't kill us all," I yelled, clamping down harder on Thane's spirit box.

"You brought a Berserker up here?" Jerry asked in disbelief over the din, his booming voice seeming small in comparison.

A magical red whip elongated from Thane's hand.

"Get back. Everyone get back!" I pushed Donovan behind me as I backed up. The others filed out onto the ledge.

"Lost another cadaver," Donovan said.

I ignored him. Animated cadavers wouldn't do a damn thing against Thane.

"Calm down, Thane," I yelled as he picked up a rock and smashed it against another.

"Should I loose the rest of the rocks?" Jerry yelled.

"No. I can handle this." I ripped into Thane's chest as he picked up another rock. This time he did aim, although luckily not at me. "Incoming, Jerry!"

Thane threw it with such speed that Jerry could barely catch it with his magic. The rock stopped inches from his face, and even from a distance, I could see his eyes grow as big as saucers. Thane roared again and turned, his whip cracking out, his manic, red-eyed stare fixed on me.

"Donovan," I yelled, stabbing into Thane's chest with my magic, ripping and tearing, trying to bring him to heal. "Keep that whip off me."

I pushed forward so Donovan could step in. The magical whip buzzed as it flew out, cracking right by my head.

"Keep it off me!" I screamed.

Terror eating me alive, I reached into Thane's chest and grabbed one of the prongs that docked his soul in place. With effort, I applied spirit and then power before crumbling it into dust.

The roar that shook my bones held equal parts pain and fear, an animal giving in to basic, primal injuries. I struck harder now. Faster.

His whip slashed out.

I didn't react, trusting Donovan to protect me, knowing that if I relented in my attack, I'd have to start all over, seconds and minutes I didn't have.

The whip stopped inches from my face. Donovan grunted behind me with the strain of holding it back.

Thane took a grudging step forward, against my battering him from the inside.

"Kill him," Jerry yelled. A rock the size of a sink

slammed into Thane's back. Thane didn't turn around, clearly recognizing I was the real threat.

"I will not kill him." I reached in and crumbled another prong. If I destroyed any more of them, his soul might come loose during his transformation back into his normal form. "He will come back from this. Come on, Thane. Fight your way back to the surface. Regain control."

The whip cracked out. The tip sliced my arm before Donovan could push it away. I gritted my teeth against the pain, still working.

Bria darted in around me. The whip cracked again, but she dodged it, lithe and graceful. She slid under Thane's leg, popped up, and stabbed down.

"Metal doesn't pierce this form," I said, having learned that from our first encounter.

"It isn't metal; it's a slab of rock with a wicked point." Bria ducked a swing aimed at her head, Thane turning around clumsily in the small (for him) space. She crawled through his legs, barely dodging a kick, and used both hands to stab his humungous calf.

I wasted no time, knowing she was doing this solely as a distraction. Doubling down on my efforts, I applied pressure on another prong while repeatedly slicing through his soul box with as much power as I could muster. Over and over I kept at it, ignoring Thane's tortured roars and the flying rocks, propelled not by

Donovan or Jerry, who was huddled in the corner, but by the Berserker himself. He was smashing and slamming and kicking anything within reach. One sped toward my chest, big enough and fast enough to crush my ribs. Donovan grunted and the rock stopped, inches from me. I couldn't help but flinch.

"Hurry, Lexi," Donovan said, his voice pained. "I'm running out of steam."

Chapter 5

ALEXIS

B Y THE TIME Thane dropped down to a knee, sweat was pouring off me, my limbs trembling from the effort. He shook his mangy head and groaned as his form reduced, slowly at first and then all at once. He lay down in human form, dirty from smashed rock dust, bloody from stab wounds and boulder battering, and clearly spent.

"Why couldn't you have just chatted like a normal guy, *Jerry*?" Thane said, using Bria's accusatory tone from earlier, looking up at the sky. His chest heaved.

"Yeah, *Jerry*, why do you always have to make things difficult?" Donovan added, leaning his forearm against the cracked wall in the small tunnel. "I'm going to be really put out if, after all this, we still die on this godforsaken mountain."

I made my way through the rocks, catching a glimpse of all the spirits sitting with Harding up on the first shelf. The woman in the purple dress sat next to him, and they were holding hands, but I doubted Jerry would want to know about that.

"Show's over, Jerry," I said as he straightened slowly with wide eyes. "Time to chat. Do you have water or anything? I'm parched."

He curled his fingers around the hilt of the knife in his shoulder and, without flinching, yanked it out. No blood gushed down his front—it only left a splotch around the actual wound. The knife clattered across the ground as he turned, jerking his head to indicate we should follow him into his cave.

A WHILE LATER, we all sat in the main sitting room of what looked to be a collection of giant-made caves. The walls and ceilings had the same polished-looking surfaces as the tunnels and Death Alley, and at the end of the living room was a little forked hallway leading to two other areas we hadn't entered.

The condition of the place proved John and I had very different definitions of "homey." Sparse and dirty, the living room didn't have much to offer beyond a single decrepit armchair on a grime-filled rug. The main attraction was staring out into Death Alley. The seat barely even had a view, with the small opening on the other side blocking most of the grandeur of the valley floor below.

Jerry sat in his chair with the rest of us on the ground, fanned out around him like children. We were too tired to care. I could feel Kieran winding ever closer, probably out of his skin with fear and worry. Without any cell phone coverage up here, the only thing I could do was pump soothing feelings through our connection.

The spirit of Jerry's fiancée stood next to his chair, her eyes rooted to him. It was clear she really missed him, and that they'd had a great love. It was such a shame they'd been torn apart so brutally.

"You really can see her," Jerry started, leaning forward so he could stare me in the face.

"Yes. I'm a Spirit Walker. That's my jam."

"She said that to me all the time when we were together. 'Wait, my knight. We must not haste today, for we'll have nothing to occupy us tomorrow.'" His smile was sad. A sheen came over his eyes. "She had plant magic. A Chloromane. She had a talent for creating these fantastic natural scenes. Each little corner had something different. Something for every mood. She helped me take life slower. Enjoy myself more. Quell the rage that springs up out of nowhere. She was my light in a dark world. I lost all sanity when she was taken from me."

"What was her name?" I asked.

"Don't you know?" he asked with an edge to his voice.

"No, actually. I haven't asked her. I don't know anything about her death, either. I was told she was killed by a Demigod, but not how or why. I can ask her, if you like. I was just giving you an opportunity to answer."

"Be my guest." He waved me on before leaning back in his chair and throwing a large leg over the small armrest. It came to my attention that he wasn't wearing underwear, and also that he needed a lot of patches for those pants.

I looked at the lady, her hand resting on the back of his chair, and lifted my eyebrows.

"I'm sorry for his behavior," she said, her face pulled down. If she could cry, I knew she would be. "He is a good man. A just man. He's in pain and he's lost his way."

"Didn't you hear him? You were the one that quelled his rage. Without you, he's fighting to keep his head above water. Sometimes we need to lose our way for a while to find ourselves again. Maybe he still needs more time. I don't know. He's not much of a talker. What's your name, before we go on?"

"Caily," she said. "But he calls me Sweet Rose."

"Well I'm not going to call you Sweet Rose." Like I'd predicted, he jumped, and like I'd only hoped, he pulled his leg off the armrest, closing up the peep show. "Did you cross over after your death, Caily?"

"Not at first. I didn't realize—"

I held up a hand. "Do you want me to tell him this, or...?"

"Tell me everything," Jerry said hungrily.

"It's not up to you, *Jerry*," Donovan said from the other side of the room.

"Yeah, *Jerry*, you get no say in ghost behaviors," Thane said.

Jerry pretended not to hear.

"You can tell him, yes," Caily said with a sad smile. "We had no secrets." I gave Jerry a thumbs-up as she went on. "I still don't know what I did to anger the Demigod. Something with the Demigod's garden, though no one would say what. My death came out of nowhere, with my back turned. Suddenly I was standing beside my body, my head rolling away, and the Demi-god's henchman was standing over me with a bloody sword."

"Good heavens, what a thing to witness," Red murmured after I'd relayed Caily's words.

"I'd prefer that over thinking I'd hurt a kid," Jack said, over with the other spirits and Harding near the entrance of the cave. Prior to his death, a Possessor had used his body to hurt Mordecai and Daisy.

Why Harding had decided to lump himself in with them, watching silently and intently, I didn't know. He didn't usually hang out with the hired help, as he thought of them.

"Soon enough, though, I saw the pulsing beacon," Caily went on. "It pulled at me, promising to soothe the trauma of the event. But seeing my ruined body didn't bother me nearly as much as knowing that I'd never see my knight again. I'd never stroll with him through our garden—a modest affair, but ours all the same. I'd never whisper secrets to him beneath the elm tree, or sneak kisses behind the sequoia grove where he proposed. I'd never get my white wedding under a canopy of vines and lilies. Worst of all, I'd never get to tell him good-bye."

I wiped a stray tear, the agony in her voice matching that on Jerry's face as I relayed her words. "You can tell him now, Caily. Through me." She stepped toward me, and I motioned her back. "No, no. Not *through* me, like possessing me. I mean I'll relay what you say."

She turned and looked at him, and I told Jerry of her positioning so he could look back.

"You made me the happiest I've ever been," she said softly, her voice like the mist before rain. "I never thought I'd be so lucky as to find someone like you, and I am forever thankful that I got to know true love before the Great Mother tucked me into the earth. Please be easy, my love. Do not mourn. For I have a great garden in the beyond, filled with all the things we loved. I've even put in your moody corner, so when you join me, there will be a place for you to retreat when the vibrancy of the colors annoys your rocky soul."

"Ask her if she thinks he should stay in this stinky

pit of despair," Bria said after I'd repeated everything. She'd gotten comfortable, stretching out on her side with her head propped on her hand. "Someone needs to talk sense into him."

"I would join you now," Jerry said, tears in his eyes and choking on his words. He wiped his runny nose. "I would join you right now."

Caily's smile was sweet. "Then you would have so very few stories to entertain me with when we meet again. Live your life. Live it to its fullest. Experience everything as though it will be your last. Find love again."

"Never," Jerry spat, sobbing silently. "I could never."

"Time does not exist where I am, my love. Live your life. And when I blink next—not before—I will see you again."

"I love you," Jerry said. "I miss you, every day. Every second. I can barely think straight for missing you."

"Be easy. I am at rest. I am waiting for you. Gather those stories, and then we will laugh once again."

He hunched over, his whole body shaking as he sobbed, great heaves of his huge body. It seemed as though he was experiencing her death all over again. This time, though, he'd have closure. This time, he *would* be able to move on, because she had allowed him to.

"Thank you for telling him," she said to me, and I wanted to remember that kind smile forever. It was so loving and sweet, so joyful and full of life, yet also so sad.

"You're welcome," I whispered.

She watched Jerry for a few moments longer before turning and looking around, obviously searching for an exit.

"Here." I summoned the Line for her, a quick portal back to her resting place.

Before she crossed, she half turned back to me. "If you have someone you love, make sure to let them know. Show them every day. Every hour. Savor each kiss, and remember each touch. You will never miss anything more than those that you've loved and lost."

I repeated her words, even as they sank down into my core. Longing, *my* longing, infused the soul link I shared with Kieran. I would do exactly as she said as soon as he arrived. With all the danger we faced, we could be taken from each other at any moment, ripped apart. While we had physical bodies, I wanted to make sure we used them to express our love for each other as often as possible, just like Caily had said.

"Give me a moment," Jack said from beside the door before getting up and walking out. Chad followed, digging his hands into his ghostly pockets. They were probably thinking of those they'd left behind, family and friends. Acquaintances they'd never sit and chat with. Jack definitely missed the times he'd cooked dinners with Donovan, the two of them cracking jokes and snickering. The other spirits stayed as they were, watching.

"Let's all take a minute," I said, leaving Jerry to his emotion and standing, moving deeper into the caves.

"Wait, are you gonna snoop?" Bria asked quietly when she caught up. "Because I'd be in for that."

Red and the guys hurried to catch up.

I waved them away. "Oh my God, you guys, no! I was going to sit down and maybe rest my eyes for a moment. I'm freaking tired. We'll give Jerry some time to calm down, but we need to have a chat with him before Kieran storms in and undoes all the bridge-building we've done."

"I just wanted to get out of that room. That guy is a buzzkill," Donovan said.

"I didn't want to be left alone with him, either," Thane admitted. "I'm all for a good cry, but not around strangers. That shit makes me uncomfortable."

I rolled my eyes, my curiosity getting the better of me. "Fine. Let's have a little peek at how far back these caves go, really quick, and then we'll chill, okay?"

We traveled through a bedroom with a worn-out mattress on the floor and very little else, beyond a small area with a bucket for a privy and a horrible stink, and into a long rock hallway with the smooth sides and a rounded ceiling customary of Jerry's rock work. Camping lanterns dotted the way, so far apart they created a very low light, hardly enough for visibility. We supplemented it with our phones, taking the first right we came to into a half-made room with rough walls. Almost like a little dug-out nook. A similar nook led off that, then another long hallway with a slight breeze.

"Did you ever hear back from those rats?" I asked Bria. My voice echoed down the hallway.

"They never came back," she replied. "I was too preoccupied to keep much of a focus on them."

"I feel a breeze," Donovan said.

"Me too," Thane said.

"I wonder if it's another way out," Bria whispered, reducing the echo.

"Or another way in. How can one guy guard two entrances?" Red asked.

"We shall see," I said.

But we didn't see. Or we just couldn't figure out how. The rooms and hallways all seemed to interconnect, twisting and turning and then cutting back on themselves. The inside of the mountain was a labyrinth, created by a bored and listless individual who had nothing to do but exercise his magic. None of the rooms or nooks had anything in them, including bones. Yet camping lanterns dotted the way. He'd need to refresh those pretty regularly.

"He must leave this mountain occasionally, or where do the supplies come from?" Red asked.

It was a good question, but we had bigger concerns. Before long, we were hopelessly lost in the tunnels, the giant not the only danger on this mountain—we didn't have the sense of direction to get us out of this jam. I doubted Jerry would come to our aid, either. We were on our own.

Chapter 6

KIERAN

"THEY AREN'T SCARED like they were a couple hours ago," Henry said as Kieran led them up the narrow road littered with rocks.

"Alexis is worried," Kieran said, trying to calm the inferno within him.

Alexis and the others were alive—that was the main thing.

"What were they *thinking*?" he said for the millionth time as he picked his way around the boulders, obviously placed as a warning. They were a damn good warning of the giant's power. Some of the boulders were massive. "I had a plan for meeting him. I had it worked out."

Silence answered his words. They all clearly thought Kieran wouldn't have been able to close the deal. Alexis and the others had put themselves in harm's way to get the job done. Commendable, but they had no idea what they were getting into.

Kieran had seen this sort of scenario play out before. People as powerful as the giant weren't allowed to disappear from the magical world. The life of seclusion they envisioned often became a life of harassment. They were sought out, taken against their will more often than not, and put right back into the rat race, bound by a blood oath they hadn't agreed to or wanted. It was a part of the magical world no one ever talked about. Binding someone against their will was illegal, but once a magical worker was bound, they could be silenced. Without proof, a Demigod wouldn't be judged for their crimes. Business resumed, the rule breaking swept under the carpet.

Kieran's father had partaken in the practice. He'd called them "pilgrimages," and he'd dragged Kieran along on a few.

This giant hadn't been taken down yet, which meant he would be exceptional in his defense. He'd be ruthless in his execution. And he'd be closed off in his thinking, assuming everyone was out to trap him.

Mostly, of course, he'd be right. That was the angle Kieran had hoped to use. Kieran wasn't there to trap the giant—he was there to offer him the choice of a new life.

Except he would kill the giant if he had so much as put a finger on Alexis.

"He must be holding them captive," Henry said as they found an inlet laden with trees. A small path led through a ravine and likely up to the ridge that would take them to the giant's lair. This route was well documented in the inner circles. Of course, the only people who'd survived to tell the tale hadn't made it very far. "They are mostly staying in the one area."

Kieran stepped up onto a boulder and followed the trail out of the trees and up. The path narrowed to the point that he had to hold on to the side and carefully watch his footing.

"If he shakes this mountain, we'll be thrown off," Henry said, directly behind him.

"That's part of his defense. I probably would've sent you all back at this point. Gone it alone."

"He wants to play with his food before he eats it," Zorn growled, taking up the rear.

Kieran gritted his teeth, remembering the rush of disgust he'd felt from Alexis a while back. One finger. If that giant had laid even one finger on her, Kieran would rip his arm off.

"She's fine, sir," Boman said with utter conviction, the only one who had been talking Kieran down. "She is like a misfit whisperer. She has a knack for making people feel understood. She probably learned it with spirits, but she's done it with all of us. If anyone can charm that giant, it is her. And if she couldn't, she would've ripped his soul out and stuffed it up his newly evacuated body's ass. Have faith."

"I'll have faith when I see her. Right now, I'm running alternative plans through my head." Kieran took it easy around a particularly tight corner, not bothering to look down. He wouldn't fall. He couldn't, not when Alexis needed him.

A slight rumble disturbed the small rocks at Kieran's feet and made the rock under his palm tremble.

"He knows we're here," Kieran said, speeding up. He called down a thick fog, blanketing the sky with it, creating a cocoon for them. He knew the giant could sense them through the rock, but if he had any sort of viewing system set up, the fog would shroud them from view. "Watch your step."

The sound of stone grinding against stone caught Kieran's attention.

"Down!" He hunched, compacting into a tight ball. Not a moment later, a boulder launched off the cleft next to them, skimming Kieran's shoulder as it passed the groove of the path. It crashed down on the slope ten feet below before continuing its descent. "Speed up. Fast as you can."

They worked along the ledge at a breakneck pace, senses alert for more falling debris. Another boulder came at them a moment later, smaller than the last, skimming past them and carrying on.

"He's not shaking us off—he's trying to knock us off," Henry said.

"He likes to play with his food, as I said," Zorn

murmured, barely audible.

"Maybe he can't shake the mountain this far down," Boman added.

Kieran shook his head as the path flattened out just a little. In a moment, he saw why. An inlet ran off the ledge into a short tunnel. Beyond that, cloaked in white fog, was an area open to the skies. Alexis was deeper in the mountain and farther right, but not higher. She must've entered through this passageway.

He ducked into the tunnel, lifting the fog just enough to see the ground ahead. Rocks of various sizes littered the way, some smashed in half, some gathered in little piles.

"Look." Boman pointed above them, where the sleek and shiny tunnel ceiling had cracked. Dirt pooled in various places, hinting that the damage was recent.

"You are not welcome here," a voice boomed out, filling the tunnel before leaking out. The ground beneath them rumbled. The sound of rocks grinding together spoke of a larger defense just out of view. A strong current of fear flooded his middle—Alexis!

He was moving before he could think it through. Rage, hot and heavy, lodged in his chest. Terror drowned him.

"Zorn, go gas," Kieran barked, wondering if the giant could feel a Djinn in gas state through the rocks. No matter: Kieran would make sure the giant was plenty distracted. "Get past him and look for the others. Boman and Henry, stay with me. If you see an opportunity, take it."

He didn't need to be more specific. They were experienced enough to read the situation and respond appropriately to whatever opportunities arose.

As soon as Zorn darted forward, Kieran tore away the fog, revealing himself to the giant across the way, standing at the mouth of another tunnel. Aside from the rocks strewn across the ground, boulders of various sizes lined the three shelves built into the sloped walls of the tunnel, funneling down to the path.

"You have granted your own demise," the giant said, and the rocks rose from the ground. The ones stacked above the path pushed off their perches and sped down the sloped stone, curving in their trajectory toward him.

Fire building within him, Kieran stalked forward and *shoved* with air, ripping the rocks back up the sides of the crevasse. He shoved again, the strain incredible, now fighting against this level five with a great mastery over his art. He thrust his hands into the sky, directing the air. The rocks cracked and splintered as they slid against each other. And then they soared up over the side of the mountain and away, falling down the steep slopes.

The ground shook beneath Kieran, and the giant's

face, strangely blotchy—was it tear-streaked?—
reddened with effort. He was trying to pull up more
rocks, or maybe alter the landscape.

He would have time for neither.

Kieran was on him in a heartbeat, lifting him up by
his neck and forcing him backward into his lair. He
slammed the taller man against a polished rock wall and
leaned in.

"Where is she?" he demanded, voice laced with
venom, feeling Zorn work deeper into the mountain.
The giant's eyes widened, but he didn't answer. Kieran
squeezed harder, digging his thumbs into the giant's
neck. "*Where is she?*"

"You are here for her," the giant wheezed out.

"Of course I am here for her, you sack of shit. If you
have harmed her, I will tear you apart so slowly that you
will feel each piece of flesh I take from your miserable,
worthless hide."

"You are the mark holder."

Kieran flung the giant around, bashing him against
an adjacent wall before grabbing him again with two
hands, silently threatening to do it again. "Tell me
where she is. *Now!*"

If the giant felt fear, he didn't show it. Instead, respect lit his eyes. "You put that mark on her for love."

"A thousand times over. Where is Alexis? This is
the last time I will ask."

"She and her companions are in my caverns, turned around. I did not have the energy to get them. Your man is showing them out now."

"Boman," Kieran barked.

Boman took off at a run, tracking the other members of the Six through the blood link they shared through Kieran.

In no time, Kieran learned why Alexis had been so worried.

"We're okay!" Alexis said, running out of a room at the back. "Kieran, we're okay. Don't hurt him. We just got lost, that's all. Let him go. He didn't try to hurt us. Okay, I mean, he *did*, but that was before we came to an understanding. And also before Thane went Berserk."

Kieran felt the breath whoosh out of him.

"Zorn," he said. Zorn took Kieran's place, pressing a knife against the giant's jugular.

Kieran wrapped Alexis in his arms, squeezing her tightly. "Are you hurt?"

"No. I'm fine, honestly, Kieran. Thane got a bit beat up, and none of the cadavers made it, but we're all good."

"Thank heavens." Kieran buried his face into Alexis's neck, rocking her back and forth. "You idiot. What were you thinking? You should be dead. He kills everyone that crosses his stoop."

"Did you really forgo binding her with a blood

oath?" the giant asked, his tone indicating he was unworried about Zorn. "Or was she lying to me?"

He ignored the giant for a moment longer, allowing his eyes to roam Alexis's face and then settle on her lush lips. He shook his head again, the fear and worry for her slow to unravel while in this place.

"How can I protect you if you do things like this?" he asked quietly, thinking about the option to meet Demigod Lydia. He could not have Lexi taking a different path than his plans, not with her. A Demigod was dangerous enough for Alexis, but a Hades Demigod was worse still. Kieran would have a hard time protecting Alexis if things went pear-shaped and he didn't have complete control. There was plenty of wiggle room in the rules for Demigod Lydia if she decided to double-cross Kieran to get to Lexi.

A thread of fear wormed through him, and he pushed the thought away. Now wasn't the time. He'd contemplate the risk to Alexis with the possible reward of a Hades ally against a strangely idle Magnus soon enough. First he needed to deal with this giant.

"How can you expect me to stand by and do nothing? Most of the danger you're in is because you're with me," she replied, resting her hands on his chest, her eyes wide open all the way down to the soul that was connected to his own. "I love you, Kieran. I'll fight to keep us in our bodies and on this earth together."

He ran his thumb across her chin and snuck a quick kiss. "I love you too. I'll show you tonight." He winked, and then let his feelings seep away so he could deal with the giant. They needed to get out of here before they lost the light. Even twilight would be treacherous on that mountain path. If he couldn't enlist the giant or part ways with him amicably, things were about to get bloody.

Chapter 7

ALEXIS

I WATCHED AS Kieran's face closed down into a hard mask. Time for business.

He turned and motioned Zorn out of the way, pausing for a moment to take stock of Jerry. "Alexis never thinks to lie," he said. "Anything she told you would be the truth as she knows it. I'm Demigod Kieran, the unofficial leader of magical San Francisco."

Which meant he led San Francisco by the will of the people but didn't have the ability to vote on issues at the Magical Summit until he presented himself there officially.

He stuck out a hand for Jerry.

Jerry didn't break eye contact with Kieran. After a tense beat, he took his hand. "You know me as Titus. But..." His gaze flicked my way. "My...fiancée introduced me by my given name. Jerry."

"Damn right it's *Jerry*," Donovan murmured from his spot near the wall.

Thane, standing beside Donovan, said, "*Jerry* is

right."

Zorn gave them a hard look, probably to shut them up.

"They're a little punch-drunk," I explained.

"Jerry, then." Kieran looked around the space, his eyes lingering on the other spirits. They narrowed on Harding, who was still observing everything unobtrusively. It occurred to me that he probably could've helped us out of the caves and clearly hadn't bothered. He was capricious like that.

"What do you want, Demigod Drusus?" Jerry asked.

My mouth bent into an upside-down smile. I'd never heard anyone use Kieran's last name after his Demigod title, and I wasn't sure if it was a slight or a form of respect.

Kieran half turned to me. "How much does he know so far?"

"I'd rather hear it from you," Jerry said before I could answer. "I want to see how well your dad has trained you."

"Very well, I assure you." Kieran's gaze snagged on the single chair. "Do you have somewhere we can talk?"

"Yes. Follow me." Jerry pushed past Kieran without reservation. We walked through a room I hadn't been in before, the others following behind, including the spirits. A kitchen table sat off to the side with two chairs, one of them broken. A horrible smell beyond the kitchen caught my attention, and I glanced into a connected room and saw the pile of bones John had discovered.

"Had a nice wander around, huh, John?" I asked over my shoulder. "Checked out all the sights while we were having a standoff with a powerful, not-super-tall giant?"

"I wanted to make sure he didn't have friends," John replied.

"I would've felt any of his friends, John, you know that."

"Fine. I was curious."

"Finally. Honesty," I muttered as we passed through the other end of the kitchen and entered a hall similar to the one on the other side, only this one was higher and broader. Rooms branched off to the right, then left, but Jerry didn't turn into any of them. We kept climbing ever higher and deeper into the mountain, until Jerry rounded a bend, took a turn, and led us out onto something sort of like a balcony—a little cutout with a rock wall blocking a dizzying fall. Two chairs were stationed in front of it, looking over the vast blue of Montana. I'd never been this high up before. It felt like the top of the world. I wondered if we could see the whole state. I also wondered if I could get an oxygen mask because of how thin the air was.

"Please." Jerry gestured at the chair before moving

to stand near the rock equivalent of a railing, crossing his arms.

Kieran motioned for me to sit down, taking a standing position at the other side of the rock railing. Bria took the other open seat without apology and everyone else fanned out, some on the patio, some tucked back into the cave.

Silence stretched as Kieran and Jerry both stared out at the view. I had a feeling it was guy code of some sort so I just waited them out.

"She was talking to a spirit back there, wasn't she?" Jerry finally said, still looking out at the plateau that didn't seem real.

"Yes. They are around all the time," Kieran answered.

Jerry shivered. "Can you see them also?"

"Yes. She initiated a soul link, allowing us to share a small portion of our magic with each other. The first morning with this new…insight was…disconcerting. The power that came with it, however, is fantastic. Very effective."

Jerry's arms tightened over his chest. "You essentially stumbled upon a Soul Stealer, is that correct?"

"Yes. The shock was great, I assure you. When I first met her—"

"Stalked, met—similar, I guess," Bria said.

"—she had no idea who I was. She was utterly clueless about the magical hierarchy. She is as green as they get."

Jerry turned to me. "You weren't lying. You weren't brought up in the magical world?"

Bria huffed out a laugh. "How dense are you? Even a reclusive nutcase who eats his kills can see that."

Jerry's eyebrows lowered.

"Yeah, *Jerry*," Donovan said from within the mountain.

"Duh, *Jerry*," Thane said.

"What the fuck is your problem?" Zorn asked them in a forceful hush, out of sight.

"She battled my father only months after learning the true nature of her magic," Kieran said, his gaze shifting to me. "Her first proper introduction to the magical world was on the news. I put her in incredible danger. You wonder why I'm here? For help. She will never be safe. Not as long as she lives. Someone will always be trying to take her, to use her. You should've seen the look on my father's face when he realized what she was. He'd always told me it would be a foolish mistake to mark any woman in my life. He was so adamant that he never told me how to do it. But the second he saw the woman I had marked, his tune changed completely. He hoped I'd done it to claim her. They'll all think like that. They'll use it as an excuse to try to rip her from me, and they'll try to kill me to make it easier. I'm doing everything in my power to give us some protection. *Any* protection."

Jerry grinned without humor. His bald head shone in the dying sun. "You are good, Demigod Drusus."

"That was the truth."

"Oh, I know it. And you knew exactly which truth to share with me."

Kieran let a moment pass, looking out at the incredible view. "Yes, I did."

"What makes you think you're different from all the other Demigods?" Jerry asked, thick arms still crossed over his chest.

"I grew up with impeccable training—training that'll make me the best. It was hard-won. As my father prepared me for a magical life, my mother was suffering and fading away. Because of what he was doing to her. I didn't battle my father for his territory, and if Alexis and her kids hadn't made me want more from life, I wouldn't have taken it—"

Jerry's gaze snapped to me. "You have kids?"

"Wards, really," I said. "They aren't biologically mine. My mother saved them off the streets, and I took up the baton after she passed. One of my wards is non-magical, and the other was a shifter with Moonmoth disease, where the human side tries to fight the magical blood. Kieran saved Mordecai before he had any claim on me. He bought us food, too, and he and his guys even showed up to cook it. You asked what makes Kieran different? It's that he is genuine when it counts. The first day he met me, when he thought I might have been hired to spy on him, he still went out of his way to buy a blanket for my very sick ward. He left it at the door without so much as a note. Kieran looks after his guys like they are family. He takes it in stride when Bria"—she raised her hand, eyes still closed—"talks back and drags me into terrible schemes, because she's family, too. He hasn't forgotten the lessons he learned from his mother."

"I probably would have," Kieran murmured. "With enough time, I probably would've turned to the only thing I knew—my training. My father's training. But Alexis keeps me level. She and her wards keep all of us sane. What makes me different? She does. She makes me a better man, and that makes me a better leader."

"*Kumbaya, my lord*," Bria sang softly. "*Kumbaya…*"

"Get the woman a lighter, *Jerry*," Donovan called out.

"Where's the campfire, eh, *Jerry*?" Thane said.

"This is unraveling fast." I rubbed my eyes, swore, then remembered I hadn't put on makeup that day. I rubbed them a little more. "We need to head down the mountain before dark. I am not staying in that cave with the poop and the bones."

"I don't eat the trespassers," Jerry said. "That's a

rumor. Those bones are from mountain goats and deer. I have a car around the other side of the mountain. I've always wondered who would be smart enough to grab me when I go down for supplies—vegetables and fruit. The people in the village at the base of the mountain are good people, though. They clearly haven't told anyone about my habits."

Silence again fell over everyone as the sun kissed the horizon, Jerry looking out over the valley, Kieran letting him mull things over.

The wait didn't do kind things to the two punch-drunk members of the Six.

"Join our party already, *Jerry*," Donovan called out.

"Sorry about throwing rocks at your head, *Jerry*, okay?" Thane said.

"I don't think Kieran realizes how different he is from other Demigods," Bria said, pushing up to standing and taking a place at the stone rail. "I've worked for a few of them here and there, and seen even more in action. He's the only one I like. Literally the only one. Regardless, hurry up and make a decision so we can get out of here. Your life right now sucks, bud. I don't want to spend any more time in it."

Laughter shook Jerry's shoulders, but it was short-lived. "If Miss…"

"Just call her Alexis," Bria said. "Formality makes my ass clench."

"If Alexis hadn't spoken to Caily, we'd all be dead," Jerry said. "I would've brought the mountain down on top of you, and she would've killed me in the process. I would be with my sweet rose right now. But I cannot ignore Caily's wish for me to do more with my life. I will join you. I will take the oath. Most importantly, I will help protect Alexis so that Demigod Drusus never has to endure what I have."

"Thank fuck." I heard a slow clap and some shuffling within the stone hallway. "Let's get out of here," Donovan said. "This place is doing my head in."

Jerry didn't want to bring anything, maybe because all of his belongings had gone to seed, or maybe because they reminded him of the empty years he'd spent seeking revenge. Either way, he left everything behind. As we made our way out a side exit, a large cave used as a garage that was blocked off with a stone slab only the giant could move, Harding fell in beside me.

"I am thoroughly impressed," he said as the giant hopped into an old Subaru, the seat pushed back so far that no one would be able to fit in the rear.

"About which part?"

"All of it. Everything. The way you all worked together, your collective courage in the face of danger, your ability to get the guy no one else was able to get—you pulled it off. I'm impressed. I've said it before, but this has cemented it in my mind—you and your Demigod are something special. Add in your team, and you've got something magical."

"Thanks." We made our way down the road, no one riding with Jerry, who lead the way slowly, lifting the rocks out of the way. I suspected that was Kieran's way of extending trust. If Jerry wanted to take off, he could. But if he chose to follow us back to our lodgings, his decision would be set in cement.

At this point, after everything we'd been through, I couldn't find the energy to care.

"I will tell you a secret, but you can't tell anyone it came from me," Harding said, putting out his hand to slow me. Zorn, at the back of the group, gave me a hard stare, but let me fall behind him. "There is a recluse I know of with fantastic power. Most of the living world thinks he is dead. Like your new giant, this recluse is hiding in a mountain, but the mountain is not his protection. His ability to disappear and don a non-magical identity has kept him safe."

"What is his magic? Espionage?"

"That's not an actual magic. Have you ever heard the term"—Harding paused for dramatic effect—"Lightning Rod?"

"No. I mean, I know what a lightning rod is, but not the magical kind."

His expectant expression fell. "No? You've never heard the term Lightning Rod? Really? Crack a book."

He sighed. "It's like how they call you a Soul Stealer instead of your actual magical name. This magical worker is of Zeus's line. He's a level-five Thunderstroke. He entered into a blood oath with a Demigod of Zeus, Gianna. Rumor has it that he was then forced to be her sex pet, sometimes chained to the bed for days on end. She died of poisoning, and the world believes that he died right beside her. Though a few people prospered because of her death, your father included, it was never discovered who actually killed her. It couldn't have been the Thunderstroke because of the blood oath. Regardless, he is not dead. He is not in the beyond. I wonder if he would be amenable to entering magical society again. Chester life can be so dull. It would do anyone's head in. But he'd need magical protection. His power is nearly as rare as yours, though far less elusive and terrifying. All of Zeus's line will want to have it, just like Hades's heirs want you. Wouldn't it be a grand joke if one of Poseidon's line had the monopoly on rare, cool magic? That watery bastard doesn't deserve it, but you're shacked up with one of his kind, so here we are."

"Why are you telling me this now? Why not when we started the hunt for a larger magical defense?"

"Lightning Rods are incredibly dangerous, and this man was done all kinds of wrong by a Demigod. Gianna was a big lover of BDSM—do you know what *that* is?"

"Yes. I don't live under a rock."

"Do you like it?" He waggled his eyebrows suggestively.

"Hurry up. We're almost to the SUVs."

"I'll take that as a maybe. Well, she didn't believe in safe words. She beat him bloody, I've heard. Cut him. Tortured him. By now, I imagine he is severely mind-fucked, and won't trust easily. He'll be more dangerous than the giant. He might be a death sentence. But maybe, just maybe, with all of you working together...*all* of you..." He paused, his gaze pounding into mine, trying to get his meaning across. He meant the kids, obviously. I shook my head, but he continued before I could object. "Maybe you'll have a shot. He would be the ultimate *score* for your party. With his ability to detect and counteract Zeus magic, he'd sufficiently cover your Zeus blind spot."

The various rocks and boulders littering the way lifted into the air as we walked down the mountain, the giant clearing the road for his car. The SUVs were parked just up ahead. Donovan would have to lift the cars and turn them around.

"Where is this guy?" I asked as Kieran glanced back at me. He'd stopped in front of the huge boulder that had blocked the cars, which was now lifting into the sky.

Harding shook his head, the shadows making his strong features more severe but not diminishing his handsomeness. "Telling you would be crossing the line.

I've given you too much information as it is. Tell the team and work it out."

"What are you even talking about?" I asked in annoyance. "How is this crossing a line? Who would know you're the one who told me?"

"If you suddenly knew everything about this guy, including his location, without creating any kind of paper trail, people would know you had an informant. They'd want to know who, because they'd want to silence or steal that informant. That's how it works in the minefield of Demigods. I do not want them to know I am whispering in your ear. I'm not back on the radar yet. I'd like to keep it that way."

I huffed through my nose. "Okay, I'll let Kieran know."

"Good. A hint should be enough for his team. They're pretty sharp. How are my kittens, by the way?"

I crinkled my nose. Back home, Harding had temporarily possessed a small white cat. He'd remained connected to the cat while it did the nasty with a feral cat. So gross.

"They are four months old, in case time got away from you. Two of them seem unnaturally big, and those two won't let us re-home them. They scratch and bite anyone that tries."

"Good. Let them hang around. They can be guard cats." He stopped me and turned, the mirth leaving his eyes. "Above all else, Alexis…" He put his hands on my arms. His touch would have sucked energy from me had he been a normal ghost, but his hands felt like actual hands, with a warmth that soaked into me. "Stay safe. He is the most dangerous of all. While I definitely want to pry you away from your Demigod and show you the incredible pleasure you've only dreamed of, now is not the time. It won't be a matter of backing off if you don't think you can get him—he'll want to kill you to keep his secret. Have a care."

With that, he was gone, his warning and his touch still burning through my body uncomfortably.

Chapter 8

ALEXIS

"WHAT WAS THAT about?" Kieran asked as he drove us back to the Airbnb.

He'd told the rest of the team to get in the other SUV, and Jerry had surprised everyone by suggesting that Bria or Red ride with him in case he got separated. He didn't have a phone.

"What, with Harding?" I asked, sliding my hand over his upper thigh.

"Yeah. You two seemed pretty intent."

"I'm not allowed to tell anyone. In other news not at all related to this, do you know what a Lightning Rod is?"

"Yes."

I leaned closer so I could slide my hand along the crease of his thigh and down over his delicious bulge. He sucked in a breath.

"Well, a Lightning Rod that everyone thinks is dead actually isn't. He would be an unbelievable *get* for your magical arsenal." I applied a little pressure and rubbed his growing hardness. I ran my other hand up over my breasts, my nipples tight, desperate for his touch.

"Do you know his name?"

"No." I rubbed back up, finding the button on his jeans and popping it. "He apparently has a human ID and is living as a recluse on a mountain in the non-magical zone. He's supposed to be incredibly dangerous, very distrusting because of a gross past, and intent on killing anyone that uncovers his secret."

I leaned in more so I could use both hands to pull down his zipper.

"Oh, baby, I can't focus with you doing that," he said with uneven breath, lifting a little so I could make room for my hand in the front of his jeans.

"That's okay. That's all the info I have. You can get Henry on it. Tomorrow." I ran my lip over my teeth, remembering what Caily had said, feeling the pinch of worry that I would lose Kieran. "Just focus on driving."

I slid my palm against his warm skin, dipping my fingers under the waistband of his boxers. His smooth shaft filled my palm, hard and ready. I moved the seatbelt out of the way so I could lean over his pant line, pulling his girth from its confinement.

"I want to fuck you so bad, Kieran," I said, then licked his tip.

"Hmm." He spread his large hand out over my back. "Suck it in, baby."

I circled the head with my tongue before taking it in and sliding my lips down his velvety skin. Sucking languidly as I came back up, I circled the tip again before bobbing back down, taking it in as far as I could. His groan spread tingles through me, tightening my breasts and making my core pound. I increased my speed, taking pleasure in his delight, feeling the desperate ache for him pooling in my gut.

The car swerved to the side and stopped quickly. He rolled the window down, but I kept going, feeling a thrill that someone might see. He stuck out his hand and waved everyone on. I continued bobbing on his hard length, working my hand in tandem, feeling him tightening up.

Once the window was back in place, he turned, clicked off my seatbelt, and grabbed the bottom of my shirt and pulled it over my head. I unhooked my bra.

"Suck on my nipples, Kieran."

He did so without hesitation, flicking one with his tongue before fastening his scorching-hot mouth around it while undoing the button on my jeans. I moaned as he moved to the other, helping his harried fingers with my zipper. He pushed my jeans down and off, my panties quick to follow.

He came back up, as desperate for me as I was for him, his kiss hard and needy. His fingers trailed a line of heat down my center before dipping in. His thumb toyed with my clit, the pleasure pounding through me like a steady, insistent drum.

"Fuck me," I urged, finding his cock again and stroking.

He pulled my leg across him as he lifted me, his strength incomparable, moving me over his lap. Once in place, I dragged his cock against my slickness before stopping when his tip bobbed against my opening. His callused hands cupped my butt cheeks, and his fingers involuntarily squeezed the moment I finally sat down.

"Heavens, *yes*," Kieran said, thrusting upward and impaling me fully.

I groaned and my eyes fluttered, the sensations always so fresh with him. I rolled my hips before gyrating forward, his girth filling me. He thrust, lifting me up, slamming me down with pleasure. I met his thrusts, crying out.

"Yes, Kieran," I said, gyrating faster now. The car rocked with our movements. "Harder."

Hands at my hips, he continued to lift and pull me back as he thrust, creating glorious friction. I held on to his massive shoulders, the muscle playing under my palms. His tongue swirled with mine, mimicking our rhythm as it picked up.

Chest tightening, unable to get enough air, I rocked, each movement sending waves of delight through me. His cock pummeled me exquisitely, hitting all the right places. He dropped his hand between us, still kissing me feverishly, and manipulated my nub.

"*Oh...fuck!*" I fractured around him as an orgasm swept me away.

He shook under me, calling my name.

"I love you," he said softly, his kiss turning languid. "I will keep you safe. No matter what happens, I will never let anything happen to you."

With every ounce of my soul, I believed him.

WHEN I WALKED into the large kitchen area the next morning, most everyone was already sitting at the huge long table. When a house could sleep fourteen, the vacation rental owners clearly anticipated large gatherings for meals. Donovan stood at the stove, steam rising from various items sizzling on pans. Jack stood behind him, watching the proceedings with a look of longing, and Bria worked at the long counter cutting fruit.

Jerry sat in the far corner by the window. He'd stayed at the house last night so Kieran could keep an eye on him, and also because he had no place else to go besides his creepy lair. His warm, golden-tan skin had been freshly scrubbed, the shower tiles probably blackened because of it, and the clothes he'd borrowed from Kieran stretched tight across his chest and fell short on his long legs. At least there was no peep show, though.

K.F. BREENE

Not seeing the kids, I looked for their souls on my radar. Both of them were moving around upstairs. They'd be down shortly.

A hush fell over the room.

"Talking smack?" I asked, beelining to the coffee pot.

"Always," Bria replied without looking up.

Kieran watched my progress from his position at the head of the table. "I told them about the Lightning Rod," he said.

"It would be incredible to have someone like that on our team," Henry said. "It would close down one of our big blind spots."

"I got the feeling that pursuing him would be incredibly dangerous. More so than going after Jerry." I poured myself some coffee.

Jerry didn't look away from the window upon hearing his name.

"From what I heard," I said, keeping it vague, "it sounds like we'll probably have to kill him if he won't join us. He's too desperate to keep his secret to just let it go."

"It was the same way with Jerry," Thane said, and it seemed like rest had made him forget his Jerry jokes. Until he muttered, "Right, *Jerry*?"

Donovan huffed out a laugh. "*Jerry* usually kills trespassers."

Jerry still didn't look away from the window. Apparently he didn't care that he'd been dubbed someone to poke fun at.

"But a Lightning Rod is much more dangerous than a giant," Henry said. "He probably has more reach than Lexi, and Kieran's magic would make his lightning more powerful instead of less, since water can carry an electrical current."

I felt Daisy before I saw her, trudging into the kitchen with her hair pillow-rolled around her head, her eyes puffy with sleep, and her silk pajamas much too glamorous and expensive, given everyone else in the house was wearing sweats and T-shirts.

"Daisy, have you heard of a Lightning Rod?" I asked. Since she wasn't magical and was training to fight in a magical world, she had tasked herself with learning all there was to know about magical types. "The magical kind, not the metal rod."

She narrowed her eyes at me and stopped walking. "It is the crack of dawn, Lexi. Attacking me about work stuff is totally messed up."

I put a hand to my ear. "What's that? I couldn't hear you through all that teenage angst."

Jerry finally turned from the window to glance at Daisy. She met his stare.

"You're not very big for a giant," she said.

"Big enough that my feet hung off the bed," he replied smoothly, before turning back to the window.

"Fair enough." She trudged to the refrigerator and took out the orange juice. "Lightning Rod is a somewhat rare magic of Zeus's line, and it almost always manifests as a level five. The actual name for it is Thunderstroke. As the name implies, the practitioner can harness the power of thunder, creating deafening booms that rattle windows and disorient the enemy. Most notably, however, is their ability to control and manipulate lightning. They can pass lightning through conductors to strike someone miles away. If they practice enough, they can rain lightning from the sky with ninety-nine percent accuracy. A strike is like that of natural lightning—almost always kills, but some people have gotten lucky and walked away. From the first strike, anyway. The magic user can basically electrocute at will. Bolts can be divided up to strike many people simultaneously, although accuracy goes way down with that method. Best way to kill a Thunderstroke is to sneak up on him or her. Unlike you, Lexi, they can't sense people outside of Zeus-like magic. They can't sense humans at all. I'd slip in right behind them and, boom, stab them through the back of the neck and into the brain stem. Then I'd bend them on top of me just in case the split second it took to die was enough to rain down lightning."

Jerry jerked back around to look at Daisy again, this time with wide eyes.

"You'd best get stronger if you hope to pull that move off," Zorn said lazily from the table.

"Okay. Fine—"

"Speaking of electricity, close the fridge door," I barked. "You're wasting it."

Daisy slammed the door harder than was necessary, orange juice container still in hand. "Yes, I'd need more strength." She twisted her lips to the side. "Fine, then. I'd get a long-range rifle and place a kill shot to the head."

"With a noise suppressor, I hope," Zorn said.

"Obviously. I'm not a novice."

"Yes, you are. And where would you get such a gun? You haven't been able to steal mine."

"I have one. Stole it off a redneck kid back home. Idiot thought he was going to get lucky with an under-age teen. I broke his jaw and took his shit. Asshole."

I held up my hand to stop all conversation and leaned toward Daisy as Mordecai entered the room. "*What?*"

"Sorry about swearing," she muttered. We had a rule that she had to watch her mouth. Apparently, she thought I was more concerned about her language than the whole creepy older guy thing.

My voice filled the whole room. "What were you doing spending time with a guy who has an obvious agenda? A guy I assume is way too old for you. What if he'd tried to force you?"

"Obviously I would've killed him and had Zorn help me cover it up." She gave me a *you're so dumb* stare while popping out a hip. "I'm not an idiot."

"You certainly sound like an idiot, taking risks like that."

Mordecai shoved Daisy out of the way and opened the fridge. "I was there with her, just out of sight. I would've stepped in if anything had happened."

"I wouldn't have needed your help with that guy," she said.

"Which is why I didn't step in."

"Why were either of you there in the first place?" I asked, my blood pressure rising. "When was this? Where was I?"

"This was a few weeks ago when Zorn charged me to increase my arsenal of unregistered weapons. That guy stole it from someone and was bragging about it on a private chat. I figured it would be a good weapon to acquire. You were at a meeting in the government building, and I knew you wouldn't be able to call and check up on me. I pulled it off without a hitch. Don't worry, that moron is too stupid to track me down, so he can't turn me in or sue me for medical bills."

"Well executed," Zorn said, his voice ringing with pride.

"She is a child," Jerry said in accusation.

"My first beating in the foster home at four years old—at least, the first one I clearly remember—stripped me of childhood, *giant*. I'm where I want to be. Mind your business." Daisy poured herself a glass of orange juice.

"*Close the refrigerator door*," I yelled. Sure, the owner was the one who'd get stuck with the electricity bill, but I'd spent my whole life trying to save money. It wasn't the kind of thing you could just turn off.

Mordecai slammed the door shut and scooted to the table without anything to show for all his staring.

"This has got to stop," I said. "Zorn, you've gone too far. Daisy can't be in those kinds of situations. She's too young for that. Too inexperienced."

"We are headed into increasing danger," Zorn replied, flipping a page in the magazine he was reading. "Daisy and Mordecai are at risk because they're dear to you and Kieran. Might I remind you that Mordecai came inches from death, and Daisy was kidnapped and had to save herself. *Not* putting her at acceptable risk decreases her chances of survival. You need to trust her judgment. From all I've seen so far, it is impeccable."

I heaved out a wary sigh. He was right; I knew he was. But the knowledge that she'd put herself in danger terrified the parent part of me, no matter what the outcome had been. I was responsible for her, and the last thing I wanted was for her to be in harm's way, for any reason.

Still, I nodded. Daisy wouldn't want to be sidelined. Neither would Mordecai. I'd tried to keep them away from our battle with Valens, but they'd both shown up in the end. I'd tried to keep them away from the battle with Aaron's people, too, and they'd both almost been killed.

Donovan started transferring bacon and potatoes into a warm oven as he prepped for a batch of scrambled eggs. I stepped in to help and was promptly shooed away.

"Regarding the Lightning Rod"—I stood at the island instead—"we know how to kill him, but sneaking up on him won't help if our objective is to talk to him. He might kill us where we stand before we can say three words."

"Not if you meet him in a public place," Zorn said. "If he uses his power around Chesters, they'll react. Whatever magical government is closest will be alerted so that he can be extracted. His cover will be well and truly blown. He will know that. He won't want to rock the boat."

"Except he's a recluse on a mountain," I said.

"So was I, and the nearby village knew about me, as I said before," Jerry said, back to looking out the window. There was no telling what he thought of our dysfunctional family.

"Everyone knew about you—you didn't fake your own death," Bria said.

"This guy might be a different character, but he's in the same play," Jerry replied. "He has to get supplies from somewhere in order to live. I don't know of any high-powered magical people who were brought up in the woods. When you're not accustomed to living off the land, you don't have the tools to make it work. He's hiding in plain sight because he's in a non-magical zone, but mark my words, someone's noticed him.

"Another thing trained magical people can't live without is their magic. On days of no activity, I still felt the need to flex my magical muscles. It was an itch that I needed to scratch. If this guy's bag is lightning and thunder, then we're looking for freak or particularly violent thunderstorms. The kind that freak Chesters out and make the papers. That, or you're—we're, I guess—looking for a place where the weather can cover up his rushes of magic. We have plenty of clues to go by."

"When did *Jerry* turn into Sherlock Holmes?" Thane said with a grin.

"Jolly-oh, guvna," Donovan retorted, his accent on the wrong continent.

Zorn shook his head and flipped another magazine page.

"If that Thundercunt is on a mountain," Jerry said softly, as though to himself, "it doesn't matter what he can do. I own him."

All activity in the kitchen stopped. Donovan turned from the stove to look at Jerry, a smile blooming on his face. Thane's eyes widened. Even Zorn looked up, respect in his eyes.

Jerry must've noticed even though he hadn't turned away from the window. He shrugged. "I was made for battle. Stone does not conduct electricity. I'm safe from his magic."

"Looks like we're going to play a game of rock, paper, lightning, eh *Jerry*?" Boman asked, beaming.

"Who's paper in that scenario, I wonder?" Bria scratched her chin.

"Alexis," Jerry murmured.

Shivers coated my body. He wasn't wrong. I could take the Lightning Rod out if he ventured close enough, but he wouldn't face the same limitation. It was a good reminder that my magic did not trump all. I could be beaten like anyone—it just took the right magic.

This stranger would have that magic.

"What are you going to do, make a rock suit or something?" Daisy asked Jerry, breaking through the churning of my thoughts.

Donovan tsked as he turned off the burners. "You're showing your ignorance, princess."

Daisy scowled at him.

"She didn't know the size of a giant, she doesn't

know anything about their magic—my, my, she is behind," Boman teased.

"Boman, why don't you get that duct tape out of your pocket and make a gag for yourself," Daisy clapped back.

Donovan barked out a laugh. "Hey, Boman, why don't you get some more fashionable pants out of your pants pocket?" he said, starting to pull things out of the oven to put on the table.

"Hey, Boman, why don't you find a new personality in one of your pockets?" Jack said with a grin, still monitoring Donovan's efforts.

I repeated it for him. The guys around the table started laughing, and Jerry turned away from the window again, his eyes darting around. Big, tough giant was just like everyone else—skittish at the thought of spirits walking among us. At least when those spirits weren't Caily.

Jerry zeroed in on Daisy for a moment before turning away. "My skin can harden to stone, *princess*." Donovan's eyes widened and his smile stretched. Jerry just might have a dry sense of humor under his rough exterior. "Most weapons can't penetrate it, and certain magics don't work against it. My movement is severely cut down, though, so it's best to use it within a battalion."

Daisy narrowed her eyes, clearly at the name he'd

called her, but nodded. I knew she'd file that away and probably think of ways to counteract it.

A light bulb went off as everyone took a seat. "That's why he told—um… That's why a flash of brilliance struck me, randomly, after Jerry agreed to come aboard," I said. "Jerry has a natural defense against the Thunderstroke's magic. He can greatly help us bag him. Why wouldn't he just say that?"

"You lost the thread of keeping your mouth shut," Zorn said.

"Now do you see why we said she doesn't lie?" Bria asked Jerry, who still hadn't gotten up to join us at the table. "She's terrible at it. World's worst. Don't tell her a secret if you want her to keep it."

"I mean, this situation isn't normal. Obviously you know I didn't randomly come up with this info," I said. "Jerry, come on. Food's getting cold."

"Come on, *Jerry*," Thane said in mock annoyance.

"Yeah, *Jerry*, come on," Donovan said.

"That's going to get annoying," Daisy grumbled.

"Hopefully the giant will give them a thump," Mordecai said.

"Yeah. I'd like to see that," she replied.

Kieran turned in his seat so he could see the giant. "When we are together, we share a meal together. Please, join us."

Jerry nodded stiffly. He probably felt uncomfortable

being around all these people in an enclosed space, after having a mountain to himself for so long. But he did as Kieran asked, choosing a seat between two vacant chairs, still a little removed from the group.

"Let us take a moment and give thanks that we are all safe and together," Kieran said, "and ask that the next leg of our journey, whatever it may be, does not lead us into harm's way."

Shivers ran across my skin and I knocked on wood.

Chapter 9

ALEXIS

H ALFWAY THROUGH THE meal, I paused in buttering my toast.

"Someone is walking toward the front door," I said, feeling the soul come nearer. It burned a strange sort of…neutral. That was the only way I could describe it. Not a bright, glowing orb, like those seated at the table around me, but not a dull, listless, or bland sort of soul, either, which usually denoted questionable morals. This one just kinda…was. I'd never encountered that before.

The person in question stopped at the front door. I waited for the doorbell. Everyone at the table watched me, clearly expecting more info.

"Seems like they're just waiting there," I said. I told them what I'd gleaned about the soul.

"They are just standing in one place?" Kieran asked, rising.

"Yes."

He nodded and headed for the door. "Our visitor is fluent enough in your magic to expect they won't go unnoticed. They are either testing us to see if we're paying attention, or seeking acknowledgement for knowing they don't need to ring the bell."

"Valens did train you well," Jerry murmured.

"That's nothing," Bria said as Red stood. "Wait until he tries a little. It'll blow your mind."

"Doubtful," Jerry replied, standing as well.

"Bet you a hundred bucks, and where are you going?" Bria asked.

"I've finally chosen to leave the mountain. It would be too much to ask that this is a coincidence."

Bria laughed and forked some eggs. "You might've been the most exciting thing on that mountain, giant, but you are not the most exciting thing in this room. That title goes to Alexis."

"If only it were a title worth having," I said, slinking out of my chair and following Kieran toward the front door. He didn't actually need backup, but solidarity looked good. If the visitor knew I could sense souls, they probably also knew about my other abilities.

Kieran pulled open the door to reveal a striking beauty with large onyx eyes, silky black hair, and plump red lips. Her thin, muscular body sported sleek curves and an ample bust, her figure displayed to perfection in leather pants and a tight, ribbed bustier. A knife hilt peeked up from between her breasts, a gun holster hugged her right thigh, and I got the impression there were at least seven other deadly things hidden from view. She had the easy confidence of someone who knew they were lethal.

The woman spared me a glance, her face devoid of emotion or even interest. She looked vaguely familiar, but I couldn't place her.

"Amber," Kieran said, his tone completely flat, not giving anything away, but surprise and wariness swirled through our various links. He clearly knew her, and he was not pleased to see her. The name tugged on a memory, but before I could latch on to it, it was gone.

"Demigod Kieran, long time," she said in a sultry voice. She was, quite possibly, the sexiest scary woman I'd ever seen.

"Not long enough," he said.

"I wondered if I might have a word." It was not a question—it was a statement of what would come next.

Kieran paused for a moment, his wariness eating through our links, before stepping back and angling to the side, silently admitting her entrance. He led her to the sitting room, which doubled as a game room for vacationers, with a pool table, poker table, and a collection of couches and chairs.

Amber chose a chair in the corner farthest away from all exits. I had a feeling that meant something. Kieran sat on the loveseat opposite her and crossed his ankle over his knee. His guys and Red filed in, spreading out around the room, and Bria, Jerry, and the kids hovered with me near the door, watching. If Amber had wanted privacy, she didn't show it.

No one spoke, the air ripe with hostility and unsaid words.

"They're waiting for you to sit with them," Bria whispered to me.

"Me?" I frowned at her before seeing Kieran's subtle nod. "Oh."

What did I have to do with this? Even so, I joined him on the loveseat, hoping it would help get the show on the road.

"Amber was in my father's Elite," Kieran told me. The Elite was what Valens called his inner circle, those who were good enough to warrant the blood oath. Now I remembered where I'd seen her—battling against us on that beach in San Francisco. "She was in charge of his intel gathering. She was the one who first brought his attention to you and Bria. And she battled against us on the beach when I challenged my father."

She inclined her head, clearly not feeling the need to defend herself.

"Why are you here?" he asked her.

"I've kept an eye on you. I wanted to see if your defeat of your father was luck, or something more."

"You should've known better. You helped design some of my training, after all."

Her lips pulled up at the corners just a bit. "You are a young playboy suddenly in charge of a large, prosperous territory. Training means nothing without the maturity to use it. Looks like all you needed was the love of a good woman." Her sensuous gaze flicked to me, and despite myself, my face heated. "I've had countless offers of employment after Valens's passing, as I'm sure you can guess. One of my would-be employers attempted to kidnap me after I turned down his offer. Demigod Aaron is starting to get desperate, it seems. He's like a child throwing a tantrum. He's too used to getting what he wants—or maybe he just hasn't wanted anything this badly for a long time. His obsession with your pretty little Soul Stealer is eating away at him. He clearly thought I could help him with that." She paused, and I knew that in itself was a comment of some sort. "You know my qualifications, do you not?" she finally asked Kieran.

"One of the top three best spies in the world. Excellent at espionage and absolutely deadly. You could get placement with any Demigod in the world, or so my father always claimed. You were his pride and joy."

"I was a prized employee that he treated very well. I was not seduced or beaten. I was listened to, paid handsomely, and given every convenience. In return, I did my best work for him."

"You killed and tortured people on his behalf."

"I found and captured the people he desired. Some-one else did the torturing."

"Why are you here?"

"You have the potential for greatness, beyond even what your father predicted. You could be one of the best in the world, and so far, you are building an outstanding force of Elite to make that happen. You have seen qualities in magical people that others have missed. Quite simply, I want to be on the winning team. Henry is great, and a real asset, but I am better. With my direction, I can take your intelligence operation to the next level. I've identified five people we could get that would make your Elite sing, and have word on a dozen more that could be a great second string. More importantly, I can start stockpiling information on the Demigods of Hades and come up with strategies for dealing with them. I am excellent at what I do, Demigod Kieran, you know that. I can make you stronger."

"I killed your boss less than a year ago," Kieran said. "Why would you possibly want to work for me?"

"Working for Valens wasn't personal. Working for you wouldn't be, either. The arena of Demigods is a cutthroat snake pit. I understand that better than most. You don't deal in secrets without knowing the risks. I want a challenge. I want to be with the best, with the most ambitious, because complacency bores me. With Alexis on your team, you don't have the luxury of complacency, particularly given how you got your start. You'll constantly be fighting, probably for years to come. I want to win that fight, starting with the Magical Summit. The blood oath will give you a leash that should quell your concerns. I'm happy to take it immediately. You know I'm not making this offer lightly—I've done my homework."

"That explains the somewhat neutral soul," I said, her gaze making me squirm uncomfortably. It made me feel like she had stripped off my outer layers and was looking at the vulnerable, squishy stuff hidden inside. Like she was gleaning all my secrets without my permission. A leash was definitely a good idea for her. "She goes where the wind takes her."

"She doesn't have a moral compass," Kieran said.

"Correct," she replied. "I am the perfect employee. My compass is defined by my employer. They take the fault, and glean the benefits, of my actions. I am simply the vessel."

"Thank you, Amber. I'll take it under advisement. Give your information to Henry and I'll let you know."

She stood gracefully, followed by everyone around the room that had been sitting. The way cleared as she passed. At the front door, she stopped and turned. "I will inevitably accept placement somewhere. If I don't take it with you, I will take it against you. On the dark offer boards, you can see who is offering what. That might help you make up your mind. I look forward to hearing from you."

Her sleek, graceful walk entranced me as she made her way to a plain Kia that in no way fit with her personality or her outfit. I had expected a sports car at the very least. Something exotic and fast.

When the door closed, I let out a breath I hadn't known I was holding.

"Henry," Kieran said, walking back toward the breakfast table. "Find that dark offer board."

"On it." Henry jogged out of the room, heading for his computer.

"Everyone, sit. We can contemplate this as we finish our breakfast." Kieran resumed his seat, and the rest of us followed suit.

"She was like a sexy viper," Daisy whispered. "I can't tell if I have lady wood or am envious."

"She's a little light on morals, though," Mordecai said. "She's not someone I'd want hanging around."

"Oh, she's totally morally bankrupt. You heard her, though—the Demigod arena is like a snake pit. Demigod Aaron tried to kidnap her. Obviously she doesn't need to concern herself with morals." Daisy jabbed a piece of cantaloupe. "I loved her vibe. Didn't you love her vibe? She's vicious and lethal and smart, and she doesn't give two fucks about being the villain."

"Daisy," I reprimanded.

"Sorry. Two craps," she said. "That one got away from me."

"My knee-jerk reaction is that I don't want anyone that worked with my father," Kieran said, lifting his plate and heading to the microwave. "But that is emotion speaking, not logic."

"You're sure the blood oath gives her a leash?" I asked, pushing my half-filled plate away. I was no longer hungry.

"A blood oath forces the oath taker to put my best interests first. I can also control or curb her actions as I see fit. Demigods alter the amount of leeway on a person-by-person basis. Amber was allowed a lot of leeway by my father. As far as I know, he never had a problem with her, and he kept his dick in his pants to ensure they didn't have any personal distractions. Something he didn't do with many of his more attractive staff members."

"How much leeway do you give your...all your blood oath people?" I asked, knowing he didn't think of the newer members of his inner circle in the same way he did his Six, the original oath takers and his friends. His family.

"I've never used the blood oath to rule the Six," he said, confirming my suspicion, "but I'm keeping stricter control over the newer members until we establish a firmer trust."

"We all know how good she is," Boman said.

"If she is wanted as badly as she hinted, and still has her freedom, she is exceptional," Jerry said. He'd barely been back in his seat for half a minute, but his plate was clean. The guy had inhaled his food. "If your goal is forming the best team possible, she'd be a good addition. But if you think she can't be controlled and might find a way to wiggle within the blood oath just enough to create problems, then the danger is too great."

"Control wouldn't be a problem," Kieran said, returning to his seat with steaming food. "As I said, my knee-jerk reaction is emotional. But it packs a helluva punch."

"You won't turn into your father just because you employ the same incredibly talented and uncomfortably sexy woman he did," I said, stabbing down to the real problem.

"Right? Like...I think it's lady wood," Daisy said, frowning as she looked out the window.

Henry stalked back into the kitchen with his laptop open in front of him. "She made it easy to find that *private* dark board." He sat down in an empty seat, ignoring his plate on the other side of the table. He whistled. "She's worth a pretty penny. The highest bidder is offering half a million a year. What did your father pay her?"

Kieran shook his head. "I never heard."

"I can look that up," Henry muttered.

"Who's the highest bidder?" Thane asked, standing with his empty plate. He eyed the plate I'd pushed away and grabbed it when I nodded.

"Give me a second." Henry leaned closer to his keyboard.

"How would you feel about her coming in, Henry?" I asked, knowing being upstaged was never any fun.

"I wouldn't mind learning from the best. It wouldn't be a bad thing for Daisy, either. We'll just have to make sure the little princess keeps her more...delicate sensibilities." He grinned.

"When the time comes, she could teach Daisy things I can't," Zorn said, and it was entirely clear these guys would do whatever was best for Kieran and the group as a whole. They would shove aside their egos for a stronger team.

The way Jerry was analyzing the others said he recognized it, too.

"Fuck." Henry blew out a breath. "Highest offer is Magnus."

The air in my lungs dried up.

"You're sure she didn't construct that board to get what she wants?" Kieran asked, leaning back in his chair.

"Checking on that now. It is possible, but...given her talent, unlikely. She wasn't kidding—she could work for anyone she wanted to. There are a lot of players on this board, only a few throwing around big money. Magnus looks like he has a few posts, each increasing in amount. I'm just checking who else is represented here. Bidders are anonymous, so I have to hack into each account…"

"Magnus is in it to win it," Thane said, coming back for more plates. "She'd know we can't allow Magnus to get her. That dame is good."

"Yes, she is," Henry murmured. "The fifth highest offer is from Demigod Aaron. Looks like that was as high as he could go."

"Hence the kidnapping attempt," Red said, helping Thane and now Boman clear dishes. Jerry stood with his own plate, looked around at the others, and then skulked toward the sink without them. He clearly didn't feel like a part of the group yet.

"Demigod Zander of London is number two." Henry's brow furrowed. "Demigod Elise of France, Demigod Ruby of South Africa… All the big-money players are in."

"It bodes well that she wants to work with you, Kieran," Bria said, leaning on the island.

"Except for the fact that she likes a challenge," Donovan said. "Her interest in working with Kieran means she thinks keeping Alexis alive will be more of a challenge than helping Magnus kill her."

Everyone around the table nodded.

Kieran blew out a breath. "She is probably wondering if I'll go with what I want, which is to turn her away, or go with what is best for this outfit."

"And what will you do?" I asked.

His gaze on me was steady. "I will protect you at all costs. I'll need to bring her on. I can't risk Magnus getting his hands on her. She's been watching me, as she said. She'll already know a few of my weaknesses. She also did help design some of my training, so she'll know how to work around some of my strengths, too. She'd be Magnus's ace in the hole, and he probably knows it."

I nodded, feeling the anxiety pooling in him. His greatest fear was turning into his father, and he worried that accepting someone his father had trusted into his fold was a step in that direction.

"Okay, then. Besides that, what's next?" I asked.

"We reconvene at home, figure out where this Lightning Rod is hiding, and decide if we go after him or not. After that…we meet Demigod Lydia. It's time to edge into the dark waters of Hades," Kieran said, and a wave of foreboding rolled over me. "It's time to stick our necks out a little and see if she is friend or foe."

Chapter 10

KIERAN

KIERAN STOOD AT the window in the living room, looking out over the beautiful, sparkling water of the Pacific Ocean, tired down to his bones. It had been two weeks since they'd left Montana, and those two weeks had been a whirlwind of power and information. He'd accepted Amber into the fold the day she'd come by, settling on the same salary she had been getting from Kieran's father—considerably less than Magnus's offer—with the same bonus structure bent on performance. It was a system that she said kept her hungry.

She'd barely walked away with the blood oath—executed in Montana before the ink had dried on her contract—and she was already performing. She'd sent Henry a list of her five nominees for additions to Kieran's team, all of whom had been on the list compiled by Bria and Red. But Bria and Red hadn't detailed the candidates' hideouts, complete with the traps they'd laid to protect themselves, or devised incredibly clever plans to infiltrate said hideouts. Amber had even suggested which talking points might hit the hardest.

Kieran had told her that he would not, under any circumstances, force anyone to accept a blood bond. If he'd expected a nod to his morality, or perhaps frustration that his way made things harder, he didn't get either reaction. She took in the information and altered her strategies accordingly, without delay or emotion. She was a machine, a highly effective, incredibly intelligent machine, and Daisy had started watching everything she did. It remained unclear if that was good or bad.

Kieran had waited until they were back in San Francisco to give Jerry the blood oath. The giant had taken the whole situation stoically, barely speaking, and when it was over, he'd made his way to the back porch, sat, and looked out over the ocean.

Alexis walked in behind Kieran and slid her arms around his waist. He relished the feel of her warmth as she leaned against his back.

"Whatcha thinkin' about?" she asked.

"The calm before the storm. Amber and Henry think they have a location for the Lightning Bolt." He heard Alexis's release of breath and turned so he could fold her into his arms. "They are doing some risk assessment."

"They work well together."

"Very well. Amber pushes Henry to get better, and

Henry has no problem stepping aside if she wants to take lead. From a few remarks I've overheard in passing, Henry gets the feeling that she's used to getting pushback from male colleagues."

"Your guys aren't like that."

"I know. And I think it's thawing Amber just a little. There might be a human in there yet."

She braced her chin on his chest and looked up at him. "Did you set up the meeting with Demigod Lydia?"

He rubbed her back and kissed her forehead. Then, because he couldn't stop himself, he kissed the tip of her nose and her full lips. "I've given her a tentative time period and laid down some ground rules. Obviously your safety is the most important consideration. I'm hoping she's trying to set up an alliance against the other Hades Demigods. While most people in their right minds wouldn't go in with her on it, most people aren't hoping to marry the daughter of a kid killer."

A flurry of excitement and nervousness bled through the soul link. A sweet smile curved her lips. She was trying to play it cool, but her emotions didn't lie. Hope flowed like a spring within him. He had the ring, he had a plan, but he really, *really* didn't want to get a no this time.

"And if your hope of an alliance is in vain?"

"My next best guess is that she's luring us in to trap

us, with the intention of delivering us to Magnus and gaining his favor. Either play would be a strong one. From our talks, it's clear she is intelligent enough to think of, and plan for, either approach. I'm preparing for both."

"Is Lydia the least politically powerful of the Hades Demigods?" she asked, gliding her palms over his chest.

"She and Aaron have about the same amount of territory and holdings. Magnus is one of the more powerful Demigods in the world. They have a subtle kind of feud, from what I've heard, but I couldn't get any additional information on it. She would never want to take him on alone, but she might want to do it with help." He kissed her again, flitting his tongue between her lips.

She slid her palms up his chest and then hooked her arms around his neck, mewing softly.

"Do you have a second?" she asked against his lips.

"I always have a second for you." He ran his hands down her back and cupped her firm butt. "What do you need?"

"You. Inside of me."

"Of course, milady." He scooped her up, but rather than bother with the stairs, he crossed into the next room and clicked open the secret entranceway. One of the kittens that refused to be re-homed darted out, nearly as big as a cattle dog.

"Four-month-old cats shouldn't be that big, should they?" He put Lexi down gently beside the door and leaned into her, pressing his pounding bulge against her.

"Hmm." She pulled his lips down to hers. "I have no idea. Without the mother or father around, I've lost all concept of cat size. I wonder why they won't let us find them homes."

Kieran reached over and closed the door. "Light it up with spirit."

Ultraviolet colors infused the air around them, visible to him only because of the soul link. The Line popped into view: a smear of black pulsing from within a starburst of bruise-like colors.

Her magic wound within him, *through* him, erotic and glorious. He undid her pants and then pushed her panties down with them, dropping to his knees to take a loving taste. She moaned, moving against his lips.

He sucked in her clit and threaded a finger, then two, into her wetness.

"Hmm, Kieran." She raked her fingers through his hair, and her hips swirled uncontrollably.

The sight of her like that, so fired up, made it impossible to wait any longer. He stood in a rush, pushing his pants out of the way and letting his cock spring free. He hooked one of her knees over his hip, found purchase, and pushed into her in a single thrust.

"*Oh!* Hmmm." She gripped his shoulders and swung her other leg up, wrapping them around his middle.

He let his Selkie magic from his mother's side accentuate her pleasure as he pulled back and then plunged into her again, sheathing himself completely. Her breathing hitched, and he drew out before shoving in again, losing himself in the sweet slide of her body. In her tight embrace.

He amped up the Selkie magic, dipping into her secret places even as he rammed into her, teasing and hard at the same time. She moaned, her skin feverish against him, her breathing uneven and her lips on his, sharing the same heated air.

"Yes, Kieran. Oh God, yes." She rolled her hips as he pumped into her, faster now. His Selkie magic tickled her nipples, vibrated her clit with pleasure, while he held her tightly, driving into her with manic desire.

Her legs tightened around him. Her core clenched. He teetered on the edge for one moment, and then an orgasm exploded through his body. He let her name fall from his lips, infused with love and longing and forever. She shook against him, crying out her pleasure, clutching him.

"Amber and Henry are waiting outside," she said softly, lowering her legs.

"They can keep waiting," he growled, soaking in her

warmth, delighting in her kisses.

"Ask me, already," she said after a moment, so soft that he thought he had imagined it.

But he wasn't imagining the soft gleam in her eyes and the love pouring through the soul link.

He tried not to let his excitement show on his face. Or leak through the soul link. He surely failed on both fronts. "We'll see."

She laughed before kissing him. Then she sighed. "They're still waiting. Can't life just take a break for a while? Leave us alone?"

"It will. We have a hard road ahead of us, but once it levels out, we'll be able to enjoy things a bit more. You'll see."

He pulled up her pants and fixed them before seeing to his own. When they were both ready, he twisted the handle and pushed open the door as Alexis said, "Oh, wait!" revealing Henry and Amber facing away with crossed arms, and Daisy darting through the room.

"Shit," Kieran whispered as he saw Daisy, about to yank the door shut, but it was too late.

Daisy's eyes widened and she came to a stop. "What the fuck is that?" She pointed at the secret passageway door.

"Daisy! Language! There goes your phone," Lexi said, walking out with her head held high.

Other than Jerry and the kids, everyone in the crew

knew about the secret hallways. Zorn had wanted Daisy to figure it out for herself. Mordecai hadn't been told because Daisy could sniff out his lies immediately.

Cat was out of the bag.

"Sorry, sir, I didn't know she'd be coming this way," Henry said.

"Well, I wondered what you two were doing coming this way when you usually take the main hallway just so you can see the pinched look on Jeeves's face when he's reminded Amber is working for Kieran," Daisy said, bracing her hands on her hips, a childlike expression of joy on her doll-like face. "Jeeves" was her name for Sodge, the old and wrinkled butler who'd served Kieran's father for years and years. The man had been one of the few to mourn Valens's passing, and although he hated that Kieran had moved into the house, he had nowhere else to go. While he did have to tolerate the new owners, his behavior toward Amber sent the message that he did *not* have to tolerate turncoats.

"Quite the payload I got," Daisy said. "Imagine, all this talk about loyalty and honesty, and here you were, keeping this from me the whole time."

"No one was talking about any of that," Alexis said. "Go. Go up to your room. No free rides for you. You should've known about that entrance long before now."

"You're saying I should have been snooping more?" A wicked smile crossed Daisy's face. "Challenge accepted. You brought this on yourself."

When she'd left the room, Amber said, "Cute kid. She's got potential. She's not magical at all?"

"No," Henry said. "Not even a little."

"She'll be better for it, mark my words." Amber nodded at Henry, who handed the file under his arm to Kieran. "We are ninety percent sure we've got him," she said. "It's a tiny town in the Blue Ridge Mountains in West Virginia. The town experiences more than normal thunderstorms for the area. They go year-round, but while they are powerful and violent, they have never produced a fatality, unlike in other places with similar storm activity. From what we've read, it seems like a Chester town—they hate magic and all it stands for. To live there, you need a solid ID. Which our guy has."

"What's the risk factor?" Kieran asked, heading back to the living room. The risk factor was all he cared about right now.

"From what we've pulled up of his past, he's a classic Lightning Rod," Amber said, coming to stand in her spiked heels in the center of the room. Henry took a seat on the couch. "Immensely powerful and exceptional at his craft. He's been hiding out for fifteen years, though, basically out of commission. Sure, he probably plays with his magic where he can, and he has explosive discharges once every month or two, but there is no regular practice for him there. He'll be rusty."

"He lives in a mountain area in a little cabin, we think," Henry said, crossing his ankle over his knee. "He's nestled in the trees. Google Maps doesn't show much, but it looks like the nearest neighbor is half a mile away on one side and a quarter mile away on the other. Nothing behind him—it's a national park."

"He might hike up in that park and work on his magic," Alexis said.

"And he probably does," Amber replied. "But he'd have to do it rarely, or on a very small scale. Lightning is bright and loud, and people in that area love the outdoors—that means hikers. Given there hasn't been any word on a magical person, he's kept everything on the down-low."

"He really doesn't want to be found," Kieran said.

"No, he does not," Henry agreed. "I imagine he'll blow like a top when he realizes it's happened."

"The risk factor is incredibly high with this one," Amber said. "Even if he doesn't kill us on the spot, there is ample room for him to kill us after the meeting. The only consolation is that he's rusty with his magic. His margin for error can only help our situation."

Amber shifted her weight as Sodge came down the stairs. Upon seeing her, he scowled, then about-faced and walked right back up.

"I will say this, sir," Amber continued with a small smile. "This guy is better than anyone I have found.

Acquiring his loyalty would set us up nicely for the Magical Summit, not to mention help shield you if the meeting with Lydia goes bad. We'd need less people around you for protection. I think we need to take a chance on this one."

Kieran shook his head and looked at Alexis. Logically, he knew this was their best play for protecting her. If anyone could sway this guy, it was his people. Just like with the giant, they would find a way.

But the part of him not operating on logic took a strong stance against the plan. The risk seemed too great, the situation too dangerous. They'd gotten lucky with Jerry, but their luck was bound to run out. He said as much.

"It wasn't luck with the giant," Alexis said, slipping her small hand into his much larger one. "It was compassion. It was offering him a second chance at a good life."

"This guy has already granted himself a second chance," Kieran said, turning away from his advisors so he could focus on her. "He's walked away from the magical world to give himself that chance."

"And we will offer him a way to have his cake and eat it, too."

"We can build an amazing team without him, love." Kieran kissed her forehead. "We don't need to put ourselves in this kind of danger."

"Yes, we do," she said sadly. "If we're going to play in the Demigod viper pit, we'll always be in danger. Even your dad had assassins coming for him, and he was at the pinnacle of power and influence. At least in this situation, we know what to expect."

Kieran sighed, but even as he nodded at Henry and Amber, giving his approval, he wondered if they actually did know what to expect, or if this Lightning Rod would blindside them all.

Chapter 11

ALEXIS

"THIS TOWN IS a hundred miles from the nearest magical area," Amber said as we sat in Kieran's private jet two weeks after deciding to go after the Lightning Rod.

The plush surroundings did nothing to soften my fear of what was to come. Despite Amber's grim confidence and Henry's assurances that this was within our wheelhouse, I had very little faith things would go smoothly. While Jerry had picked a hideout within a magical area, and had met with his trespassers before disbanding them, the Lightning Rod had completely cut himself off from the magical world. This guy did not want to be found.

Daisy and Mordecai sat behind me on a cream leather couch, sipping non-alcoholic cocktails and wearing the smug looks of previously dirt-poor kids in the lap of luxury. I wished I could've worn that same look, but I couldn't be smug about anything when I knew I was putting my kids in danger.

Harding had visited me again, remarking fondly on the (enormous) white kittens, and warned me that if I didn't bring all of *my* people when going after the Lightning Rod, they'd likely never see me in the flesh again.

He'd meant the kids, and because his customary smirks and eye twinkles had been notably absent, I'd taken him at his word. He'd never led me astray. Besides, the one time I'd tried to keep them out of the fighting, they'd both nearly ended up dead.

I hated that they loved being included.

"This is good and bad," Amber said, sitting forward on the chair across from the small table where Kieran and I sat, fancy finger foods arrayed on a silver tray between us, untouched. "Good, because it's doubtful the people that live there will be able to identify magical people from sight. From my research, it seems many were born and bred in that small town. The town generates income from tourists who wish to hike, camp, or otherwise use the resources of the mountain. There are a lot of rock climbers at this time of year, for example. Properly dressed strangers won't stick out. Unfortunately, our guy *will* be able to identify magical people on sight. To him, we will stick out. Most of us, anyway."

I couldn't tell who she thought would stick out. Kieran hadn't brought any of the new people except for

Jerry, who would be useful because of his lightning-resistant skin and affinity for rock.

"We have about an hour till touchdown," Henry said, sitting up close to the cockpit with his computer.

Amber nodded at him and then refocused on Kieran. "The original plans still stand, for the most part. You and Jerry will lead most of the team through the mountains, coming in the back way. The few we talked about will enter the town the traditional way. Our aim is to raise his suspicion. Make him jump at shadows."

"Wait…" I put out a hand. "We're basically going to alert him we're there? When was that decided?" I'd been left out of a few discussions, but this seemed like something I should've been let in on.

"If we come at him completely by surprise, he'll likely react on impulse," Kieran said, "in a way that relies on muscle memory and training."

"It'll turn violent, basically," Amber said.

"But if he suspects there is danger," Kieran went on, "he'll probably think things through. He might even set up a place for us to meet. Only Jerry will be able to meet him in that place, but it'll make him more rational. Less trigger-happy."

"It sounds like it'll make him more dangerous," Mordecai said.

"Only if he's smarter or more prepared than us," Amber said, and amazingly, despite how highly I knew she thought of her abilities, she didn't sound overconfident. Her voice held a bit of gravity, suggesting she would be on her toes with this one.

My stomach churned. That wasn't good news.

"Did you guys come up with some ideas for recruiting him over to the dark side?" I asked, eyeing the champagne chilling in the silver bucket at the edge of the table. No one had touched it, but now I wondered if I shouldn't just glug some for courage.

Amber leaned back, looking to Kieran.

"Harding is under the impression you should handle that," Kieran said with a grim expression. "You and the kids."

The blood left my face—I could feel it. "Harding is… Me…and the kids? Why was he talking to you? He never talks to you."

"He figured you'd kick him out of the house for suggesting it. He thinks it's the safest approach."

"I would agree," Amber said. "You don't have the ability to blend in. That mark, for starters. The Lightning Rod wore a mark when his mistress was alive, although not by choice. He'll recognize it immediately. Soon after, he'll figure out who you are. The kids will be with you, so he might think you're on the run. Or, if he's smart, he'll realize the coincidence is too extreme but assume you're there to speak with him in a non-threatening way. People don't bring their kids when they think a meeting will turn violent. If he's very smart, he'll know it wasn't your idea to meet with him. Maybe he'll take pity on you, or at least try not to make you a target. As soon as I know which way he's leaning, I can work on the next steps."

"Wait." I stood up in a rush. "You don't even know the next steps? You're going to send us into incredible danger—you're going to send *my children* into incredible danger—and you don't even know what comes next?"

"We're your wards, and we're almost adults—"

"You speak again and I will make you wish you hadn't," I said to Daisy, who'd turned fifteen not that long ago and acted like she'd turned twenty. Her teeth clicked shut. "Kieran, what are you thinking?"

He shook his head slowly. "We can pull out right now if you can't resign yourself to this idea. We do not need to go through with it. But I've heard all the details about how you handled the situation with Jerry. The things you said. The way you approached it. You never think about trying to get something for yourself, and it shows. You're the best chance we have. I told you that before we left."

I bit my lip, knowing he might well be right. But the kids—I couldn't put them into danger like this. I couldn't cart them right up to the front line and shove them forward. I said as much.

K.F. BREENE

"There's something else Harding said...something we haven't been able to verify," Kieran said. He was not taking this lightly. "He thinks Zeus himself must know about the Lightning Rod. That maybe Zeus had a hand in the Lightning Rod's escape. Gods aren't supposed to interfere in the lives of humans, but it's always been said that some gods develop favorites. A person with a rare magical ability, treated unjustly, would certainly draw the eye of their god. Now, this next part is just speculation, but Harding suspects Zeus would be pleased if the Thunderstroke were better able to show off his mighty magic. It is not a bad thing to please a god."

"That..." I balled my fists. "That sounds crazy. Zeus knows of this dude? Zeus. The god?" I rolled my eyes. "The gods haven't walked the earth in...forever. And even if they had, Zeus wouldn't leave one of his favorites to flounder."

"The Thunderstroke's not floundering," Bria said before popping a grape into her mouth. She was just as calm as she always was before an extreme clusterfuck. "He has been given a second chance. Look at the facts— not even Amber knew about him. No one does, despite the fact that he has used his magic in a Chester town. He was once high-profile, and he's got a rare, eye-opening kind of magic. Guys like him don't get confused for being dead. An expert would've checked to make sure the poison had done its job."

"Maybe the guy who reported his death was in on the escape," I said. "The Thunderstroke had to have some friends."

"Maybe, but secrets that big have a habit of coming out. The Thunderstroke's body would've passed under a great many eyes as he was transported around the palace. Only after he was declared dead would he have been left alone. If anything was amiss, it would've been talked about."

"Maybe he killed the person that helped him," I reasoned.

"Maybe so, but no other deaths except his and the Demigod's went on record. It's just...too clean for a high-powered magical type," Bria finished. Red nodded, which was annoying, because they hardly ever agreed on anything.

"Fine. Assuming that ridiculous notion is true, do you guys really think it's a great idea to mess with divine intervention? You'd be pissing off Zeus. You would literally be pissing off the king of the gods. Besides, what does Harding know? Even though *he* had a rare and interesting magic, Hades didn't do a damn thing for him. He's nothing but a nosey ex-Spirit Walker. I'll bet he only went to you guys because you're gullible. He knows I'd see sense."

"Probably, yeah," Bria said. "You're so rational when it comes to your kids."

"I'm allowed to be in that town," Daisy said, crossing one leg over the other. She wore plain jeans, a cropped black T-shirt that let her midriff peek out, and her hair in a ponytail. She looked cute, her age, and dressed down to blend in, as though she'd known about the plan in advance. "I'm a Chester."

"A Chester is a close-minded moron who either doesn't believe in magic or hates all things magical. You are not a Chester," I snapped. "And I don't think Chesters would be thrilled to have a Demigod's ward in their town."

"To put you at ease, I have laid out many next steps," Amber said. "I just won't settle on one until after I see how our man reacts to you."

I slumped down onto the edge of the couch. "Was everyone in on this but me? I mean the details. The stuff with Harding."

"We didn't tell *Jerry*," Thane said.

"Yeah, *Jerry* would tattle," Donovan added.

"Freaking *Jerry*," Boman muttered with a grin. They'd all taken up teasing Jerry, largely because he never seemed to notice, or if he did, he didn't care.

"I can shelter you and the kids from a lightning storm," Jerry said, staring out the plane window. His plate of appetizers had been picked clean. "I don't care how wondrous this fool's magic is. I own the mountain he lives on."

"Damn right you do." Boman put out his fist for Jerry to hit. Jerry ignored him, and Donovan and Thane snickered.

I ran my fingers through my hair. "Fine. Sure. I'll do it. But when he threatens my kids and I rip his soul out of his body, *you're* going to answer to Zeus, Kieran. Not me."

"I'll answer to Zeus. I hear that guy is hot," Amber said.

"Ego's too big—he's probably bad in bed," Bria responded.

"You'll have spirit surveillance all over that town," Jack said from his corner, the only spirit I'd allowed on the plane. "We'll call in everyone and set up shop. We'll start our perimeter at the edges of your magical awareness so we can account for his possibly larger range."

I nodded, relaying what he'd said. Amber nodded with me.

I knelt in front of my wards. Their expressions were guarded. "You are somewhat trained, but not for this."

"Speak for yourself," Daisy said.

"I am," I replied. "I'm definitely not ready. I'm now really thinking this is a terrible idea."

"Actually, Lexi," Mordecai said, "going to the Magical Summit without more firepower is a terrible idea. I've been doing a little research on it. Everyone might say it's just about magical politics, and for the Demigods and leaders, that's probably true, but for the staff, it sounds like the Wild West. Everyone challenges one another with their magic. A lot of people die."

"Without a good defense, that place will be the ultimate risk for you, Lexi," Daisy said. "A lonely Lightning Bolt—"

"Rod," Mordecai corrected her. "It's Lightning Rod."

"Whatever. He's just a steppingstone on the dangerous path Kieran dragged you onto."

"Don't pretend like you don't love it," Mordecai said.

"I do, but I don't want to take the heat for it," she replied. "This is all Kieran's fault. I'm just doing my part to lessen the horror."

Amber huffed out a laugh and murmured, "Cute kid." She was starting to say that a lot. It made me nervous.

Kieran reached for the champagne.

"Besides, Lexi—"

"Shut up," I said, pushing to standing. It wasn't nice to say that to a kid, but Daisy was getting on my last nerve. She was talking too much sense.

I went to the back of the jet and tucked myself into the bathroom for a while. I needed a second. This was my life now, yes, but I still hadn't adjusted to the constant danger. And no way did I believe that nonsense about Zeus. The gods hadn't messed around with humans for countless years. There hadn't been a new Demigod baby sired from a god in forever. It had been even longer since a goddess had birthed one. A big part of me wondered if Harding was just messing with me to see how far I could be pushed. The same big part of me wondered why the hell I had already decided to rise to the challenge.

Chapter 12

ALEXIS

"T HEY THOUGHT THIS would help us blend in, did they?" Daisy asked as we stood in front of a large house pushed back into the woods.

The three-year-old Jeep Wrangler that Kieran had purchased sat in the driveway, not a scratch on it. The rock-climbing supplies we didn't know how to use and wouldn't be unpacking sat in the small trunk area behind the back seat. The rest of our bags rested on the ground around us, Daisy's pristine rolling suitcase with a designer label standing out next to Mordecai's and my beat-up travel gear. Neither of us had thought to buy new stuff, so we'd used my mom's old luggage, a pink suitcase without wheels and an army duffel someone had probably stolen along the way.

"It looks *kinda* like a cabin," Mordecai said, looking up at the three-story structure spanning out within the trees. The For Sale sign still stood in the front yard.

"It looks like a rich person's idea of a cabin, yeah." Daisy shook her head, grabbed her rolling suitcase, and headed up the walkway. "We're the bait."

I hoisted up my pink suitcase, which had given Bria no end of amusement, and followed Daisy in. "Well, yeah, they told us we'd be bait. They weren't mincing words about that."

"No, they said the mark's reaction to us will help Amber decide on a strategy. Which is probably still true." Daisy held her hand out, and I filled her palm with the keys. She unlocked the door and shoved it open, clearly annoyed. "But they acted like we'd be drawing him out. Being bait is different. Staying in this fancy place—a house Kieran bought instead of rented— we won't need to go to him."

I set down my suitcase on the stone tiles in the grand entranceway, decorated in beige and gray and rust. Peeled log beams stretched across the pale wood ceiling, the dark knots a stark contrast to the lighter background. Simple and elegant wooden furniture in the same neural tones gave the area a subtle elegance, and the deep gray stone around the fireplace enhanced the grandeur. I didn't bother voicing my surprise that Kieran had managed to find and close on a home, not to mention furnish it, so quickly. Rules didn't apply to Demigods, even in the non-magical zones. Or maybe it was Kieran's wealth that had paved the way. Money and power talked, wherever you were.

"This place looks like the inside of a tree," Daisy

said, leaving her suitcase at the bottom of twisty stairs made of finely polished logs. Stone of various shades and sizes lined the stairwell. The décor was weathered and rustic, yet very classy.

"Drawing out the mark, acting as bait—I don't see what the difference is," I said, opening the fridge. My heart sank. The interior was bare. The cabinets were equally empty. "We need to head into town for dinner."

"Pizza might deliver," Mordecai said, standing near the large window in the open living room, staring off into the trees. Deep shadows draped the branches as evening stole the light from the dying sun.

"Why bother? Let's just go into town and get this rolling." Daisy opened the cabinet and then scoffed. "Really, Kieran? No glasses or anything? Why put in furniture and not some freaking glassware?"

"Because he secretly hates us," Mordecai said. "He probably put our names on the deed, just out of spite."

"What's gotten into you?" Daisy asked as I headed down the hall, marveling at the oak floors, polished to a high shine.

A quick perusal of the other rooms on this floor told me that glassware wasn't the only thing Kieran had forgotten. No curtains or shades lined the windows. Outside, shadows pooled around the tree bases and branches dusted the dirt. A lurker would have plenty of places to hide. Thankfully, the trees were pushed in close. To get a glimpse of us, the Peeping Tom would need to venture onto my radar. I'd know if someone came sniffing around, and if I didn't, the spirit surveillance I'd soon call in would catch them.

"Nothing." Mordecai was still looking out the window when I returned. "It's weird, though. Being on our own again."

"We're not really on our own, Mordecai. Give me a break." Daisy grabbed her suitcase and paused, clearly waiting for us to head upstairs with her and pick out bedrooms. "Kieran's team is just getting into position, that's all."

"His team, yeah." Mordecai grabbed his bag. "The team we're not a part of."

"What do you think bait is?"

"I just thought maybe I'd be in their group rather than pulling non-magical detail." Mordecai followed us up the stairs and then stepped in the first room in the hall. He dropped his bag.

Daisy stalled next to him. "You're his girlfriend's ward, Mordecai, and one day you'll be alpha of a wolf pack. You're not one of his Six. Welcome to reality."

"He needs a new name for his crew." I stopped by the next bedroom so Daisy could put her stuff inside, though she jerked her head to keep going.

"Looks like the master's at the end of the hall," she said. "I'll take the one next to you in case you don't wake up if someone comes in."

I rolled my eyes but didn't say anything. It was like they didn't realize they were teens and I was the adult here. Then again, had they ever?

My phone rang as we reconvened downstairs. I rescued it from my purse.

"Alexis, it's Amber."

"Hel—"

"Head down to the diner to eat while we get in position."

"Okay, do you guys—" I realized the line was dead before I finished. "That woman is really intense."

"That woman is insanely talented," Daisy said. "She's got Henry running in circles. Even Zorn is impressed, and he still hates her from when she worked for Valens."

"Stop brown-nosing." Mordecai grabbed his light jacket. "She doesn't like kids—she won't be training you."

Daisy pointed her finger in Mordecai's face. "Your attitude is starting to piss me off." He slapped her hand out of the air. She jabbed him in the chest. "How am I brown-nosing, huh?" She jabbed him again. He bristled, his jaw set, and leaned toward her.

"Do not fight in this house," I berated.

Daisy continued as though she didn't hear me, fire in her eyes. "She's not here, genius. When they can't hear you, it's not brown-nosing, it's just talking about them. And I'm not a *kid*."

"Well, you're not an adult," Mordecai shot back.

"What, and you are? Your balls probably haven't even dropped yet."

"Daisy, knock it off!" I shoved them toward the door.

"Well?" Daisy retorted, heading to the car. "Everyone knows girls mature faster than boys."

"You two are both still knuckleheads despite your age—"

"Shotgun," Daisy yelled over me, then punched Mordecai in the arm. "Slowpoke."

I rolled my eyes and locked the door behind us.

"Why wouldn't they get glasses and flatware if they got everything else?" I mused, climbing into the Jeep.

"Because they clearly want us to go downtown to get the stuff we need, duh," Daisy replied, shoving Mordecai out of the way and climbing into the front passenger seat. "We're going to basically throw ourselves in the Lightning Bolt's path, but they gave us a solid excuse. We aren't pretending that we need water and ketchup, though freaking glasses might've been nice. I'm thirsty."

"We should make a list, actually," I muttered, handing my phone to Daisy.

"Yes, exactly. If we were pretending, we wouldn't

think to make a list. See?" She opened the notes app, then looked at me. "What should I put on the list?"

"You guys need to learn to shop. This is ridiculous."

It was only three miles to the tiny downtown strip, populated mostly with single-story, cabin-like buildings. Green and red Open signs blinked from a few windows, and one dark storefront featured a brightly lit Coors sign. I pulled into the middle of three open spaces in front of a building whose sign declared it to be a café.

"She said diner, not coffee shop," Daisy whispered, looking down at my phone. "The diner is down the way—can't you see it?"

I knew that, but I really needed some good coffee first.

"We don't know this guy's name," I realized with horror. "We don't know what he looks like, either."

Daisy's fingers froze and Mordecai pushed up a little. No one said anything. What was there to say? Not one of us had thought to ask for details. We were flying blind.

"I told you we were bait," Daisy said, her fingers again flying over her screen.

"I'll be checking that list." I stepped out of the Jeep.

"What do you think I'm going to put on it? Vodka?" She rolled her eyes at me.

"Well…yes, I hope so. And a bunch of wine. But no

sweets. The teeth will rot out of your head."

I reached the sidewalk and looked down the dimly lit street, tiny pools of butterscotch light circling the cracked and faded concrete. Red maples dotted the way, their usually vibrant red subdued in the failing light. Mountain peaks rose in the distance, pressing in on the town. The cool air delighted my senses, rich with floral and evergreen fragrances, carrying the dewy chill of the coming evening.

"Look, there's a grocery over there." I pointed across the street at a shop down the road. It had large windows facing the street and curved brass light fixtures fitted onto a green strip painted across the red brick exterior. The white letters read, "Mitchel's County Store."

"It's a good thing we aren't looking for extravagant," Daisy murmured.

"The money has gone to your head," Mordecai said.

"Yeah. It's nice to have. Being poor was no fun, or don't you remember?"

"I haven't forgotten my roots so easily as you."

"I swear to God, Mordecai, I will rearrange your stupid face if you don't can it. You're getting on my last nerve."

"And you're both getting on *my* last nerve," I hissed. "Stop fighting, would you? Here, let's just go in here. We can play bait later. I'm not in the mood."

I ushered them both into the no-name café.

Daisy stomped in after me, muttering, "It's a good thing he loves you, or you'd get fired."

"It's a good thing I have an aversion to jail, or you'd find yourself in an unmarked grave," I replied, holding the door open. "We'll get a quick bite and then get some supplies."

The deep aroma of coffee was even better than the crisp night air. I nearly floated up to the counter, anticipating the warmth and comfort of a cup of joe.

A plump woman with graying hair and a warm smile greeted me. "May I help you?"

I glanced at the chalkboard, advertising open-faced sandwiches, pastries, pies, and the various coffee offerings. "A slice of quiche and an Americano with a double shot, please."

"You're going to be up all night," Daisy said, sidling up next to me.

I gave her the flat stare of a coffee addict who knows what she can handle. The woman's smile stretched wider and she nodded.

"May I please have the open-faced chicken sand-wich and a glass of apple juice?" Daisy asked sweetly.

"I'll have the same," Mordecai said. "Can I also have a side of fries, a hot chocolate, and a piece of blueberry pie?"

"Ew, you glutton, get dessert later. You don't need

to order everything at once." Daisy elbowed Mordecai. "And you ordered apple juice, so take that off if you're going to get hot chocolate."

"If I'm going to eat it all, what's the point of making two trips?" Mordecai elbowed her back. "I'll drink them both. Stop micromanaging me."

"You guys," I said between my teeth, my face flaming. "Go. Sit. Down."

"But the—"

"*Go,*" I said to Daisy, and I knew I had crazy eyes.

"It's a hard age," the woman said as the two found a table in the back corner and continued to bicker. "Are they your…siblings?"

The woman let the question linger. I smiled, knowing why she was confused. With only ten years or so between us, there was no way I could be their biological mother. Besides, our appearances didn't bear out a connection as simple as blood, what with Daisy's pale-as-snow complexion, Mordecai's dark skin and flashing hazel eyes, and my various shades of beige and brown.

The half-truths and outright lies were ready on my tongue.

"My mom took them in as foster kids, but she died a few years ago. I didn't think they'd let me keep them, but my uncle—my mom's brother—homeschools them, and I have a steady job that I can do from home, so I guess it's a team effort." I shrugged. "We thought we might try a little rock climbing, but I suspect we'll instead do some rock dangling."

The woman laughed and stuck a handwritten green ticket in a clamp on the circular ticket holder for whoever was in the kitchen. "That's really noble of you, a young woman like you looking after those kids. God is smiling down on you for your charity."

I shrugged again, now feeling bad for lying. "I couldn't, in good conscience, turn them away." At least that was the truth.

"Whoever is generous to the poor lends to the Lord, and He will repay him for his deed," the woman said, her eyes kind.

Guilt flowered within me. Here I was, invading someone's refuge for personal gain. This Thunderstroke guy had escaped a truly horrible life in a world so corrupt and disgusting that it had been openly known—and accepted—that his Demigod had kept him chained to a bed as a slave. What was I thinking? I couldn't, in good faith, take his second chance, especially since I was offering nothing but danger as a substitute. Because the truth was that I had no idea if he'd be safe with us. If someone took out Kieran, everyone on our team would be vulnerable. I couldn't protect this guy any more than he could protect me. He might find himself chained to someone else's bed, and honestly, I could, too. The future was bleak if things went wrong. I couldn't force someone to endure that with me, not when they'd already been granted their freedom.

I took the coffee and food back to our table, lost in thought. I didn't interrupt the kids' bickering, and shrugged them off when they asked what my problem was. By the time Mordecai took his last bite of pie, I'd made up my mind. Being here was a lot of risk, and a lot of selfishness, and the latter wasn't a good look on me.

"Come on, finish up. We're leaving." I piled my dishes together for easy cleanup. "We'll stay in the house tonight, but we're leaving first thing tomorrow."

"Where are we going?" Mordecai said, his mouth full.

I sighed and gave him a flat stare until he closed his mouth. The door opened, and fresh air swirled through the coffee shop. Daisy put her dishes in a tub near the napkin and flatware stand.

"Here." I motioned for her to get mine, too.

"I'm not your minion."

I lifted my eyebrows. "You're my kid. Kids do stuff. Get to it."

"I'm not your kid."

"Daisy, so help me God, if you—" Mordecai's kick nearly loosed my power on them both. I was in that kinda mood. I turned my scowl on him. "Do you want to sleep outside, is that what—"

"The guy who just walked in is standing in the

doorway and staring at us," Mordecai said under his breath.

I glanced over, only to freeze solid, my hands hovering over my dirty plates and my eyes rounding like saucers.

The man looked about Kieran's age, late twenties or early thirties, and extremely handsome. His hair, a little wavy and a lot messy, went from light brown at the roots to wheat and then gold, natural highlights women would spend oodles of money for in a salon chair. A light dusting of scruff adorned his angular face, tilting him from pretty boy to pretty damn hot. Brows arched over clear baby blues, framing a gaze as direct as it was beautiful. A tattoo of fire rose from his neckline like actual flames crawling up his skin.

I gulped, not sure what to do. Not sure where to look. This had to be the guy. I could see the conflict in his knowing stare. The rage. He was clearly wondering if he could burn me dead on the spot.

Chapter 13

ALEXIS

"DYLAN, HELLO," THE woman at the counter said.

He shook himself slightly, as though waking from a trance. His deeply hooded eyes, like a man in the throes of sex, blinked twice quickly, and then he was walking toward the counter again, fluid and easy.

The small hairs stood up on my arms.

Too easy.

Sweat broke out over my brow. All I could think about was getting my kids to safety. But where the hell would they go?

My mind whirled, going over everything I'd heard about this guy. He could only detect people of Zeus's magic, but that didn't mean he couldn't put his other senses to use. He clearly knew something was up. Still, he wouldn't light up this whole town. No way. Given the way he was talking to the woman, he liked her. They were friendly. In a small town like this, he was probably friendly with a great many people. He wouldn't want to rain lightning down on everyone just to get to the kids and me. It wouldn't be smart, either. A Chester would cry magic, people would figure out what magic, and the game would be up.

"Go," I said softly, passing the kids the keys. "Go. Drive away. Get out of this town. Right now. Do not come back for me."

"No," Daisy said, her body moving like liquid grace as she walked back to the table. Her movements screamed *lethal training.* "We're not leaving you here."

I reached in and grabbed her soul. "You will get out of his town right now. Both of you. You will run."

She gritted her teeth, fighting the pain in her middle. Mordecai didn't even have to grit his teeth. He was too used to pain for that—his entire life had been riddled with it until recently. He just watched me placidly, refusing to get up.

"This is the second double-shot Americano I've made in the last hour. You young people." The woman tsked with a smile, moving to prepare the coffee. The man, Dylan, turned and looked at the person who'd obviously ordered the last one, the warning in his suddenly dangerous glare sending tingles scurrying across my skin. His soul, once bright and alive, pulsed dark. Throbbed, even. I had never seen a soul change like that. I wondered if mine did the same thing when I prepared for battle. Like right now.

"What about you?" Mordecai asked.

"Get the fuck out of this town, right now," I said, standing and yanking him up with me. I shoved him toward the door. "Take your sister. Make her go."

Daisy yanked her arm out of Mordecai's grasp. She blinked away the moisture in her eyes, the only remaining sign she'd felt my attack on her spirit box. "We've done this before, remember? When you took off to protect our house and left Mordecai and me in safety? Remember how that turned out? We both nearly died. I'm not doing that again. I'm not leaving you or him. We stay together. We've always done okay when we're together."

I shook my head at her in utter disbelief. This was not the sort of thing heroes had to deal with, their freaking kids refusing to get saved.

Dylan slid a bill over the counter and turned gracefully, heading toward the sugar station behind Daisy.

"Then sit down," I said through clenched teeth, watching the woman behind the counter busy herself cleaning. "Daisy, go order something. A hot chocolate. Keep that woman in the room."

"I could do with another slice of pie," Mordecai said as though we weren't in extreme danger and Dylan wasn't slowly loading up on sugar while he worked over why a magical worker with a Demigod's mark was hanging out in this Chester town. The fact that we were here meant we had fake documents good enough to get us past the very thorough highway patrol station. Only dual-society zones allowed magical people in, and this was far from one of those.

"You're going to get sick if you eat another slice of pie," Daisy said.

I shook my head in disbelief for the second time. "Really? Arguing *right now*? Get the fucking slice of pie. Throw up. Whatever. *Just get it now.*"

"She does not handle pressure well," Daisy murmured as they both turned for the counter.

"She's never come back from the dead, that's why," he replied, much too loudly, because I could still hear him and now they were closer to the Lightning Rod than I was.

"I haven't either," Daisy replied.

"Yeah, but you were nearly there. You just managed to save yourself before you had to be saved. She's the one that always saves the day, so she doesn't ever have to sit and stew in danger."

"Yeah. This is kinda good for her."

I couldn't do much more than stare at them with my mouth open. I honestly couldn't. Was I dreaming?

Dylan turned from the sugar station before fixing his lid in place. A couple of slow strides and he was at my table. He lowered into Daisy's chair.

"I can kill you where you sit," he said softly, like a lover whispering into my ear. My stomach flipped and then cramped in fear.

"I will take your word on that. I don't honestly know much about how your magic works. But I'm pretty sure I could kill you about as fast as you could kill me." I rested my touch on his soul casing, light as a feather. His eyes tightened. "But let's keep this between us. Don't harm those kids. Please. I tried to make them go, but they are too damn stubborn. They are no threat to you. One isn't even magical. They were with me before…any of this."

He leaned forward, baring his teeth just a little. "And what is *this*?"

"Living in the magical world. I haven't been in-volved with it for very long."

A wry grin twisted his lips. "Maybe not, but you've made a loud entrance. I know who gave you that mark. It's not hard to get around the Chesters' block on magical news."

I couldn't help my brow furrowing. "They have a block on magical news here?" I whispered. "I didn't even know that was possible. And yes, I did make a loud entrance. It couldn't be helped. I wasn't about to let a loved one face Valens alone."

"How'd you find out about me? Don't try to say you're running away with your kids and happened to pick this town. I don't like being called stupid."

"Then we won't get along." Daisy stopped beside

the stranger. "You're in my seat."

"Just get another chair," Mordecai said, sitting with his pie.

"No. He's in my seat. That's rude." She stared down at him. "Please move."

"Daisy, have you lost your mind?" I motioned her away. "Just sit somewhere else. Quit antagonizing him."

"Being afraid is a waste of one's last minutes. I refuse to give in." She set her hot chocolate down, crossed her arms, and lifted her chin.

I stared her down, promising pain, until she finally huffed and grabbed another chair. Wood groaned as she slid it across the floor.

"It's that age," the woman behind the counter said before chuckling softly.

"Well now. Isn't this just a happy little family. Where's the rest of it?" Dylan asked, his gaze rooted on me. He was asking about Kieran and his crew.

"Around. We weren't given specific information," I said. "Honestly, I'd decided to leave without letting you know I was here. We were supposed to run into you in the diner. As you can see, we aren't in the diner. I was going to head out at first light."

"That right?" He sipped his coffee, and I could tell he didn't believe a word I said. "How did you find out about me?"

"I'm not allowed to say, but the person isn't living. I

can see and hear spirits, and—"

"I know what you can do," he whispered, "but you'd do well to lower your voice. There is plenty of room in the mountains to speak plainly. Let's head out that way."

Daisy snorted. "About being called stupid…"

I glanced up as an older man with thinning gray hair and a stoop entered the café. He smiled when he saw Dylan, and his smile only grew when he noticed me.

"My goodness, young man, you sure do meet the pretty ones." He gave me a nod in hello, and nodded at the kids in turn.

Dylan's soul pulsed brightly, radiantly.

"You like it here," I said, clasping my fingers. "It has changed you. You're a better person when you're here."

His eyes smoldered blue fire. "I do like it here, yes. I will not jeopardize these people or this town."

"I get it. I was told about someone with your"—I glanced up at the people talking at the counter— "affinity for hiking. I wasn't told where you liked to hike, but when you know what to look for, it's not hard to put things together. I mean…" I put my palm to my chest. "Not for people like me. For people who do this kind of thing for a living."

"And your Demigod is hoping you'll sweet-talk me into joining forces?"

"No. My Demigod is very uneasy about this situation, but this spirit told him that I should be the front man. Me and the kids. This news was broken to me on the plane ride here. Being that I'm a gullible jackass, I went for it. That is, until I talked to that woman at the counter." I explained what she'd said and what I'd decided. "But now things are awkward. I'm not sure where we go from here."

"Where do we go from here?" He sneered, and somehow that didn't make him any less handsome. "*We* don't go anywhere. You will go into the ground and take these teens with you. Otherwise their blood will be on your hands."

Daisy giggled. "Way wrong answer, buck-o. Should've left us out of it—"

I held up my hand to Daisy, who thankfully listened for once and stopped talking.

"Right." I leaned my elbows on the table, looking deep into his hateful gaze. "There are three things I will tell you, and your response will set things in motion. Here are the facts. The person that told me about you was the last…" I pointed at myself. "Terrible rock climber." I lifted my eyebrows to make sure he understood that I was talking about my magic. "We still don't know how he knew about you. He comes and goes as he pleases in my life. I have zero control over him, but I keep his home base safe. It is very well hidden, at his request, so it doesn't fall into the wrong hands. But he can be called with other objects. If I cease to…sow my wild oats, and he is called by another, your secret is not safe. While I am sowing the oats—"

"Oh my God, stop with that. The people at the counter aren't listening," Daisy said, rubbing her temples.

I sighed. "While I'm alive, your secret is safe. Everyone who knows it has a blood oath to Kieran. He will ensure they *cannot* break their silence. I say walk, and the whole team walks. No questions. You will not be bothered again, and if you are, I will personally show up to help you. I swear that."

He crossed his arms over his chest. "And what do you think your word is worth to me?"

"I'll tell you what my word is worth to you." I leaned forward a little more, knowing the fire that was in his eyes earlier was now raging in mine. I wondered if my soul was pulsing the same deep blacks and reds I felt from his. "Fuck with my kids, and I'll make this a zombie town, and you can fry your friends as they hunt for your soul. Do I make myself perfectly clear?"

His eyes had widened and a muscle pulsed in his jaw. He might've thought I was lying before, but he didn't think I was lying now.

"Mordecai, finish that pie," I said. "We have the roof on the Jeep and it has rubber tires. Lightning can't get us while we're inside."

A small crease worked between Dylan's brow, and suddenly I wondered if that were true.

"One thing," he said. "Did you want that mark? Be honest. I'll know if you lie."

"Truth—it was first applied accidentally in the heat of the moment. The second and subsequent times have been on purpose, and yes, more often than not, I have asked for it."

"Very loudly sometimes," Daisy said. "It is so gross. When we were in the old house, we had to wear ear-plugs. Thank *God* we're on separate floors now. So much better."

"Would you stop?" I asked her, my face flaming. To Dylan I said, "I love him. I wear his mark, and he is connected to me through my soul link. Both connections are permanent."

Dylan's stare beat into me, but he didn't further comment. Silence hung heavy over the table. Nervous tingles spread over my body.

I spread my hands. "What's the score here? What happens next?"

"You were right about one thing," Dylan said. "You coming here was selfish." He took a sip of his coffee, eyeing me over the rim of his paper to-go cup. "I've read about you. I find your story hilarious. You didn't bring the stylist with you, I see."

I looked down at my jeans and plaid shirt. They weren't that much different than his.

"I've often wondered how different things would've been if I hadn't been brought up in the magical world," Dylan said, a little more softly than before. "Or if I could meet someone who wasn't tarnished by the life people like me are forced to endure."

"What's the difference? I've still ended up here, desperately looking for someone to help me so I don't get kidnapped, mind-wiped, and used as an assassin."

"Not to mention forced into the situation this guy survived if Aaron gets you," Daisy said. "You know, since you're not Aaron's blood relation. I heard he'd probably make you his mistress, whether you wanted it or not. That got Jerry all riled up the other day."

"Stop talking or no more phone," I said through clenched teeth.

"I'm already on phone restriction."

"Then no more allowance. No more money. Or nice things."

"Just tell her you'll pick out her clothes for a week—that'll shut her up," Mordecai said.

Dylan looked slightly bewildered. We could derail anyone.

"Look…" he said.

"Okay, Dylan, see ya later," the older man said, lifting his hand in goodbye as he headed for the door.

"See ya, Chuck." Dylan nodded.

"Say goodbye to your pretty friend and her foster kids for me." Chuck pushed open the door.

"I'm not a kid killer," Dylan whispered, leaning in so his voice didn't carry. "When I had the choice, I drew the line at kids. As soon as I got a chance, I walked away from my past life and never looked back. Just…leave. Leave at sunrise, like you said. Don't leave, however, and I will kill every last one of you. Do *I* make myself clear?"

Relief such as I'd never known flooded me, because I believed him. His soul was back to pulsing brightly. His shoulders had relaxed. He didn't want a confrontation any more than I did.

I nodded, allowing myself to smile. The woman behind the counter wandered into the kitchen, but I didn't increase my volume. "Thank you, and I apologize again for even showing up. I'll try to figure out how to bind spirits from telling secrets. I don't know if it's possible, but I will try."

Daisy stood when I did, but Mordecai didn't move so fast.

"If you never looked back, why are you so fervent on keeping up with our world?" Mordecai asked in that soft, solemn way of his. His rational tone was hard to ignore. "Why do you still do magic in the hills, and read about women experiencing the world of magic for the first time?"

"I need to make sure my whereabouts remain hidden," Dylan said.

Mordecai nodded, as though he took the lie at face value. He didn't push, or try to talk the other guy around, but that was the thing with Mordecai: he didn't have to. The way he delivered words sometimes made people think. Time would tell if he'd just planted a seed within Dylan.

Unfortunately, time was the one thing we did not have.

Chapter 14

KIERAN

FROM KIERAN'S VANTAGE point, he could see the Lightning Rod sitting on top of a large rock, looking down over the mountainside through night-vision binoculars. A large canteen sat beside him, holding more of the coffee that now steamed in a white travel mug held in a steady hand. He clearly planned to be there for a while.

Amazingly, the Lightning Rod had found one of only a few vantage points that provided a clear view of the new house, not an easy accomplishment in a wild national park full of trees. That meant this man knew his way around the mountain. He'd clearly spent a lot of time roaming or trying to work his magic away from prying eyes. He had to miss using his ability freely. Any highly trained level five would. But the unspeakable horrors he'd been through probably kept the longing at bay.

It wouldn't keep the madness at bay, though.

Kieran had seen it with his mother. He'd watched

the slow decline of a magical worker unable to use her craft, to release the pressure building inside. This man would blow eventually, and the whole world would watch the fallout in horror.

"Make the first move," Kieran said into the phone. Jerry, on the other end grunted. He wasn't much of a talker anyway, but in rock form, he rarely issued more than a grunt.

Kieran had spoken to Alexis soon after dinner. She'd made it home after her heart-to-heart with the Lightning Rod just fine. The rest of her evening had been spent assigning positions to her spirit sentinels. A precaution, not a call to battle. Alexis's resolve had hardened—they'd leave in the morning and never look back. The Lightning Rod, who'd been through so much already, would be allowed to live in peace.

A decision Kieran had agreed to—except here Dylan sat, looking down on Kieran's love, within striking range. This section of the mountain was in Chad's jurisdiction, and he'd been the first to report on the Lightning Rod's location. Kieran had alerted the team, only to learn Jerry was already on the move, having sensed Dylan's movements through the rock.

Jerry currently sat directly above the Lightning Rod in plain view. Well, plain view if you realized the odd-looking boulder was actually a large, hunched-down giant. A large pool sat a hundred feet away from him, newly formed from water diverted from mountain streams. Kieran would use that water as a sort of shield, holding it around his body. When lightning hit it, the electrical shock would spread out over the surface, directed toward the ground. He and Jerry had a solid defense in place. The rest of the team had been kept away.

The rock Dylan sat on wiggled. Dylan startled, his coffee sloshing over his hand, but he didn't seem shocked. Kieran knew what that meant.

Alexis had mentioned that Dylan was keeping tabs on the magical world. He likely knew Kieran had procured the giant. He now knew the giant was powerful enough to wiggle a multiple-ton rock that had probably been there since the beginning of time.

The rock bucked up out of the earth, and Dylan flew into the air. In a shock of sound and light, lightning zipped down around Kieran like raindrops, each bolt small, concise, and with enough of a punch to fry someone from the inside out.

Kieran shielded his eyes, unable to help it. The movement surely gave him away.

Water sailed through the air, surrounding him in an arc before the next blast rained down. Just like before, it was a cluster of smaller bolts, none of them digging down far into the water before spreading out, finding ground, and dispersing.

Dylan hit the dirt beside the rock, his head thunking on the hard ground, but he scrambled up quickly. Light crackled between his fingers, ready to blast out at a moment's notice, and clouds gathered overhead, carrying much larger charges.

Zeus wasn't the only one who could affect the weather, though, and while his Demigods were stronger with storms and cloud formations than Poseidon's, this guy was not a Demigod. He was no match for Kieran.

"I don't mean to harm you," Kieran called out, scattering the clouds above. "But you watching my girlfriend is something of a sticking point for me."

Jerry stood slowly, clearly unaffected by the lightning that had just rained down on him. Dylan flinched and altered his position, now only needing a slight turn of his head to focus on one threat or the other. He'd had good attack and defensive training.

"Clever, with the water," Dylan said, and Kieran could tell he held no love for Demigods. Not that anyone could blame him. "I partially chose this location because there *weren't* large quantities of water readily available."

"There aren't...unless you work with someone that can literally move mountains." Kieran walked to the right, forcing Dylan to take his eyes off Jerry if he wanted to remain focused on Kieran. Dylan wasn't the only one with training, after all. "Why are you watching

Alexis?"

"I didn't realize her magic could reach this far. Or was it the giant that felt me coming?"

"Hers doesn't, and he did, but not before Alexis's army of spirits noticed you getting within striking range. Why are you watching her?"

"Isn't it obvious? I don't trust her. Or you. Since when does a Demigod allow the mouse to get away?"

"Who is the mouse, her or you?"

"Both. Either. Aren't we all mice to a Demigod?"

"I prefer to think of things as a game of chess. To me, you are a pawn, and she's the queen. My queen. She has decided you will be left to your life. I will gladly honor her wishes." Kieran held out a hand. "Unless you endanger her or her children. Then I will allow Jerry to play a game of rock, paper, lightning with you."

"Giants don't move very fast in rock form," Dylan said with a smirk.

"Jerry?"

Rocks rolled down from heavens knew where, large and small alike, crowding in around Dylan in perfect formation. They blocked him from bolting in all directions but one—straight back to Jerry.

"He doesn't move very quickly in that form, no. But trust me, he can magically throw a rock much faster than you can run. He owns this mountain. You're but a squatter."

Dylan scanned the rocks gathered in front of him, chest high, then looked over them at Kieran, hate filling his eyes. He didn't speak. Thunderclouds tried to form overhead, blocked by Kieran. Rage was getting the better of him.

Kieran put up his hands. "As I said, I don't wish to hurt you. If you remain peaceful, I'll remain peaceful. We'll leave tomorrow. You'll never hear from us again."

"You expect me to believe a Demigod who needs me will just walk away?"

"I don't need you. You'd be an incredible asset, don't get me wrong, but I can fill that hole in different ways. Look, it's very simple. I need a team to help protect her. If you don't want a place on it, then great. Been nice knowing you. We won't hang around."

"Yet you just bought that big house on the hill."

"You guys don't do Airbnbs up here. That was the next fastest option for what we needed."

"Must be nice."

"Watching my mother die slowly at the hands of my father? No, not really. That wasn't exactly the highlight of my life. Killing my father in vengeance and taking his money and his job? It's actually a shitty, hollow feeling, if you must know. If I hadn't met Alexis, I'm pretty sure I'd be the horror you currently think I am. But I did meet Alexis, and she's taught me that anyone can change their stars. Anyone can turn things around.

Anyone can have a second chance."

Jerry grunted his assent.

Dylan scoffed. "I have my second chance. Guess you're out of luck."

"This second chance is going to kill you," Kieran said softly. He pushed the water away, standing without armor in front of this man who had obvious, unhealed emotional scars. Kieran knew what that was like, and for the first time that he could remember, he felt a deep, profound connection toward a stranger. They hadn't had the same circumstances or life situations, but they'd both suffered in a magical system beyond their control. Kieran had been saved by Alexis and her misfit family, but this guy still had nobody. He had nothing to fight for. To live for, really, since he was living a lie.

"Is that a threat?" Dylan said, lightning crackling between his fingers.

Kieran put his hands in his pockets. "Alexis has devoted her whole life to helping people. As you probably know, altruism doesn't come naturally to me, yet I find myself wanting to help you. I know what it's like for a level-five magical person who can't use their magic. My mother would stare out at the water and twitch, desperate to be in it, needing to allow her magic to swell and feed on the ocean's currents. My whole life, she needed the release that was denied to her. You know what I mean. You are using your magic in increments, but the pressure is building. You can feel it, I know you can." The nearly full moon cast light on Dylan's falling, knowing expression. Yes, he definitely felt it. What a terrible way to live. "My father was keeping my mother's skin from her. She couldn't release any magic, no matter how desperate she got, but you can, and when you blow, this whole town will feel your wrath. By then, though, I'm not sure you'll care."

"What about Alexis? She's a level five and didn't even *know* her magic until she met you. She was fine, and you've basically given her a death sentence."

Kieran spread his hands in a sudden flash of rage. The thunderclouds rolled back in, boiling and building. Electricity filled the air from Dylan, but fog moved in around them, easily turned to liquid if Kieran required it.

"Why the fuck do you think I'm here?" Kieran yelled, losing his cool. "Why the hell do you think we went after Jerry? The most important person in my life is in danger *constantly*, and she's not strong enough to handle it on her own. By the time I was smart enough to send her away, I wasn't strong enough to go through with it. And now I question whether I can protect her. So yes, I'm here, begging help from people who hate everything I stand for. That's the situation I have to bear, and I will bear it, because I'm the one that created it.

"But don't fool yourself into believing you're safe. Alexis used her magic constantly to contact and communicate with spirits. She had access to the Line before she knew what to do with it. You don't have enough of a release. You crave the power in your blood, and the effort to keep it at bay is messing with your mind. Deny it until this whole town burns. I don't care. It's nothing to do with me. But if you let us leave without hassle, I'll transfer that house to you. No strings. No paperwork leading back to me—or anyone. Sell it and pocket the money, if you want. Get the local government to accept Airbnb and start a business, whatever."

"I don't want your house or your dirty money."

"I don't give a shit, you arrogant twat." Kieran threw up his hands and turned away. He was done. "Fuck me, how does Alexis deal with people? What an annoyance."

"Why weren't you strong enough to send her away?" Dylan asked, sounding suddenly unsure.

"Because I loved her too much. A good woman has the power to make a strong man helpless. She is my world, and I will skin you alive if you go after her."

Chapter 15

ALEXIS

"AFTER WHAT KIERAN said, I feel like we should've warned the townspeople or something," Mordecai said the next morning as the small motor brigade left the Chester village, headed for the airstrip that housed Kieran's private jet. Amber drove an old, beat-up Bronco at the front, with everyone else following in various newly acquired vehicles that couldn't be traced back to real identities.

"If they are too stupid to see a magical person in their midst, then it's their own fault," Daisy said, riding in the back seat. She'd been too slow with calling "shotgun" to procure the front. "The only reason that guy didn't show up at our door this morning is because Kieran messed things up. *This* is why Harding told Kieran to let us handle it. We turned Dylan's mood all the way around last night. He relaxed a lot. If we'd just gotten one more chat in…"

In an unexpected burst of chattiness before they'd left that morning, Jerry had told us what had gone down on the mountainside last night. Dylan had apparently sat on a rock for a long while afterward, staring at nothing until the small hours of the morning. He hadn't bothered telling Jerry to get lost.

Despite what Daisy said, I didn't think anyone could've talked Dylan into joining us. If I'd been in his shoes, I doubt I would've even kept my cool long enough for a chat. So no, I didn't think Kieran had made or broken anything. From what I could tell, Dylan would never be willing to work with another Demigod.

Maybe, though…just maybe, meeting us, experiencing our dysfunctional but loving dynamic, would change things for him down the line. Maybe he'd venture out and try to live a magical life again. A good life, with a boss who treated him well and deserved his respect. I hoped I'd get to meet him if that ever happened. I'd definitely say, "I told you so."

"Is Amber set on going after the ones on her list?" Mordecai asked, his hands clasped in his lap.

"Yeah. We still need a bigger, stronger crew," I replied, somewhat dismally. "I don't think we'll get it by the time we need to meet Demigod Lydia, though. So…"

"Demigods are a serious hassle," Daisy said, falling back against the seat. "All the maneuvering and strategizing…"

A line of shiny black SUVs passed us, headed *to-*

ward the Chester town, starting with a Hummer and decreasing in expense and awesomeness down the line. Chrome sparkled in the climbing tangerine sunlight. Fresh paint and dealership plates gleamed.

"It's only a hassle when you're the one lacking power and prestige," Mordecai replied. "For them, all the strategizing is probably a nice break in their monotonous, never-ending lives."

"Yeah. But since we always seem to be the ones lacking power and prestige—"

Thane, driving the Ford pickup in front of me, swerved into a pullout area on the side of the mountain road. His brake lights screamed red, and dust and rocks blew up behind him. Amber had stopped just in front of him, and behind me, Kieran pulled in as though he'd expected the sudden stop.

My phone rang, patching through to the Jeep's speakers.

"What's up?" I asked Kieran.

"Demigod Flora just passed, leading a train of seven SUVs."

The kids and I both turned in our seats, looking behind us. "That was a Demigod?"

"The Demigod of New York, yes. She has a pinched face and wears her hair in an outrageous beehive. Amber and Bria both agree that it was definitely her. First six SUVs are full. The last is probably carrying supplies. She has a large team on the ground, and I wouldn't doubt a helicopter will be flying over shortly. She doesn't do things by halves. Never has. There is no way she is up here for a holiday." He paused for a moment. "She's a Demigod of Zeus, Alexis. She'll want Dylan like Aaron wants you."

A chill froze my blood. "How could they know about him? You said we were careful."

"We were. But not everyone around us has taken a blood oath. Amber will be looking into this when we get back, trust me." A growl rode his words. "I'm calling because you promised Dylan that if someone found out about him, you'd show up and save the day, correct?"

"I mean...not in those words, but...yeah, I did promise I'd help if we were the reason he came under fire. If we led people to him, we owe it to him to help. This is crap, though. We obviously have a rat."

"I agree, but here's the thing: given how well he knows that mountain, there is a strong possibility that he'll be fine. Much of her force is of Zeus's line. They won't be able to feel through rock—if he stays hidden, Demigod Flora will go home empty-handed."

"If we show up, will we just aggravate things?"

"The problem is that, traditionally, the people of Zeus's line don't hide," Kieran said. "They are brave to a fault and their ego is maddening. They'd rather stand and fight in pure bullheaded stupidity than resort to what they deem *cowering in a bush*."

"Careful, your rivalry is showing," Daisy murmured.

"Okay, but Dylan is hiding from the magical world," I said. "His life is basically cowering in a bush."

"Right. Which is why I give him a strong possibility of being fine. The issue is...Demigod Flora is arrogant to a fault. It's easy enough to get fake IDs, but I doubt she'll try to sell the identities, like we did. She'll raise suspicion without trying. Unless, of course, she has already called the local government and alerted them to a magical person in their midst. If that's the case, they'll provide her with an escort and she'll be free to hunt the mountain."

I stared at the speakers for a moment. "How does any of this result in him being fine?"

"The more resourceful magical types, like Jerry or Amber, have the training to escape situations such as these."

"Dylan wouldn't have done a bang-up job of escaping you."

"I am not the average Demigod."

"Are you sure Zeus is the only one with a penchant for an ego?" I muttered. "You're talking in circles. Will he be fine or not?"

"I don't know. The odds seem evenly split."

"Well...I mean, we have to help. What if he's rusty

with his magic against so many people? What if he doesn't escape? Hell, what if he *does* escape? Then what? His whole life has been turned upside down. This is our fault. We have to fix this."

"Fixing this will mean taking on another Demigod. A strong Demigod."

"Would you stop stalling? All we do anymore is take on Demigods, it feels like. I made a promise. *Let's go!*"

"Sounds good. Follow Amber. Just in case Demigod Flora rats me out to the Chester officials, we'll go around their checkpoint. We will not be heading to the house. We'll meet up in the cabin in the woods and go from there."

The cabin had been another property Kieran had purchased in the area. A moment later, Amber pulled ahead, going another half-mile before she could turn around.

"They got here just one day after we did," Mordecai said as we cut off an oncoming car to pull into traffic. The honk nearly drowned out his words. "Careful, Lexi."

"Yeah, yeah. I got it."

"All those SUVs must've been bought in advance, but not far enough in advance for them to get all the same kind," Daisy said, nodding as she continued to lean toward the front.

"They had one SUV just for supplies, Kieran said,

which means they expect to be in the wilderness," Mordecai said, and it was clear the kids were treating this as a sort of high-stakes training session. "They expect to hunt for their prey. They know more than just a generalized location."

"Could Harding have told other people?" Daisy asked me. "He seems like a dirty player. I wouldn't put it past him."

"I wouldn't either. He likes to watch me in action," I replied, having already considered the matter. "But he *is* tied to that pocket watch. I know he is. Besides, *I* can hear spirits, but there is only one of me, and Demigod Flora doesn't have any Hades hard hitters on her team. It can't be Harding."

"Well then, it is someone that is in deep with Kieran," Daisy said. "None of the secretaries have oaths. Red and Bria don't. Aubri—she's a snoop. She's always listening for gossip. Mordecai and I don't."

"Jerry," Mordecai said softly. "For the first week or so he still didn't have a blood oath, but he was always around."

I shook my head as our SUV train turned off onto a small road following a cliff face on one side. "Why would he double-cross us when he'd have to deal with the fallout?"

"Yeah, true." Daisy chewed her lip. "Red and Bria don't necessarily have to deal with the fallout, though.

Not if they are still double agents."

"There is no way Bria is double-dealing," I said. "We've been through too much."

"Maybe she's just giving you the shove she always thinks you'll need?" Mordecai said, and goosebumps spread across my skin.

We turned off another road, and then another, turning onto a seemingly barely used dirt road. My ability to think about the problem evaporated as I caught sight of the swiftly moving river directly ahead of us. "What in the holy—"

Amber slowed to a crawl before venturing in, the Bronco's front right end lifting as it encountered a submerged rock and then splashed down into the water. The front bumper bobbed as the current lifted the vehicle. In a moment, the chassis lowered again, the water pulling back from the Bronco and then lifting over the top in an arc before touching down on the other side again.

"Why can't he just stop it from flowing for a few minutes? Why does he have to make it go over our heads?" I whispered, nearing the glistening riverbed. "What if he passes out or loses his grip? We'll be swept along."

The larger rocks rolled out of the way, Jerry helping out, leaving big holes in their wake. I followed Amber with trepidation, never having off-roaded in my life.

The tire instantly found one of those holes, and I screamed, making both of the kids jump. The car crawled out with steady pressure on the gas, then the underside scraped something hard.

"Please keep going. Please keep going," I urged the Jeep.

The other wheel dipped, and the Jeep tilted forward wildly, as if we were on a ride in an amusement park. The forward right wheel clipped the side of a rock Jerry hadn't moved, and we slipped sideways, the rock battering the underside of the Jeep. The top corner bit into the stream of water overhead, showering us.

"I can't see!" I hollered.

"Use your wipers, Lexi," Mordecai yelled, clutching the dash. "It's just like rain."

"It is a freaking river, not rain," I muttered, fumbling with the wipers. The Jeep dipped into another hole. Water sloshed off the windshield. "I can take on a freaking Demigod in the middle of the night, and I'll run to the aid of a perfect stranger against another Demigod, but driving through a river is not my idea of awesome. Why couldn't we take the road like normal people?"

My grumbling got me the rest of the way across the riverbed. I urged the Jeep up the small incline and onto a mostly grown-over set of tracks leading into the trees. Either that riverbed dried up at certain times, or someone had bigger balls than I did, because there was no way I could have made the crossing without Kieran.

After another half-hour of taking back roads that were increasingly easy to traverse, we emerged onto a small highway nestled into the thick canopy of the mountains—sugar maples, beeches, hemlocks, and tulip poplars all struggling for a place in the sun. Below, ferns and ivy tangled together in the brush, creating a few little patches of brightly colored flowers to help decorate the beautiful tableau.

"What can Demigods of Zeus do?" I asked Daisy as we drove.

"They'll also be able to manipulate lightning, of course," she said, sitting back and looking upward, thinking. "They can either throw it from their hands or, for more power, use the sky. Kieran can combat their ability by messing with the weather, although Zeus's descendants are likely more experienced with storms. They can mimic people's voices and apply glamor to look like other people, so watch for mannerisms—"

"I can just use the soul," I said.

"Right, yeah. Nice. You can get around one of their most sneaky magics. They can also force land creatures to shift or stay shifted unless the creature is strong enough and can resist. Watch yourself, Mordecai. You probably have the power to resist, but not the experience. They won't have any power over your shifted form, in any case, so it is probably only an issue for people like Thane. Hopefully he's strong enough to resist."

"I'm sure he's trained for it," Mordecai said.

"We'll know soon enough, I guess," she murmured.

I bit my lip, remembering Thane on the mountain. Or even Thane in training. When he went Berserk, he was never a fun time.

"Anything else?" I asked.

"Big schlong, big ego, very brave, and a distinct rivalry with Poseidon and Hades. Zeus thinks he's the best, and while he's a little more powerful than his brothers, it's offset by his tendency to think with his big schlong instead of the thing between his ears. That trait has been passed down in his lineage, and it goes for the ladies, too. Big lady schlong. It shows in their attitude."

"I think you have to be born into the magical world for any of this to seem remotely normal," I said, the incline growing.

"Probably," Daisy said.

"Any idea what lesser magics are traveling with Demigod Flora?" I asked.

"No idea whatsoever," Daisy replied. "I'm not there yet. Zorn says I need to learn all the magics and how to combat them first."

"How would you combat Zeus?"

"Personally, I'd look helpless and fragile and pretty

and let him play hero or else take pity on me. A mortal taking on a god is just stupid. Anyone taking on a god is just stupid, actually, unless it's another god. It's best just to make sure they don't kill you. Although I am curious about the schlong issue. The internet didn't have any pictures. I mean, of his. They had plenty of pictures—"

"No!" I held up my finger and made eye contact in the rearview mirror. "You are barely fifteen. No thinking about schlongs, no matter how big. Do we need to have another sex talk?"

"Nah. Your embarrassment embarrasses me. I know how that stuff works. But honestly, don't you wonder if it is as big as the legends say?"

"No," Mordecai and I said together.

Daisy shrugged.

"How would you combat Demigod Flora?" I asked.

Daisy's mouth twisted to the side. "In this situation? Do whatever Kieran says and hope he has the experience to take on the most powerful line of Demigods in the world."

Chapter 16

ALEXIS

A COOL EVENING breeze kissed my exposed skin as I sat in a lonely fold-out chair in front of a small, two-room log cabin deep in the trees. It might've been serene if not for the beat-up SUVs and mighty fine Jeep choking the isolated property. Daisy sat at my feet with a collection of five cell phones piled in front of her. They belonged to the people in the group who hadn't taken a blood oath. Including me. No one had objected to the confiscation, except for me—I would've really liked to play a game to calm my nerves.

A motor cut off somewhere behind the cabin. Bria jogged in a moment later.

"The cadavers have been moved," she announced, wiping her cheek and smearing dirt across it. It added to the other smears already present. "We can use your spirits to fill them, but we need to wait for Kieran's go-ahead. Won't be long until we confront Flora now."

I eyed my phone. "What's the status?"

Bria glanced off to the right. "I have to pee, and

there is only one outhouse for a handful of large, stinky men. I might just use the bushes."

"No," I said with a scowl. "I mean the overall situation."

"Yeah, I know, I just wanted you to feel my pain." She braced her hands on her hips and rolled back on her heels. "It's official. That bitch Demigod Flora tried to sell us out. She knew about Kieran buying that house. Given there are no records linking him to it—Amber double-checked his work, but you know he's good at hiding his electronic trails—someone is definitely passing along our sensitive info. We don't have time to figure that out, though. She's got the sheriff and his cronies looking for us and Dylan—sounds like she had no idea we were pulling out of this Popsicle stand. Dylan's picture is up all over town, wanted for magic, and we're being portrayed as the fugitives helping him hide. At least he knows we aren't at fault here."

"We are at fault," I said. "Because of us, his cover has been completely blown."

"Well, yes, but we're not trying to screw him, is what I meant. We didn't go all Zeus in this joint. We went in quietly. Flora is trying to make it sound like she's doing the town a great big favor. She's got the local news telling people to look in their sheds, check their land, guard their kids from the evil magic man—the whole shebang. She's a real piece of work."

"She's setting it up so that she can drag him out of here?"

"Yep. He broke the law—he forged documents and moved into a strictly non-magical zone. The Demigod that captures him can punish him however she deems fit. Obviously we're not going to let Flora capture him, though. Shithead. We'll extract Dylan, hopefully knock Flora down a peg, and help Dylan disappear again. Presto change-o. In the meantime, we already took a couple of their guys."

"How'd you manage that?" Daisy asked.

"Get this—those fuckers snuck into the house to ambush Alexis. They were huge guys—big chests, big arms—as big as Jerry. Apparently size matters in their thick heads. Those idiots thought they could take down a Soul Stealer—no biggie, I guess—and her two teen wards. Easy-peasy." Bria laughed. "What absolute tools. I wish Kieran had let you go with me. I swear, Zeus's people are the Ken doll crew of the magical world. Attractive, but big, dumb idiots. I did them a favor."

"How's that?" Daisy asked.

"I had Jerry take out the foundation underneath the whole front of the house and collapse the thing. Smoosh-ville. It'll be an insurance nightmare, but that's not my problem. I had to get those cadavers, after all. Can't fault me for protecting myself, and Jerry was just doing what he was told. We're in the clear."

Daisy's mouth dropped open. Amber might've been the sexy viper of our group, but no one could beat Bria's flare.

"Why does every house Kieran buys have bodies buried and waiting in the yard?" I asked, a little numb. I knew a grisly battle was coming. Flora played to win, that was clear, and while I knew killing a Demigod was typically off-limits, everyone else would be fair game. I'd have a target on my back, Bria, the guys...the kids.

Fire smoldered in my belly, but I doused it. I needed to stay numb until the last possible moment or adrenaline would rage through me until I was worn out. I had put my neck on the line for this one, and I would not lose. Not the battle, and not one person. I'd obliterate Flora's forces and send them marching back at her before I let that happen.

"Necromancers magically store bodies everywhere we think we might run into trouble," Bria said. "With you, that is literally everywhere. I had Jerry help me unearth everyone while the Ken dolls were being squished. That guy is fiercely handy. No digging necessary—he just works the rocks within the dirt until they churn up the cadavers. Not sure why he threw up those few times, what with the state of his cave, but he'll get used to it."

"You have a screw loose," Daisy said with a grin.

Thane and Boman broke through a thicket of bushes on the side of what passed for the front yard. A moment later, Mordecai trotted out behind them in wolf form, his tongue lolling as though he'd gone for a good run. They'd recruited him to help them scout out various areas. Thank God Mordecai hadn't seen any action.

Yet.

A flare of fear fueled the fire bubbling just below the surface of my consciousness. The battle would come soon enough.

Behind them, Jack put out his hands to move the tree branches to the side, didn't notice his hands going through them, then jerked back like he was about to get *thwapped* in the face. He'd probably been shadowing Mordecai and would have training tips for Kieran when there wasn't a battle on the horizon. Maybe one day.

"Flora is setting up to comb the mountains," Thane said to Bria. "She's got the sheriff and some townspeople helping. Thank heavens the village is tiny. Where's Jerry?"

"Here." Jerry emerged from the side of the cabin, his bronze-toned skin three shades lighter than usual.

A smile spread across Thane's face. "What's the matter, *Jerry*? I thought you liked playing with your food?"

Jerry's mouth formed a grim line.

Thane's smile dripped away, any humor short-lived,

given the situation. "Can you feel the Lightning Bolt?" He grimaced. "Now she's got me doing it." He nodded at Bria, who had heard, secondhand, Daisy's question about the legend of the big schlong and decided it wasn't prudent to use the term Lightning *Rod* until Dylan could prove its relevancy.

None of the guys had found her comment particularly funny, but I'd never seen Red actually guffaw until that moment.

"He's been in the same place since about two o'clock," Jerry said. "It's at the very farthest edge of my power. If he moves any farther east, I'll lose him."

"Until you get off your ass and walk a little, *Jerry*," Bria said.

The guys cracked a grin. Jerry didn't seem like he'd heard.

"What time is it now?" I asked.

"Seven," Boman said, checking his watch. "Full moon tonight. We'll be able to see until Kieran and Flora battle for the sky."

"That's a battle Flora will win," I murmured, looking up at the deep purple sky hole-punched with two stars. "I need to think about which spirits to summon and get Jack organizing everyone. Maybe Mia will pop back in. I've still heard no word about her or the others." I shook my head and then pushed the thought away. Now wasn't the time to worry about spirits leaving without saying goodbye.

"Summoning spirits? Did someone ring?" Harding popped up next to me.

I jumped and then released my breath in a slow hiss, turning away a little. Guilt swam through me like minnows over how this situation had turned out. I'd be lying if I said I didn't blame Harding a little for it.

"No," I replied, then told the others, "Harding just popped up out of nowhere, probably to watch the show."

"Clever girl." He grinned at me. "I do so love the way you get yourself out of tight fixes. Your tactics are so strange and ingenious. The world needed someone like you to come along. So what's the situation? Armed and ready, I trust?"

"Did you do this somehow?" I asked, facing him now. "Did you tell someone else?"

"Who could I tell?" He palmed his chest. "My cat has run off and your Demigod has hidden the pocket watch. My other artifacts are under lock and key with Demigod Zander. To get that stuff, someone would have to steal it, and he's a real tight sonuvabitch. Zeus breeds 'em difficult, to say the least. I couldn't tell anyone if I tried."

I passed the information on. Truthfully, I'd already figured that was the case—I had just wanted a justifiable reason to be angry with him.

"Fine," I said, thinking through the situation. "Jerry, can you feel Dylan's surroundings?"

"Feeling through rock and stone, as I do, doesn't translate to seeing," Jerry replied. "He is in a half cave, so I have a good idea of his surroundings, but any picture I drew would be made up of a lot of blank space."

"Is there anything you can do to make him more comfortable? Some way of showing him we're still around, and we want to help?"

Harding grinned, and his eyes sparkled with pride. I scowled at him, wiping the grin from his lips.

"On it," Jerry said.

"Classy guy, that *Jerry*," Boman said.

"A real class act, eh, *Jerry*?" Thane replied.

"You guys sound brain-dead." Bria shook her head.

"It is such bullshit what the magical world allows Demigods to get away with," I said. Distantly, I felt Kieran break away from Zorn somewhere in the trees and head back toward the cabin. "Jerry would've been forced into a blood oath if people could've gotten to him. They would have done the same for Amber and me. Why is this allowed to happen? It's against the law! No way should this practice be this prevalent."

"It's not, really," Bria said, leaning against the side of the cabin. "I'm an experienced level five in good standing with the community and plenty of job offers, but I've never had a problem turning jobs down. No one minds when I do freelance work. Most of the magical world is comprised of people like me—we're too common to be chased or stolen or forced. We can be replaced.

"But there are a few rare gems that *can't* be replaced, and when it comes to them, to *you*, we're in the Wild West, so to speak. Normal laws don't apply, or at least they're not regulated, and no one knows how to change that or cares enough to bother. Now, Amber really shouldn't have been in this camp. She's exceptional, yes, but not so exceptional someone would force her into a position against her will. She's basically CIA—Chesters can do that job. Spitting acid, her actual magic, doesn't factor in here. Her attraction lies in how she might help with you, and Demigod Aaron lost his mind for a moment. Jerry made himself invaluable by basically becoming an urban legend. He was the king of the mountain, and Demigods are competitive enough to feel the allure of being crowned the new king, basically.

"Then there's magic like yours. Like the Thunderbolt's. Priceless, rare magic that promises to give a Demigod an edge over everyone else. With magic like that, you'll always be forced to deal with the underbelly of our world. You have to harden up just to survive. It's not awesome, but it's your lot in life. Thank your mom when you see her next for hiding you for so long. It was a shit existence, but it was probably better than this."

When Bria fell silent, I didn't rush to fill the gap. Murmuring reached me from around the cabin, where Kieran had connected with Henry and Boman in the backyard. The kids were both in the house, playing cards at a small table. They'd changed so much over this last year, really blossoming into their own people despite all of the danger and uncertainty. Maybe because of it. Thane and Red stood off with Jerry in the trees, and I could feel Jack moving to the edge of my perimeter, heading toward a collection of what I knew were spirits. He was in charge of getting them organized.

Harding sat to my other side, staring at me with a flat expression—analyzing me, I knew, as he'd done the day I talked Jerry out of killing us.

"It wasn't better than this," I said, part of me knowing it was this answer Harding had been waiting for. "My old life was a pale comparison to this one. I wouldn't go back for anything. I have friends now. A man I love with all my heart. A nice home and nice things for my kids. I have a community and a purpose. I have a place in the world where I fit, as strange as I am. As strange as my magic is. Despite the danger, I wouldn't trade this life for the existence I had. I know for a fact my kids wouldn't, either. I've even accepted Harding and his enormous kittens. My life is full, and

I'm blessed to have it. I'll fight for that."

"Just wait until you consent to taking those cats around with you," Harding murmured, finally looking away. "You'll take strange to a whole new level. Death on a pale horse is for losers—give me a cat lady in her pajamas any day. You can ride next to Poseidon's Demigod on his goldfish steed."

Bria crossed her arms and looked strangely uncomfortable, and since she couldn't hear Harding, I wondered what she was reacting to.

Amber and Donovan cut toward us before I could ask, though, through the trees, moving fast. Clouds built on the horizon, flashes of light interrupting the boiling dark mass. A peal of distant thunder rolled through the sky.

"Someone is making a move," I said, standing. Kieran and the others moved my way. Expectancy fell over our group.

The fire within me, kept contained all day, emerged with a roar, filling me to bursting.

I cracked my muscles and pulled power from the Line. "It's time to see what Zeus's people are really made of."

Chapter 17

ALEXIS

"**S**HE'S GOT DOGS looking for him," Amber said as she ran toward us, out of breath. Kieran had just come around the cabin.

Donovan had sweat running down his face, clearly in worse shape than Amber. "She's trying to flush him out. Demigods of Zeus can sense their kind, just like the Lightning Rod. She's on horseback following the dogs. All she has to do is get close."

"He's moving." Jerry braced his hands on his hips. "He's left the rock chair I made and moving out of my range. I need to head that way to get traction on him again. There are over two dozen others that I can feel, too, moving slowly. They don't seem to be disturbing many rocks. They must be on the hunt."

"Can you feel if people are magical or not?" I asked. Jerry shook his head.

"She'll use townspeople," Kieran said, ducking into the cabin before reemerging with a leather vest to match the leather chaps he was already wearing. He was preparing for fire. "If they die in the crossfire, she'll shower the town in money while talking about their bravery in bringing a dangerous magical person to justice. This town is tiny, not influential, and the people here already hate magic—their lives mean nothing to her."

"Or she can blame everything on us and wash her hands of it," Amber said. Kieran nodded his agreement.

"They mean something to Dylan," I said, remembering his bright soul when he was around them. Remembering how warmly the woman and man in that café had greeted him.

"He'll play the Zeus hero card if those he favors are in harm's way," Amber said.

"He'll light this mountain up," Thane said, gathered with everyone else.

I felt Jack sectioning the spirits off into groups. The stronger ones were organizing into lines, while the others gathered into a cluster out of the way.

"We're going to have to stay fluid out there." Kieran crossed the group and exited the other side, seeking open space. Confidence and determination surged through the soul link. "We'll be running over rough terrain, and we'll be playing for keeps. They will not hesitate to put you into the ground. Get them first. Do not kill innocents if you can help it, however. Keep this a magical fight wherever possible. Now that Dylan is on the move, it's only a matter of time before he's discovered. The second we can extract him, we will. Got it? Our goal is to join forces with him."

Everyone nodded or murmured their assent.

"We're outnumbered, but that's nothing new," Kieran continued. "Alexis and Bria will load up the cadavers right after this. Everyone else will get into their battle gear. When we're all ready, we'll head off together, led by Jerry and myself. Bria and Red, stay near Alexis. I won't be able to feel your positions, but she will. If one of you does something that looks shady, I have faith that Alexis will happily turn you into another cadaver. Got it?"

"Yes, sir," Red said without hesitation. Bria hooked a thumb into her pocket. Kieran looked at her hard for a moment.

After a moment he continued. "Thane, you'll fight with steel until I say otherwise. After that, you will go Berserk. You will be aiming away from the town before you change form. You know the drill."

Fire lit Kieran's eyes as he surveyed all of us, his large shoulders squared, his posture powerful. Although he stood in the wilderness with only a handful of his people around him, his aura of unblinking authority said he could've been standing in front of a golden throne speaking to the masses.

Confidence wound within me, shared through the

soul link, bolstering my spirits. This situation wasn't new, anymore. Loading up cadavers and marching into danger wasn't an unknown experience. The terrain had changed, but the people I fought with remained the same. We had something Flora couldn't dream of—love and loyalty for one another. This tight unit fought for one another more than we fought for ourselves. We were stronger because of it. Even Jack, who had taken a fall, had insisted on joining us. He planned on taking a body for the first time since he'd lost his life.

"That Demigod of Zeus has no idea the hornets' nest she has kicked," I said softly, fire eating through my middle. "This will be the last time she tries to roll up on us, throwing her weight around."

A grin pulled at Thane's lips. Zorn shifted his weight, nodding slightly. Donovan outright laughed.

"Get it, girl!" he said, and clapped. "Show that ol' Demigod of Zeus how gross Hades can be."

"Way to ruin a good thing, *Donovan*," Jerry said quietly, looking away with a small grin.

I laughed and hurried toward the spirits, now completely organized and staying in their formations.

"Bria, a word," Kieran said behind me, his tone hard and rough. "I'll send her to you when I'm done, Alexis."

I frowned at him, not sure what that was about, but turned and hurried toward those spirits. Kieran was an excellent battle commander—he saw things in people they sometimes didn't even see in themselves. He was probably warning Bria not to step out of line during this battle or risk lightning crashing down on her. It was a good warning.

Nervousness stole my breath as I reached the small clearing. Jack greeted me with a resolute nod.

"How terrible is this going to be?" he asked.

I looked at the bodies tied on the backs of two small flatbed trailers Bria and Jerry had towed through the trails on four wheelers. They looked somewhat fresh, with mostly no missing parts or obvious rot.

"Not as terrible as it could be," I answered, and Chad, standing directly behind Jack, shook his head. He clearly didn't agree. He probably always thought it was terrible. "Okay, everyone, buckle up. I'll slap you in and shove you off. We're about to wage a battle with lightning."

AN HOUR LATER, the clouds were thundering overhead, flashes of light streaking the sky between them. The moon only rained down in small patches, just enough for us to see.

When Bria and I returned to the cabin, Kieran and crew were waiting for us in the front yard, most of them having donned the leather vests and chaps. Mordecai waited with them in wolf form, but Daisy sat in the lone chair off to the side.

"Apparently, I'm not ready," she said when I gave her a questioning glance. "Not for guerilla warfare."

"Sometimes we need to come to grips with acting as an anchor for our team," Zorn said. "She and Mordecai will be fine in the woods behind the house. If they get taken this time, they're on their own."

I frowned but said nothing. Obviously that wasn't true, but if he was keeping them out of the fight, and giving them a little feeling of danger in the process, he was my hero.

Zorn handed Bria and me our leathers. We pulled them on as the spirit-filled cadavers shambled after us, shaking and jerking. Jerry turned away, and I had no doubt the color was leaching from his face again.

"He'll get used to it," Bria said as Kieran turned toward the trees, heading in the direction of Dylan's previous hideout. "As soon as he sees their effectiveness, his tune will change."

"I wouldn't hold out hope," Boman said, one of the few not wearing chaps. He had on his black cargo pants, the pockets no doubt stuffed with anything and everything he thought would better prepare the whole crew for battle.

Red was the other one not wearing leather (besides a silently watching Harding, obviously). Instead, she wore a Spandex suit with an armory of weapons strapped to her person—a gun holster on one thigh, a circle of throwing knives around the other, and a leather belt packed with pouches and pockets around her waist. Most of the contents were hidden from view, but I saw the tops of a few throwing stars. A larger knife was fastened to her calf. I'd heard along the way that her magic had to do with hand-to-hand combat, but I hadn't seen it in action. That was clearly about to change.

When the path through the trees narrowed into a deer trail, Jerry took the lead. The ground beneath our feet trembled as though something was going on under the surface. Rocks shook within the weeds and brush we passed. Thunder rolled across the sky.

"Got him," I heard Jerry say as Jack broke for the trees.

I yanked his spirit, forcing him back in line, twitching and jerking more than the rest of them, bringing up the rear of our crew.

"What's gotten into you?" I heard Bria ask, the last of the living in our single-file line.

"Don't know. My brain is saying to abort mission and get the hell out of here," Jack said, and I repeated for Bria. "My legs thought it was a great idea."

"Keep it together, man," she said in an undertone.

"I kinda like it when Lexi does it for me," he said.

"Well, put on your big-boy pants," Bria said after I relayed his message. "Soon she's going to have other things to do. Lexi, use that creepy spirit wind once they can see you. These bastards mostly deal with their own magical kind. Your hair blowing when there's no wind will freak them out."

"If the storm kicks off, there's going to be plenty of wind," Boman said, glancing upward.

A large rock, the height of my thighs, rolled from the right, cutting across the front of the line and trampling the plant life in our way as it rolled off between the trees. When Jerry reached the intersecting path, he took it, his pace increasing even more.

"He's on the run and they're on his trail," he said, his long legs eating enough ground that some of us had to jog to keep up. "He seems like he's heading toward a few people who aren't moving as much. Not sure what to make of that."

A peal of thunder vibrated across the hillside. A moment later, I realized it wasn't thunder at all. It was a gunshot.

"That has to be a townsperson," I said. The twisted canopy above us strangled the moonlight even more. I blanketed the area in spirit to help me see the divots and pitfalls in the deepening night. Bria bumped into me and grabbed my shoulder, not so lucky with the extra sight.

A bolt of lightning blistered down from the sky. The compression of power nearly took me off my feet.

Thunder roared all around us, drowning out sound and shaking my bones. It was entirely too clear that this was not a natural storm, and also that I might've misjudged what a Demigod of Zeus could do.

I gulped as we hurried through the trees, rocks rolling with us now, following beside us like Jerry was the pied piper on his golden flute.

Souls popped into my awareness. I slowed, putting up my hand for Bria to stop. I needed a second to feel these people out before engaging.

Thane, directly in front of me, slowed as well. Boman, in front of Thane, slowed, and on down until everyone had stopped with me, including the rocks.

Another thick bolt of lightning slashed through the darkness. Sound and light hit me at once, the force of it blowing my hair back and making me stagger. The spirit-filled cadavers took off running in all directions, stomping through the brush and trees, one getting caught in a bush and flailing.

I pulled them all back in, happy enough with them in a jerking, shaking cluster.

The strangers on my radar pushed away from us, predators in the night. A single point in front of them hunkered down, at the very edge of my awareness. Had Dylan stopped? Was *he* attacking us?

"Tell me this lightning is from the Demigod," I whispered to Thane as Kieran made his way back to me.

"Definitely. Not even the Lightning Rod can create lightning this intense, but he'll be close. Same idea, just less power, like pitting you against the Demigods of Hades."

"What's up?" Kieran asked, coming in close. Power hummed within his body, I could feel it. He was ready to duel with the other Demigod.

The moon dappled the treetops and occasionally the ground, turning on and off like fairy lights as the thick clouds shifted and rolled above us. I closed my eyes, memorizing those souls. Gearing up for what was coming.

For what I would need to do.

"I'm pretty sure Dylan stopped running," I said.

Kieran nodded slightly. "Jerry said the same."

"I'm within striking range," I whispered, my stomach churning at the thought. "I can assume control of the two closest and weakest. They're on the—"

Another slash of light lit up the world. The thunder stopped my heart. My hair blew back, but I didn't stagger. If that bolt had hit anywhere near me, it would have killed me. Or at least ensured I didn't run away. This was why Zeus's descendants preferred to battle face to face. They needed to see their targets. Their blunt force worked best when all the players were represented on the board.

"I can assume control of the ones on the outskirts of

the battle, and use them to create chaos within their ranks," I said.

"Not yet," Kieran whispered, looking at the sky. "I want to get a little closer to Dylan. Right now Flora is just testing the waters. She's goading Dylan into action. This is a pretty standard game of chicken among Zeus magical workers. So far, Dylan is not rising to the bait. I'm not sure if that means she's got his back against the wall—Jerry says there's a big cliff face not far behind him—or if he's decided to make a stand. I know a lot about the training and theory behind Zeus magical workers, but I've never worked with one. I want to strip away some of the guesswork before I engage. We're going to watch them from under cover."

Another bolt of lightning hammered the ground, and I gritted my teeth against the sound and feeling of static electricity in the air.

"But when it kicks off, Alexis, give it everything you've got." Kieran covered my shoulder with his large hand, the heat of his touch grounding me. "The Demi-gods of Zeus can be some of the greatest war lords outside of Ares. They can handle some chaos, but there are very few who can efficiently maneuver in an absolute clusterfuck."

"I can do clusterfuck," I said, suddenly out of breath, adrenaline throbbing. "I can do clusterfuck better than most."

"Yes, you can." He squeezed my shoulder. "I love you." He stayed with me for a moment longer, not even flinching when another thick bolt of lightning slammed down what must've been a hundred yards away, a distance I'd once thought respectable.

Kieran moved away, taking the lead again. Strings of lightning spiderwebbed through the clouds above, shedding light onto the world for an instant. The tree canopy flickered like a projector. Smoke curled up in the distance, barely seen through the trees. Thunder growled all around us, cutting out all other sound, making it impossible for us to communicate over it.

Jogging now, Jerry designing our route to get us around the Demigod's team without being seen by them. We eventually cut back in, heading back toward the solitary soul whom Jerry had thought was backed up against a cliff and that was why he wasn't moving on. And while there was a cliff face a ways behind him, that wasn't keeping him here. As we got closer, more souls pinged onto my radar. Dylan was standing in front of six tightly clustered. I recognized two of them as the older woman and man from the café. Somehow they'd gotten mixed up in this mess, and Dylan was trying to make sure they didn't go down with the ship.

My heart ached for him. He'd come here for a quiet, peaceful life, trying get away from the pain and suffering of the magical world, but the magical world had come for him.

A shadowy figure stood in a clearing with others loosely gathered at her back and sides, facing the way in which we were quietly working. Light from above flickered on creamy skin and carrot-tinged hair. The woman had her hands out, palms facing each other, as though she were ready to clap. Something horrible would probably happen the moment she did.

I gritted my teeth as Kieran ducked between two hemlocks, Jerry after him, neither of them disturbing the reaching branches of needles. My band of zombies would crash through it, probably taking half the branches with them and making it rain pine cones or whatever else existed on that tree.

The rolling thunder cut off as though a switch had been flicked. I froze and forced the zombies to freeze with me, not an easy task when their normal operating procedure was to jerk and convulse. The lightning above dimmed. A woman's voice rose into the uncomfortable silence.

"I don't want to hurt you, Amell," she said, her tone deep and commanding and brimming with arrogance. This whole situation was clearly a waste of her time. "I know about your past. It wasn't pretty, and I understand why you'd run like a coward. But this isn't the answer, living out here with Chesters like some wild mountain man of little status. This existence is beneath you. You were made to be great. You were made to be the right hand of a Zeus Demigod. I will make sure you find your rightful place."

Dylan's voice rang out. "What happens if I don't want to take what you think is my rightful place? If I don't want a job in the magical world at all?"

She laughed, the sound condescending and haughty. I balled my fists, doing everything in my power not to grab her soul.

Thane stared at me from five feet away. He jerked his head just a little, signaling for me to walk on.

"And waste a Zeus-given talent like yours? Ridiculous," she spat. "But have no fear: you will want for nothing. I will make sure you can slowly acclimate to your new life. Your duties will be light. Your body will be your own."

I shivered in disgust, thinking of the alternative.

"If you come peacefully, I will not hurt those repugnant Chesters," she said, and her soul moved forward a few feet, indicating she was advancing on him. "They will be free to go."

"And if I don't?"

"Sadly, if you do not come quietly, there will be casualities. It cannot be helped." She obviously meant she'd kill them out of spite. "You will lose, Amell, we both know that. You are a marvel, but I am a Demigod. You are no match for me."

I took a step, and my foot crackled in the dried un-
derbrush. I froze and grimaced, looking at the shadowy
figure with the red hair, standing erect with her hands
out, at the ready. She didn't look back.

"How'd you hear about me?" Dylan—or was it
Amell?—shouted. Thunder rolled overhead, and I
jogged into the trees, branches slapping me in the face
as I worked closer to Dylan. I made my zombies jog
after Bria.

"That child of a Demigod isn't as locked down as he
thinks. He's made enemies out of those he thinks are
loyal, and enemies talk. He's nothing. He's already run
from here like a little coward, in fact. He is no match for
me. The descendants of all other gods bow before the
line of mighty Zeus."

I rolled my eyes. She was *mighty* hard to listen to.

Silence drifted through the scene, my senses saying
it should be peaceful but for the ominous flickering of
the lightning overhead and the expectation for violence
pounding silently through the unsaid words.

My heart thumped as Thane slowed. He stepped
back, motioning me on again. Dylan's soul waited fifty
feet away.

"Come out, Amell, don't make me come in," the
Demigod demanded, losing her patience.

A bolt of lightning seared my eyes as it dropped
down, smashing into a rock not far in front of where I

knew Dylan waited. The boom of impact rattled my bones. I took a step back, my primal senses telling me to run, the zombies trying to break free.

Body shaking, ears ringing, I felt Thane's strong hand on my arm. He escorted me past Boman and behind Red and Donovan looking out through the branches, and to a waiting Kieran at the front with Jerry just off to the side.

Instead of staying close to me like Kieran had directed, I was momentarily distracted as I felt Bria move in the opposite direction, through the ranks of zombies and beyond, out of my range. I looked back, but the trees obscured my vision. Where the hell was she going? Had Kieran changed her role in this?

Before I could inquire, I caught sight of the large cliff face Jerry had mentioned. Rough rock rising high into the sky, there was no way to climb it without serious supplies. A small shelf stuck out near the bottom, and around it were piled various-sized boulders and rocks, creating a small alcove. Within that alcove waited all six souls Dylan was clearly guarding.

"Come out, Amell. I won't give you another chance," the Demigod called.

Twenty feet in front of the alcove, hunkered down within a collection of trees and rocks, sat Dylan. If not for the placement of his darkened, smoldering soul, I would've missed him completely, so still was he within the branches and immobile rocks. With a start, I realized that the plane of his face was pointed directly at me. Although we'd been careful not to attract attention, sneaking up from the side, he knew we'd come.

I hoped he didn't mistake us for the enemy, because we had nowhere to hide.

"Don't I get to the count of ten?" Dylan called, and something had changed in his tone. His soul throbbed, a flash of beautiful brightness, before reducing back to smoldering ash.

"Must we play these games?" the Demigod answered.

Kieran gave a thumbs-up. Nothing happened for a moment, but then I caught Dylan flashing a handsome smile in the flickering light from above. He mimicked Kieran's gesture.

Kieran countered with five fingers, counted them down, and then made a fist. I wasn't sure what he was trying to relay, but Dylan seemed to understand, giving Kieran another thumbs-up.

"It's on," Kieran said, turning to me. "Time is ticking. Cause havoc, Alexis. Bring out the big guns."

"When? Now?" I asked, putting my hands out like I was bracing for something. Truth was that I fell into a momentary slide toward terror. He was turning me loose? Did he *know* how easily I could mess everything up?

"Go—"

"Sure, if you want," Flora said, and a dirty, frayed lightning bolt lit up the sky. When my ears stopped ringing, I barely heard, "One."

"—go, go, go!" Kieran's hand was at my back, urging me on.

I hurried in the direction of the zombies, expecting to feel Bria pop into my radar, for her to be with them and waiting for me. As I neared, though, she was still nowhere to be felt or seen. It was like she'd slinked away when she thought I'd be distracted.

Confusion stole over me. That wasn't like her. There had never been a battle where she wasn't in the thick of it with me. If Kieran had told her to be somewhere else, if it wasn't on the front line, she would've gone against his wishes by now. She didn't have a blood oath—he couldn't control her. Not now, not ever. Her slipping away right when things were getting hairy wasn't her MO.

Flora's words seemed to echo in my head.

He's made enemies out of those he thinks are loyal, and enemies talk.

Chapter 18

KIERAN

KIERAN WATCHED ALEXIS hurry away, her face screwed up in terror. The fireworks were about to begin, and she would send this whole place scrambling in a way no one else could.

"Wait for it," Kieran said to Jerry, putting his hand on the giant's shoulder. "What she did on the mountain was nothing. Wait for…"

He paused as a flash of power rolled through his flesh and bone. The lightning cracked down, this bolt a little closer to Dylan than the last. Great god of the sea, the Demigod of Zeus had some mighty power with that lightning. It felt like it was drawn directly from the heavens and aimed together with Mother Nature herself. The spectacle set him on edge.

Then again, dealing with a Demigod of Hades, cloaked in invisibility, had been terrifying in its own way. He'd gotten used to that. He could get used to this.

"Wait for her signal," Kieran continued, "walk away from us so we don't get blasted with you, and then turn this mountain into your playground." He held up a finger. "If you can lock those non-magicals into a stone safe room a Berserker can't break through, I'd be grateful. One thing, though…"

The next flash and boom was a little closer to Dylan, the countdown its own warning. Dylan watched Kieran, not moving, not even showing concern. The descendants of Zeus did arrogant indifference in their sleep.

"If you think Demigod Flora will force you to shift back—"

"She can't force me to do shit," Jerry said, his voice a deep growl. "What's the signal?"

"Absolute chaos. You won't be able to miss it."

Jerry grunted and stepped forward, moving deeper into the trees, his skin mottling as he did so, turning to stone.

It had been damn lucky getting that giant. He'd made things ten times easier than Kieran could've imagined. No wonder he'd been so sought after.

"Thane, the second you think Flora might regain control of the situation, go Berserk."

Thane nodded and jogged back through the trees. He'd find a trajectory that set him directly against the enemy, ensuring he didn't get distracted by his own people.

"Boman, bend your light around yourself and Alexis to keep both of you hidden. Alexis can work through the haze. Spirit will help her see."

Boman nodded and took off.

"Donovan." Kieran paused for the next flash and explosion of lightning. Electricity built in the air and sizzled across his skin. Dylan was preparing to act, Kieran would bet his life on it. Hopefully the guy didn't try to take Kieran out with the other Demigod. He seemed smarter than to try, but a cornered man was a desperate man, and Kieran didn't totally trust him. "Stay with me. You might need to rip me out of the way of lightning. Flora's lightning is powerful enough to punch down multiple feet into water before it spreads out. I might not have feet, especially not at first. Shove or yank me out of the way. Whatever it takes."

"Yes, sir."

"Zorn—" Kieran paused again for the lightning. Dylan kept his eyes on Kieran. They needed to start soon. Zorn waited patiently for his instructions—his magic was incredibly useful and didn't get the credit it deserved. Had he been nobility and able to grant wishes, his magic would've been as sought after as Alexis's. "Take out as many as you can. I doubt they've dealt with someone like you. Keep out of sight until you need to strike, and then kill them as fast as possible. Getting hit with lightning will kill you in your gaseous form, too."

He nodded without comment.

"And Zorn, if she forces you to change—"

"She won't." Zorn curled his lip and pulled out a precision knife. His body blinked out, shifting into his gaseous state, only visible if you knew the signs, which most people did not.

A clap of thunder from the side made Kieran flinch. No lightning followed. Flora had a Thunder Clapper, annoying but not much else. It wouldn't compare to what Dylan could do.

A cut-off scream made Kieran's small hairs stand on end. The next scream crawled up his spine and turned his blood ice cold. A ball of white light flew into the sky and exploded, sending out fissures of electric shock. Alexis was messing with someone's soul, and the feeling of it was sending them into hysteria. It never got easier to hear. It would never be easy to beat. The love of his life was a fucking boss on the battlefield.

Thunder clapped in a constant stream, the sound echoing off the cliff face, the originator running through the trees and laughing manically. Alexis apparently had control over that one. Another ball of light went into the air, the scream turning grating, the voice box fraying as surely as the soul's casing, Kieran had no doubt. Something popped and fizzed. Another scream, this one earthly. It wasn't an injury of the soul but the flesh.

"Report!" Flora yelled. "What is happening?"

Kieran called down the rain, the storm clouds heavy

with it. He scattered the clouds, breaking apart their energy. With air, he turned the rain into stinging pellets that slashed and wounded exposed flesh.

Yells rent the night. Electricity dissipated somewhat from the air.

"What—" A weak blast of lightning streaked sideways, and Flora was clearly caught by surprise. The bolt hit a tree off to the right, exploding the trunk.

The mountain bucked like a great beast, trees and plants rising into the sky as the rocks and soil rose beneath them, and then falling as both of those things gave way. The great roots of oaks and hemlocks and beeches pulled up out of the earth, sending the massive trunks thrashing toward the ground.

Lurching and shambling shadows streaked the space between the rolling rocks and the grinding boulders. Hands out like claws, Alexis's zombies slammed into the enemy forces, ripping and tearing at flesh.

Thunder clapped as the coopted spirits danced to Alexis's tune. Balls of light exploded against trees. Something sizzled and someone else screamed. She had a few people under her power now.

"Kill them," Flora yelled, her voice growing like the thunder from which it was made. "Kill those cowards, hiding in the trees like goblins!"

Clouds rolled above, fighting against Kieran's hold,

ripping from his grasp. It did not stop the rain, though, or the accompanying wind, slashing through Flora's people.

He sprinted toward Dylan, hoping against hope that Dylan would accept that they were on the same side. That Kieran and Alexis were keeping their word, and they would continue to do so after this was all done.

The ground shook beneath him. A great crater opened up not twenty feet away, splitting the mountain open at the seams. Water pulsed within, an underground river cutting through the rock.

Control of the sky was finally ripped from his grasp. Within moments, electricity throbbed around him, standing his hair on end. A streak of raw power broke from the storm-laden clouds, zipping directly for him.

He pulled up the water as he tilted his head to the sky. She was going to kill him. She was actually going to push this to the next level and take him out.

She was going to succeed.

Chapter 19

ALEXIS

I STAGGERED MID-STRIDE as I saw, in slow motion, the streak of burnt yellow light rip down from the sky. Kieran's face had tilted up, but I couldn't see his expression. I felt it, though. Shock and certainty. Earth-shattering sorrow. He knew this was it.

I didn't have time to open my mouth to scream. Or to react at all.

His body yanked to the side at the last instant, and the blast of lightning rammed the ground right next to him. The concussion sent him flying, though, and he hit the rock next to Dylan and came crashing down.

Heart in my throat, not thinking, I sprinted toward him. A soul popped into my radar. Hands up, the person was ready to come at me.

Boman shot out a beam of light, slicing through the enemy's chest. I yanked the enemy's soul free, even as I directed my zombies to file in around me. They guarded me as I ran across the small clearing, now in plain sight.

Boman ran to catch up, but a blast of fire exploded

at his feet, knocking him back. Someone must've realized he'd been shielding me from view with his Light Bender magic. Divide and conquer.

Red caught up a moment later, blood splattering her face and knives in her hands. Not knowing I had just turned the enemy into an ally, Red spun and threw out a leg, connecting the sole of her boot with the vulnerable throat, the attack so graceful it was beautiful. A crunch said the blow would've killed the man, but the confused soul in a newly dead body was under my control and wasn't allowed to sink to the ground in misery. Sorry, Charlie.

Fire shot from the cadaver's fingers and rolled along the ground, quickly doused by the driving rain. I sent him and the other enemies I controlled running at Flora, the red-haired one who clapped thunder, one who emitted blasts of white light that didn't seem to do much, and the fire spitter—the magic was fun to execute, but not as dangerous as it had originally seemed.

That lightning, though…

Flora lifted her hands, building those clouds. Building her power. Another searing blast zipped through the sky.

Halfway to the ground, it forked and then bent, doubling back on her. It snapped into a tree ten feet from her, and rage crossed her face within the flashing light.

"Are you okay?" I yelled as I reached Kieran, clutching him.

He stood and rolled his shoulder. "Donovan is on point. I'm good."

Dylan stood from the other side of the rocks. The ground near Flora bucked, throwing her to the ground. Massive boulders rolled toward the rapidly scattering cluster of enemies, dodging the felled trees. I sent my zombies after them, belatedly seeing Bria rushing through the trees from whence she'd gone. *Finally* she'd showed up.

After a moment, though, relief turned into horror, stealing through me. She held a knife and a determined expression. She wasn't rushing for the enemy or running to help with the zombies…she was rushing toward Thane. I'd seen that look on her face before—she was getting ready to take out the enemy, and that enemy was the threat of the Berserker.

I hesitated in reacting, my heart dying a little, not believing what I was seeing. I knew she'd slunk away from the battle, which wasn't customary for her, but Bria did strange things all the time. The element of surprise was her greatest asset.

There was no rational explanation for attacking Thane, however, and from the way her leather vest flew open to reveal her Monster High T-shirt and the dog collar around her neck, there was no denying it *was* her. She must've been the leak. She was the only one who had been around for all of our talks, even in the wee hours of the morning.

Tears came to my eyes as I grabbed her soul, not sure what I would do, not sure if I could bear to hurt her, my first real friend in the magical world. My teacher, and my buddy in arms. I squeezed her soul a little in warning, willing her to fall to her knees, to come to her senses.

And then I yelled in frustration and ripped the soul from its casing.

How stupid was I? That woman looked like Bria, definitely, and she even held herself with the same loose shoulders and *I don't give a fuck* confidence, but the soul throbbing within her didn't match. Assholes. I'd almost let my eyes fool me.

I slapped that bastard back in, sent a command through the new connection, and watched the image alter into that of Demigod Flora. Thane stared at her in slack-jawed shock, watching as she turned around and jogged back the way she'd come.

More enemies pushed forward, seeing me exposed and ready to take their shot. They hadn't battled someone like me, though. They hadn't asked around to see what my radar was like, much smaller than theirs but ten times more effective. *Fools.*

I grabbed the little ribbons connecting all of their souls, waving gleefully within the spirit that surrounded us. With a hard yank and plenty of energy and adrenaline to spare, I ripped them all out. Bodies fell like sacks of skin. Newly freed spirits blinked at me in confusion.

I shoved the spirits at the Line, not giving them a chance to choose if they wanted to hang around or not. This was battle, and they knew the score—I didn't need all the confused faces standing around, and I didn't have enough energy to secure them all in bodies.

I raked across Flora's soul box. Punched the casing. Shook and squeezed it.

A peal of thunder drowned out whatever sound came out of her open mouth. Lightning streaked across the sky with no real target or purpose. I'd knocked her off her game.

"You are fucking sensational," I heard behind me, only to see Dylan flicking lightning between his fingertips. He shook his head slowly at me. "Terrifying, but sensational. You took control before I could even warn you about the dog-collar chick. I've read the legends, but nothing could prepare a guy for all of this." He gestured, indicating the zombies scrabbling over and around boulders to get at the enemy. One misjudged a boulder's trajectory, accidentally getting in front. Its bones crunched under the weight. I pushed it to get back up, ruined body and all, and hobble toward its targets.

The mountain bucked again, throwing Flora onto her butt. More of her people pushed forward, but they were slower now than before. Cautious. Most were a little too far from me to pull their souls out. The few who *were* close enough were a little too strong for me to disable them at a distance. I could only slash at their souls, the feeling uncomfortable but clearly not enough to drop them to their knees.

I was within their range, though. I was within Flora's range.

"Stop congratulating me on being terrifying and help out!" I yelled at Dylan.

"You're cooler than me, but I'll give it a go," he replied, his voice even and steady, his movements slow and precise.

Meanwhile, I was sweating and swearing like a trucker, and adrenaline and fear was making me jerk about as much as my zombies.

Power built as Flora crawled to her feet, one hand directed toward where Jerry was concealed in the trees, the other pointed at the sky. The ground stilled. He had to split his focus to keep his rock skin, and she was probably trying to force him to shift back to his normal, and breakable, form. Another bolt of lightning broke from the clouds.

"Kieran," I yelled, diving out of the way.

The lightning painted the sky fire-white, coming at us in a deathly streak, until it hit a halfway point and then forked. Each leg bent, one side burying into a tree, the other punching the ground five feet from Flora.

Her eyes narrowed. Zorn manifested right next to her and she flinched away. Working with a knife in each hand, he peppered her with strikes, faster than I could process. Definitely faster than Daisy had ever witnessed in training. His blades sliced through ribs and across her stomach. He leaned around and jabbed her repeatedly in the kidneys. And then he was gone, back to gas and probably drifting away.

Lightning rained down all around her, smaller bolts but plenty effective. The mountain bucked again, Jerry freed from her attentions.

Heart in my throat, I hoped to hell Zorn had gotten free. That he hadn't been caught in that sudden, ferocious blast of electricity.

"Here we go." Dylan's hands shot out. Lighting curled around his fingers before flying out, each finger throwing its own bolt, and each of those fracturing into several, like a spray of electric water. Some of the bolts slammed into Flora's middle. She jerked and her body went taut. The rest of the spray continued on, hitting zombies and the enemies alike, his range larger than mine but his targeting not great. Screams and shrieks filled my awareness, and then a peal of thunder rendered me deaf. It *boomed* all around me, *within* me. It took me from my feet and laid me flat on my back.

Ringing silence followed.

I was struggling to get up, just like everyone else in the vicinity, when Dylan snapped right next to my ear. That snap brought back the sound as though it had never left.

He did it for Kieran next, who was shaking his head, probably to rid himself of the same ringing.

"Sorry, I'm extremely rusty with that one," Dylan said, having leveled the battlefield. "My targeting has gone to crap."

"Holy fuck," I said softly.

The reprieve was short-lived. Zeus people knew how to deal with Zeus magic. They knew how to combat it, or at least push through it.

Flora waved the effects away, her manic expression flickering in the storm of light building within the clouds. Her head tilted, and I knew she was done playing.

"Bring her down!" I yelled, digging into her middle, slashing.

"Here's a conductor." Kieran lifted his hands, and water rose from the deep chasm Jerry had created in front of Dylan's rock barricade. He unleashed it across the ground, pushing it across everyone's feet and then holding it there, keeping the enemy standing in a half foot of water.

Dylan wiped his hand through the air, palm down. Lightning sprang to life along the top of the water like a living thing. Like fire, almost, but a current instead of flames. A raging, fizzing, burning current that sailed across the surface of the water. When natural lightning struck water, it usually dissipated within twenty feet, but this was magic, guided and controlled by Dylan himself.

Flora screamed, wiping at her chest—my magic— and then flinched as Dylan's magic washed over her ankles and the electrocution crawled up her legs. She was a Demigod, though. We weren't enough to keep her down.

Jerry must've known that. A huge boulder, waist-high, rolled uphill toward her. It pinged off a tree, flattened a bush, and barreled into Flora, crunching over her ankle.

Then stopped.

"Take cover!" Dylan roared, jumping over the rock barrier and standing next to Kieran and me. He lifted his hands into the sky. "This is her last-ditch effort."

A monsoon of lightning crashed down around us, the power distributed across the sky enough to dilute each strike, but if any of them hit me, they'd be plenty powerful enough to send me to the emergency room. Bolts that were aimed right for us curved at the last moment, Dylan acting as our umbrella. But the others weren't so fortunate.

Donovan dove into the cover of the rock shelf housing the cowering non-magical people. Red dashed through the trees in Jerry's direction. A rock fort sprang up, bending trees and branches out of the way. Hopefully she'd get there in time. A scream from an unlikely source caught my attention. Amber's leg had been caught in the crossfire, but she quickly dove into a tiny rock crevice in the bottom of the cliff face and pulled her knees in.

I redoubled my efforts, crumbling one of the prongs attaching her soul, then the next. I scrabbled at the squishy middle. I banged on the casing like a drum, working with her primal instinct that *had* to have been making her want to curl up to protect her middle.

Kieran lifted more water from the crevice. Then more. He pushed it forward, rolling it across the ground, slopping it over Flora, submerging her. Caging her without air. He lifted his eyes skyward next, working on the weather, trying to force those clouds away, fighting her power while multitasking with his.

"Incredible," Dylan said, still keeping that lightning off us. "You win the most trained award."

"It came at a steep price." Kieran, his muscles bulging, rain soaking his light shirt, kept up the pressure.

Flora's soul casing loosened, her body probably

fighting for breath. The prongs weakened. My grip slipped in past her protections. I grabbed her soul.

"Oh shit—"

Chapter 20

ALEXIS

"ARE WE TRYING to kill her?" I asked in a panic.

"No. We are making her submit," Kieran answered.

"Then stop. Stop! Pull back. Quick!" I tried to keep absolute focus so I didn't do something stupid, like sneeze and accidentally pull her soul out of her body.

The lightning cut off suddenly. The thunder died and the clouds cleared away. The black sky, holding a full, heavy moon, lifted its skirt and showed off all its stars.

Dylan lowered his hands, one perfect eyebrow arched.

"Pull away the water," I told Kieran, not relaxing, my fingers out like claws.

Kieran did as I said. Silence as thick as death settled over the scene.

"Do not move, Flora," I yelled, feeling another prong disintegrate within my magical grasp. This time I hadn't been trying. "You gotta give in to Kieran right now, but *do not move*! I will pull my grip out of your chest, but I need a very calm second in which to do it. Your life is in my hands right now, and I am not trained nearly as well as everyone else in this clearing. I repeat, I am very new at this, and your life is literally in my hands. I know you can feel that."

"I submit," she said, pain lacing her words. "I submit. Stand down!"

"Jerry, keep that rock on her for a moment," I said, dribbling the power of the Line through my magical touch and repairing the first prong. "I'm trying to fix a couple of things, Flora, and then I'll get out, okay? Just hang on."

"You're a danger to the magical community!" Flora screamed, her primal terror clearly overcoming the pain of the boulder pinning her in place.

"I am not trying to minimize your situation, Flora, but honestly, you started it." I released the prong, and sighed when it held. "Just one more. I'll leave the last one broken for insurance purposes in case you act up."

"It'll repair itself," Harding whispered from ten feet away.

I jumped—and then let out a ragged breath when Flora's soul stayed put.

"Way wrong time to pop in, Harding," I said, re-building the second prong. Most of the time, when I got this far in ripping out a soul, I went through with it. I was fighting against muscle memory right now, and more than a little worried I'd mess up."

"I've been around, watching from a distance. You have a certain *way* about you, you know? It's thrilling."

"No, I do not know," I said through clenched teeth.

"That is why Hades was banished to the Underworld, with his disgusting, cowardly magic," Flora spat, her arrogance helping her fight her fear.

"Did it ever occur to you that maybe the reason Hades slipped under the earth and Poseidon dove into the deep oceans was to get away from Zeus carrying on about himself, his courage, and his schlong? That must have gotten old. I'd find somewhere else to be, too. Honestly, you and your people are about as dumb as a box of hair. I'd take Hades magic over yours any day."

Harding laughed. "Good one. You're definitely one of us. Sure wish you'd been a Demigod so they'd care more."

Sweat dripping off my brow, I slowly disengaged from her soul, then took a step back. I took a long, steadying breath. "It's good. We're good."

"Jerry, roll the rock off her foot," Kieran said, lowering the water back into the crevice and walking around it to get to Flora. I went with him. "Zorn, anyone left?"

Zorn emerged from the rock fort Jerry had created as we neared Flora. "Of theirs? Six. Three are very badly hurt and might not make it. The others will need medical attention but should be fine."

"Bria should be waiting a couple of hundred yards down the hill with the four-wheelers and the flatbed trailers," Kieran said. "The injured can be transported on those."

"When did you give her that directive?" I asked, my heart squishing, remembering the moments when I'd thought she had turned. "It's not like her to skip a battle. Not for any reason."

"And she didn't skip this one. I told her to take out any transportation Flora might have, then go along the outskirts of the battle on the way to checking on the kids, taking out anyone she ran across. I'm sure she took out one or two enemies, at least."

"But...why her? Were you worried she was the leak?"

"I knew she wasn't. Bria's too smart to betray a Demigod. In her field, she'd run the risk of becoming unemployable. I knew she wouldn't want to fight another Demigod unless we were going in for the kill, and that you'd be handling cadaver duties, so I figured I'd use her in another way. She saves face, you get your kids checked on, we have transportation for the injured, and she still gets to take out some enemies. Wins all around."

I touched his arm, not really able to believe my love for him could grow even stronger. Bria was great in combat and we'd had less people than the enemy, but instead of pushing his own agenda, he'd put her needs first and given her an out. From what I was learning, not many leaders would've done that. Not many leaders would have allowed people as intimate with our plans as Red and Bria to hang around without a blood oath, either. He was one of a kind.

He smiled at me. "Let's get this all cleaned up, and we can get out of here. If we don't leave soon, I have a feeling this town is going to chase us out."

"He's of Zeus's line," Flora said, sitting up with a pained wince as we stopped next to her. Her leg was in bad shape, and I kept from looking at it to avoid losing my last meal. "He belongs with me."

"He belongs with whomever he chooses," Kieran said, looking down on her coolly.

"Noble words coming from someone that's here for the same reason I am. You Drususes have always thought you were above the rest of us. Well, I have a prosperous territory, too. And I—"

"Let me just stop you right there." Kieran lifted a hand. "I am not here to secure the Thunderstroke. I am only here to prevent you from unlawfully forcing a magical worker to join your organization. After this, if he is willing, I will transport him wherever he would like to go, and there I will leave him, in anonymity if he so chooses. If he would like to join you, he will contact you. If you try to force his hand, you will, once again, come up against me. Next time, however, I won't stop the Soul Stealer from turning you inside out and using you like a puppet. Think it through."

Flora stared up at him with a moving mouth, no sound coming out. I was pretty sure it was the last thing she'd expected Kieran to say.

"We'll round your wounded up and deposit them in town," he went on. "Hopefully you were nice to the townspeople, since you'll now be in their care. See you at the Summit."

He turned away, thoroughly dismissing her, and scanned his people. He might not make arrogance an art, but he sure could turn it on when he wanted to.

Amber stood with her weight on her uninjured leg, the other blackened badly where the bolt had struck. Thane leaned against a tree, his perfectly cut torso on display, marred with charred smudges. His vest lay at his feet, and I could just make out a blistered hole in it, plus the blackened remains of what had to be his shirt. He'd obviously been struck, but while his shirt had literally gone up in flames, he didn't appear to have sustained any lasting damage.

"Are Berserkers immune to lightning?" I asked as Kieran inspected a large gash down Red's back. Boman stopped beside them, his pants only singed at the ankles, already digging for supplies to patch Red up.

"Not totally, no." Thane rolled his massive shoulders, and a ripple of power ran through his muscles. "It still hurts like an absolute beast. I barely stopped from changing."

"Wait…" I bent to touch the scorched hole through the vest. "You were still in human form when this hit you?"

"Yes. I sure would've liked to get free, but you all had it locked down. I didn't want to piss on your parade." Each word was laced with a growl. It sounded like he was still resisting the urge to go Berserk.

Dylan waited just beyond the tree that Thane was using as a leaning post, his hands in his pockets, watching Kieran move through his people.

"Hey," I said, stopping beside him. I'd just get in the way if I tried to help the others. I was better at causing the mess, not cleaning it up.

"Hey," he replied softly, no longer as cool and confident as he'd been in battle. The training had fallen away and now he was just a guy again, maybe not quite sure where he stood or what he wanted.

"You okay?" I asked.

"I'm not hurt, if that's what you mean." He pointed toward Thane without looking. "Did I hear that right— he got struck by lightning and didn't go Berserk?"

"Yeah. Crazy, right? The hole in his vest was pretty big."

He let out a slow breath. "I have never, in my life, heard of a Berserker who could take a hit like that without tearing the whole place apart. That's incredible."

"Kieran has gathered a pretty incredible team." I chewed my lip as I stood beside him, both of us watching the others. "Look, I'm really sorry. We tried to be careful. I fucked up your life, and I realize that. I'm in your debt."

"I checked your house this morning, to make sure you'd gone."

"So did Flora's people, apparently."

"Biggest mistake they ever made."

A glance revealed his lopsided smile. "Bria isn't subtle when she takes care of business. Poor Jerry probably doesn't know what he's in for, hanging out with her."

"How'd you know Demigod Flora had found out about me?"

"They passed us on the road. They weren't subtle about who they were."

"That's the funny thing—Demigods usually aren't. They're so used to being on a pedestal that they never think to hide their talent or their status. Even the Demigods sitting over failing territories puff up like peacocks. A level-five leader of a prosperous territory is still just a level-five leader. It isn't specifically called out, but they are deemed lesser than."

"Yes, well, thank God, right? Because it helped Kieran and his people identify her."

He turned just a little so he could look at me. "My point is, your outfit didn't come in that way. You tried to fit in, and you accomplished that goal perfectly. I didn't even know you were in town until I physically saw your mark. I'd heard about the Hammermil house selling, but that was it. No one knew anything else. The names on the paperwork didn't lead anywhere—I checked."

"Kieran is good."

He shook his head. "I don't think you realize how strange Demigod Kieran's outfit is. When you came back, I figured it was some sort of trick...until you started ripping souls out."

"Right." I tightened my lips, feeling like he was making a point that I just wasn't getting. I said as much.

He huffed out a laugh. "Something isn't adding up, that's my point. I don't understand this, and I don't trust what I don't understand."

"Fair enough. For the record, *I'm* the one that's not adding up. I'm sure Kieran's situation would make a lot more sense if he didn't pander to me. My life has always been a mess. He probably thinks it's easier to just go with it than try to fight it."

"That's the thing. Demigods don't just *go with* things."

"Most of the Demigods you've known probably weren't sequestered on small islands with their tortured and slowly dying mothers, either. We all have bad crap in our lives. Sometimes you just have to make the best of it and push on. Anyway, look, I know you have a lot to think about"—his expression closed down—"but we both know you can't stay here. Kieran can help you disappear again, if you want. You can start over. That doesn't cover the debt I owe you, obviously, but it's something. It's an apology."

He was staring at me again, perplexed. "I thought you guys wanted me in your crew?"

I frowned. "I thought you didn't want to work for a Demigod again?"

"I don't."

"Right, well… Sorry, I'm confused. What's the problem?"

He threw his head back and laughed. "It's just…I was in the magical world for a while. I took an immortality blood oath, so I'm older than I look…"

"Most people seem to be, yeah."

"I've never run across someone like you. I might not have left if I had."

I rolled my eyes. "First, you were chained to a bed by a psycho half the time. How could you have met someone like me? That's not my jam. Second, *you were chained to a bed by a psycho.* No one would've decided to hang around after that. No way."

Bria walked past before doubling back and spreading her arms at me. The hair at her temple was matted with blood and a dribble had dried down the side of her cheek. "I heard you killed my lookalike? What a bitch, seriously. That could've been me."

"Imagine my disappointment when I learned it wasn't. What's up with your head?"

"Yeah." She fingered the wound. "I'd just taken out one of theirs, and I look in the trees and see my face staring back at me. It was a trip! I jumped out at myself, clubbed me in the head, and took off running. I'm not going to lie, I could've killed her, but I hesitated. It's a weird damn situation trying to kill yourself. What a trip!" she repeated, and then laughed. "Hey, Dylan, what are we doing with your Chesters? Do they need a ride back? I don't want to ask them myself—the old guy keeps aiming shotguns at everyone. I don't have fast healing powers, as you see, so I'm not trying to get shot."

"I'll be right there." He turned to face me and then enveloped me in a tight hug. I could feel him shaking, as if the touch was an unwelcome feeling but the act of a hug was worth it. It probably had something to do with that psycho. I accepted it gladly. "Thanks for coming back. You evened the score. No debt to repay." He held both of my shoulders. "Tell Kieran thanks, but no thanks. I'll make my own way."

I nodded at him, feeling a tinge of sadness at parting. I hardly knew the guy, but I felt for him. "If you ever need anything, look us up. We have a place to stay if you ever want to slip back into the magical world."

He winked. "Maybe I'll take you up on that, some-day."

I watched him stride away before glancing off in the direction of the cabin. I needed to check on the kids. They were probably worried sick. Then we needed to get out of here before the townspeople went for their pitchforks.

It wasn't until I turned to join the others that I noticed Harding sitting off to the side, his lurking well past creepy at this point.

"Don't go telling me about some other rando that needs saving," I said, striding past him. Weariness dragged at my bones. "This was not worth the risk."

"Are you so sure?"

"Yes. Yes, I am so sure. Bugger off, Harding, would ya? I could do with a few days without you."

He put a hand to his chest, his customary smirk never far away. "That's hurtful."

I shook my head and kept going, thinking over the battle. One Demigod down, one more to navigate before we even made it to the Summit. I just hoped the next one was a little nicer. I was tired of fighting for the right to freedom.

Fear coiled in my gut. Dare to dream.

Chapter 21

DYLAN

D YLAN SLIPPED INTO the café right before closing, his muscles sore and fatigue dragging at his eyelids. He couldn't rest yet, though. He had a lot of work still to do.

Demigod Kieran, Alexis, and their group had left shortly after all the wounded were transferred into town. True to their word, they hadn't pushed Dylan to join them. Kieran had simply given Dylan a card, wished him good luck, and walked on.

That would've been that, too. Had nothing else happened, Dylan would've gladly pushed them from his mind. Something about their group didn't add up, and Dylan didn't want to be on the wrong side of a blood oath when he figured it out.

But Alexis's feisty young ward had hung back as the others walked away. She'd pulled from her pocket a folded-up piece of notepaper, the edges torn, as though it had been hurriedly ripped out of a notebook.

Looking straight ahead, she'd held it in front of her

stomach between her first two fingers. "Kieran didn't think you had much in the way of funds."

"I have enough."

"Enough means very little. Here." She didn't move, continuing to hold the paper low and between them, although her expression was studiously casual, as if they were having conversation about birds or trivial matters.

"What is it?"

"A fucking bomb." She rolled her eyes. "Don't tell Lexi I swore. It's an account number. Just take the bloody thing and slip it into your pocket so those yuk-ups behind me don't realize what I'm doing."

Wrestling with a smile, he did as she said. Despite her age, he was half afraid not to. There was a raw, ruthless quality about her, like a feral cat.

"You don't need a Demigod in your business, I get that," she said, stepping back a pace. "You don't need him trying to set up a new life for you, because then he knows your shit. That's smart. But you still need money, and these guys don't travel with nearly enough cash. On that paper is sign-on information for an offshore account. There is also the login information for a generic email. Log in to the email, change the password. Log in to the bank, change the password. That will effectively remove me from the equation. Transfer the funds to an account you set up. Close this one down. I won't use it again after you touch it. No offense, but you get where I'm coming from. The account has two hundred grand in it. Choose a cheap town and it's a good start. Good luck."

She turned without another word.

"Wait, wait," he said, lunging to pluck at her shirt. "What are you talking about? Did Alexis put you up to this?"

She turned back, looking annoyed. "They were right—Zeus's line is filled with a bunch of plastic-headed Ken dolls. You're cute, but that isn't enough to get by, bro. No, Lexi didn't put me up to this. You better not tell her, either, or we'll have a problem, you and me. I don't know if you know this, but Kieran's dad was a lunatic. If Kieran goes down the same road, we gotta get out. She's thinking with her heart, so she's not preparing for the worst, but I'm thinking with my head. If we need to lose that Demigod, I'll have the funds and know-how to do it. You've lived my worst fear. Least I can do is help a dude out. Hide your magic a little better, huh? Now that people know you're alive, they'll be hunting for you. Lexi fucked up your game—I'd call her on her debt, one day. Until then, though…" She nodded at Dylan's pocket. "Good luck. I hope I never see you again."

"Hate me that much?"

Her dead-eyed stare was a clear message of Dylan's idiocy. For some reason, he thought that was hilarious.

"If I don't see you again, it means you got free," she said. "If that's what you want, then I hope you get free."

"But what about you? This is a lot of money for a girl your age. How'd you even get it?"

"I leaned hard into Kieran's generosity—or his desire to impress Lexi, whichever—and started hiding the money away. I'm pretty sure they know I'm doing it now, but they don't know exactly how or where it's going. They see it as a fun little game that helps the poor little Chester feel a bit more secure. Fine by me. It's only a game to those not used to surviving." She nodded at his pocket again. "That was the first account I set up. It's clunky. It's time to let it go, anyway. Might as well give it to a good cause."

"I'm not a charity."

"Good thing, or you'd have to claim the money on your taxes. Good luck. Sorry we screwed all this up for you." A moment later she was walking away, leaving Dylan standing there, dumbfounded.

She'd been a hundred percent genuine, he could tell, and she'd spoken in Dylan's language. Her situation was the reverse of his—a Chester in a magical world instead of the other way around. The money was all there, exactly as she'd said. The telephone access code and account specifics had been in an email sent to and from the email account earlier in the day. He'd had everything he needed to transfer the money to his second alias, and then close it all down. He'd done it quickly and without hassle.

He'd taken two hundred grand from a teenager who'd stolen the money from a Demigod and then given it to him without strings because he needed it.

Was this real life?

He'd gone from a nightmare to a lonely, solitary life, to…what? Where was he now?

He was saying goodbye to the life he'd lived for the last decade and a half.

Dim lights greeted him as he entered the café. At ten o'clock, few people in the quiet town were awake, let alone out and about, especially with all that had gone on earlier. Thank heavens, because most of the populace had wanted to hang him. Literally hang him, like in the olden days. Acquaintances he'd had for the last ten years, who'd served him food or bagged his groceries, had spat at him as he helped deliver the wounded into town. They'd sneered at him, treating him like he was some sort of dangerous animal.

With Kieran's help, the town had given Dylan twenty-four hours to vacate. He would do it in less than that. He didn't trust that the townspeople would leave him be. Jeremiah's truck was down the street from Dylan's cabin. That old redneck didn't need much of a reason to get violent.

Dylan stopped at the counter and flattened his palm

on the rustic wood. With a deep sigh, he hesitantly chimed the little round bell, polished to a high shine.

"We're closed—Oh!" Mag's face appeared through the kitchen window below the silver ticket holder. "Dylan!"

He smiled in relief, having half wondered if she'd changed her mind after the battle on the mountain. It still baffled him that six of his friends had shown up to defend him, firearms in hand. He'd already said good-bye to the other five who had shown up, but she was the last. She was the most special.

Fifteen years ago, Dylan had woken up in the morgue in Gianna's palace, dressed in a suit as though he were being prepared for a casket. The last thing he'd remembered was trying to breathe through a closed-up throat and seeing black. He'd woken in the middle of the night and the night watch wasn't on duty. No one seemed to be on duty, actually, which had allowed him to slip out undetected. Guards slept at their posts. Someone had left a service van running in the delivery area, which he'd easily stolen. He'd driven until it ran out of gas, no money to buy more or even something to eat. But a stranger had taken pity on him and given him a ride.

He'd been dropped twenty miles outside of town and hiked his way in here, somehow managing to slip past the non-magical checkpoint unnoticed. Mags, the only person out on Main Street that morning, had ushered him into the café. Just like that, she'd taken him under her wing. She'd fed and clothed him, helped him find a place to live, helped him find a job as a town gardener—she'd saved his life. He could never be too thankful for her, or for the driver who'd picked him up.

"Hey, Mags."

Her smile was sad as she stopped on the other side of the counter. "Want a cup of coffee?"

"Nah. I came to say goodbye. I have to get going. I'm not welcome here anymore."

Her eyes misted and she nodded, biting her lip. "Well, come on, give me a hug."

She came around the counter and held out her arms.

He calmed the quailing in his mind and pulled her close for a moment. Gianna would not have a hold on him forever. He would not lose himself to the horrors of his past. Not anymore.

"I'm sorry," he said, dangerously close to letting emotion overcome him. "I never meant to lie to you. I wanted to tell you so many times, but I didn't want to put you in an uncomfortable situation." That, and he'd feared she'd cast him out. He wouldn't have been able to bear that.

"Don't be silly," she said, and cupped his cheek in her weathered hand. "I knew you were magical. The number of lightning storms in the area quadrupled the year you moved here, yet no one was injured and there was zero damage. Even trees stopped getting struck and falling on houses. That's the sort of coincidence that needs more of an explanation than the Almighty."

"You...you knew? Why didn't you say anything?"

Her smile was comforting. "I figured you'd tell me in your own time."

"Instead I was hunted down." A flash of rage stole his breath. He'd run like a coward. He'd hidden. He'd tried to slip away without being detected. If his old trainers had heard that, they would've spat in his face. The only reason he'd stood up to fight was because Mags and the others had gotten stuck in the crossfire.

He hated that his life was now running.

"What about that lovely young woman and her foster kids? Now, she seemed very pretty and put together." Mags walked around the counter and headed for the coffee machine. "Turn off the sign and lock the door, would ya, Dylan?"

He did as she said, his heart aching at her use of the name he'd given himself. He'd made it up on the fly when she'd asked for it all those years ago. With that name, he'd become a new person. A better person. A *free* person.

"She has a heart of gold, that one, sweet and fierce." Mags polished a mug. "I think you should look her up.

She's magical too, right? You'd have a lot in common."

Dylan laughed and leaned on the counter. "She has a boyfriend. The powerful Demigod that can control water, remember him? When he lifted you over the rocks, I believe you said, 'Oh my lucky stars.'"

She pursed her lips and her face turned red. She turned to busy herself again with the coffee machine. "I was just surprised, is all."

"By the muscle, yeah. We all caught on when you squeezed his bicep."

"Oh, pish! Well, that's too bad. She seemed sensible. As sensible as a magical person can be, of course."

"Naturally."

"Well, I think you should find someone. You've been alone for long enough. It's time to get matched up. You're magical—*be* magical. God didn't intend for you to hide what you are. Find a place that makes you happy, and live true to yourself. No more sneaking to the mountaintop to put on secret light shows—let everyone see. It's beautiful."

He chuckled and shook his head. "And I'd always thought I was so secretive."

"It's hard to hide what you are from people that pay attention," she said, laughing softly.

Her words filtered into his awareness, merging with the things that young girl had said. He'd have to get better at hiding his magic, or people would find him.

They knew to look now; it would be easier.

He accepted a cup of coffee from her. "That Demi-god and his girlfriend want me to work for them."

"Oh? See? Now that's a good idea. They were very nice people. Not like that other one. I'd always thought magical people were like the blonde with the beehive"— she meant Flora—"waltzing in, waving their money around, barking at everyone to bend to their whims— but the dark-haired man and his people were very sweet. So generous, too. The tips!"

Dylan nodded, sipping his coffee. "He and his people are certainly different, you're right about that. I told myself I would never...work for one of them again. Never. But if I go back into that world, I'll have to. Either I'll choose who to...work for, or someone, like the beehive lady, will choose for me."

"Hmm. That doesn't sound right."

"I have a special kind of magic, and the magical world is a brutal place."

"Now that I do know. That's why I live here. I'm a simple woman, and I want a simple way of life. I can't keep up with all the other stuff. But no matter where you end up, you'll find two sorts of people—those who want to help others and those who would rather just help themselves. I think if you find the sort that want to help others, you won't go wrong."

He sipped his coffee in reflection.

Her little chuckle brought his focus back to her.

"What?" he asked.

"Well, that kinda fits, doesn't it?"

"What's that?" he asked.

"That man has magic over water."

"He's a Demigod of Poseidon, yes."

"Yes, Poseidon, that's the one. And your name is Dylan."

"And?"

Her brow furrowed even as she smiled at him. "Haven't you ever looked up what your name means?" In response to his blank look, she shook her head, her gray curls waving. "I love learning the meaning of names and seeing if they match the person. Your name means 'son of the sea' or 'born of the ocean.' It didn't seem to fit, but now… Well, maybe that's your calling."

× × ×

KIERAN

TWO DAYS AFTER returning home from West Virginia, Kieran sat in his library, urgent business tugging on his mind and an uncomfortable feeling squeezing his heart. He did not take any pride or satisfaction in what he was about to do. He hated that it had come to this.

It couldn't be put off any longer, though. He had one month to plan the meeting with Demigod Lydia, and there were a lot of moving parts to that situation.

He needed to plan for every eventual hiccup, every possible outcome, and navigate every possible strategy Lydia might have developed for him and/or Alexis. He'd be taking his love and his people into a pit of flames, and he somehow had to make it out without catching fire.

Kieran stood when he noticed the ancient butler had answered his summons. He lurked by the open double doors, holding a silver tray laden with a tea set. "Sodge, come in."

"Yes, sir." Sodge's jowls shook as he moved, slowly lifting his chin and pursing his lips the closer he came. The man needed to work on his poker tells.

"Take a seat, please." Kieran closed the doors.

Sodge finished placing the tray on the coffee table between two stylish though comfortable leather arm-chairs. "A seat, sir?" Sodge looked around in surprise.

"Yes, Sodge. Please." Kieran retook his chair and waited for the butler to uncomfortably take a seat. He wasn't used to being talked to as an equal, or sitting in the same room with the master of the house. He'd been a servant for two of Kieran's lifetimes or longer, and he'd always been treated as one. It was the only way Kieran had ever thought of him, either. The silent help, always underfoot but never in the way. It was the reason for Kieran's major slip-up—the reason he had let everyone down.

"Please, sir, this is unseemly. Who will pour the tea?"

"The…tea." Kieran had asked for coffee.

As if hearing Kieran's thought, Sodge pursed his lips again. "Civilized people drink tea. Cultured people. Your father drank tea until the day he died."

"My father was lactose intolerant and hated coffee without milk or creamer in it. He quit out of spite for milk, and drowned his tea in sugar. I hardly think that is the sign of a civilized and cultured man."

"You never did understand the finer things in life," Sodge muttered, turning his face to the side.

"You may pour the tea, if it makes you happy," Kieran said.

"Yes, sir." Sodge stood with effort, clearly feeling the years now that Valens's blood oath and the accompanying perks had been ripped away.

"Sodge, it has come to my attention that someone in my employ has been talking to Demigod Flora of New York."

Sodge stiffened. "Oh?"

"She and her crew showed up in West Virginia barely a day after I did."

"That sounds most unfortunate. Her team must be nearly as good as yours." He finished pouring the light brown liquid into a dainty cup painted with purple flowers—something Kieran's mother might've picked out. He reached for the silver spoon sticking out of the silver sugar bowl, something his father had liked. Valens never missed a chance to show off his wealth.

Kieran put out a hand. "No sugar for me, thanks. Milk will be fine."

Sodge sniffed. "I didn't bring milk, sir. It's bad for you."

Kieran sighed. Sodge wasn't making this any easier.

"Fine. And no, her team is not nearly as good as mine. Most of them are now dead, despite the fact that she brought her best and brightest. She'll be in the market for some new oath holders. Is that something you'd be interested in?"

Sodge stepped to the side and clasped his hands behind his back. He hadn't poured himself any tea, and he didn't plan to sit again. Kieran let it go.

"I have no wish to enter a strange Demigod's rat race, thank you very much," Sodge said haughtily.

"Then I wonder why you would consistently feed her private information overheard from discussions in this house, Sodge."

Kieran placed his elbows on the arms of the chair and steepled his fingers against his lips, waiting.

Sodge straightened a little more, although no remorse showed on his face. No fear or regret, either.

After a moment of silence, it was clear he did not plan to deny the allegations. Kieran gave him a little credit for that.

"You've put me in a tight spot, Sodge," Kieran went on, dropping his hands and leaning back. "I would like to honor my father's position for you—I'd like you to keep your home—but I simply cannot allow you to stay here if you plan to share sensitive information. After this, I cannot trust you."

"I didn't do anything you haven't," Sodge said. "You came slinking into your father's house under false pretenses, learning his secrets and spying on him, like a filthy rat."

"Yes, I did. And when he found me out, he planned to kill me. I do not plan to kill you, Sodge."

"Go ahead. It will be a hero's death."

"You are not a hero. Because of you, many people died. Because of you, a man's future has been jeopardized."

"Yes, well, the Demigod of New York has always been lacking in her ability to close a deal. Your father always said that."

"Then why go to her?"

"Because she is of Zeus, and I thought she would jump at this chance."

"She did. Good call. If you do not plan to take up a position with her, I must decide what to do with you."

Sodge stood there stoically, looking straight ahead, and offered no help or direction.

"You liked working for my father," Kieran said to stall, wishing Sodge would give him something, *anything*, to work with. His mother had thought Sodge was good at heart, though irrational when it came to Valens. Kieran didn't want to kill another little piece of his past if he could help it.

"Of course I did. He was fair and just. If I had gone around your father's back and done this, he would've tortured and then killed me. He was not a soft man, like his son has turned out to be. He was an exacting leader in this uncertain age."

Kieran sighed. "Shall I ask you to leave, is that what you'd like?"

"I have nowhere to go. That must've crossed your mind."

"It has. It has also crossed my mind that you'd rather die than give a blood oath to me. Which leaves me at an impasse, I'm afraid. I can't have you in my home without some way to control your scheming. I can make some calls—see if anyone else will take you."

"Only a few in the world can live up to Valens's status. He was one of the best. I wouldn't degrade myself by entering the employment of anyone lesser."

Kieran shook his head, at a loss. The old man was leaving him no choice but to cast him out.

He opened his mouth to promise the man a healthy retirement and a home of his choosing, but Sodge continued.

"Your father thought you had the potential to be as good as him, someday. That you two would control half the world, magical and otherwise."

"Yes, well—"

"He was not wrong, though your methods would make him turn over in his grave. I do not claim to understand the world of the Demigods, but it is my place, and so I will embody my place. I will accept the blood oath, on the condition that when the Hades woman"—his nose curled—"figures out how to grant immortality to both of you, you will renew the blood oath with that ability embedded."

Kieran did a bad job of containing his shock.

"If that's all, sir, I will come back to clear away the tea." Sodge turned to leave without a formal release, something he had done with Valens. "Oh, and..." Sodge turned back at the door. "I knew, of course, the woman from New York would not pose a threat. That is why I called her instead of Demigod Zander, who would've taken the boy right out from under your nose. Despite Flora's high standing, she has always been mostly useless. And now she knows the son is as good as the father. You will have no more trouble from her."

With that, Sodge let himself out of the library and closed the door after himself.

Kieran could do little more than blink in amazement.

Sodge had orchestrated the entire situation that had led to this meeting? How could it be?

But there was no denying the truth of what he'd said. Flora had been no match for Kieran and his team, and he did not expect her to stand up to him again. He'd realized that shortly after the end of their battle. He'd even thought, fleetingly, that at least *one* good had come out of the failed journey to grab the Thunder-stroke.

Sodge had set out to get a blood oath from someone he hated but deemed as good as Valens, and in so doing had helped Kieran remove some of his competition. But his genius hadn't ended there—he'd also bartered for a better deal in the future.

"Did I just get manipulated by a butler?" he asked the quiet room. "I just got manipulated by a butler. And fed a slew of backhanded compliments. What the…"

He let his mind wander. With this taken care of, he was free to spend all his time on the upcoming meeting. He doubted it would be anywhere near as easy as dealing with Flora had been.

He also wondered what Sodge knew about Demigod Lydia. He'd take any information he could get. First, of course, he'd hurry up with that blood oath. He didn't need Sodge hatching some other elaborate plan without his knowledge.

Chapter 22

ALEXIS

A FURRY HEAD rubbed against my knee. I jerked away, not having expected it, and then stared down at the absolutely enormous snow-white cat that would apparently be staying. Not even six months old, he was as big as a medium-sized dog. His sister was the same size. I wondered if Harding's possession of the father cat had somehow muddled the DNA of two of the kittens in the litter. Otherwise, it was genes gone wild.

Deep forest-green eyes surveyed me patiently. His tail flicked.

"I suppose we should probably name you now," I said, leaning forward to run my hand over his fuzzy head. His fur was downy soft and puffy. "Where's your sister? Tell her we don't want any more mice left on the white carpet. Sodge will kill you before you can make it outside. I'm not kidding, that guy is grumpy as hell."

Grumpier than hell, actually. He'd had the blood oath he'd basically orchestrated for two weeks. If anyone had thought that would settle him a little, or diminish the hard scowls, they had been sorely mistaken. His expression nearly put me off the meals he delivered to me. And the guys making dinner? Sodge wouldn't stop muttering about how unseemly it was. Turned out it was about as unseemly as Bria and I swearing or not sitting with our legs crossed.

"We got one!"

I looked around in confusion. It was Frank's voice, but I had no idea where it was coming from.

"Watch him, boys, he's up to no good," he yelled. "Where's he going? I said watch him, goddammit! Follow him."

I set aside my laptop, which I'd been using to study the goings-on in Demigod Lydia's section of the world, a type of desert oasis within Egypt, mostly removed from any of the larger cities. She'd fashioned herself a large palace in the desert, from which she ruled an area that boasted a few resorts lining the Red Sea. Since the resorts hosted both magicals and non-magicals, it almost seemed like a dual-society zone setup, but unlike the dual-society zone in San Francisco, which was dirty and mostly ignored by both sides of the divide, this one looked busy, with high prices and clean sidewalks. Her territory dollars seemed mostly to come from tourism.

Frank stood with his back to the patio doors, fists on his hips, looking out to the right. "Do you see him?

Where'd he go, John?"

"Around to the front," I heard. "Let Alexis know. He's not a paparazzo."

"But he has a camera, John. What else could he be?"

"Tell Alexis to go to the front door!"

My magical awareness always encompassed the house. If someone dared to come inside without permission, I'd feel them. But I'd pulled back from monitoring the yard because of the paparazzi. My spirit sentinels did it for us, saving me from having to jump at every false alarm.

Kieran's compromise had been a press conference last week, warning everyone that he was beefing up security for the neighborhood, and especially for the house. If someone trespassed, they'd suffer the consequences.

Meaning me.

If this was a paparazzo, he was going to get a punch in the spirit box.

Frank turned around as I pushed out my magical awareness. When he saw me on the other side of the glass, his eyes widened and he screamed. He scrambled backward, flailing his arms.

A soul popped onto my radar, working toward the front, John close behind him. My heart jumped in my throat, and I turned and ran, dodging around Sodge and thundering down the hall.

"I got it," I yelled, ignoring his grumbling about ladies running in the house.

I reached the front door just as the doorbell rang. I ripped it open, a smile already spreading across my face.

The early afternoon sun beamed down on Dylan's golden highlights. He wore a plain white T-shirt that hugged his defined, wiry muscles. The look on his face indicated he still wasn't sure if he should be here. A cheap camera on a canvas strap hung around his neck, not even a good disguise. Though good enough for Frank, clearly.

"Come in," I said, standing back and waving him in. "Kieran is at the government building with most of the guys."

"Good news. We can duel in peace without the Demigod altering the outcome."

"Exactly."

"And the kids?"

"They're training. Separately, but they're both gone. It's just me and the really old, really ornery butler that will make you feel bad if you ask for anything."

"Now wait just a minute," Frank said, having recovered from his scare and followed me to the front. John stood off to the side, keeping an eye on the street. He must've recognized Dylan from the battle in the woods. "No, no, no, this is not right, Alexis. You can't entertain a man like that without a proper chaperone. What would Kieran say?"

Dylan passed into the house, and I put a hand on my hip as I stared Frank down. "A proper chaperone? What would Kieran say? Frank, did the various moves over the last year mess with your mind? Since when do I need a chaperone to invite a man into my house? Kieran's Six spend more time in this house than they do their own."

"Kieran's Six are moral, *loyal* men. They wouldn't prey on a young lady like this handsome buck probably will."

"And what if he does, Frank? You think I'm helpless, do you?"

John huffed out a laugh and shook his head. "I think it's about time for that old coot to cross the Line," he said. "He's lost all his marbles."

Frank put up a finger, his lips tight. "Alexis Price, don't you sass me. You can't just go inviting paparazzi into your house. The handsome ones have a *way* about them. You don't want to accidentally slip up. You can't afford to lose Kieran. He—"

I slammed the door in his face. John could enlighten him about Dylan's real identity if he saw fit. Not like it would matter. The only thing Frank cared about was getting me to seal the deal with Kieran so I would finally, after all this time, have someone to look after me. His gumdrop dreams were becoming a problem.

Dylan waited just beyond the foyer, between me and a surlier-than-usual Sodge.

"Might our *guest* want anything to drink while he is here?" Sodge asked. "Tea, perhaps?"

I looked at Dylan, whose brow had furrowed as he surveyed Sodge. "I'm good."

"Tea is fine, Sodge, thank you," I said, taking the lead toward the living room at the back of the house. When Sodge trudged off toward the kitchen, I said over my shoulder, "That's his thing. Serving tea. You can ask for coffee, but you'll still get tea. It's best just to let him do his thing."

When we reached the living room, I gestured to the seats and waited for him to pick one. Instead, he walked slowly to the large bay window overlooking the sparkling blue ocean. In the distance, a storm brewed, gobbling up the horizon.

"That you?" I pointed as a bolt of lightning broke from the tumultuous gray. It separated into three prongs, the side bolts bending before all of them streaked toward the water, like a huge trident. A homage to Kieran.

"Yeah. I figured that was as good of a message to Demigod Kieran as any. Unless it pisses him off, in which case I should probably leave. Quickly. He's got all the water around him he needs."

I sat on the massive couch, the central piece of furniture in the room around which the other pieces were arranged. Sodge entered a moment later carrying the gleaming silver tray. He set it on the coffee table in front of me and straightened, not looking at Dylan but *looking* at Dylan.

"Go ahead and pour, Sodge. He'll sit when he's ready," I said. Dylan glanced back, appearing unsettled. "Oh, Sodge, I didn't mention. This is the guy whose life you messed up. He's the one we went to see in West Virginia."

"Charmed, I'm sure," Sodge said. It was clear he was not charmed, and also that he didn't much care about his impact on Dylan's life.

"So, to what do we owe the pleasure?" I asked as Sodge finished up, halfheartedly bowed, and trudged out of the room.

Dylan waggled his finger around. "You don't have any guards or anything? It's really just you here?"

"Unless you count Sodge as a guard. Which you should. His dickface would scare away even the burliest of enemies."

Putting his back to the ocean, Dylan glanced around the room, then through the doorway to the den and up the stairs. "Kind of small for a primary residence. This was Valens's?"

I smiled. "Poseidon is cheap, yes. I've heard the jokes."

Dylan chuckled, looking back up the stairs. "Where do Demigod Kieran's people stay?"

"They all have their own places in the magical zone. Usually one of them stays here with us, since the Demigods of Hades like to spy on us from time to time in their spirit form, but they don't have permanent rooms here. I mean, except for Jack."

"Jack is…" He grimaced. "You keep a room for the deceased?"

"His spirit. It's just a private place for his spirit to hang out if he wants. He's gotten pretty used to his new form, though. He usually patrols the grounds or swims in the ocean when we're sleeping. We'll probably use his room as a proper guest room soon, and just not tell anyone a ghost lives in it."

Dylan grimaced again. "A ghost, yeah. You were talking to a spirit at the front door, right?"

"Yeah, but not Jack. That was Frank, an old neighbor. It's weird, I know."

"And you did that when you lived in the dual-society zone? Talked to ghosts?"

"Not so obviously, no. I had to hide it. Frank hung out there, but I couldn't, like, openly talk to him. People sometimes got run off by their neighbors if they were too open about what they could do. It didn't happen very often, but I was careful to keep my weirdness under wraps."

"Can I see it?"

"What?"

"The neighborhood you used to live in. Can I see it?"

I hesitated, realizing I hardly knew this guy, and he was powerful. If he'd come for revenge, he could fry me before I knew to react.

He must've seen the indecision on my face. He put up his hands. "You're safe from me. You'll…" He took a deep breath. "You will always be safe from me. I've thought a lot about what you said. About what your ward said."

I nodded, remembering Mordecai had asked Dylan why he watched the magical world.

He paused. "She told you?"

"She…" I furrowed my brow, trying to remember what Daisy had said. Nothing came to mind. "Which ward said what?"

His eyes lit up, and he smirked at the ground for a moment. He shook his head slightly before shifting his gaze back to me and furrowing his perfectly arched eyebrows.

"It's only a matter of time before I'm found again," he said. "Mags, the woman that owned the café?" I nodded. "Turns out she knew about me. A few people in the town had guessed. And then you guys found me… I'm done running. It's time for me to carve out a new path. The problem is, my magic isn't the kind that allows me to be a free agent. Not forever, anyway. You saw what happened with Demigod Flora."

"I'm in the same boat. I get it."

He pointed at me, his hands large and rough-looking. A working man's hands. "Yes, exactly. But I just…" He looked around the house again. "I've only known… I haven't had a good experience with blood oaths, you know?"

"I've heard, yes. Not the particulars, but…"

"I came here to go through with it, but…I'm still not sure. So much doesn't add up with Demigod Kieran. I thought that things might…fall in to place if I could learn a little more about your story. See your world. I don't want to make another mistake." He ran his fingers through his hair. "I don't know why I'm telling you all of this. Nothing like telling a potential enemy your plans, but…you were true to your word before. You seem legit. Your kids seem legit. They tried to help me."

"They did? When?"

He turned back, checking my face again. A smile showed off his straight white teeth, and he shook his head again. "It's madness, all of it. All of this. It just feels like there is no order to your life at all."

I leaned forward and braced my elbows on my knees. "There isn't, kinda. There never was. It's hard to have order when you're taking life day by day. You want to see where I grew up? Sure, why not. Try to kill me and I'll take you with me. If we both survive, we'll grab a beer. Kieran just got done fixing up this pub I used to go to. I haven't been back since it was revamped. May as well see what it looks like now." I reduced my voice to a mutter as I stood. "I might need a shoulder to cry on if he messed it up."

"You are leaving with this man, I take it?" Sodge said as I led the way to the garage.

"Yes. I'm running away with him. You'll just have to find someone else to figure out immortality, give it to Kieran, and then somehow put it in a blood bond and pass it on to you. Good luck with that!"

"I called Demigod Kieran and told him your...friend was here," Sodge said. "I called some of his staff, as well, in case Demigod Kieran was detained."

"Narc." I hit the button for the garage door and motioned for Dylan to get into the passenger seat of my sleek Maserati.

"I'm not sure if we'll be safer together, or in more danger," Dylan said as I backed out of the garage. "We each have a highly desired magic."

"It'll take a Demigod some time to organize a crew to come after us. Anyone else doesn't stand a chance. If they get in close, I'll take their soul. Otherwise, you can blast a hole through their head. Nothing to it."

"There is that."

"The others will probably meet us for a beer, anyway. Bria never misses an opportunity to belly up to a dive bar." Something in my stomach twisted, and I added, "Even though it's probably all sleek and shiny now."

My stomach did some more twisting as we neared my old house. The house I grew up in. I hadn't been back in months. I'd never rented it out, or even fixed it up. I'd just left it. Half of me was glad the memories had been left intact, and the other half felt sad that I'd just walked away. All that time in this place, and I'd taken off and never looked back.

I parked next to the cracked curb. A moment later, I stood on the walkway, looking at a place that seemed so much smaller than I remembered.

"Wow." Dylan stood behind me, taking in the lack of view.

Two steps led up to the faded wood of the old door. I took out my keys as I stepped up, peering down at the bush beside me, where Kieran had placed the bag containing Mordecai's blanket. At that time, I'd had no notion of what he would come to mean to me. Of how my life would change. I said as much with tears filling my eyes.

"He saved my kid. Mordecai never would've made it to adulthood. And Daisy..." I licked my lips. "I didn't have any paperwork for her. She would've been completely unprepared for adult life. She would've had to hustle for the rest of her days. I was merely keeping them alive. Kieran gave them a future." I wiped the tears from my face. "It's so strange to stand here, thinking about all of this from the right side of things. I might be in a lot of danger now, but at least my kids are comfortable. At least they have a future."

"I saw your kids with you in that café," Dylan said softly, and I felt him gingerly touch my shoulder. "They love you. Whatever you were doing was plenty. More than plenty. I've lived in luxury for most of my life, but I was alone and unhappy. You gave your kids a family, and that's not nothing. In fact, it's worth more than all the money in the world. Please trust me on this."

I wiped my face again. "I'm going to have to. I can't go back and change it now."

The key slipped into the well-used lock and I turned it, ready for more bittersweet memories.

"You lived here all your life?" Dylan asked.

"Until Kieran found me, yeah. I considered myself lucky to have a place at all."

I pushed in through the front door, hit with stale air and the damp smell of home. The itty-bitty round kitchen table spanned the line between the teensy-weensy kitchen and the tiny living room. The low ceiling pressed down on me, reminding me of its trademark popcorn texture. Down the short hall I found my bedroom, so small that I fleetingly wondered how I'd even turned around in it. The kids' room was next door, their two beds crammed into the tight space. Mordecai had nearly died more than once in there, coughing up blood and keeping us up half the night nursing him.

Tears came to my eyes again and my chest burned.

I took a deep breath and traced the scuffed paint where Jack had rammed my head into the wall. He'd attacked me as part of a training exercise—and found himself facing a harder fight than he'd anticipated. "Kieran saved my wards, but I couldn't save his brother in arms. One of the Hades Demigods came for me, and Jack got in the way." Tears trailed down my cheeks. "I miss him, so much. It's not the same when a person is in spirit. I miss watching his big arms flex whenever he cracked an egg. It made me laugh to see *all* that muscle used on something so benign as cracking an egg. I miss the way Donovan and Jack always bantered when they were putting together a meal, and the way Jack coached Mordecai. I miss him calling Daisy a little gremlin. I hate that Kieran gets a pang of sorrow every time he sees Jack in spirit."

A sob broke free, along with the realization that I'd never properly grieved for Jack. I let a few more emotions roll through me and then tucked them away again.

Now wasn't the time. The right time would probably be when Jack officially crossed the Line, and I couldn't bear to think about that.

I took a deep breath and checked out the bathroom that we'd all shared. One sink, one medicine cabinet, a few drawers. The lack of space hadn't mattered because we hadn't owned much stuff to keep in there anyway.

Back in the living room, I wiped my face and lowered into a chair at the kitchen table. It creaked with my weight.

"At one point we had five people living in this house. My mom, me, and three other kids, including Mordecai. All of us squished in together."

Dylan finally took a step away from the front door. He glanced in the kitchen before taking a seat opposite me. He leaned his forearms on the scratched and beat-up wood before clasping his hands.

"None of us minded. We didn't know any better," I said with a sad smile. At least those were pleasant memories. "Well…" I shrugged, picking at the wood. "My mother might've. She's the one that had a hard go of it, I guess. She had to give everything up when she realized I was Magnus's kid. And she must've realized it, or else why would she have hidden me away like she did?"

"*How* did she hide you away, that's my question," Dylan said. "She must've been at least partially powerful to produce you, even with a Demigod father. She would've been on the books. How'd she keep you from getting tested?"

"She didn't. I altered my results."

He tilted his head to the side. "What does that mean? How'd you do that?"

"She taught me. You just…like…focus your magic on muddling the outcome. I always envisioned a red needle dancing within a green screen, and that was what my magic would do to the testing machine. I wasn't as good as my mom—she could skew it so the readings would be about the same every time. I always had to be tested a few times, and when two of the results were close together, they'd take that. The results were always low—level one and two—so they didn't take more time than they needed to."

He leaned over the table. "I've never heard of altering the machine readouts."

"I don't think many people have done it. No one questioned it until I met Kieran. He felt my magical level and got suspicious when my records didn't match up."

Dylan leaned back and looked around again. "I'll be damned. No wonder he followed you around. This is a mind fuck. All of that magic"—he made circles with his pointer finger before jabbing it toward my chest—"and you lived here. *Here!* This is poverty."

"Yeah. We took a lot of handouts and charity."

"Demigod Kieran pulled you up out of this."

"Well…" I frowned at him. "It's not like it was a Cinderella story. The kids and I helped him when he went to war against his father. We earned our keep and held our own. He paid for the privilege."

"Hey, whoa." Dylan put up his hands. "That's not what I'm saying at all. Sorry. It's just that rare level fives like us…we are usually born into a certain lifestyle, and if not, it's given to us as soon as we are tested. We're given the best, we live in luxury—we never want for anything."

I spread my hands to indicate the house at large. "Before the kids became my responsibility, what did I want for?"

His gaze lingered on the far corner. "A TV, for starters. Maybe a rug that doesn't smell like mold. I don't know."

I chuckled and wiped away the rest of my tears. "My mother kept me away from a child killer. I'm fine with my lot in life."

"Yeah, I can't fault you for that. And it explains why you don't really care about living in such a small house. Kieran got lucky, finding a woman that doesn't expect much. People of Poseidon hate parting with their precious coin."

"Such a bad rap!" I said, laughing with him. "The

guy is super generous!"

Our laughter died as I let the memories of the space float through me.

"Kieran and his Six—five now, I guess—would kill for my kids. Even if I don't make it, my kids have backup now. They won't ever be alone. Eventually, when he's ready to be challenged, Mordecai will return to his pack. I have no doubt he'll be alpha someday. I don't know what Daisy will do eventually, but she has the tools for happiness. She can choose whatever she wants. It might've been hairy for a while, but at least the kids are in a good spot now. That's all that counts, small house for a Demigod or no."

Dylan chuckled before sobering. "Living like this taught you to protect the people you love against all odds. Those feelings are primal. They're powerful. Clearly Kieran is a man who recognizes that. Thank you. If you don't mind, I'll just wait outside. The emotion is starting to make me uncomfortable."

I barked out a laugh and sprayed him with spit. "Sorry." I wiped my mouth and laughed a little more, standing. It felt better, remembering the past. Sad but sweet. Like I'd dodged a bullet, quite frankly. And maybe I had. My mother had clearly been wise to protect me from my father. To keep me hidden away.

But I was not guarding a child from a ruthless ty-rant... I was the child. And I was done hiding. Let him come. I would not go down without a fight. If my mother came back from the grave to yell at me, well, it would be nice to see her again. I had a few questions.

"Let's get that beer."

Chapter 23

ALEXIS

I STOPPED IN front of the red, gleaming door on top of the freshly poured concrete without one line or crack in it. Cars lined the street, as they used to, but these were the immaculate cars of people who could clearly afford nice things. Bulbs shone from artfully curved poles over the entrance.

If there had been a red carpet leading up to this joint, I would've turned around and walked away.

The inside was even worse. New wood adorned the glossy bar, and the stools lining it had leather seats and seatbacks. The spirits that used to haunt this place, wilting over the bar in never-ending sadness, had been replaced by living people excited to drink in a place owned by the Demigod of San Francisco. The floor had been redone in fresh rustic wood, the height of trendiness, and clean round tables backed up against the far wall. At the other end of the posh space was the pool room, packed with laughing and chatting people.

"This is..." I felt increasingly annoyed as I ducked

between two women who couldn't have talked any louder if they'd been yelling. It wasn't until I reached the other end of the long, lively bar that I sighed in relief.

Mick, a regular from the old bar, sat on a rickety old barstool with a surly expression and an empty seat next to him. Kieran had come through with his promise to keep Mick's spot and stool intact. Given the fact that the rest of the bar was packed, his personality had clearly scared away anyone who might want a comfortable seat. Some things hadn't changed.

"Mick!" I gave him a wide smile as I came around the corner.

He glanced up, and then did a double take. In classic Mick fashion, he grunted, "Well," in his thick Irish brogue and resumed hunching in his spot, his big hands, scarred from manual labor, curled around a bottle of Bud.

"Big change with the bar, huh?" I sat down, the plush seat much nicer than the crappy stools from before, although Mick's seat had been saved as a relic. "I hate it."

He huffed, his whole upper body rising to do it. "Bunch o' *coonts*."

"Was that…" Dylan was at the corner of the bar, half squished between me and some woman who was chatting up a reasonably attractive guy on her other side. He leaned over the non-rounded point so he could see Mick's face better. "Did he just say…?"

"Yeah. The c-word. Stick around, he gets much more colorful. Do you want me to get you a seat?"

"How?" He glanced at the woman beside him, who seemed quite content.

"I could probably just tell them to move. Actually, let's wait for Bria. She's on her way with Jerry. If I let her handle it, then maybe I won't get gawked at. Hopefully. I didn't have Aubri come today, so it's inevitable someone will snap a picture and put it on social media titling it *hot mess* or something. Do you want a seat while we wait? I don't mind standing."

Dylan leaned toward me a little and dropped his voice. "I have a question."

"Hey, ye fecking bastard, ya." Mick leaned over the bar in order to look at Dylan. He waggled his finger in front of his temple while squinting an eye. "Be careful where ye aim, eh? She's not fer sale, ye *coont*. She landed the *fooking* Demigod, *boi*."

I didn't have time to wonder what the hell he was talking about, or why everyone was getting so nuts over Dylan—he was attractive, yes, but not enough to make a woman lose her mind. Liam, the bartender from the old bar, sidled down the bar, one of three on duty and the only one who probably wouldn't bother to move faster if someone put a burner under his butt.

"Alexis, hi, nice surprise," he said. Although he was non-magical, he'd taken up residence in the dual-society zone because he didn't want to be bothered with law enforcement. "You ended up giving in to the Demigod, huh?"

"Hi, Liam. I did." I hung my head. Kieran had followed me into this bar once, before we knew each other well, and Liam had applauded me for standing up to him. It felt like a lifetime ago. "He didn't take a subtle approach that day, but he turned out to be not so bad. Could I have a Guinness, please?"

"Sure, yeah." Liam surveyed the crowded bar. "You want me to clear you some space? I don't think they know you walked in."

"No." I waved the thought away. "I have a friend coming. She'll do it in a less authoritative style."

Liam nodded and looked at Dylan. Dylan lifted his eyebrows.

"He's silently asking what you want," I told Dylan.

"Oh. Uh…" Dylan looked at the large blackboard above the bar with various specialty cocktails and wines artfully written on it.

"Just get a *fooking* beer, man," Mick grumbled. "Good God almighty, you'd think he'd never seen alcohol in his life. Young man, young man, young man."

I'd heard him say that a million times, but I still had

no idea if he was actually saying "young man" or something else. If he was, I also had no idea why. I'd never bothered to ask.

A grin creased Dylan's lips, and some of the tension seeped out of his shoulders. "Stella. Please," he finally said.

"Now. Feck's sake." Mick resumed his hunch over his beer.

"Demigod Kieran came in here?" Dylan asked me. "Is that what the bartender meant?"

"Yeah. It was during Kieran's stalking phase. He came in here and…" I remembered the things he'd said to me on that occasion, the pull of his body. My face heated and my core tightened. I cleared my throat. "He was pretty arrogant and I wasn't having it."

What was a tiny lie amongst friends?

I told Dylan the story of how Kieran had bought the bar out from under my ex-boyfriend.

"I liked it better before," I said, watching Liam pour my pint.

"He didn't kill your boyfriend?" Dylan asked.

"He was an *ex*, not a current boyfriend—"

"I realize that, but the guy was paying your tab and lording it over you. I'm surprised Kieran didn't kill him."

I rolled my eyes. "He's not his father."

"Most Demigods are his father, Alexis. You need to

harden yourself for that. And the best Demigods are *your* father."

Dylan started and then stepped away from the bar, turning back to glance at the woman beside him. He muttered an apology. Apparently she'd gotten tired of his presence and shoved him away.

She threw him an annoyed scowl, but her gaze changed the moment it landed on his face. Her eyes rounded and her breasts jutted out, as though someone else had suddenly assumed control of her body and didn't know how to work the thing. She turned toward him, the man next to her completely forgotten.

"Excuse me, I am so sorry. Did I bump you?" she asked in a breathy whisper.

"Good Christ," Mick muttered, watching the exchange.

"No, it's okay," Dylan said, shrinking away from her notice.

"Honestly, I'm sorry. Hi, I'm—"

"No." Mick waved her away, his arm crossing in front of my face in large, sweeping movements. By his animation, I was pretty sure he'd been on the whiskey earlier, fallen asleep at the bar, and was on round two. I was pretty good at guessing his moods. This was the surliest. "Don't even bother. He's too good looking for you. Move along." He shooed her. "Move along. Never gonna happen. He's way out of yer league. Know when yer beat. *Git!*"

"Is this real life?" Dylan said quietly, standing away from the situation with a cockeyed smile. "Did he just tell her to 'get,' like an animal?"

"This is my life, actually, yes," I said. "Welcome. It gets weirder."

The woman, probably terrified of Mick's manic stare, turned away.

"Stand closer to Mick," I told Dylan. "No one will bother you there." Mick grunted his agreement. Our drinks landed in front of us a moment later.

"On the house, Lexi, like normal," Liam said. "Different owner paying this time, though." He winked.

"I'm not sure if I should bother making a statement by paying," I mumbled.

"Am I on the house?" Mick slapped his hand down.

Half the people lining the bar jumped and fell silent, shooting him nervous looks.

"What's funny is, he isn't magical," I murmured to Dylan. "He doesn't even throw his punches straight. Yet they are all terrified."

"You datin' the owner?" Liam asked Mick.

"I will for a whiskey," Mick replied.

Liam rolled his eyes and moved away.

"Did you know my name?" Dylan asked me after things had calmed down and Mick started grumbling to himself. Definitely on round two for the day.

"No, the woman said it in the café." It dawned on me what he was asking. "That one Flora yelled out? No, I didn't know that one. Honestly, Dylan, people don't tell me all that much. It's my fault, really, because everyone else asks about stuff except for me. I've always just…kinda taken things as they come. You'd understand if you'd known my mother. There was some new kind of crazy every day—you dealt with what was in front of you, and you moved on. So no, I knew very little going into your town."

Bria emerged from a throng of people and spread out her hands. "Kieran ruined this bar. *Ruined* it! I can't drink here. Who are any of these people?" Bria leaned over the woman who kept sending furtive glances at Dylan despite Mick's warning. "Hey!" She hooked a thumb at me. "That's Alexis Price." She directed the thumb at herself. "I work for Demigod Kieran." She pointed at Dylan. "He's not interested. *Move!*"

The grin twisting Dylan's lips widened. "This is not real life. It isn't. No guards or anything…"

The crowd shifted and swayed. Bodies parted. Jerry emerged from the throng, his wide, flat features closed down. He stopped behind the woman and man, now staring at me with wide, excited eyes.

"Move," Jerry said in his deep, earth-shaking baritone. His muscles popped out on his frame, turning him from large to imposing.

The couple scrambled off the barstools, muttering their apologies. Their smiles and excited eyes said we'd made their night. They'd been told to leave by the magical elite, the next best thing to seeing Kieran himself.

News of our, or rather my, presence spread across the bar like wildfire. Faces turned and people clustered closer, trying to get a look at me.

"We should leave," I said to Bria. I grabbed a loose strand of hair and tucked it behind my ear. "I'm not dressed to be noticed. Let's go back to the house."

"Fuck 'em." Bria motioned for another couple to leave. "We need a seat for a giant." She pushed Dylan down into the seat the woman had evacuated and pointed for Jerry to sit farther down.

"I'll stand," Jerry said, taking up residence behind Dylan. "He probably needs a wall behind him. Every woman in this place is staring. It's distracting."

"Well, yeah, he's liquid sex," Bria replied. "Look at the guy. He looks like a sweaty, dirty night in satin sheets. No offense, bud, but you do. Change your image if you want people to perceive you differently."

Dylan, clearly uncomfortable, spread his arms and looked down at himself. "I'm wearing a white shirt and jeans."

"Yeah. A *tight* white shirt, showing off your muscle, and snug jeans, showing off your ass. That is what hot guys wear. As a hot guy, you are clearly asking for it." She put up her hands with a grin, obviously joking. "Hey, no one can accuse me of double standards."

Jerry chuckled. Bria had apparently grown on him.

"Maybe try a faded, wrinkled blue shirt," she added. "That's a bad look. Or a bag over your head. That might help."

"He keeps asking if this is real life," I said, and glugged down some of my Guinness. I needed it in this place.

"Nothing with Alexis is real life," Bria said as Liam sauntered up. "She will change your whole perception on things, trust me. Nothing will be normal after she and her kids trample all over your life."

"Why don't you have a blood oath?" Dylan asked after she'd ordered and been given her drink.

"In the beginning...because I didn't want one," she said. "I didn't want to be permanently attached to a Demigod, especially one that shared genes with Valens. I accepted the job because he paid well and I'd be training a Spirit Walker. How could I pass that up, you know what I mean? I was ready to walk the second things got weird."

"And now?"

She shrugged. "He hasn't made it a requirement. He hasn't asked, either. It's probably for the best. I'm here for Alexis, mostly. He's a good guy, I will admit, but I'm loyal to her. I'd do the oath to stay in the circle, but I don't feel the need. I don't have your issues, though. Someone might try to kill me just because I'm in the way, but they won't try to force me into their inner circle. You need a powerful Demigod at your back."

Bria sucked down her drink like it was water. She pounded the bar with her fist.

"Mick, how the hell are ya? Nice to see ya," she said. "Now make yourself useful and call down Liam. Your next drink is on Kieran."

"Feck off," Mick muttered, before raising his hand. "Liam! Ye *fookin'* deaf bastard. Liam! Get a round, will ya? Yer *useless*! Like tits on a bull, ye are. Fuck sakes. Liam!"

A ripple of excitement rolled through the bar. I smiled, knowing what it meant—I'd felt Kieran drawing nearer. Someone shrieked in the back, but the voices in the front of the bar had lowered to respectful murmurs.

From my vantage point I could see the crowd parting. Kieran emerged from the throng of bodies like a ship parting the tides, his broad shoulders swinging as he strolled through the crowd of staring spectators. Strength and power oozed from him, filling the bar like a savory aroma. His smooth grace screamed debonair, especially with his pinstriped, tailored suit, but his intense, intelligent gaze and coiled strength spoke of danger in a way that dried up all the spit in my mouth.

As he approached us, his stormy blue eyes focused on me, and my heart surged and then melted down through my middle. I couldn't help but smile at his deliciousness. His guys walked in behind him, also wearing tailored suits, projecting strength and power and silently promising pain to anyone who stepped in their way.

"*That* is sex on a stick," I said in a breathy whisper, watching Kieran draw near. "A bag wouldn't do much to hide his sexiness. He'd still have the style and the body."

"Not to mention the power and prestige, yeah. The difference is, he knows it," Bria said, turning back to the bar. "Soon we'll find out if he can sell it to the big dogs. Lydia will have all of her people, and Kieran will only be allowed a select few. That's how it's done. He'll be protected, but his people won't be. We'll all be put to the test. Soon we'll see if he's as good as we all think."

Kieran stepped around Jerry and slid his arm around my shoulders. "Hey, baby." He kissed me on the temple, sending my insides into a flutter again. Heat throbbed in my middle at his touch, his proximity. "How was your day?"

"Liam, we're closed," Zorn said, leaning over the bar next to Bria. "Close out the tabs and get everyone out. You can stay on. The other bartenders can go home. They'll be compensated for the tips they lost."

Liam turned, waved a dingy white bar towel, and yelled, "Get out! We're closed. Demigod is in residence. No last call. Put your drink down and leave. Out!"

Mick didn't move a muscle, but none of the guys seemed to notice or care.

"Dylan." Kieran stuck out a hand. "Good to see you again. I didn't expect you."

Dylan shook it. "I'm still not sure if I'm staying."

Kieran nodded, replacing his arm around my shoulders. "There's a place on my team, should you choose to stay. No hard feelings if you go. You need to make up your mind quickly, though. We're meeting with Demigod Lydia in two weeks. We have a lot to plan still."

Bria caught Dylan's focus, and then brought him over to the rest of the guys, already cracking jokes and having a good time. The second they could let down their hair, they did. I had a feeling Bria was helping sell Dylan on that blood oath by showing him the kind of camaraderie he could expect. Jerry edged down a little to join them, leaving Kieran and me with a little space.

"Everyone acts really crazy with him," I said as Kieran trailed his fingers through my hair. I soaked in his warmth, not able to think about much more than his touch. About wanting to get him alone.

His smile was languid, his eyes hooded. His sexy Selkie magic curled within my body, stroking all the right places and bringing a gasp to my lips.

"How so?" he asked.

"Apparently, everyone thinks that if he gets me alone, I won't be able to resist his not-at-all-seductive ways."

Kieran laughed and reached toward the bar to grab the Guinness Liam had delivered. "Yes, I got that feeling when Sodge called me. He hinted that it would be best to send someone to watch you when Dylan is around."

"Tell me you didn't hurry here for that reason."

He kissed my temple. "I didn't. I hurried here because I was shocked as hell to hear he'd come. I'm hoping it means he wants to join our team. While I am possessive to a fault, I have absolutely no fears where you and Dylan are concerned."

I sighed. "Good. Frank and Sodge—and even Mick—were acting like such idiots. It was really embarrassing."

"Do you want to know why I have no fears?"

"Because you're rational and not prone to hysterics?"

He laughed again. "We share feelings through the soul connection, and I've never once felt any arousal from you when you're in his vicinity. I've never felt any sexual nervousness or even appreciation for his appearance. The only time I've noticed those things through our bond are when I enter a room."

I ran my fingers down the edge of his suit jacket. "I think I'm going to need to be marked again tonight."

He slowly let out a breath and squeezed my shoulders. I could feel the desire pooling hot within him. "Come here for a moment."

He set down his drink, then stepped back and guided me off the stool. He threaded us through the lingering bar patrons, slow to make their way out. Their gawking didn't seem to bother him as he led me down a hallway, past the bathrooms and to a door that said "Staff."

He flicked on the light, pulled me inside, and locked the door behind us. I didn't get a chance to look around as he pushed me against the door, his lips on mine and his fingers at my jeans.

His Selkie magic pounded pleasure through me as I hurriedly unbuttoned and unzipped his pants, moaning. I pulled up the Line and heard his answering groan as he felt my magic.

He shoved my jeans and panties down my thighs before turning me around. My palms flattened against the door. Cool air kissed my wetness, interrupted by the heat of his tip. All the air exited my lungs as he filled me in one glorious thrust.

"Oh God, Kieran," I moaned, his magic blazing under my clothes and across my skin. "Yes, Kieran."

He grabbed my hips as he pulled out with deliberate

slowness before ramming into me again. Aching pleasure coursed through me. I couldn't get enough air. I couldn't get enough of him.

He pulled out slowly again, but I couldn't wait for the next thrust, wild with need. I jerked my hips forward and back, impaling myself, seeing stars from how good it felt. I swirled my hips and jerked forward and back again, shoving against the door to get more traction. His fingers tightened against my hips. His pace increased.

"Yes," I whispered, repeatedly filled. Pounded with sensation. The pleasure built, filling every inch of me until it felt like my skin was stretched too tightly. The sensations were overwhelming. "*Yes!*"

I hit a peak and shattered around him. He shuddered against me, groaning my name.

Panting, love glowing within me, I leaned back against him. He circled me with his arms, holding me tightly.

"I needed that," he said, his hot breath feathering my neck. He trailed his lips up the slope of my neck and along my jaw line. It was only then that I realized one of the bartenders was knocking softly on the door. She probably needed to get her stuff so she could go home.

"To be continued," I said, and turned so I could kiss his full lips. "We're holding people up."

"Let them wait." His kiss was deep and sensual.

I smiled against his lips. "My drink will get warm."

He laughed softly. "To be continued, then."

Hand in hand, we walked back to our places. I sat, and he stood by my side. The bar, once incredibly loud and obnoxious, now only held our crew, chatting and laughing together. Jack had joined us on an empty barstool, listening to the banter with a smile, although he couldn't actually talk to anyone but me. Mick was also still there, minding his own business, exactly like any other day.

"I'll join you," Dylan said during a lull in the conversation. He didn't look away from his beer.

"You'll take a blood oath?" Kieran asked, his arm resting on my stool back, curved around me. "You'll join my team?"

"Yes." The word was so quiet that I almost didn't hear it.

"What made you change your mind?" Bria asked.

Dylan shrugged, and it was clear he was struggling with some demons. "A lot of things. Most importantly, I trust this." He waggled his finger, basically pointing down the bar and back. "I didn't at first. I didn't understand how a bunch of misfits, led by a green Demigod and backed by the magic of someone that doesn't seem to understand the magical world, could be so incredibly effective. I figured I was missing something."

"Nope. We're just that screwed up," Donovan said, sitting between Thane and Jack. I wondered if he knew his buddy was next to him—if maybe he'd sat on the end to leave a place for him, just in case.

"And I think what I was missing was the sense of family," Dylan went on. "I've never really had one. My parents didn't spare any time on my upbringing. Their pride was in producing my magic, not as parents. I doubt they cried at my funeral. I was raised by nannies until I was old enough to be tested, and then I went to boarding school to be trained. After that, Gianna got a hold of me. The mark applied to me was not my choice. My bed was a holding place and her bed was my cell. The horror of that existence gave me a very warped view of what it meant to pledge service to a Demigod. This is…night and day." He shook his head, hunched over his beer. "I would rather die than be tied to someone like Gianna again. Heaven help me if I'm wrong, but this is probably my safest bet. It seems like it, anyway. It is at least *very* clear Alexis does want that mark. She looks ethereal, a woman in love. I trust that."

Silence greeted his words until Mick said, "*Jay*sus. Talk about airing your dirty laundry. What da *fook*?"

The Six, Jack included, roared with laughter. Even Jerry chuckled helplessly.

"Well"—Donovan splayed his fingers across his chest—"*I* don't want you in my bed. You're safe there."

"I'm a nope there, too, brother." Thane raised his hands.

"No man meat in my sheets except mine," Boman said.

"Man meat?" Thane turned so Boman could see his full scowl.

"Would you have preferred if I'd said dick?" Boman retorted.

"Not really, no."

Zorn huffed. "I had to get saved, too. It's hard on the ego."

The guys laughed again, and in response to Dylan's obvious confusion, Zorn stood and peeled off his jacket. "We all got shit in our pasts." He unbuttoned his crisp white shirt and took it off. Silvery white lines crisscrossed his torso and back. Some scars were long and straight, possibly from lashings, and some were jagged and bent, as if a knife had slowly cut into his flesh.

Dylan's eyes widened. "Did they douse you with some kind of magic that didn't let you heal?"

"This was before the blood oath. I didn't get the luxury of healing between sessions. I'd hang from the shackles for a month, drenched in spit, blood, and piss. It would've been easier just to die, but I didn't want to give them the satisfaction. I wanted them to know that they could try as they might, but they weren't going to get a word about the Drusus family out of me. I didn't give a shit about Valens, but even then, I would've died ten times over for Kieran. You want to talk about dirty laundry? Being ignored by my parents would've been a luxury. I was beaten by them. Tossed downstairs. Blamed for their troubles. I can't seem to maintain any sort of normal relationship—I drive everyone away."

Bria picked up her drink and took a long sip. As far as I knew, they'd been on the outs lately, it having been just physical in the beginning, gotten confusing a couple months ago (Bria's words at one point), and now it looked like Zorn was revealing what was going wrong. My heart squished for the guy.

"But fuck it," Zorn went on. "You live, you learn, you keep going. It does no good to dwell on it. You will be safest in this team, that's no lie. Even the dead watch our backs."

Zorn shrugged back into his shirt, his expression flat.

"He wins," Jerry said, his arms crossed against his chest. "He one-upped you, bud."

"Way to kill a moment, *Jerry*," Donovan said.

"If this shite keeps on, I'll need to find a new bar," Mick muttered.

Everyone erupted into laughter again, and I wished we could stay like this forever. But I couldn't forget that danger awaited us outside this door. Now that we had Dylan, the Zeus Demigods would probably take a new interest in our team, just like the Hades Demigods. At this point, all someone had to do was kill Kieran and divvy up his team.

Then again, part of our job was to make sure that didn't happen.

Regardless, one thing at a time. Next up was Demigod Lydia. Two weeks and counting.

Chapter 24

DYLAN

"**W**HAT THE HELL are you doing here?"

Dylan turned away from the railing on Kieran's back deck to find Daisy standing in the open sliding glass door, one hand on a slim hip and the other against the doorframe. Her expression wasn't cross or even expectant, but her tone and words told a different story.

"Didn't they tell you I was here?" he asked, letting the lightning fade away behind him. "I got here yesterday afternoon. Demigod Kieran is letting me stay in the non-ghost guest room until I get a new place lined up."

"Yeah, they told me." She slid the door shut and walked to a spot beside him, looking out over the ocean. "They told me you showed up, had a few beers, and let Kieran give you a blood oath. Now you're trapped. What happened?"

Dylan sighed, turning back toward the railing. Then started chuckling. He couldn't help it. This kid was like no other teen he'd ever met, and he'd met a lot of

Chesters at this point. She quite clearly liked her situation and the people around her, but not to the point where she wanted to give them any authority over her. Only two people had her total and complete loyalty, it seemed—Alexis and the other teen, Mordecai. That was it. She kept a layer of distance with everyone else, even her scarred-up trainer, Zorn. If circumstances compelled it, Dylan bet she'd have no problem cutting off ties to this life and leaving with no one but Alexis and Mordecai to go with her. She wouldn't say goodbye, and she wouldn't look back.

He let the lightning rain down over the ocean. The bolts zigged and zagged and created loose and rather clumsy designs. He was incredibly rusty. He'd been nearly useless in that battle a couple of weeks ago. He had to blow the dust off his magic if he hoped to contribute to the team.

"I would've been a hunted man, thanks to you all," Dylan said, trying to twist the lightning in the sky while also rolling a sheet of lightning across the ocean surface. Sweat beaded on his brow and the lightning dried up in the clouds. The distance was too great. He'd need to work back up to that.

"Cut the crap. That's not why," she said.

He grinned. "If you cut and run from this life, you'd still have family. I have no one. I couldn't even properly use my magic. Being alone gets old after a while. It gets lonely."

She didn't respond for a while, instead watching him start up the lightning again. "Any regrets?"

He pushed back the thick black clouds, a dead give-away that there was someone with Zeus's magic on the scene. Instead, he tried to pull lightning down from a puffy white cloud. The bolt splintered and spiderwebbed across the darkness, mostly useless by the time it finally touched down. That might give someone a jolt, but it wouldn't kill anyone.

"No," he said, which had shocked him when he first realized it. "I used to always feel suffocated with Gianna. But even though Demigod Kieran said I'm in the probationary phase, and he's exerting more of his will than usual to make sure I color within the lines, it's nothing like I'm used to. Nothing. I barely notice his influence. I don't feel put out at all."

"Yeah, Kieran doesn't lead by being controlling. He leads by example, and people generally want to please him. Don't fool yourself, though. Just because you aren't being watched through that link, however it works—"

"By magic."

"—doesn't mean you aren't being watched. We live on a cliff made of rock—if you wander around, Jerry will feel you. Alexis will feel you if you're within her range. Zorn has eyes in the back of his head. Henry just randomly shows up places, destroying traps intended for Mordecai. Mind your Ps and Qs, because right now, you're set up to stay in the inner-inner circle. That's the Six, Bria, Alexis—we're the good circle. You want to be in this one. Jerry's pretty much in, but the other new people—well, I barely even know what they look like. Kieran keeps them at a distance. If you're looking for inclusiveness, don't end up with those people."

Dylan shoved the cloud away, annoyed with himself. He let out a hard sigh before taking a seat in one of the chairs. "How did Jerry get in the inner-inner circle?"

"Playing hard to get." Dylan couldn't tell if she was making a joke or not. She pushed away from the banister. "Alexis helped him with his life, and apparently people are like spirits in that they try to stick around after that. Well, I hope your life doesn't start to suck. Or that Kieran doesn't go crazy like his dad. Also, you owe me money."

With that, she made her way back into the house.

Chuckling, he stared out at the horizon for a while, feeling the chill of fall. The area was temperate, but even still, there was a bite coming off the water.

This was his new life. These people. This area. The ability to use the full range of his magic, if he could wipe away the cobwebs. He never would've guessed he'd be answering to a Demigod of Poseidon. Soon, he had every belief that Kieran would marry Alexis and make her a co-ruler. That would mean Dylan was also answering to a mistress of Hades. A Soul Stealer, no less. His parents would be severely disappointed in him. Most higher-powered people of Zeus stayed with their own kind. He'd always been taught that was the strongest way, because Zeus was the strongest god. After witnessing how Kieran's people had handled Flora's... Well, their assurances of being the best wouldn't help them much when Demigod Kieran dominated the playing field.

The problem was that Dylan didn't have a clue how to combat people of Hades, and that was exactly what he'd need to do if he accompanied Kieran and Alexis to Demigod Lydia's territory. Hades didn't play by the rules—Dylan had always been taught that. They were underhanded, stacking the odds in their favor whenever possible. They said one thing and did another. They fed you sweet words and, when you turned your back, stabbed a knife through you. Hades, by and large, was not to be trusted.

Alexis was supposed to be their resident expert, and she didn't have a clue about anything magical. Dylan wondered if Kieran was actually leading them to the slaughter. Was he too green—too new—to take on someone of Lydia's caliber so soon?

Ready or not, though, it was happening. Dylan had only just returned to the magical world, but he was headed into a possible battle.

He'd best be ready.

Chapter 25

ALEXIS

THE SPRAWLING PALACE lit up the desert like a beacon, all three stories well lit on this moonless night. The large drive up to the residence was flanked by flower-laden bushes that couldn't be native to the area, what with their leafy green foliage and bright, sweet-smelling flowers. The palace itself was nestled amidst palm trees, artful landscaping, and strings of fairy lights.

Men wearing tuxedos waited at the top of the drive and in front of the large double-door entrance, their white gloves spotless and their souls as shriveled as old, dried-up prunes. Souls stood inside the doors—the second leg of attendants to our arrival, I had no doubt.

Our caravan of stretch limousines slowed and then stopped beside the men, the driveway now running parallel to the entrance and leading to an enormous garage that might be better described as a warehouse. I sat in silence. Although the limo was likely big enough for the entire crew, the only other passengers were

Kieran and my kids. The rest of our main crew followed in an unnecessarily large number of matching limos, the name of the game clearly a display of wealth, both by Demigod Lydia and Kieran.

I'd felt out of place many times in my life, but this was competing for one of the most notable occasions.

"Just be yourself," Kieran said, holding out his hand for me.

"Lexi is going to make an ass of herself within the first five minutes," Daisy murmured, turning to look behind her. "I can't wait to see what Bria says about the style. Talk about *gaudy*!"

"This is certainly...distasteful," Mordecai said, his lip curling. "She won't make an ass of herself in their eyes, though. She'll do something they didn't expect, and that will put them on their toes."

They were both right, I had no doubt. "As long as I don't incite war, we'll be fine," I murmured, feeling our people climb out of their limos.

One of the white-gloved attendants opened our door and stepped aside. Kieran stepped out gracefully, pausing to button the jacket of another of his delicious tailored suits before offering me his hand. I climbed out...not as gracefully, hating the height of my heels and worried my boobs would fall out of the low-necked dress.

Daisy and Bria had made adjustments to the attire

Aubri had chosen. Aubri, sadly, had been left behind. While Lydia's invitation had allowed for me to bring a certain number of service staff, Kieran had insisted on bringing only people who could help protect me. Namely Bria, Red, and Jerry. My kids got to come because they were kids, and the rest of the available spots went to the "famous" Six, which now only numbered five and allowed a spot for Dylan. Amber had been forbidden, and although the explanation we'd been given was that she was untrustworthy due to her former service to Valens, I suspected Lydia had just been worried Amber would unearth all of her secrets. Little did Lydia know that Henry was nearly as good at this point, and had an uncanny ability to be in the right place at the right time.

So while my protection was in good standing, my style was not. I hoped there wasn't much of a media presence.

One thing at least I could boast for my style was that I'd denied Harding's strong suggestion that I bring the cats. Other Demigods' partners brought around magical beasts or little dogs—why not take a couple of cool cats? I had to own my mantle as the pajama-wearing cat lady.

When Kieran had seemed on the verge of relenting, probably thinking two enormous cats would help protect me in some way, I'd threatened to sleep in the other room. I had enough problems with my image and looking after two wards—I did not need to add to either plate, thank you very much.

"Demigod Kieran, welcome." A short, slight woman stepped out of the door in a flowing black gown with what I hoped were *fake* diamonds lining the neck and dipping down to her tiny waist. If they weren't fake, then the dress was a ridiculous waste of money.

"Demigod Lydia, hello. Thank you for having us." Kieran dropped my hand so he could bow and then graze his lips across her knuckles. I knew that meant he was proclaiming himself to be lesser in status. "Let me introduce Alexis." He turned and put his hand out to me again.

I'd been filled in on a few things, like how to enter the room and what he and his guys might say and do, but after that, I'd received no instruction. Nothing. Kieran wanted to play me as a wild card, and he suspected my gross negligence of magical decorum would make people even more unsettled than simply knowing my magical type. Since I'd probably mess up regardless, I'd agreed to go along with it.

"Hello," I said, stepping forward and taking his hand. I didn't curtsy. I probably should've, but the thin four-inch heels were hard enough just to stand in. My ankles kept trying to mutiny, buckle, and dump me on my face. "Nice to meet you, Demigod Lydia."

"My, my." She took me in, from my sleek, fashionable dress showing too much skin (but not as much as she was showing) to the new ruby and diamond necklace Kieran had bought for the occasion, then down to the horrible designer shoes that were in the process of sawing off a toe. "The rumors are true—you wear his mark."

"Yes. Reapplied several times over." I entwined my fingers with his.

Lydia noticed. Her dark eyes surveyed me, her black eyebrows heavily tweezed and her long raven hair so dark that it held a blue shine in the dim glow of the exterior lighting. In contrast, her skin was paler than Daisy's, somehow lacking the hue of the living. She almost looked like a fabled rendition of a vampire, complete with blood-red lips and a hungry gleam to her eyes, a more romantic look than the mottled corpses that prowled the dark places of the world. There was an otherworldly vibe about her, as though part of her had been left in the spirit realm.

"You are a striking beauty. There is a regal quality to your bearing. A gift from your father, I would imagine." Her smile was slick, like oil glistening atop the waters of a rippling pond. "Magnus has the same...*way* about him."

A surge of feeling rushed through my links with Kieran. Lydia had clearly spoken with Magnus, because Kieran hadn't made my heritage public, and from what

Henry and Amber had said, Magnus hadn't either. Unless she was guessing, and if so, I hoped I'd kept the grimace off my face.

"And Kieran, just as dapper as your old man. Such a shame, how that worked out for you two."

There was that smile again, and it took everything I had to not punch her in the spirit box.

"We shall see," Kieran replied, his double meaning clear. It would be a real shame for her indeed if she kept this up.

"Please, come in. You must be tired from your journey. I've prepared rooms within my palace for you. I hope that is satisfactory?" Lydia turned with flair, her skirt swirling around her legs and the gems catching and throwing the light.

Kieran kept hold of my hand as we crossed the threshold. My first look at the inside of the place made my stomach drop and my knees wobble. I staggered to a stop, thankful for Kieran's steadying grip.

Giant, glittering chandeliers dropped down from the high, domed ceiling within the long two-story hall. No doors lined the sides of the bottom level, but a large double door was nestled between two wide staircases at the end. The stairs led to twin corridors that ran along the outer sides of the hall, encased by a gold railing stretching between marble columns.

"So…she's rich, then," Daisy murmured next to me.

Although she was probably supposed to be walking farther back for reasons of etiquette, she either didn't know or didn't care. "That's what I'm taking away from this. She wants us to know she has more money than sense."

"She got her point across," Mordecai said from behind us. "Too bad money can't buy style."

"Totally. This is gross," Daisy replied, a little too loudly for Lydia's distance. I wondered if that was on purpose.

"*Shh.*" I turned to glare, and caught a glimpse of someone on the second story, looking over the gaudy banister. A hollow-faced man with a moth-eaten suit and sorrowful eyes watched our progress. I wondered how long ago he'd died, and why Lydia, who should be able to see spirits, let him hang around.

The click of high heels and dress shoes echoed against the walls, an aggravating sound. She'd do well to put down a rug or two. The doors between the stairs opened as Lydia reached them, and we passed into another long hall, this one with high-vaulted ceilings and another set of enormous, glittering chandeliers. The cream walls had gold-plated panels, and pinkish couches and chairs sat within large, arched alcoves. A line of people waited to either side, their expressions hungry and a little manic. None of them were living.

The first few reached out to Kieran, already moving

to keep pace as he passed them. An older woman on my side reached out as well. Those behind readied to touch the living as we moved through.

They wanted our energy, that was clear enough. It was equally clear this wasn't their first time haunting these halls, waiting for a feast of energy. Judging by their expectant expressions and the excited anticipation in their eyes, this was a regular occurrence. Lydia gave them the living, and they gave Lydia weakened guests, tired and weak from the spirit siphoning.

Some fucking welcome.

I scanned faces quickly, my heart thumping, wondering if I'd see Mia or any of the others stuck within these spirits—wondering if it was Lydia that had nabbed them or if they headed for eternal rest. Not one face was familiar, however. Not one soul.

I gritted my teeth but refrained from blasting out my repellent magic. I could send all these spirits hurtling through the hall and out of sight easily enough, but it would be equally easy for them to collect themselves and wander back. That was no good—Lydia had pushed these spirits at us, and now she could either collect some more, or go fishing in the spirit realm to retrieve them.

Still walking, putting in the barest amount of magic into keeping the spirits off us, I pulled up the power of the Line. It pulsed to life, the bruise-like colors flaring from a strip of black. Little soul ribbons waved from the various spirits, and I grabbed them all up as they scrabbled to get away. On an impulse, I grabbed Lydia's as well, fluttering in spirit like everyone else's. Demigods had souls, too. They were not immune to my tampering—they could just withstand it better than everyone else.

I tied all the soul ribbons together with Lydia's, using power and spirit to do so, Harding's teachings feeling incredibly natural at this point. Once I had them in a big knot, I strained, shoving all but Lydia's spirit through the Line and deep into the beyond. I pushed them as hard as I could without losing my body.

They sailed out of the room, swallowed by the abyss. The ribbons connected to Lydia went taut, yanking at her center. She staggered to the side, as though an anchor had just been dropped on a moving ship. Her face came up, and she looked into the Line—probably looking Beyond, following the line of soul ribbons that had caught her up.

I moved the spirit around the room, letting the wind catch my dress and my hair and fling them in the opposite direction, just to make a statement. *Yeah, I did that. We both know it, and now I'm showing that it was on purpose.*

Lydia's eyes narrowed as she looked back at me. The spirit wind around me calmed. The soul ribbons dragging at her snapped.

She was very good with her magic, and I felt like a novice again. I barely stopped from gulping.

Without a word, she straightened up and continued on. But while I could feel her trying to pack the Line away, it didn't fade or diminish. It was as if it had chosen which master to listen to—and it had picked me.

I wondered if that was my imagination getting the better of me.

"I've prepared a small supper for you." Lydia put out her hand, directing us through another set of double doors to a sort of parlor, comfortable couches and chairs arranged on thick rugs. A card table sat off to the side and a grand piano adorned the center of the room. She continued on through another set of double doors.

"Is she expecting a crowd of elephants?" Daisy murmured to Mordecai.

"Why have just one door when you could have two?" Mordecai whispered. "I wonder why there is only one card table."

"I wonder why all the upholstery is either pink or purple," Daisy said. As we walked into the dining room, she added, "Ah, here is some obnoxious red, what a nice surprise."

"*Shh!*" I said, glancing back with a scowl.

The dining room could've easily sat thirty, and the spread of food could've fed twice as many. The long oak

table was laden with meats, cheeses, breads, and fruit—
so much food it nearly put me off eating. It was like an
entire buffet restaurant had been laid out for a handful
of people.

"Here we are." Lydia stopped at the head of the table, laying her arm across the chair delicately. "My men
will attend to you. If you need anything, just ask." She
looked at Kieran's guys, her gaze appreciative as it
traveled across shoulders and lingered on handsome
faces. When it came to good looks, the "birds of a
feather" rule definitely applied to Kieran and his guys.
Except for maybe Jerry, who was looking at Lydia like a
mongoose would a snake. "*Any*thing at all." Her gaze
found Dylan last, lingering in the back. Lust lit her eyes
and her tongue darted out, wetting her lower lip.
"Hmm, you can stop by at any time. I'll make time for
you *all* night."

Dylan went rigid, and though he didn't visibly quail,
his eyes said he wanted to. Flashbacks were probably
hounding him.

A surge of protectiveness stole over me. I was essentially forcing him to deal with his past by dragging him
into this new life. I would damn well make it as easy for
him as possible.

"Gross. That's not appropriate." I curled my nose at
her. "Don't address Kieran's guys like that. It makes you
look desperate. Have a little respect for yourself."

Dylan's eyes widened. Thane, Boman, and Donovan all grinned.

Silence hung in the room, and Lydia's eyes beat into mine. I held her gaze, knowing I'd just totally screwed up the status quo, but honestly, I didn't care. She was gross. Dylan didn't need yet another creepy woman seducing him, and I didn't want to spend the next week listening to double entendres. It was best to nip the situation in the bud. If she took offense, well…she was already on thin ice, given the way she'd greeted us. We didn't need friends like her.

"Well. I'll leave you to it, then. Kieran…" Her smile was sweet, her voice still held a note of seduction, and that thin ice was starting to crack. "I'll see you tomorrow."

She slipped her arm off the chair and sauntered out of the room, her dress swirling, her probably real diamonds sparkling, and her presence tedious. A door closed with a deep thud and an echo, and we were alone. No souls existed inside or directly outside the lofty dining room. I said as much.

"Daisy, Zorn, Henry, scan for electronic surveillance," Kieran said.

The three moved off, Daisy doing a bad job of hiding her delight at being included.

"That was…" Donovan burst out in laughter. "There are no words."

"Lexi, Lexi, Lexi," Thane said, his eyes sparkling. He shook his head. "Only you."

"It isn't uncommon for the resident Demigod to overtly proposition the staff of a lesser Demigod," Bria said, laughter riding her words. "Or to assign them menial chores. Shining shoes or doing laundry. The resident Demigod is basically making a statement. They hold the power, they hold the status, and the staff of the visiting Demigod are no better than playthings or hired hands. That's the message, anyway. Usually the visiting Demigod just handles the taunting in silence."

"Usually the visiting Demigod doesn't bite back and make the resident Demigod look about two inches tall." Boman laughed. "What happened on the walk in here? Did you do something, Lexi?"

I paused behind a chair in the middle of the table. "This won't be poisoned, will it?"

"This meal? No," Donovan said, his smile stretching across his face. "The next one? Probably." He started laughing again.

"We have a few mediocre surveillance devices," Henry said, setting his laptop down in the corner. "For now, I've simply hacked into their system and disabled their audio. Like most of the older Demigods, she hasn't gotten with the times technologically. Tomorrow, I'll have Amber do it remotely. They'll know we're messing with their systems, but given we'll only affect the surveillance spying on us directly, there isn't much she can say about our interference."

"And if she tries, we'll just have Lexi deal with it," Bria said, pulling out a chair on the other side of the table. The guys all laughed.

Kieran pulled out a chair for me and motioned for me to sit down. "She won't poison our meals because in inviting us here and offering us a place to stay, she is putting us under her protection." He toggled his hand back and forth. "For the most part. Something 'beyond her control' might befall us if we were to leave the compound, but a Demigod in her standing cannot afford to have something happen to us here. She'd look incompetent. It would lower her status."

"Well…except you don't officially have any status, so you're in a bit of a gray area," Bria said, looking over the food options.

"I doubt she'd risk attacking another Demigod, especially one with an actual territory, even if that position hasn't yet been sanctioned by the Magical Summit." Kieran shook his head. "Not unless she had help and an elaborate plan."

Shivers slid across my skin. Magnus would be plenty helpful, not to mention great at coming up with an elaborate plan. I didn't voice that thought, though. I knew Kieran had already pondered it.

"You are safe, but not all of us are safe, especially

those without a blood oath." Bria picked up a cube of cheese and popped it into her mouth. "Most Demigods don't care about their people as much as you do. The replaceable ones, I mean."

"It would be in bad form," Kieran replied, taking his seat. "Like I said, she will be concerned about her status. It would be easy for me to turn any hiccup here into a reason why she cannot be trusted by other leaders."

"You'd need to come out of the Magical Summit with a good status of your own to make that stick," Zorn said.

"I will." Kieran's confidence left no room for argument.

I sank into the bright red velvet chair, wariness settling into my bones. Traveling by private jet was a luxury I'd probably never get used to, but it had been a long flight and my body was feeling it. Kieran sat beside me and everyone else filled in around us, all of us in a cluster at the top of the table.

I told them what had happened with the spirits arrayed in the corridor, my explanation cut short when servants streamed into the room with colorful jackets, white wigs to match their gloves, and important expressions.

"I don't know that I've seen one woman working here," I whispered to Kieran as the staff positioned themselves around us.

"I noticed the same thing," he replied. "I wonder why."

"First the chairs, and now this getup?" Daisy was looking at the servants. "It's like the leftovers of a circus."

Boman started chuckling, hiding his smile behind his hand.

When we'd been given drinks and our plates were loaded up, Kieran excused the servants.

"Alexis was tested first thing, and I assume that's just the beginning. Tomorrow, we will be split up. I'll talk politics and my plans for San Francisco with Lydia while Alexis gets to wander the grounds with her wards and 'experience the delights of the palace.' Lydia's words, not mine. Given Lydia will be entertaining me, it will be up to her people to test you, Alexis. Go ahead and give as good as you get. Remember what I said about staying on the grounds—Lydia will not allow herself to look incompetent, so no"—he did quotation marks with his fingers—"'freak accidents' will happen if you stick close. Bria, guide Alexis in protocol. Let's not pour salt in any wounds. Okay?" Kieran squeezed my thigh. "I will be shortening our trip by a couple of days. Urgent business will call me away. We got this. On the other side of this meeting, I have every reason to believe we'll have a Hades Demigod in our court."

I smiled with him, willing myself to believe his positive outlook. But all I could think about was that hall filled with hungry, eager spirits, groping for energy. Their mistress had known I could see them, but she'd given them free rein.

I wasn't sure Kieran was reading Lydia right. I wondered who else she would allow free rein. What other horrors awaited me in this place?

Chapter 26

ALEXIS

THE NEXT MORNING I sat in what I could only call the living room in Kieran's and my elaborate suite, the place nearly the size of our entire bottom floor in San Francisco. Breakfast had been served in the suite's dining room, the table large enough to fit six, and I'd been waited on by Lydia's very colorfully dressed service staff. Daisy didn't have enough terrible things to say.

I'd dressed in what Aubri had chosen for the day and tried to do my makeup and hair like she would've, but her written instructions were crazy and I'd lost interest halfway through.

Now it was ten o'clock and I could think of nothing else to keep me in the suite. With me were Jerry, Bria, Red, and the kids, my crew for the day.

"It doesn't make sense," I whined, strapping a knife to my inner thigh so it wouldn't make a bulge in the side of the loose, flowing dress. I had a pair of kick pants on under the dress in case I had to grapple with someone, and a tiny tank top in case I had to rip the dress off altogether. The shoes were the only problem. The heels were three inches of impractical and the straps would be a time waster to undo. "Kieran is here to talk politics. He's doing that with Lydia. Fantastic. Why do I have to wander around and pretend to have a good time when we all know that's not what's happening? Why can't I just stay in the room and read until Kieran is done?"

Bria adjusted the throwing knives hugging her hips. She and Red hadn't even pretended to hide their dangerousness. Given the state of my makeup and hair, they weren't pretending to be my fashion consultants, either.

"This is how things are done," Bria said. "*I* wouldn't even hide in my room. I'd wander around, staring at people and checking out the wealth on display. That's what's expected when you're in a place like this. You're paying homage to Demigod Lydia. The fact that you've been hiding in your room until now sends a clear enough message. We don't want to push it."

"What message is that?" I asked, adjusting my cleavage and the knife tucked within it.

"You do not give a shit about Lydia's wealth or her furnishings," Red said, waiting by the door. "Not like your constant grimace last night didn't make that message clear. Or the mutterings of your wards."

"But, like...it's gaudy," Daisy said. "It's super gross. All this money, and *this* is what she does with it?"

Bria lifted her eyebrows and put out her hands. "I know, right? Haven't I always said that? They're all like this. They don't seem to understand that fine things actually come in palatable colors. Valens's taste was just as bad. Kieran did well, asking my advice."

"We need to go," Jerry said, standing from a dainty wooden chair with gold trim. The contrast between him and his seat was comical.

"Here." Red dug something out of her back pocket and handed it to Bria. "Items of interest around the palace. There's an itinerary, but we've already blown that to hell."

"Any Demigod's girlfriend would've done the same. That's nothing." Bria looked down the list as she walked toward the door. "Okay, here's something. The skull room. That sounds rad. Let's check that out." She turned the paper over, then back again. "Map?"

"Oh." Jerry patted his pockets.

Bria rolled her eyes. "Hunt and walk. We probably have miles of hallways to go."

Two people were in the hallway outside of the door, a man with a utility belt and a woman wearing an apron, probably getting ready to straighten the quarters of some of our crew. Everyone besides us and the kids had junior suites down the hall.

"At least there are finally some female staff members," I murmured as Jerry directed us. "Last night it was all men."

"Yeah. That's because Lydia is notoriously horny and diddles the help," Bria replied, not keeping her voice down. "She likes a good selection."

I couldn't tell if she was joking. I decided not to ask.

We stayed on the second floor and traversed several wide hallways and rooms with gold plating, many of them adorned with those large, hanging chandeliers. I couldn't tell the various rooms apart by their décor alone. There were probably some subtle differences I should've noticed within all the awfulness, but honestly, I was too bored to hunt for the clues.

Servants tilted their heads with respect or bowed as we approached. Some stepped to the side and clasped their hands, holding the bow until we passed.

"She has been placed on a very high pedestal," Red said, her lips barely moving. She analyzed the people we passed. "Something is wrong here. Alexis is being treated like a high-standing Demigod."

"Or maybe a high-standing Demigod's prized possession." Bria's words and tone sent shivers racing down my spine. Although Kieran wanted and deserved a high position within the community, he did not yet have one. "Something smells fishy."

"Voices down," Jerry said from behind us, guarding

the rear.

A soul caught my awareness, moving a little faster than we were, coming up from behind.

"Watch your six," I whispered.

A moment later, Jerry said, "Nothing is there."

I chanced a look back, greeted by empty air. Until I lowered my eyes. A tiny white mouse ran along the spotless white baseboards, given away by its feet and nose. Well, that and the human soul occupying its body. That mouse looked alive, but there was no mousy soul in there. It must've been killed moments before a human soul was shoved into it.

I wasted no time in yanking the soul out of the body. The mouse dropped and a gaunt woman popped loose, blinking in confusion at the change in perspective. A meager presence drifted away from her soul, as though someone were still trying to hold on. I waved it away, brought forth the Line, and shoved the woman across.

"Necromancy," I told the others, starting forward again.

"Must've been a weak soul. I didn't feel it," Bria said.

"The spirits here all look like they're starved," I said. "Their bodies look starved, I mean. Spirits can take any form they want, so why would they choose to look gaunt and half-dead?"

"Maybe Demigod Lydia keeps them in her service even though they'd rather move on, and that's how they feel about their lot in life at this point?" Bria offered as Red motioned for us to turn right, having overtaken the guide duties from Jerry. With his size, he was better off at our backs.

"You said the spirits in the hall last night were desperate for energy—do spirits lacking in energy look like that?" Mordecai asked.

I shook my head. "Usually they just get wispier or disappear altogether. I don't feel any traps keeping people here, either," I whispered, taking yet another set of stairs. I hadn't realized this place had four stories. "Red, you're on our side, right? You're not taking us into a dark corner so someone can attack us?"

"I'm not the one that chose to go to the skull room," Red replied, not really answering my question.

"Lydia is a Demigod of Hades," Bria said as Red slowed, looking at a nondescript closed door. She glanced down the hall, eyeing the next door down, clearly unsure which one led to our destination. "She doesn't need to trap the spirits. She can hold them, just like you can. I wonder if she didn't realize you could send spirits across the Line—the spirits she is holding, I mean. That would explain the setup in the hall."

"It wouldn't explain the ghosts," Red said, trying the nearest handle. It clicked and stopped, locked.

"I got this." Daisy stepped forward, digging into a little pouch at her waist.

"Wait, wait, wait." I held up my hands. "No. We're not going to break into the skull room. Or any room. We're supposed to be sightseeing guests. Let's not piss anyone off."

"You mean, let's not piss *anyone else* off, right?" Bria's lips curved into a sly grin. "Besides the resident Demigod you openly dissed last night?"

I ignored her as Red tried the next door down, finding it locked as well.

"Why would they put the room on the map if it isn't open for business?" Bria asked, clearly disappointed.

"Why would they have a skull room in the first place?" Mordecai gave her a bewildered look. "Why would anyone want to look at skulls?"

Bria *tsked*. "You just don't get it."

"No. I don't."

Uncertainty filtered through the soul link, followed by wariness. Something was bothering Kieran.

My own uncertainty pooled in my gut. "Let's head for something we're supposed to be interested in."

"You and I are people of Hades—we're supposed to be interested in skulls," Bria said.

We headed back down to the second floor, to the middle of the house, where a gallery was supposedly *to die for*. I didn't miss the pun. As before, staff greeted me like someone of note, stopping and bowing respectfully, some murmuring "ma'am" and some "miss." An older gentleman in a blindingly colorful jacket told me I was "supremely welcome."

"Something is definitely off," Bria said, pushed in close to me. "They shouldn't be greeting you like that. They're treating you like one of Lydia's top staff."

"What's your theory?" Red asked as Bria tapped the screen of her phone and put it to her ear.

"I don't know. Is Lydia going to make a play for Lexi?" Bria replied.

"No way. She'd have to kill Kieran to do it, any fool can see that," Jerry said. "She's probably using the servants to mock Alexis behind Kieran's back. Their pandering is making Alexis uncomfortable, which in turn makes it clearer that she was not raised like the rest of us. She was raised poor."

"Yes, giant, we get it," Red growled. "You don't need to rub her nose in her own shit. She knows where she came from."

I could feel my expression souring at their conversation.

"Yeah, hey. How are people greeting Kieran?" Bria asked whoever was on the other line. She listened for a moment, and her lips tightened. "They're giving Lexi the preferential treatment. Something is amiss." She listened for a moment longer before nodding and hanging up.

"What'd he say?" Red asked.

"What I thought he'd say: Kieran is being treated how he should. Lydia knows the right etiquette; she's just not using it with Lexi. The question remains...why?"

"She's not making a play for Lexi," Red said, once again barely moving her mouth. If we hadn't been standing so close to her, I wouldn't have even known she was talking. "She can't be that stupid. If she didn't know Kieran would defend Lexi with his life before yesterday, she does now. He was very clear in his possessive mannerisms last night. Lydia wouldn't dare take him out, either. The magical rulers wouldn't let that slide, because it would open the door for the other Demigods to do something just as crazy to make a play for half a dozen other rare talents around the world that are currently securely locked down. The magical world would be plunged into magical mayhem as fast as you could blink, which would then affect the Chesters. Setting up the rules we currently have in place stopped all that Dark Ages crap. No, Jerry is right. She's mocking Alexis to make her look stupid. Alexis is gorgeous, but she cannot hide her roots. When she gets flustered with the servants, it reveals her poor bumpkin roots—Cinderella without the elegance. Lydia has all the cameras watching to make sure it's caught digitally, too.

Thank heavens Amber is at the other end of that noise."

"Now who's rubbing her face in shit?" Jerry asked.

"I really wish you'd *both* stop," I grumbled, trying not to sink into myself.

"What a fart-box-licking piece of crap," Daisy spat, and I couldn't do more than stare. She'd managed a really foul cutdown without any technically bad words.

"Right, fine, whatever," I said, trying to get this situation back on track. "She's trying to make me look like I don't belong. It wouldn't be the first time. Let's just look at...whatever is next on the list and hope this day doesn't drag on forever."

"I've got bad news," Jerry said, almost like it was an afterthought.

"Please don't enlighten me any more about my situation," I said, rubbing my face.

"This place is built on sand," he said. "Sand for days. Very little natural rock. I won't be much help if something happens."

Chapter 27

ALEXIS

THE AFTERNOON JUST got weirder. After lunch we visited the mortuary, where Lydia stored magically sealed dead bodies. That in itself wasn't odd, per se, since Bria hid bodies in the yard of every new house I moved into. The strange thing was that the bodies were stored upright in glass cases filled with dirt. Only the faces had been left visible. We walked down the rows, looking at dead faces, with their lidded eyes and sagging skin. It was more grotesque than I'd expected, which was saying something, given we'd just toured a collection of stuffed animals that would give a child nightmares, including created animals pieced together from various parts.

Everywhere I went, eyes followed me. People smiled and bowed. They muttered reverence. Staff asked if I needed anything, offering ridiculous things, like to carry me in a chair if I needed a rest but didn't want to stop. At lunch someone had actually cut my meat for me, like a child. It was a wonder they hadn't attempted to feed me while they were at it.

When I finally saw Kieran walking down the hall toward us, an hour before our scheduled dinner with Lydia and her choice people, I heaved a great sigh of relief.

His jacket buttons were open and his hair disheveled, as though he'd repeatedly run his fingers through it. His smile was brief and eyes tight. Although I'd already gathered as much through the soul connection, his day had clearly turned out little better than mine.

"Hey, love, how goes it?" he asked, his tone and mannerisms easy, loose and confident, but the wariness within him set me on edge. He waved his finger at the air around us. "What's with this?"

The Line throbbed not far away, pulsing with power that sizzled through my blood.

"Oh, sorry. Hang on, I was just about to—"

I turned and spied what had to be the twelfth white mouse that day, scurrying toward us with yet another spirit tucked inside. The woman that I ripped out looked around, her hair limp around her gaunt face and her faded eyes not seeming to register the scene around her. She seemed like she was on her deathbed...but she was already dead. Did she not realize she could change her image? And if so...why not? From my understanding, it was the kind of knowledge that was automatically imparted to the dead. If I weren't so afraid of what

Lydia might do to Jack if she found or felt him wandering around, I would've called him to me and asked.

"I tried to talk to a few of the spirits lingering in the halls and a couple of the ones I've taken out of the mouse bodies," I murmured. "It's like they don't even hear me. They look right through me. Except for one, who reached out for me, but I could tell he was just hoping to glean a little energy. I just don't know what is directly causing it, or how to fix the situation."

"And the mice?" Kieran asked.

I shoved the woman across the Line, as far as I could manage. Hopefully that would solve the problem. I was half inclined to go check, but we'd told Harding to stay away too, and I didn't dare cross the Line while in the dominion of a Hades Demigod.

"The Necromancer around here keeps sending white mice after us." I took Kieran's arm and walked with him back to our suite. Mordecai and Daisy followed behind, as quiet as the death lingering in this palace. The others walked with them, equally as silent. "Sometimes it is just the one and sometimes it's a few of them all scurrying down the halls together. It's weird. I get sending the first couple, trying to sneak up on us and hear what we're saying, but after none of them succeeded, why keep it up?"

"Bria?" Kieran asked as we reached the suite. He led the way inside, scanning with his eyes while I was checked the place with spirit.

"Clear," I said. Kieran nodded, but kept the lead until he was in the middle of the room, his power oozing out around him. He worried about an attack, and he didn't trust his eyes or my senses. Something had gotten to him.

"It seems like a joke," Bria said, following us in with everyone else. "There's no other reason for it. The souls didn't do any magic. I couldn't even feel them, they were so weak."

"Lydia doesn't have a sense of humor," Zorn said, his voice deep and gruff. He scanned the windows and the corners.

"Right. Exactly." Bria sank onto a delicate chair, huffed, slid off, and melted onto the ground. She stretched out and propped her head up on her hand. "The way they've been treating Lexi doesn't add up, either. Jerry and Red agree that it is probably intended as mocking behavior, but I just don't see Lydia encouraging her people to treat someone lesser as someone of high status."

"Hades people are never what they seem," Dylan said, taking a spot at the window. "Even if something is against their personality type, don't rule out the possibility. They will bend a lot to get what they want. They are cunning and treacherous with their words, and they will take greater risks than others. Hades is the king of the dead—what do they have to lose, you know? They already rule the dead. At least, that's how it has always been described to me. I don't know much about Lydia, but Magnus is the master of trickery. He has no honor. All the Zeus Demigods are wary of him." He shot me a glance and mumbled, "That I knew of, anyway."

"That's a very Zeus way to see Hades, that's for sure." Bria huffed out a laugh.

"Could the mice have been a distraction?" Thane asked as Henry clacked on his computer keys. He'd be making sure there was no surveillance in this room. There hadn't been earlier that morning...but that had been hours ago. Apparently no one cared enough to halt the conversation.

"In a different setting, sure," Bria replied. "But we weren't doing anything interesting. There was nothing to distract us from."

"There was plenty to distract us from, but a few mice wouldn't do it." Daisy rubbed her eyes.

"If anything, the mice made it worse," Mordecai said. Daisy nodded.

"What about how they were treating Lexi? I'd like to hear more about that," Kieran said, sitting on the couch.

"We're clear," Henry said, leaning back in the chair pushed up to the little round table that held his laptop. He didn't close it, though, clearly intending to keep monitoring.

Bria explained how people had been greeting me and waiting on me, all while mostly ignoring Jerry, Red, and her. I felt the uncertainty within Kieran grow, and he rubbed his fingers along his chin, his dark five o'clock shadow giving him a rugged look.

"What's your take?" Bria asked him when she'd finished.

Kieran shifted and propped an ankle over his knee. "The reason she invited us here was because we caught her loitering in spirit. At the time, she seemed appropriately abashed and receptive. I had high hopes of good communication. That's not what I'm getting. I am getting a Demigod firmly entrenched in her territory and status, who speaks of politics delicately, who speaks of the future with the correct amount of vagueness, and who is carrying on how I would expect someone to carry on with a Demigod of my standing. She's doing everything by the book."

Grim expressions covered faces, and as usual, I felt like a dunce.

"Why is that bad?" I asked in a small voice.

"She is a Demigod of Hades—she invited us here because she fucked up and got caught on Demigod Kieran's territory without permission, and you are of particular interest to her and her kind," Henry explained. "She hasn't spoken to any of that. It's the proverbial elephant in the room."

"She is actively *avoiding* speaking to any of that," Kieran added. "I am here because of a few specific reasons, and she is acting as if we're paying her a visit to acknowledge and admire her status. She is not generally thought to be inconsistent in her dealings, which means something fundamental has changed with regards to her invitation or her motives. I'm just not sure if the change is cause for alarm or annoyance."

"It seems like there is a plan at work here, sir," Thane said.

Kieran nodded slowly, staring out at nothing. "I am inclined to agree, but again, is that plan cause for alarm, or annoyance? Mocking my girlfriend is not enough of a slight to incite retaliation. She could still be feeling out my connection to Lexi, trying to suss out if the mark is legit. Alexis has no blood oath—that mark is my only claim right now. That mark, and her word that it was applied willingly." He paused for a moment. "Until I know more, I will remain cautiously optimistic. There is still a chance I can turn this meeting around to our benefit. I've thought of a few ideas I can plant. At the same time, there is *not* a chance we can pull out without it reflecting badly on us. We don't have cause. Until we do, we have at least two more days before I can make an excuse."

"You might be green, but by Athos's mountain cap, you have been trained incredibly well," Jerry said.

"Athos's mountain cap?" A smile spread across Boman's face.

"That's not in Canada, eh, Jerry?" Thane said, and Donovan started laughing. Jerry cracked a grin.

"This isn't just training," Dylan said from his place in the corner. "He has an affinity for it. If he had adopted Valens's ruthless style…"

"I didn't adopt my father's…style, and if I ever try, Daisy has promised to burn my house down," Kieran said.

"With you in it," Daisy said.

"Right, yes, with me in it," Kieran said. "How silly of me to forget that detail. But training and natural ability will only get you so far." He rose and loosened his tie. "It won't be enough to get us out of a trap. Only my crew can help with that. Look sharp in this place. Lydia has a firm handle on the rules of the magical world, and if things go poorly, I wouldn't put it past her to use that knowledge against us. She mentioned the mark and said that many of the Demigods wonder if it was legally applied. Demigod Zander was one of those, apparently. His wife bears his mark, something he gave her on their wedding day, and because he had to defend it, he's touchy about others who have it. I knew this, of course, and I expected he'd want me to speak on Lexi bearing my mark. That's not a problem—he's a sensible man, and Lexi's testimony will do plenty to appease him. But for Lydia to bring it up in a meeting of the minds…"

"Through torture, one of the Hades Demigods could break Alexis," Zorn said. "At that point, they could easily make her claim you gave her that mark against her will. That would be enough to discredit it, and since she doesn't have a blood oath, they'd say she's not really yours. They could make the claim that she wanted a new home with those of her kind. That's that issue filed away for them."

"Precisely. I'd then have political problems after I hunted them down and killed them all," Kieran said as he shrugged out of his jacket. The confident, blasé tone he used when talking about violently avenging me sent a warm chill racing through me. I couldn't say if it was fear or arousal. Maybe both.

"Except everyone who knows Lexi can vouch for her," Mordecai said.

"Everyone who can vouch for her would be killed," Donovan replied, his smile from earlier long gone.

"I'd like to see them find me," Daisy replied.

"Nice sentiment, but you're not magical, kid," Bria said. "You don't matter in their eyes."

"I matter, and they wouldn't find me, either," Zorn ground out, his eyes flashing. "Even if they took out Kieran, I would not forsake you, Alexis. I would still protect you and your wards. And I'd get to do it *my* way."

I gulped. Zorn was clearly not someone anyone wanted to piss off.

"That's all well and good, but by then…" Kieran turned away, and agony ate through the soul link.

I pushed Zorn's scariness and Kieran's fear away. "Then why not give me the oath? You've already started it by giving me your blood. Just finish the procedure, or whatever it is. Then, even if they break me, I'm claimed. It's official."

Kieran shook his head slowly. "If you take that oath, your impulse will be to protect me. I need you to protect yourself. I can't let you take that oath."

Dylan shifted against the wall, his eyes rooted to Kieran, looking incredulous. No one else was surprised.

I felt like stamping my foot on the ground in frustration. "Right, fine, awesome. I'll have a bad future if they get a hold of me." I braced my hands on my hips. "We've always known this. It's not news. So instead of thinking or analyzing all of the horrible ways this can go wrong, let's prepare for the possibility we may need to fight our way out of here. It's not like we haven't had practice."

"I'm good with that." Donovan shrugged and grabbed an apple out of a golden bowl.

"Question." Daisy raised her hand. "How thorough do you think their inventory is of this place? For example, just hypothetically speaking, would they miss something like a golden ashtray inlaid with rubies just randomly left on a low shelf in the library behind a chair? They probably don't even know it's there, right?"

The bubble of tension in the room popped. More than a couple of people took deep breaths. Smiles creased previously tight expressions. Chuckling, Kieran headed toward the bedroom and probably the shower.

"Is she being serious?" Jerry, not one of those smiling, asked Dylan.

A big smile lit Dylan's face. "I think so, yeah."

"Of course I'm being serious," Daisy replied. "That clown Demigod doesn't need all this."

"That's no way to speak about a Demigod," Mordecai said. "Even in private."

"She made her bed, with all the colors she chose. I just noticed it," Daisy retorted.

"You shouldn't steal," Jerry told her.

"I heard about that mountain lodge you made for yourself," she replied. "Bones in the corner? Filth everywhere? Who are you to give me advice on how to survive?"

"They won't notice the little things, but you cannot get caught or give them a suspicion you took anything," Zorn told her. "That would reflect badly on Demigod Kieran."

"Unless we have to drop the hammer on this bitch." Donovan pushed away from the wall. "Then grab whatever you can carry. Rob that bitch blind. *Bam!*"

"This outfit will take some getting used to," Jerry murmured.

"When it comes to surviving, there are no rules," Dylan said, still smiling. "You might take a lesson from her. That kid seems to do it better than most."

"I learned from Lexi," Daisy said. "If you want an example of someone good at surviving, look at her. You'll see. If these idiots turn up the heat on her, they won't know what hit them."

Chapter 28

KIERAN

KIERAN HELD LEXI'S hand as they made their way to the main first-floor lounge to await dinner. The servants they passed acted exactly as Kieran would've expected, nodding to him before stepping to the side to give him more room. Lexi got a glance, which was correct, and the rest of his staff was ignored. Whatever had gone on earlier in the day was not happening now.

Given Bria and Red were not prone to dramatics, and Bria was especially knowledgeable of the rules of hierarchy within the Demigod world, he wondered what Lydia was up to. Was she testing Lexi, ridiculing her, or were there darker forces at work? It troubled Kieran that he didn't have a clue.

Once they were in the lounge, a servant approached wearing a hideous, colorful jacket and one of those strange white wigs. Kieran had no idea what sort of fashion statement Lydia was trying to make with the getup. Surely her tastes were laughed at behind closed doors. If not, and if things went poorly here, Kieran would make sure to start the talk. That was an easy button to push.

"Would you like a drink, sir?" the man asked.

"Yes. A whiskey on the rocks, please." Kieran angled a little to show he would like Alexis to order for herself. By deferring to her, he was making it clear that she would eventually be his co-ruler, with an equal say in all decisions for the territory and a status similar to his, if not that of a Demigod. Making that point now would hopefully dispel some of the rumors surrounding the mark he'd placed.

"And for you, miss?" the man asked.

"Pinot Noir, if you have it," Alexis said, looking away and lifting her chin haughtily. The soul link said she was annoyed and wary, reacting unconsciously to all the speculation surrounding them, but Kieran wondered if these people believed she was acting up because the special treatment from earlier had been toned down. If so, was that the reaction they'd hoped for?

So many threads to this intricate web. So many nuances. Kieran didn't have nearly enough information. At present, he would be blindsided if someone made a move. He and all his people would be vulnerable to an attack if one came.

But would Lydia really go to such extremes? Even with the support of an intricate strategist like Magnus, it would be a dangerous gambit. If she were to kill Kieran, she'd be expected to pay the price. If not, the rules of the Magical Summit would be undermined at every turn. He doubted Lydia was foolish enough to try anything.

"Surveillance in this room has been cut out entirely," Henry said when the man had left, and Henry waved off a different servant that drew near. Only the head servant would wait on Kieran and now Alexis, his sole duty to make sure they were comfortable. Other, lesser servants would see to the rest of the group. "Amber is monitoring the other areas of the house. Nothing is amiss that she can see so far, but certain rooms aren't accounted for. A block of guest rooms in the east wing are dark, and a second dining area and the rooms surrounding Lydia's bedroom."

"Is that cause for alarm?" Kieran asked, looking down at Alexis.

"It doesn't appear so. There's little activity in the halls around the guest rooms, and we wouldn't expect Lydia to allow her people to monitor her in that way."

Kieran nodded and turned away, excusing Henry for the moment. There was always some suspicion amongst Demigods, even between allies, but Kieran had to be careful not to go overboard. He didn't want to cause offense, and he certainly didn't want Lydia to guess he suspected any of her possible plans. If she changed things up, the few hints he'd gleaned so far would be rendered useless.

Lydia sauntered through the lounge, headed his way, her bright pink dress blowing in an unseen wind, her mostly exposed chest layered in diamonds and pearls, and her arms clad in fishnet-type gloves decorated with multicolored gemstones. She glittered and sparkled, and even if he hadn't checked up on her holdings, he would've guessed that the extreme show of her wealth hinted at sagging finances. Old-school Demigods weren't hard to read when you knew the signs, and it seemed this one hadn't changed much with the times. Her financial ego was incredibly fragile, another thing people must talk about behind closed doors.

"Demigod Kieran, you're looking almost good enough to eat." Lydia's smug and sultry smile was all for Alexis, trying to get a rise. Alexis stared at her blandly, and it was clear she was bored and waiting for all this to end.

He stifled a smile. "Demigod Lydia, those jewels are fabulous."

"Why, yes, thank you." She lifted a hand, turning it as she did so, letting the light shine and sparkle as it hit the various gems, before stroking her extravagant necklace.

She took a moment to shoot Alexis a look, clearly taking note of the simple strand of pearls at Lexi's elegant neck, her formfitting dress without any frills or embellishments, her sparkly flats, and her mostly natural face. She'd put on only enough makeup to enhance her already striking beauty, just like when he'd first met her. Alexis hadn't put in half the effort Lydia would've expected, but instead of making her look *lesser*, it made her natural beauty shine. Her somewhat unruly hair created a halo around her angelic face, and her simple but well-made dress accentuated her perfect curves, at the same time athletic and feminine.

"Hello," Alexis said, as though completely oblivious to the scrutiny.

Lydia's pencil-thin eyebrows dipped. She huffed, barely perceptibly, before turning for the dining room. The doors opened from the inside, allowing her to stroll in.

"How do you feel now compared to this afternoon?" Kieran asked Alexis, hesitating before they followed their hostess.

"Like we're being watched." Alexis scanned the baseboards of the room. "I can't figure it out…"

"It isn't a Demigod in spirit form?" Kieran turned toward her, like he was stealing a quick kiss. He hadn't expected that answer.

"No. I've seen this before, but at the time I didn't know my magic well enough to suss it out. Forms appear in the corner of my eye, but when I turn, they scamper beyond the veil before I can catch more than a passing glance. They aren't normal spirits. They're shadows, but with even less substance than a Demigod. More wraithlike. I don't know what they are, but they're adept at staring when I'm not looking and zipping away right before I turn. It's driving me nuts."

Kieran ran his lips across her chin, his gaze darting around the shadows and into the corners. With his ability to see spirit, he might be able to see them too. "Keep your senses open." He straightened and ran his fingertips down her cheek. "What about the way the servants are treating you? Lydia?"

"The servants earlier today treated me quite a bit differently. Lydia's behaving exactly like she did yesterday. Exactly. I'm pretty sure she doesn't like me."

"You're beautiful and elegant—you're competition. She doesn't seem like a woman that savors competition."

"She doesn't seem like a woman who is playing her cards where everyone can see them."

Truer words had never been spoken.

Kieran turned and slipped an arm around her waist.

Lydia was cunning and devious, and if her enterprise was flagging, even a little, maybe she was also growing desperate. After living in wealth for hundreds of years, the most experienced Demigods could be thrown by even a gradual decline in fortune. When you lived many lifetimes, there was no such thing as too much money. Eventually, if you lived long enough and mishandled your territory, you could find yourself without a penny.

If that was the issue—and Kieran didn't know that it was—would it be so far-fetched to assume Lydia would risk grabbing Lexi, breaking her from Kieran, and trading her to Magnus for some large political favor? Perhaps the servants' reverence this morning was all part of the plan—butter Lexi up in the hopes she'd leave willingly.

Kieran blew out a breath and tried to school his expression.

No, it wasn't out of the realm of possibility that Lydia had gotten stars in her eyes with a legendary Soul Stealer so close at hand. Someone who could maybe tilt the earnings back toward an upward trajectory.

Kieran could only hope Lydia knew how foolish any of that would be. He could only hope she was still in her right mind.

Chapter 29

ALEXIS

ECHOES DRIFTED THROUGH spirit, tickling my ears but taking no shape. A feeling of urgency pushed at me, imploring me to do something, to get moving. But where would I go? What was needed?

Ghastly faces swam through my dreams, gaunt, hollow-cheeked, eyes milky and sightless through a layer of glass. Their bodies bowed, even young people looking old and weathered, their vitality gone. Their will to live dried up.

Only they weren't alive. They were dead, all of them. They solely existed in spirit, but they were trapped as surely as the spirits Valens had imprisoned.

The Line pulsed, sending a surge of power through me.

The feeling of urgency persisted. It drummed through my body, matching the beating of my heart, as the horrible faces swam toward me, greedy fingers pulling at my clothes and scraping across my skin.

I sucked in a breath and jerked up to sitting, a

strangled scream caught in my throat. The dreamscape cleared away in a flash. Sweat plastered hair to my forehead and my whole body shivered uncontrollably.

"What is it?" Kieran sat up beside me, sleep evaporating from his eyes. "Are you okay?"

I pushed my hair out of my face. "Yeah. Just a bad dream." I willed more spit into my mouth, trying to keep my tongue from sticking to the roof of my mouth. "It's fine."

It took me a moment to realize the Line pulsed within the center of the room. Its power filled me, and just as in the dream, it held a strange sense of urgency. Something danced across my magic. Daisy stirred, in the bedroom next to ours, before getting out of bed. A tapping against my magic caught my attention next, in a different place than the odd dancing.

Knock, knock, knock.

I jumped, a scream escaping my lips.

"It's the door," Kieran whispered, and laid a hand on my back. "It's the outside door of the suite. Can you feel who it is?"

My heart thundered in my chest, and I swung my legs over the edge of the mattress. "I don't recognize the soul, but I do recognize the two animal souls with the person. What the—"

Daisy met me in the living room area, staring at the door. "Something feels off in here," she said, rubbing the goose-pimpled flesh on her arms. "It feels like when you have a bunch of spirits hanging around."

I frowned at her. She'd never mentioned feeling a certain way when I had a bunch of spirits around, although it wasn't uncommon to feel spirits. Most people did, whether they realized what they were feeling or not.

"We're protected from spirits in here." My magic lined the perimeter of the suite. I stopped by the door, waiting for Kieran to catch up. He had on a robe and slippers, provided by Lydia, of course, and handed a set to me.

"I'll get it," Kieran said. "What's out there?"

"A person and a pair of cats."

"A pair..." A crease formed between his eyebrows as another knock sounded at the door, muted and respectful.

Kieran opened the door to a man in a colorful tux and gloves, his face a mask of confusion and a note in his hand. Two enormous cats waited beside him, the green-eyed male sitting and licking his front paw, and the luminescent bronze-eyed female staring at me expectantly.

"What are they doing here?" Daisy asked, peering around me.

Kieran took the proffered letter. "It's from Sodge. He says they are of better use to us here than at the house."

"He…shipped the cats to us?" I asked in utter confusion, my question directed at the staff member, who was looking at me for answers. "What help could a couple giant cats be? Also, and I know I've asked this before, but why are they so giant? The mom and dad were regular cat size. Their siblings were regular cat size. Seriously, it's been two days—are they even bigger? What grows that…"

I lost the thread of what I was saying as I glimpsed what was happening behind our late-night messenger. People ambled through the hall, slow and aimless, dragging their feet as though they couldn't be bothered to lift them up. Some hunched or stooped, some curled to the side a little, some just let their heads loll. They looked like zombies, but they didn't have bodies.

"What…" I stepped out of the door, joined by Kieran. The staff member stepped back, confused.

"See if you can find some cat food," Kieran told the man. "And a couple of bowls of water. We have no choice but to keep them here. My house man sent them."

He walked away, but my gaze had already shifted back to the spirits. An older man down the way raked his fingers against the wall, ricocheting off my spirit repellent. A younger woman, probably barely more than eighteen, patted the wall on the other side of the door. She, too, hit my magic and was pushed away.

The Line filled the hall with its ultraviolet colors, illuminating yet more spirits, barely more than wisps, their clothes holey and haggard and their skin translucent. They had hardly any energy.

"Why are they all here?" Kieran asked, stepping in front of me.

I wasn't sure what he thought he'd do. Scare them with his stare?

The Line pulsed, beckoning. None of the spirits so much as glanced at it. It pulsed again, and again, beating that drum, calling its spirits home. I'd never seen this kind of insistency. I'd never felt this severe of a tug. Yet none of the spirits so much as glanced up from their directionless wandering.

This is my job—I have to help.

A Spirit Walker didn't just take lives—Harding had taught me that. We could save lives. It was also our duty to help spirits find rest, wherever possible, something I'd been doing all my life. The sudden appearance of the Line, in addition to the way the spirits were clustering around me, made it perfectly clear that it was time for them to go home. Whatever Lydia was doing to keep them here, it was shitty.

A shape appeared at the edge of my vision. I turned my head, but it zipped away, moving beyond the veil—only to return on the other side of me. Or was that a different one? I couldn't tell. I couldn't feel it specifically.

The second I flicked my eyes or turned my head, the bugger took off. A strange sort of awareness fell over me, like at dinner. I was being watched. This felt different from the Demigods who'd shown up at my house in spirit.

Those shapes had shown up before, like I'd mentioned to Kieran. I remembered seeing them back when I first started learning my magic, usually when I was heading into or escaping from danger. Part of me wondered if it was Harding. He liked to watch me work. Was sending spiritlike wraiths as spies in his wheelhouse?

The writhing spirits in front of me reminded me that I had work to do. Power pumped through me, and I pulled Kieran back. I grabbed a couple of spirits at a time, just to see if any would rouse and talk to me. None did, and over they went, one by one, shoved as far beyond the Line as I could possibly get them while remaining firmly on this side of reality. While I worked, I watched out for any souls creeping up on me, stuffed in mice or whatever else. I waited for a Demigod's spirit to appear out of thin air, or to grab me from the beyond, yanking me in after the spirits I was sending over. All was quiet.

After the last one sailed over, the Line gave one final

pulse of power, re-energizing me, before its colors seeped from the hall. I stood panting, staring, a little amazed.

I'd never interacted with it like that. Although I'd been using its power for some time, it had never seemed like an entity in and of itself. And yet it had acted like it was looking out for those spirits. Like it wanted me to be its ally in saving them.

"I might've just picked a really big fight with the resident Demigod," I said, wiping my brow. One of the cats purred loudly, and I realized they were lying on either side of me, like sentinels. "I'm not even a cat person. I think this is Harding's idea of a joke. Somehow he did this, he must have."

"The spirit world is just as much your domain as it is Lydia's," Kieran said, leading me back into our suite. "Your magic makes it so. This house might be hers, but the souls in it do not belong to her. The spirit world is not hers to claim. You have every right to exercise your ability freely." He grabbed me a bottle of water from the snack fridge. "But yeah, that will probably really piss her off. So we have that to look forward to."

I laughed, though it wasn't really funny. I could've just created a problem. At the same time…the Line had basically asked me to. I didn't know what its deal was, but I was pretty sure that it was best to do what it wanted.

I heaved out a sigh, ushered Daisy back into her room, and let Kieran wrap me in his arms.

"We'll see how it goes tomorrow," he said, then planted a kiss on my head. "If things remain this strange, I'll take offense and we'll leave, cats and all."

I chuckled and shook my head. "What the hell was he thinking, sending those cats? They don't even have names."

"I have no idea. More importantly, who did he get to help him, because he doesn't have the authority or control to get those cats here. The whole situation is incredibly strange. But as long as it doesn't get danger-ous, it'll be fine. For now."

THE NEXT MORNING, I didn't bother with a dress. I pushed my heels to the side with the toe of my running shoes. I had on stretchy leggings that looked like jeans, a knife strapped to my ankle, a shirt that said, "I'm your huckleberry," and a can-do attitude. I didn't know what was going on in this monstrosity of a house, but today I had a mission. I would seek out more of those spirits, see if any would talk to me, and then send them across the Line. There was bound to be a somewhat fresh one coherent enough to spill the beans.

"My, my, don't you look tired." Bria was peeling a banana in the living room of the suite when I walked out.

I told her what happened during the night. As I was finishing, both cats trotted out of my bedroom.

"They tried to sleep on the bed," I said. "The bed is big, but those damn cats are bigger. Look at them!"

"They're huge, yes. Their eyes don't seem like the eyes of a normal cat anymore. They kinda…glow."

I gestured at them, mouth hanging. "Nothing about them is normal."

"They smell like normal cats," Mordecai said, twitching his nose. "I hate that smell."

The male cat made a sound like a growl deep in its throat.

"It's probably time for us to name them." I checked the battery on my phone before slipping it into a small cross-shoulder bag. "Why do you think Sodge sent them? Did one puke on the carpet or something?"

"He sent them because I told him to." She flicked off the coffee pot. "Kieran gone already?"

"Wait, what? *You* told him to? Have you lost your mind?"

She shrugged. "Didn't Harding say you should bring them? That guy has not steered you wrong so far. I figured I'd help push the envelope."

"You're fired, number one—"

"Don't work for you."

"—and he hasn't steered me at all. He's done a good job training me, sure, but he has a weird thing about those cats. It's madness. Sending them here like this is crazy. I mean...it's crazy!"

"Yeah, sure. What about Kieran?"

I stared at her, wanting more than an offhanded assent. After a moment, it was clear I wouldn't get it.

"Where did I go wrong with my life? He left at nine." I checked my watch. Ten o'clock. If nothing happened today, it would still be a long day. I was not looking forward to it. "We're going to go spirit hunting."

"Awesome."

The door to the suite opened, revealing Dylan and Red.

"No Jerry today?" I asked, heading for the door. I shouted for the kids to hurry up and finish getting ready.

"He's mostly useless here, so they sent the trainee." Bria followed me. "How do you feel about skulls, Dylan? I hear the skull room is open now. I got a special invite from her ladyship, who likes you so much. I had to trade you, though. I hope you don't mind. She requested you wear leopard print. Any time is good—she will be up *all night*."

"Pick on the new guy? Is that the hazing style around here?" Dylan asked as the kids came into the living room. We all left the suite in single file.

"It's a new tradition." She evened up with me and

held out her banana peel, still chewing. "Why didn't I throw this away when I had the chance?"

"Anyone bring the map?" I asked, continuing the same way we'd gone yesterday.

"Yup." Red pulled it out. "Are we really bothering with the skull room? Because yesterday that looked like a regular, nondescript room, and all the other stuff was in halls and had big to-dos."

"It is where we're going, yes," Bria said, "and I was just kidding. I didn't get a special invite. We're going rogue. We'll trade Dylan if we get caught."

"What is your fascination with the skull room?" Mordecai said.

"You need to turn here…" Red pointed.

I ignored Red, heading straight instead, wanting to wander a bit to see if I could find another soul or two. I didn't remember seeing any on the way to the skull room.

"This leads toward the lower-status servants' quarters," Red said. "The ones that cook and clean and stuff. They aren't used to dealing with guests or important magical staff."

"Good." The hallway reduced down and lost much of its glitter. After a while, the walls weren't even lined with gold anymore. Staff members startled when they saw us, offering awkward bows or curtsies, then looking down and hurrying by. Their movements held none of the flourish from yesterday, none of the pompous, forced offerings of respect. These were true working people, paid less than they were probably worth and trying to make the best of it. I'd spent my life working around these types of people. I *was* this type of person. This area made me feel more comfortable than any other place in the house.

As I expected, there were also spirits here, sometimes reaching out to rake their hands across one of the workers. They were stealing energy from the people who needed it most.

I stopped in front of one of the spirits, a sad sack like all the others. I was sick of seeing them this way. Their suffering was just so unnecessary.

"Hey," I said.

His dazed eyes roamed the wall to my right.

"Hey!" I prodded him with my magic.

His gaze swung my way, but it drifted on by, like he was in a drug coma and couldn't focus.

I called the Line, pulling power from it, and reached out to the spirit.

"It's okay, she's crazy. Ignore her," Bria said to a staff member who had slowed to watch me.

Laden with magic, I pushed my hand through the spirit's middle and sent a pulse of magic into him. Nothing happened. A ribbon waved at me, attached to the spirit's soul, and I rolled my eyes at myself. With my magic, I grabbed the soul ribbon, but instead of pulling it to me, I pumped magic into it.

The spirit inflated like a child's plastic swimming raft.

His eyes shifted back to me, passed me, and then returned, like a blind person trying to gauge what lay in the path ahead with a walking stick.

I gave him another shock of magic.

His image changed, from middle-aged and stooped, standing listlessly, to young and broad-chested, his head held high and his magical power throbbing around him. He felt like a level four now, but back in the day, I suspected he'd been a weaker level five.

His focus snapped to mine. His eyebrows lowered.

"What'd you do?" Bria sidled closer. "I can feel that soul. Was that there this whole time?"

"What's your deal?" I asked the guy as he brought up his hands, probably to do magic.

I sapped power from him. *I giveth, and I taketh away.*

"I'm not your enemy," I said. "I'm just a girl, standing in front of a spirit, wondering what the fuck?"

"Yeah, good people skills," Bria said, and she was serious.

The man looked around, blinking, like he didn't know where he was.

"How come you haven't crossed the Line?" I felt it

throbbing beside me, its tug uncomfortable, even for me.

He turned his head, looking at it with longing, and touched his chest. "I…can't. I…" His expression turned panicked. "I can't."

"Are you trapped here? Do you remember why you're here?" I fed him more energy.

Staff members slowed, watching.

"Red, move them along," I said distractedly, watching the man's face. The more power he had, the more his eyes hardened. The more defiance crept into him. "And pass out business cards. Maybe they want a better Demigod to work for."

"She holds me," the man said. "I failed her. She holds me here. Keeps me. I can't…leave…this place."

"I'll set you free," I whispered, closing my eyes. "Can you give me a second to figure out how she's keeping you from passing over?"

He said something, but I'd already fallen into the trance of spirit so I could better judge how Lydia was holding the spirits. It could require a lot conscious concentration, given the number of spirits in this place.

Deeper into the trance I went, barely noticing Bria's attempt to get my attention. My soul felt light, like it wanted to rise out of my body, but I kept it rooted, barely slipping into the beyond so I could see. I just needed a peek, and then I'd be right back.

A person-sized shape materialized almost immediately, as though it had been waiting. Actually, it wasn't a person so much as a shadow—*the* shadow, the one I'd encountered with Will Green and his shifters, and again when I'd needed help with Valens. The grumpy guy who pushed me out of this plane more often than he helped me navigate it. It wasn't Harding, though, I could feel that right off. It—he?—didn't have the same presence. The same easy glide through this abstract place.

He stared at me for a moment, and just like with Harding, I knew what he was asking without needing to hear the words. Surprisingly, it wasn't "Why are you here?" That seemed to have been established—I was here because I belonged. My magic granted me a pass to this place. Instead, I heard/felt, "What's the situation?"

I shared my thoughts about the trapped spirit, and how I wanted to find out what was anchoring it to the world of the living. The shape nodded. He turned, almost lazily, and pressed his palm between the upper chest and neck of the soul. Spirit wound around the contact in bright violet, revealing a string starting from the soul and leading through the world of the living, cutting through the wall in swirly loop-de-loops and finally disappearing.

A strange feeling trickled down through my belly. It reminded me of my mom, and crazy situations, and everything working out unexpectedly. Without thinking, knowing it was a bad idea but used to just going with the flow when I felt like this, I grabbed that string and, using it as a guide, I left my body behind. Touching that cord, I felt energy surging in the same direction I was going, being pulled from the spirit and the magic I'd injected into him. In no time, that guy would be back to his sad state, listlessly hovering, looking at nothing.

Frustration overwhelmed me, followed fast by anger. Where did it end? This soul had been ripped from his body, stripped of everything he'd known, and left to find his way through the unfamiliar plane, alone. Surely he'd paid the price for whatever he'd done many times over. If not, she could have dissolved his spirit entirely. Lydia had the power to do so. But *this*? This was an exhibition of moral bankruptcy. She kept those spirits in the halls for her own benefit. Any energy they siphoned from her guests and staff went to *her*.

My brain couldn't wrap around how gross that was. A Demigod of Hades could just take power from the Line—why would she siphon it from people unless she got off on it?

The string led into a large room with cream walls lined and accented with gold. Three groupings of furniture created little discussion pods, one set upholstered in black and white, another in forest green, and the third, where Kieran and Lydia sat, was stark white. A thought curled up, unbidden—*Thank God I'm not in that meeting. I'd spill coffee and crumbs all over the pristine furniture.*

None of their guards or inner circle members waited in the room with them. Instead, I felt their souls in the room next to this one, all spread out, none of them mingling with the unfamiliar souls who were probably Lydia's crew.

Two staff members in their stupid coats and wigs entered the room from a door on the right, one carrying a golden tray laden with little sandwiches, chips and pretzels, and chocolates, and the other rolling a silver drink cart. The staff member with the cart stopped when he was close to remove a tray of leftover pastries from the small table in the conversation nook. The other put down the new plate of food and refilled Kieran's nearly empty glass with some sort of purple drink.

Kieran's soul gleamed, bright and beautiful, but he was troubled and scared. He'd been fine before I took flight, so I could only assume he felt me now, not in my body where I was supposed to be.

Lydia turned her head slowly toward me. She sat on the couch, her dress's slit parting around her crossed legs. The violet string I'd been following disappeared into a halo around her chest.

Hating myself, knowing how incredibly stupid this was, I acted quickly. I had to know the extent of what she was doing! I had to figure out a way to stop her.

I darted toward her and did what the shadow guy had done, only I didn't have a hand. How did I get a hand in this place? I improvised with the *idea* of a hand, slapping spirit against her upper chest. Violet lit up my world before settling. Strings of power blazed through the room, lots of them, some connected directly to her and some detouring to the room next door. She wasn't keeping all the power; she was feeding those who protected her, as well.

The string—more of a rope now—I had followed was thicker than most of the others, laden with the power I had supplied. I wondered if she'd felt the influx, or if it had just replaced the lost power from the spirits I'd sent into the beyond last night. There'd been so many of them, but they were weak.

Closing my eyes, acting fast, I used spirit and power and *clipped* the smaller strings connected to her. Instead of snapping off, however, they slowly dissolved, the beautiful purple tarnishing, darkening, then dying. The string didn't pull away—it disappeared entirely, and I vaguely felt the Line throb.

Had I just set the soul free, then? Was clipping those connections enough to let them drift away? It certainly seemed easier than forcing the spirits over the Line.

Before I could back away, spirit coalesced around me, trapping me, sticking me to the spot. A smile slowly curled Lydia's lips and a new violet string formed. A connection that she intended to attach to me!

I struggled to get away, to break free. This was why I had, up until now, avoided leaving my body. Why I hadn't wanted Jack or any of the others to come. She dealt in spirit like Demigod Flora dealt in storms and lightning. I was now in Lydia's sticky web of spirit, caught, without my body to keep me grounded.

I was at her mercy, and I had every reason to believe she had none.

Chapter 30

ALEXIS

KIERAN STOOD SLOWLY, his eyes rooted to Lydia. I knew he couldn't see me in this state, but I'd ripped out his soul six months ago and brought him into this plane with me. After that, he'd always been able to *feel* me when I traveled in spirit. He knew I was hovering right around Lydia, and I was quite sure he also knew what her sly, triumphant smile meant.

His people started moving in the room next door, surely feeling the incredible panic that was rising in him like a tide. His power, surging through the room. But what could he do? The only option was to kill her.

I pumped a shock wave of power into the beyond, attempting to reach the world of the living. Spirit shook around me, but I was still stuck. If Lydia felt the assault, she didn't show it. I thrashed and turned, chopping at her connections, hacking at the deep violet rope slowly creeping toward me through the air.

Jack appeared next to me—then Frank, of all people. John came next, followed by Chad and Mia. All of the spirits from back home, the ones who'd helped me fight or just hung around, populated the room.

"Help!" I cried, not sure what to do. Air gathered in the room, Kieran readying to fight, trying to save me even though he couldn't know what was actually happening.

I could not let him kill her. His father had been one thing—they'd battled, face to face. They'd pitted themselves against each other, Kieran the underdog. But to accept a Demigod's invitation and then kill her? The other superpowers of the world wouldn't stand for that, especially since he was so new and untried, and given his history. His future would be over before it had properly begun.

"Tell Kieran no," I said to Jack, who was staring down at Lydia with a mask of rage. "Tell him not to touch her."

"Careful there," Lydia drawled, victory in her eyes as she looked up at Kieran, unable to see me with my being across the veil. "Harm me, and I will end you. I have the connections to do it. You are already thought of as a rogue child. If you don't play nice, you'll be put down for a rabid dog."

"Hard to end me when you're dead," he said.

Her laugh was throaty. "How many glasses of that grape tea have you drunk? Enough to bring down a small elephant, I'd wager. You can already feel it, can't you? The dwindling supply of power, the sleepiness? That elixir was a special concoction, gifted to me by a sorceress. It was in your food, too. Night, night, my handsome prince. You'll wake up refreshed and won't remember your little Soul Stealer at all. Maybe then you'll rethink my suggestions regarding the way we should pass the time."

He huffed out a laugh. "You think you can hold me? Break *me*?"

"Not at all. I paid a handsome fee to the Wicked King in order to grant me attendance with one of his court. You've heard of the Wicked King of the dark fae, of course. He was expensive—nearly broke my operating budget—but to get a Soul Stealer, it was worth it. With her, I can rebuild my dynasty."

"*You* would try to keep Magnus's daughter?" Kieran asked. "You'd pit yourself against him?"

"What's the saying? You break it...you bought it?" She laughed. "What they did to the last Soul Stealer was highly effective. The blueprint is laid out—I only need to apply the practice. Once she is bound to me, he will have no claim." She tsked at Kieran. His eyes drooped and he swayed. He shook his head and straightened up. Her smile grew. "No one ever expects a woman. Play nice, pretend to be the peacemaker or the doormat, and men will believe the candied lies. No woman could ever outsmart them, after all. Well, now you know that some of us were made to be villains."

"They weren't lies in the beginning. Your surprise and embarrassment at being caught in my territory was genuine, we both know that. You must've known at that time that you had no chance to get Alexis. What changed your mind?"

"Yes, true. I must admit, I was surprised to be found out that day in your garden. I did not fully appreciate what a Soul Stealer could do. Legends only paint part of the picture. To answer your question, speaking to Magnus greatly enlightened me." Her eyes narrowed and she leaned forward. The cloud of violet around her intensified. She was pulling more power—clearly the energy draw was conscious when she wanted it to be, and she was managing all the connections just fine. "When I sought information, he treated me like a dog begging for scraps. He offered to help me acquire her, but the benefit would've been all his. His offer was nothing short of condescending, the arrogant prick. He needs to be taken down a peg." She sat back again, and her power gathered around her. "So I decided to take a chance. A gamble. I was a good gambler back in the day. It's how I climbed high in the social ranks. Who is removed from our magical laws? The fae, of course. And who would gladly accept money without caring that their customer intended to demean a Demigod and enslave his beau? The Wicked King of the dark fae court, obviously. And now you come full circle. Go ahead and sit down. I can see you're struggling, as surely as your men are ailing next door. And yes, by demean, I mean that when you are temporarily stripped of your mind—that is how the fae get at the memories, I gather—I will have you for my plaything. You are quite a prize. I don't think there is a handsomer Demigod. I am fertile for these next few days—you will give me a Demigod baby. It will join us together. My empire will be as it once was."

Kieran's power built even as he staggered. "The fae operate with tricky words and misleading contracts. Dealing with them is risky, at best. Even if you managed to navigate their courts, you're not smart enough to pull this off. Mark my words, you have just cemented your ruin. And I will never, ever lie in your bed."

Air slammed into Lydia, but she was already up and moving, hitting back with spirit and magically induced fear. The walls around us shook as he battered her. I suspected he was trying to pull the water from the pipes, but nothing was happening. Even the air slicing across her barely left a mark. Whatever the elixir was, it was having a devastating effect.

Fear such as I'd never known stopped my heart. The fear of losing him was so much more powerful than any fear I might have for myself. If Lydia won, he'd forget me. All our memories, all the time we'd shared, gone.

The feel of my body would be removed. The evidence of his love, his mark…

I froze as understanding dawned.

My spirit friends piled onto Lydia, sucking at her energy, some of them clawing at the violet strings. She laughed delightedly, and I knew they wouldn't be enough. Not without something to distract her.

"Remind Kieran of my mark," I yelled at Jack. Although my voice still didn't work here—the words were soaking into his awareness through spirit—it felt like my physical ears could hear sounds. "Tell him to remind her that even if he forgets me, he'll still see his mark sparkling across my skin. He will feel me deeply inside of him, connected by our souls. She can break me, but she cannot tear his mark from my flesh. She can strip me from his mind, but she cannot tear down the evidence of our love, because it is written within us. As soon as we meet, we'll fall in love all over again. I am his, and he is mine. We will always be one, and no amount of damage to our minds or physical bodies will ever change that. *Tell him!*"

Jack relayed the message to Kieran, yelling over the building magic and the screaming and shouting of spirits trying to suck the energy Lydia was stealing from others.

The door burst open. Zorn sprinted into the room, and the cats bounded in right behind him. One cat roared—so similar to a big cat cub on the African plains that it was startling—sending out a shock wave of spirit. It crashed into my soul and sent me careening to the other side of the room, still caught in Lydia's web but more distant from that creeping violet thread. The other cat launched onto Lydia as air from Kieran continued to batter her. Its claws sprang from its large paws and raked down her face. Huge gashes opened up and blood immediately pooled in them before dripping down her cheek and onto her neck.

She screamed. My spirit friends continued to pile onto her. Zorn reached her and picked her up before tossing her across the room. Her back hit the wall before her head and she slid down to the floor. Her hands flung outward and a huge blast of magical fear doused the room. Zorn froze, his knees wobbling but not buckling. He moved a leg forward, his exertion obvious.

"Guard Alexis," Kieran yelled, waving Zorn out. "Forget about me. Find Alexis's body and guard her. Set Thane loose."

The first cat jumped onto the coffee table, knocking away the food and drinks. It hunched, watching me through eerie, glowing bronze eyes—the female cat. She roared again, and another shock wave of spirit pounded into me. Lydia's invisible web hung on to me for a moment, reluctant to let go, but the cat's calls finally sent me hurtling from the room.

I punched through a wall and sailed out into dead silence. The bright desert sun beat down on me, and a bird lazily sailed through a blue sky. In the distance, a storm brewed, building quickly. Lightning would come with it, I had no doubt.

Panicked, hanging out in nothingness, I floated through the sky. I had to get back to my body. I felt it calling, and Harding had taught me how to pull myself back. There was only one problem: the shortest path to my body would take me past Lydia. I doubted I'd be allowed to escape twice.

"Lexi." Jack popped into existence next to me. He looked down before his eyes widened and his hands started to windmill. "*Oh shit!*"

"It's fine. Calm down." The words reverberated through the nothingness around us. "Spirit is holding your soul. Besides, you're already dead. What's the worst that can happen?"

"I fall, lose my shit, and end up back at your house feeling helpless, that's what." His chest rose and fell, not needing air but going through the motions of taking deep breaths anyway. "You need to get back to your body. Only Henry, Thane, and Zorn are mobile. Everyone else is fading like Kieran is. They were given a drug or something. So only three are running around trying to find you, but this place is huge and it'll take them forever. Meanwhile, one of Lydia's people can just call you in from behind the Line. They can snatch you real easy. You need to get back to your body and fight your way to the guys. You need to stand with them until Kieran is back online."

He stared at me expectantly.

"I don't know how to get back to my fucking body," I growled. "Lydia's in the way." Except there had to be a way around her, didn't there? Maybe if I just created another path…

"One step at a time," Jack said as I drifted through spirit, pulling myself along. This method of movement seemed to deplete my energy more quickly than using something else to pull me.

"I don't have any feet," I said, continuing to move.

"I know, it's a trip, right? It was really hard to get used to that. I don't mind this flying bit, though. That's not so bad. Did you see what those cats did? Something is up with those things. The thump Zorn gave Lydia didn't seem to bother her for long, but when I left, she still had blood dribbling down her face from those scratches."

Chad popped up beside us, looking harried, eyes bugging out. "Why are you out here?" he demanded. "Get back to your fucking body or you'll be permanently in this space with us. Lydia sent her team to recover you, and Kieran is down for the count."

Mia popped up next to me, her eyes wild, the air about her panicked. Her spirit looked sunken and weak, almost inflating like being slowly pumped up.

"Mia!" I cried, barely stopping myself from lurching for her and trying to wrap her in a hug. "Mia! It's you! Where have you been?"

Her eyes focused on me, and then seemed to notice Jack and Chad. Her eyebrows lowered. "I don't know. That bitch Demigod grabbed me out of the blue. Me and a couple others that were on duty. It happened so fast—we saw her, and before I could say anything, we were...tethered... It felt like she tethered me or something. I heard you call, though. I heard you...call...and the ropes disappeared..." Her eyes clouded. She shook her head. "What's happening? Where are we?"

I kept pulling myself toward my body, hopefully far enough to the side that I wouldn't sail past Lydia. My energy sank fast.

"She needs to get back to her body," Chad said.

"Her body is in some strange hall with Bria and a really handsome man. I popped up there first. I can get back there." Mia grabbed my shoulder as though I actually had one.

Lights and colors speckled my vision. A *whoosh* washed over me. The world stopped spinning, and Mia let me go, the two of us now hovering in spirit back where I'd started.

Dylan held my lifeless body in his arms, standing in the middle of the corridor with Red on one side and Bria on the other, both of them brandishing weapons. Daisy stood behind them, a dagger at the ready, her eyes hard and fearless, and Mordecai waited not far from his pile of clothes, in wolf form. Several grim-faced men and women were slowly advancing on them, the same way a gardener with a shovel would creep up on a poisonous snake. They'd found me fast.

There was no sign of the shadow man from earlier, but I had no time to spare. I dove back into my body and gasped for air, the transition seamless, before pulling on the Line and filling myself with power. I rolled out of Dylan's arms, startling him, before grabbing up our attackers' fluttering souls and yanking. The souls slammed against their casings, and the dozen advancing enemies staggered but didn't go down.

"Take them out!" I yelled, my body shaking and sucking as much as I could from the Line. It pulsed quickly, matching my beating heart again, sending waves of power through me.

"What do you need?" Jack asked, falling in at my side. John and Chad were there a moment later, followed, unbelievably, by Frank.

"What's the status here?" Frank asked as Red ran at the enemy. She flung her hands forward, one after the other, alternating. Knives appeared between her fingers before blooming in enemy bodies, so fast that I couldn't keep track, and neither could they.

"Ah yes. Battle. Your mother was a great fighter. Attack them!" Frank motioned me on.

"I can't yet," I yelled, sucking in more power, feeling it bolster my body. Just a bit more, and I'd be back in business, I could feel it. I might not have done an oath, but I still had the benefits of the blood bond, and healed at faster rates.

"Yes, you sure can, young lady. Your mother said you had a sprinkling of her in you, and I've seen it. Go on, now—don't be the lame duck of this battle party."

Red ripped a falling body to the side, punched forward, miraculously found and produced a knife in her fist at the last moment, and sliced open a neck. She punched with her other hand as she whirled, sticking out a foot and slamming her sole into a nose. The crack made me wince. The man fell with blood already running down his lips.

Bria followed Red through the group, her own knives ripping and stabbing, finishing off whoever Red hadn't.

Magical fear tingled across my body and bit into my skin, but it was absolutely nothing compared to what Lydia or Aaron could do. A slim slice of spirit slashed my skin, and Dylan sucked in a startled breath.

"Gotta be about time," I said, running forward.

"That's my girl! Give 'em hell!" Frank shouted.

I ripped across the soul casings of a few of Lydia's minions I could feel running toward our skirmish, saving my strength in case the others flagged. Red pulled a gun out of God knew where, stood still for two beats, and shot three times. The last three bodies fell. Bria glanced up before plucking her knife from someone's eye.

"Bria, do you have your Necromancer stuff with you?" I asked, jogging after Red and making sure the kids were keeping up.

Red descended on the group I'd slowed like a falling star, clearly in her element with her fighting magic in close quarters. She cracked someone's neck, dodged a punch, grabbed an arm and bent it the wrong way, moving all the time.

"The one time I'm without it," Bria said. "You don't have the energy?"

"I don't have as much as I'd like," I answered.

"We're bound to encounter another Necromancer in this place," she said, falling back with me. "Or a few. Find me one and I'll take their shit. I don't think it's wise for us to go back to the suite."

"We need to work toward the meeting room Kieran is in. He's been drugged. He's out. Three of the guys are heading toward me. Us. And the cats." I felt five more people coming, running our way. "Low-level fours coming," I hollered. I punched their spirit boxes as we turned a corner, heading for the stairs.

They stood in the way, recovering from the attack far faster than most people would. We were dealing with Hades magical people now, and they were no strangers to having spirit used against them.

Lightning rained down from the ceiling, striking each of them in the head. Three screamed. The other two didn't get a chance before all five started convulsing, electrocution not a fast or pretty death. Suddenly I didn't feel so bad about the things I could do.

The lightning slid along the ceiling and crawled down the wall like a live thing. It seeped into the carpet, leaving scorch marks in its wake. The hall smelled like burned skin and hair, and I needed a second to stare in shock and keep from retching.

"Well, what are you waiting for? A red carpet?" Frank said, jerking me out of my daze. "Get moving."

"That was gross," I said, pausing at the landing.

"That *was* gross." Bria nodded. "Poor Jerry isn't going to like that one bit."

"Lightning isn't always pretty," Dylan said.

"Which way?" I asked.

Bria took the map from Red, who was quickly cleaning weapons and tucking them away. "He's on the third floor at the other end of the building. If we go this way"—she pointed down the hall—"we'll pass that weird stuffed-animal asylum and maybe I can get some of them active, eh? Just need to find a Necromancer. Too bad they usually hide from the action."

We started jogging, passing lower-level staff hiding behind plants, in doorways, and one crouched behind a potted plant half her size.

A roar shook the foundation of the building. It echoed down the corridor we'd chosen and tumbled across the floor above us.

"Thane has gone Berserk," Bria said. "Watch for him, Lexi. Do not cross his path."

"You're talking to me like I don't know what he's capable of. Two ahead, high level three."

Mordecai loped ahead of us, and I didn't try to stop him. I couldn't hold him back forever—I'd save that for when the enemy was more powerful than a level three.

He snarled as he leapt on the first of the crew, the sound competing with another of Thane's roars. Daisy darted ahead of us with a burst of speed. She threw a knife mid-stride. It flew, end over end, and dug into the chest of the second interloper, a woman dressed in spandex. She stopped and clutched at the knife hilt, looking down in confusion. Mordecai slammed her to the ground.

Zorn's soul popped onto my radar, on the same level but at the other side of the building. Henry ran with him.

"That way," I said, pointing before jumping over the newly downed enemy and racing through the hall beyond her. Suits of armor lined one side, each in its own glass case. Along the other were elaborate dresses of the same time period, and I sure wished we'd strolled through this room yesterday instead of the nightmare stuffed-animal room.

We burst out the other side, directly into a throng of people running down the corridor toward Zorn and Henry. A roar ripped through the air, and something heavy fell on the floor above us. The sound of it banging and then rolling filled the air.

Red stabbed a guy and ripped him to the ground before he knew he was being attacked. A woman cracked Red over the shoulder with a steel pipe, and Red turned, gun suddenly in hand, and shot steel-pipe woman in the face. Crimson sprayed those behind her.

I grabbed the spirit boxes of anyone I didn't recognize while yelling, "Zorn! Over here, Zorn!"

"Sure, yeah, alert the whole world." Bria bent and scooped up the dropped pipe. She turned and *thwacked* a woman in the face with it before clunking a man in the forehead.

A woman appeared at my side and reached for me. I startled, immediately reaching for her soul.

An arm wrapped around my middle and yanked me back against a strong chest. Dylan. He brought his other arm around in front of me, stretching it forward. Lightning ran from his elbow, down to his hand, and then out through his fingertips. It blasted into the woman's middle, flinging her back. She hit the wall and started to sink.

Dylan released me, and I grabbed the soul as it left her body then shoved it right back in. Power pumped through my blood. The wobbles in my knees were mostly gone. Time to use the full gamut of my magic.

And not a moment too soon.

"She's coming," Zorn said as he reached us. He hacked down on a man's shoulder with a machete, of all things. Zorn definitely did not fuck around. "She's weakened, but she's still too strong for you, Alexis. We need to hide you."

The cats ran around him in their eagerness to get to me. They rubbed up against my legs, sleeker and less pushy than dogs of their size. Done with their greeting, they took their places at my sides, battle cats. My life kept getting weirder, somehow.

"How are you going to hide me?" I shoved another soul in a body and sent the two commandeered minions running in the direction Zorn had come. They wouldn't last long, but they'd be a small distraction. "She can find me in spirit and send people to my location. Or just ask the staff. We can't run, either. No one is just going to hand us cars. We have to fight, Zorn."

"She's a Demigod, and Henry and I are strangely weakened. Neither of us ate or drank anything provided, but we're still sluggish. We can't take her."

Lydia must've unleashed the spirits on them to harvest their energy. That was probably why they'd been kept in a different room, out of sight of Kieran. He would've been able to see the spirits hanging around, if nothing else.

"We cannot win," Zorn said above the din, the crashes and screams from upstairs now farther away. Thane was moving around.

"We have to try," I said, my heart breaking at the thought of what would happen if we failed. "We have to try to get to Kieran. If we can hold them off until he wakes—"

"We have no idea when that'll be," Henry said, shoving in. Sweat and blood coated the side of his face. Desperation clouded his eyes. "We have to hide you."

But there would be no hiding me, and we all knew it.

I pushed them away and held my head high. I would fight, and if I lost, then my only hope was that Kieran would see me again someday, recognize the mark, connect that with the feeling in his soul, and we'd find a way to be together again. I had to hope.

Chapter 31

ALEXIS

"WELL, WELL, WELL." Lydia stopped fifty feet down the corridor, each side of her face sporting bloody claw marks, and the space opening at her back into a hall. She could dive out of harm's way if she needed. That wasn't ideal.

My team fanned out around me, Zorn and Henry flanking the cats and everyone else behind, surrounding the kids.

"My little plan worked, in the end." Lydia's smile pulled at her wounds.

"There's more to winning than the acquisition of assets," I said, having heard that from Kieran at one point. "You'll never pull this off."

"What do you know, girl?" Lydia sneered, walking toward me. "Have respect for myself, isn't that what you said?" Even from this distance, I could tell she was looking me up and down. "Look at you. Your ridiculous clothes, your plain face—getting attention from the servants made you uncomfortable yesterday, didn't it? I knew then that you could never sit at my table in your present state. You'll welcome my attentions, trust me. I'll teach you how to be a lady, how to treat those lesser than you, and how to be so much more than this blunt tool Kieran brought me. And in return, I'll let you play with the baby Kieran puts inside me."

Pain ate through me. I blinked away tears.

"It is not wise to taunt a Price woman," I heard from somewhere in the back. Frank was still on the scene. "Just you wait. Taunt a Price woman, and you are toying with your life."

"Let me through." Dylan pushed his way in front of Henry. "There are level-five leaders that can take a Demigod."

"Yes, with their full arsenal. We only have a few," Zorn murmured.

"You could've killed Flora." Dylan side-eyed me. "Couldn't you have?"

"Yes," I said, licking my lips. Souls in bodies came up behind us, her people blocking us in.

"A few is all we need," Dylan said. He fisted his fingers and electricity zipped around his knuckles. "The others can keep her people off us. I'll distract her. You can pry out her soul."

Lydia's smug grin made it seem like she'd heard us. Or maybe just read our plan for a last-ditch effort. She motioned, and her people surged around her, running at us.

Dylan stepped forward and flexed his hand. A peal of thunder rolled from him, thankfully muted. It hit the enemy almost like a tangible thing, and it was clearly not muted for them. They cried out, grabbed their ears, and blew back, their backs slamming into the ground.

Lydia visibly recoiled, staggering backward with her hands halfway to her head, her face slacking in shock.

Dylan stepped forward and electricity rolled up his arms, around his torso, and then danced on his whole body. It moved and fizzed over him, some parts sparking, others spitting.

"Is that…" Lydia's eyebrows pinched together. "Is that a Lightning Rod?" She either wasn't well informed, or Kieran had done a good job of hiding some facts.

Dylan showed her the answer.

Lightning rained down on her and her people in sheets, and he shot out his hands, spraying targeted bolts of lightning from his fingertips. Electricity sprang up on the walls to either side of Lydia before zipping down behind her, arcing across and around in the shape of rounded bars.

She screamed, pushed forward by the bars, and nearly landed in one of the sheets of electricity raining down.

"Get to it," Dylan said, and I could hear the strain in his voice.

Red and Zorn wasted no time, running forward with their weapons meeting Lydia's forces head-on. I tore out the souls at our backs and shoved them back in, sending them away to fight anyone that should come. It would buy us time. I dug into Lydia's chest, going to work on her prongs, scrabbling at her soul.

"Thanks for the help, but there are too many coming back here," I heard Bria shout.

"Put your back into it," Frank yelled.

The female cat roared, flapping my soul in its casing. The line of enemies cowered for a moment and the other cat launched, attacking with the gusto of a young tiger.

Dylan turned, looking behind us, every muscle on his body flexing. Another wave of thunder rolled through the corridor, making our people flinch, even with it muted, and those flanking us from behind were flattened. The bars behind Lydia wavered. Dylan's breath was already coming fast. He was out of magical shape.

I disintegrated one of Lydia's prongs and quickly moved to the next while also trying to soak past her soul casing.

"The books didn't say you'd be so powerful," Lydia screamed, one hand clutching at her chest, the other flying out, sending magical fear to drown us.

"The books didn't account for a soul link and a

blood bond with a Demigod of Poseidon!" I gritted my teeth against the fear. Dylan's knees wobbled and he sank, curling in on himself. "Fight it, Dylan. It isn't real. Fear is a pathway to greatness." I'd probably gotten one of Bria's fear quotes wrong, but it would have to do. "Fight it to save your life!"

I kept trying to get past Lydia's prongs and soak into her soul, thwarted by the colossal power continuously pouring into her from those purple strands of power. I had to cut her contacts with the souls.

A blast made me flinch back, and I was losing hold of Lydia.

Thane crashed through the wall up ahead, between us and Lydia. Brick and plaster flew, striking Red and knocking her to the side. Two enemies fell. Thane looked down then roared.

In his Berserker form, he was just as likely to kill us as he was the others.

Fear shook me to my very roots, not magically inspired this time, and infinitely more effective because of it. I ignored my primal side urging me to run.

Thane bent and clubbed the two enemies, who'd made the mistake of struggling to their feet, with a huge fist. He smashed them still. I watched as their souls popped out, still looking terrified.

Red didn't move, her eyes wide, her muscles flexing.

She was probably shitting herself, but she was doing the right thing: play dead and it would go away.

Dylan struck Thane with a bolt, eliciting another of those terror-inducing roars. One more bolt struck down, just beyond him, then another, and some of Lydia's minions started running down the corridor like ants to avoid being struck. It was all the incentive Thane needed.

He thundered toward them, nearly taking up the whole space on his own. He swung his great hand, slamming an enemy's back and sending him hurtling. Then he did the same with another, tossing them like stones.

I caught a glimpse of Lydia throwing out her hand. Thane slowed a little, shaking his head. His next roar was pained. And pissed. She'd probably tried to use spirit of some kind, but Thane was used to combating spirit. He was used to pushing through the misery of it. It made him harder to defeat, and ten times more dangerous for people of Hades.

He picked up his pace again, trampling five people in his wake. He slashed at Lydia with his whips, then barreled right into her, knocking her through the bars of lightning and away left, taking them both out of sight.

Zorn ran to the hole in the wall. He stopped there, looking through.

"Need…help," Bria shouted, and Mordecai yelped.

Dylan turned, thrusting his hands forward and sending lightning racing across the walls, creating more bars. His face was red and sweaty, and his chest rose and fell quickly. He was dead tired.

"Run." I waved everyone after me. "Red, are you okay?"

She got up slowly, obviously in pain. "I'll live."

"Run! Let's get to Kieran." I reached Zorn and stopped dead, my heart in my throat.

Dozens of Lydia's forces littered the great hall. Half of them were already running to help Lydia with Thane, but the other half were staring at Zorn, who was staring at them.

"Is there another way?" I asked desperately as Bria and the others pushed us forward. They were running from yet more enemy forces. They'd clearly managed to break through Dylan's flagging magic.

"Maybe we're faster," Zorn said. "Kill everyone you can. We can't take Lydia and all of her people. Just kill everyone you can and we'll make a break for it."

He puffed into gas, and I ran through the hole in the wall, looking at all the dangling ribbons and grabbing them—feeling those behind us and grabbing those, too. I pulled as hard as I could, using all the power from the Line I could muster. I pulled at them and just barely tugged most of them free. Bodies dropped like flies.

Spirits rose in the aftermath. I didn't have the energy to put them back into their bodies and use them.

Zorn rematerialized and slashed down his machete, cleaving a chest in two. He hacked at another and took down one more. Lightning fell down from the sky, striking six more dead. I took up another six ribbons and yanked. The souls hit against their casings. I yanked again, giving it everything I had. Only one popped free.

"Hurry," I said, out of breath, my legs made of jelly.

I chanced a glance behind me and nearly cried. Thane lay facedown, his limbs spread out to the sides. Lydia climbed to her feet, and although she was unsteady, her arm at the wrong angle, she was still alive. Fucking Demigods were hard to kill.

"It is useless," she shouted, and I could hear the pain lacing her words. "I prepared for this. I hired dozens. There is nowhere for you to go. You are outnumbered! Give yourself up now, and I will not kill your friends and children."

She'd said the magic words.

I slowed, drooping. Dylan bumped up against my back and then staggered away, as tired as I was. The cats slinked around me. Mordecai and Daisy shuffled in close, the first time I'd seen them show defeat.

This was it. It was over. She might not be able to carry this off in the long run, but in the short term, she was doing a bang-up job of ruining my life.

"You win," I said, pain bleeding through me. "Give me a moment."

I turned and looked at the faces of my kids. Daisy looked so sweet and innocent, except she was splattered with blood. Mordecai had such kind eyes, even in wolf form.

"Forget me," I told them, tears running down my face. "Forget you ever knew me. Get clear of here and go into hiding. Get out of the magical world and stay that way. You don't want to see what I will become."

"She will not get away with this," Daisy said through gritted teeth. "We've lost the battle, but we will *not* lose this war, Lexi. We won't lose you." Tears filled her eyes and she couldn't blink them all away. Her lip trembled. "We will not lose the war," she whispered again.

Mordecai shifted back to human, his eyes already welling with tears. "She won't kill Kieran, Lexi. She can't. He'll fix this. He will. If anyone can fix this, he can."

I didn't tell them what she had in store for him. Couldn't.

Sobs choked me.

"Look after Kieran," I told Bria softly. "He'll need it."

Her brow furrowed. "She won't get away with this, Alexis. Demigods aren't untouchable. Don't let them break you. Keep your wits so you can give us time. We'll get you out of this."

Zorn stared at me, his machete lowered, his face flat, and his eyes on fire.

"You're a damn fine man, Zorn," I told him. "Stay prickly. I'm glad to have known you."

He didn't respond.

I laid my hand on Dylan's shoulder.

"I'm sorry," I told him. "I'm sorry I fucked up your life."

"You gave me something to fight for," he replied. "Someone to fight against. I'm done with Demigods doing shit like this. Done with it. It has to stop. It *will* stop. Give us time, as Bria said. Don't give in. We'll get you out."

"That's enough. Take her," Lydia said. She hadn't moved, beyond getting to her feet, and looked close to collapsing.

I turned to say goodbye to Red when I heard, "That won't be necessary."

The voice was smooth and confident. The crowd parted, giving me a view of the man as he entered the hall. His strut suggested money and power in large quantities. He held his shoulders back and his head high, not hurrying, taking time to let everyone see him. One hand was in his trouser pocket, and the other swung gracefully at his side. His three-piece suit was black on black, perfectly tailored and without a wrinkle or spot of lint. A silver tie dipped into his vest, and a matching silver pocket square accentuated his jacket pocket.

His soul pulsed strangely, bright one moment, and thick and dark the next, somewhat erratic. Something looked vaguely familiar about him. Although it was hard to judge his age, he looked to be in his late forties, with a strong, square jaw devoid of stubble, lips on the thin side, and a nose that was a touch too large. Despite that, or maybe even because of it, he was incredibly striking. He drew the eye and then kept it interested, his charisma unmistakable.

"What are you doing here?" Lydia spat, pulling herself up straight despite the pain it clearly gave her.

"I've learned the hard way that it is important to get with the times." His people followed him into the room, all wearing suits, women included, not here to fight, or if they were, they would look very stylish as they did so. "Your surveillance feeds have been live streaming for the past hour. All of this"—he gestured around the room—"has been recorded. Demigod Kieran's people are excellent in this field, and they made sure to cover their asses as soon as this started going down. I was close by, so I thought I might lend a hand. Your people didn't do a great job of keeping him contained, by the way. You gave him way too little of whatever drug you used. Rope to hold a Demigod of his caliber?" He laughed. "He might be young, but he is Valens's son."

"It would've been the right dose if he had continued consuming it all day, as I'd planned," she ground out. "This ridiculous, untrained, irrational little girl disturbed my plans."

"Yes." The man gave a tiny smile. "She has a sprinkle of her mother's Chaos magic in her blood. Level fives sometimes have a smattering of the recessive magic within their arsenal. It is a handy magic to have on one's side in these situations. Not so fortunate when it is used against you, as you saw, Lydia."

With the slow, deliberate way he talked about my mother's magic, it felt like he was explaining it to me specifically. I couldn't breathe. He'd obviously looked me up in the files, which was all well and good, but I'd never known what my mother could do. We'd never talked about magic growing up, and because of that, I'd never thought to ask. I'd never thought to dig into her past life.

So many things suddenly made sense. How she could turn up at a store, and something would happen to throw the whole place into disarray, allowing us to grab a few things we couldn't otherwise afford and hightail it out of there without being noticed. Or bills that would randomly be forgiven because of some crazy mix-up with the company. The list was long, and I'd just always assumed she was eccentric. It had been fun, truth be told, living in all that chaos. I'd never really minded. Now I knew why.

"You should've done your homework. You are out of touch, my dear," the man said as I came out of my shocked stupor. "Your people upstairs are all dead, and, last I saw, Demigod Kieran was making his way out of the room. This was moments ago. I think I might've just saved your life. From what I understand, he is not entirely rational where his mark holder is concerned."

"You didn't save my life! You caused my ruin!" Lydia screamed.

"My goodness, it is not a good look when a Demigod loses control." He spread his free hand wide, his smile giving him a little something extra that really suited him. Why did he look so vaguely familiar? "One must not blame others for one's downfall. Rather, one must learn to play the game. I simply outmaneuvered you, Lydia. Had you not interfered with my plans a century ago, I would not have had to usher you out of my way. And here we are, at your downfall. What a treat, for it all to be recorded on video."

The man stopped in the center of the hall, below a chandelier that was catching and throwing the light streaming in a far window, and framed by a high arch sparkling with gold trim. It would've been an excellent photo op. He seemed like the kind of guy who knew it.

"Escort her out," he said, talking to a petite woman

with tight curls and a pink suit. She smiled pleasantly, motioned at a few others, and headed toward Lydia.

"You have no authority here." Lydia pointed behind him. "You will leave. Now!"

"Not until we have this situation rectified," the man said patiently, but steel lined his words. "Attacking another Demigod in this underhanded way is highly frowned upon. You know that, Lydia. I wouldn't be doing my duty to the magical community if I didn't step in. As the closest Demigod on hand, I have an obligation to keep order."

His soul burned black and his smile said this had nothing to do with helping another Demigod and everything to do with *checkmate*. Which was fine by me, all things considered.

The previously pleasant-looking woman with the tight curls grabbed Lydia's broken arm and twisted it brutally. Lydia screamed before the woman's team bodily picked her up and hustled her out.

"Stand down," the man said to Lydia's people. "This is Demigod business. It is not worth you dying over."

Her people shifted and swayed, exchanging furtive looks, but the man didn't seem to notice. He was already crossing the room to me, just as self-assured as when he'd walked in.

I stiffened when he stopped in front of me and his gaze roamed my face. Something changed in his eyes, but I couldn't quite put my finger on.

"You've created quite a mess here." He gave a glance around the room to punctuate his words. "You certainly have your mother in you. She could turn the most organized situation into a madhouse, laughing all the while. You look just like her. Except for the eyes, of course. Those you got from me."

Chapter 32

ALEXIS

I GAPED, MY mouth opening and closing like a fish's. I'd seen a couple of pictures of him, but he'd been younger in them. Diminished, somehow. They hadn't at all done him justice. Despite a vague sense of recognition, I hadn't even recognized him!

"Magnus." Kieran entered the room from the far right. In all the commotion, I hadn't felt him coming. His face was pale, he'd lost his jacket, his shirt was wrinkled and his hair stood on end, but for all that, he looked just as cool and collected as the man standing in front of me.

"Ah." The man turned slightly, allowing for Kieran's entry. Could this smooth, collected man really be Magnus? He didn't at all seem like the horrible tyrant kid killer whose staff member had caused Jack's death. Being around him put me at ease rather than set me on edge. Was that his gift—no one saw his ill deeds coming? It had certainly worked with Lydia. Perhaps it was a trait of Hades Demigods. Dylan had tried to warn us.

"We finally meet." Magnus closed the distance to Kieran and stuck out his hand. "So glad to make your acquaintance."

"Likewise, of course." Kieran's shake was short, and he quickly brushed by Magnus, his eyes landing on me and devouring every inch. "Are you okay?" he asked.

Jerry, Donovan, and Boman entered the hall, looking a good deal more shaken than Kieran. Boman jogged to Thane, and so many emotions were already running through me that I didn't allow that to distract me. Thane's soul still glowed as it should. He wasn't critical. Not yet. I'd hold his soul in place later, if it came to that.

"Yes," I said, grabbing his arms. "Are you?"

Kieran slid an arm around my shoulders and pulled me in close as he turned to face Magnus, who had resumed his place in front of me.

"What went on here today has been recorded," Kieran said, and Magnus raised his hand.

"I am well aware. And you are aware, I'm sure, the unedited version was sent to me. I will not deny that, when presented with an opportunity to get my daughter and her incredible magic in my house, I was all ears."

Amber, who likely orchestrated all of this, must've edited the live stream to remove the part about Lydia contacting Magnus. Only she'd kept the footage to let Magnus know he owed us a favor. Kieran now had something to keep Magnus in line for a moment. Or so I hoped.

"I assume the desire to...grab Alexis is why you are here now," Kieran said, his voice hard. "You were looking for an opportunity."

"I had an opportunity." Magnus's subtle smile held dangerous secrets. "A perfect opportunity came and went before any of this even started. She stepped into spirit to solve a riddle. I could've easily grabbed her. Instead, I helped her figure out another little slice of her magic, and then off she went to find the source of the problem."

My stomach rolled and my mouth dropped all the way to the floor.

The grumpy guy!

Magnus was the grumpy shadow guy who had been lurking around in spirit, helping me?

It couldn't be!

My mind spun. He'd shoved me out of spirit and back into my body countless times. At first, I'd considered those interventions an annoyance, but ultimately I'd come to realize the shadow person was helping me, saving me from dangers I didn't yet understand. He'd saved my life! He'd also helped me figure things out, pushing me in the right direction or showing me how to do something when the concepts were complex.

I couldn't do anything but stare as my mind tried to

fit this information into the larger picture. Magnus had sent someone to kidnap me! He'd spied on me at home and devised a plan to take me away from Kieran, and said plan had gotten Jack killed. My kids had very nearly been casualties too. Not to mention he could've stepped in to help me today way before he had. He'd hung out in the area because of this meeting, probably hoping to poach me from Lydia if she succeeded. He was not a good guy—his history and reputation made that perfectly clear.

So why had he helped me?

Another thought shook my world.

He'd known about me before the battle with Valens had introduced me to the world. He must've. He'd helped me before anyone beyond Kieran and our group had known about my magical type. I didn't know how to disguise myself when in spirit—I wasn't a shadow there. No one else had magic like mine, and I could've only come from a few people. If he knew I had his eyes, and he knew my mother...

"Now what?" Kieran asked Magnus, holding me tightly against him. "The cameras are still rolling."

"Yes, they are. My team is trying to wrest control from Amber. They aren't having much success. She started out excellent, and Valens made her exceptional. He had a knack for seeking out those with potential and building them up to greatness." Magnus paused for a moment, and the pointed look he gave Kieran said it all. Valens had done the same thing with Kieran, and Magnus recognized it. He was giving Kieran a nod of respect. "Did you know I offered her a job?"

"Yes. She used it as a bartering chip."

Magnus chuckled. "Of course she did. Clever woman." His gaze slid to the side, landing on Dylan. "And you've resurrected the dead. You're Amell Maccini, correct?"

Dylan said nothing, just held Magnus's gaze.

"Gianna's prized Thunderstroke alive, all this time, and no one was the wiser. Somehow, miraculously, Demigod Kieran found you. What a lucky fellow to find a Spirit Walker *and* a Thunderstroke, all before he has even proved himself." Magnus's gaze landed on the cats next. They were flanking me, the male licking his paw and the female lying on her stomach, looking at Magnus judgmentally. "Where did you get those cats?"

"A stray had kittens," I said. "These two wouldn't let us re-home them."

"What magical beast has enhanced their genetics? As we can all agree, these are not from a normal stray." Magnus narrowed his eyes at me, and I could see the wheels turning.

"Honestly, I have no idea," I said. "They are from a normal stray. Two normal strays, actually. I, unfortunately, saw them…in a private moment." My face warmed under Magnus's calculating stare.

"Coming back to my question," Kieran said, "now what? Where do we go from here? You won't be leaving with Alexis, as I'm sure you know."

"Now what, yes. Good question." Magnus tucked his hand into his trouser pocket. He looked around, and it was clear he was making note of the cameras. "I will say this: Alexis raised some good points while in spirit. Whatever your reasons for giving it to her, she has your mark, and she has created a soul link between you. The only way to successfully separate the two of you would be to kill one of you. And if someone were to kill you, Demigod Kieran, it would severely affect Alexis's performance. I've felt what it's like to lose a soul-link partner. It is a hard thing to come back from. Even if Alexis were to be...retrained"—his tone said he meant reprogrammed—broken down and built back up, as Lydia had said—"she would feel the loss. She'd feel it, but she wouldn't understand it, and so she wouldn't be able to properly grieve. It would drive her to madness, and that would create a very dangerous situation. Controlling someone with Chaos blood is not easy. Combine that with the power of a Spirit Walker? People would die. Many people. Then they would come back, controlled by her, and wreak absolute havoc. She would need to be killed, like the last Spirit Walker. She'd do more harm than good in the long run."

Magnus was basically using the cameras to get out a warning—killing Kieran to get to me wasn't a good idea. He was saying the words that would essentially protect me. It would've been a relief, if Aaron were the type to admit defeat, and if there weren't the past to consider.

Kieran must've had the same thought, as he asked, "Does any of that matter to you? Given your past, I'd assumed you wouldn't be interested in keeping her around."

"My past, yes." Fire burned in Magnus's eyes, so hot and ruthless that I tried to take a step back. I saw something else in his eyes, too, though. A wound. Raw, weeping loss. "As I said, it is not easy to control someone with Chaos blood. It is not legal to kill someone because of a grudge, either, even for a Demigod. I well understand the importance of law and order in these modern times." His tone was lofty, and it was clear he was not speaking to us, but talking to whoever might be seeing the footage. It was also quite clear he hadn't answered the question. "I find I am in a bind. So this is what I propose, Demigod Kieran. If the two of you do not continue to harm the interests of my territory, I will see no reason to dig up past family grievances of which she played no part. She has existed this long without being troublesome, and if you keep her...coloring within the magical lines, we'll say"—his eyes crinkled with his small smile—"then we can coexist as any two Demigods and their staff—"

"Significant other," Kieran interrupted. "She is my significant other, whom I hope will one day wish to co-lead with me. She is not on my staff. She has no blood oath. She is of independent mind and soul. I can no more control her than any man can control his partner."

"Be that as it may, the events that have come to pass have put you in charge of her magical upbringing. You are tasked with teaching her our laws and making sure she follows them. Her failure will fall on you both, and if it impacts my territory, I will be forced to act. I am sure you can understand that."

Kieran nodded once, almost a bow. "I can. That compromise is fair."

"In addition…" Magnus paused again, then raised his voice. "If anyone shall threaten her, or strive to take her from you unlawfully, I will feel it is my duty to intercede." This pause lasted longer, and I held my breath. "After all, if I can't act on a grudge, or even welcome my flesh and blood onto my staff, I certainly won't let someone else force the issue. The rules of *dibs* are well known."

Kieran's laugh was forced, as was Magnus's. I held my breath, trying to sort through all of the emotions running through me.

K.F. BREENE

His gaze on me was kind, and it was hard to understand how such a ruthless man could have such a comforting presence. I found myself wanting to know more about him. It was a foolish thought, given who he was, but my mother was gone, and so help me God, I wanted to know what it was like to have a father.

But I had to remember that he was a Demigod of Hades. Lydia had been able to trick us, and Magnus was *so* much better at his job than her. We'd thwarted him this time, but I couldn't be so naive as to think he'd given up the battle. Magnus's strength was in the long game—I'd heard that from Kieran and his people often enough. Building up a relationship with me was a good foundation for snatching me up if something were to ever happen to Kieran. Something he might make happen to Kieran. Then Magnus could swoop in, helping me grieve and securing his claim on the Soul Stealer these people had apparently always wanted.

I swallowed down the aching in my heart and held on to Kieran. Why wish for a thing that might be your ruin, when you already had the thing that was your salvation?

"Until we meet again," Magnus said to me, his focus acute. "And remember, when you go into spirit, make sure your body is safe and guarded. Trust very few with the whereabouts of your body when you are outside of it. You will learn ways to break out of someone's hold in spirit. You are strong enough to escape even a Demigod, but if someone gets your body, it is game over."

Kieran laughed. "You don't know Alexis and her wards very well. When it comes to them, nothing is game over. We'll speak more, Magnus. For now, we need to pack up and head home."

"Of course. Yes." Magnus took a step back. "I'm glad I was able to help."

"It is Lydia you saved, not Alexis. Hopefully Lydia will see her way out of the trouble the dark fae are sure to bring to her doorstep."

Kieran led us away, and Magnus—my father—watched us the whole time.

No, not us. Me. His gaze was rooted to me, and I could see the turbulence in the dark depths of his eyes.

Kieran walked us through the hole Thane had created, cutting off my view of my father. That was when reality dawned on me. I jerked forward, trying to get a look at him. I was too tired and low on energy to feel more than my immediate surroundings.

"Thane!" I said.

"What?"

I started, completely off my game. Then again, with the fatigue dragging me down, I didn't have a game just now.

Thane sat in the ruined corridor with his back against the wall, his knees pulled up and his head in his hands. Boman stood next to him with a fading bruise on the side of his face, as though he'd fallen face first.

Thane turned his head, his bleary eyes finding me. "You made it," he said.

"I made it? *You* made it! Are you okay? I felt your soul, but you were lying facedown." I stopped beside him and bent, putting a hand on his hard shoulder.

"That ol' Demigod rang my bell." He groaned as he moved, slowly inching up the wall until standing. "Can we go home now, sir? I'm done in."

"Yes. Daisy?" Kieran turned to the quiet teen coming up behind us, her eyes puffy, looking unsure.

My heart broke. Daisy had thought she would lose me like she'd almost lost Mordecai. She had thought I would be taken from her. The fear hadn't yet faded, and it was written across her face. She was as tough as they came, but she was still a kid, and I was her lifeline. In the turbulent world in which she lived, I was her rock, like any parent would be.

Tears came to my eyes, and emotion filled the soul link. Kieran had pieced together what I was thinking.

"Thane blew this place to hell," he told Daisy softly. "Go ahead and take whatever you want. On the sly, mind. Just make sure you can fit it in a bag and get it out of here."

Daisy's eyes lit up. She'd make the most of it.

"I call dibs on some of those weird stuffed animals,"

Bria said quickly, and limped back the way we'd come. "I'm not going to be sly about it, either. I earned it. Fuckers."

Kieran started forward again, quiet for a moment. "I felt how you reacted to Magnus," he said, glancing at me. "I'm not going to entirely warn you away from him. There is definite strategy at play in what he's doing, but he just put a 'do not disturb' sign on your head. He protected you in a major way. He didn't have to—there were other ways to get me to back off—so his choice should be acknowledged."

"But?" I whispered, the tears flowing. All the emotion of the last few hours was catching up to me.

"But...Magnus will always have an end game in mind. He will always look for the thing that benefits him most. He has lived a long, prestigious life doing exactly that. With him, it is always wise to exercise caution."

"Says the man that had a big blind spot to Demigod Lydia," Mordecai grumbled.

Thane and Donovan laughed.

"He's got you there," Donovan said, rubbing welts on his wrists that hadn't healed yet. Apparently they'd all been tied up, not just Kieran.

"This is a lesson I won't soon forget," Kieran mumbled, turning toward the guest suites. "I think I'll wait until after the summit before I visit anyone else. I need alliances. Solid, concrete alliances. Despite what Magnus said, the magical laws are only as good as those who enforce them, and those who enforce them have to know something is going on first. Demigods are good about operating behind closed doors. I need people who will cry foul if someone does me wrong. Otherwise we'll never be truly protected."

"Remember that shadow that helped with Will Green and Valens?" I still couldn't get my mind around it. "It also kicked me out of spirit the day we fought Valens, preventing me from coming to, gasping and then drowning before you were there to save me. If it hadn't, that would've been the end of me." I blew out a breath, preparing myself to even say it out loud. "That was Magnus."

Kieran looked down at me with a furrowed brow. "You're sure?"

"Yes. It was the same guy I saw here today, He was helping me before we battled Valens. Before anyone knew I existed."

Back in the suite, Kieran ignored everyone working around us, packing up and getting ready. He stared down into my eyes. "He must've known what you were."

"Yes."

"Can't you find anyone in spirit, no matter where they're physically located?"

"You have to know the person, or have something of theirs. He wouldn't have been on hand to help me if he hadn't been keeping tabs on my activities." I took a deep breath. "He wouldn't bother keeping tabs on a stranger."

"But…" He shook his head. "He could've grabbed you anytime back then. I was keeping watch on you, but not to the degree I would've needed to protect you from a Demigod. Our greatest defense was my father not knowing about you. If Magnus knew about you back then, why is he only showing an interest now?"

"He showed an interest when he first started to help me. He's only doing something about that interest now…after I went public with my magic. After people started wondering whose daughter I was."

Another thought curled through my head, and I knew Kieran was thinking the same thing. Had my father known about me before Kieran did?

Kieran wrapped his arms around me. "He wouldn't have known your specialty before we tested you," he said, answering my unspoken question. "No one could've known that, not even your mother. Powerful in magic, sure. Some sort of Necromancer or Medium, definitely. But not a Spirit Walker. The abilities you knew how to use weren't enough for someone to classify your magic without the test. Given my father didn't even know about the test, there's no way Magnus knew.

The question is, when Magnus did figure out what you were...why didn't he act? Why help, but leave you as you were?"

Tingles ran through my body. Only Magnus could answer that question. And one day, when we did have that protection Kieran spoke of, I desperately wanted to ask.

Chapter 33

ALEXIS

I HELD KIERAN'S hand as we walked along the sandy path leading to the cliff overlooking the ocean. It was the overlook where I'd first agreed to work for him. It was now one of the few places we could escape a life in the limelight and steal a few quiet moments alone.

I sorely needed it.

It had been one month since the incident with Lydia, and even though Amber had only sent choice bits of the footage to a select group of powerful people, someone had leaked. Maybe even Lydia's own staff had leaked it. Regardless, various parts of the battle had gone viral. Among the favorites were a few clips that showed the more terrifying aspects of my magic. In one, I looked at a group of Lydia's people and they dropped bonelessly to the ground. In another, a few of the enemy forces fell, only to rise again and charge back against their own people. I'd embodied the tales and legends of old and wrapped them in modern times. Any fear of my magic that had died down had found a resurgence.

Some called for my death, some thought I should be locked up, and some thought I was actually Satan. The last two were primarily cries from Chesters.

Surprisingly, magical San Francisco had come together to cheer me on. They combated the naysayers with their pride in me. The magic wasn't as scary when you were protected by it, I wagered.

It was Dylan who'd really blown the world away, although not solely because of his magic. For the first time, the magical world at large learned that Amell Maccini was still alive. That he'd chosen to join Kieran's team over anyone else's. His videos were watched over and over, but it was the video where he jerked me back and fried the enemy that had gotten the most engagement. He was dubbed a white knight, incredibly handsome and gallant. He was the savior of the mistress of magical San Francisco. He was the most eligible bachelor of the year.

He was not happy with all the publicity, and now all of the guys made fun of him ruthlessly.

My magic had won "scariest" and "deadliest" in internet polls, but his had won for "best all-around magic." Lightning was pretty; corpses weren't. It wasn't a fair competition.

Thane was the third favorite, hitting biggest with younger men. I had watched his videos multiple times. That guy was crazy fun to watch! Best viewed from a distance, of course. He'd made mincemeat of that place. He'd thrown people out of windows and smashed through walls, furniture, and glass. At one stage, he'd jumped up and grabbed a chandelier, torn it down, then used it as a bowling ball across a hall filled with glass cases. People had run from him in every room, not even trying to tear him down.

Strangely, the cats didn't appear in any of the video feeds. Although there was plenty of evidence of their presence—people were tackled and mauled on camera—they didn't show up. Harding hadn't come around for a while, so I couldn't ask him about it, and because of my promise not to control him, I didn't want to summon him. We still hadn't named the cats, but it was clear they'd be staying with us. Also, they were both well past my knees now. I only hoped they'd stop growing soon.

"Have you heard from him?" I asked Kieran as a gentle breeze mussed my hair. My long, light blue colored dress flared out behind me.

"Magnus?" He glanced at me for an affirmation. "Not a word. As promised, I lightened up my meddling with financial and trade matters concerning his territory. I wasn't doing anything against the rules, but I was intentionally badgering him. I pulled back on that to just…being present in those respects. He's pulled back on some aggravating things, as well. We're just circling each other right now. There's been no direct contact. Anything with you?"

"Nothing." We wound through some scraggly dune bushes. The pounding of the ocean against the cliff filled the air with sea salt. "I'm not sure what I was expecting, but whatever it was...it didn't happen."

"That's not to say it won't. You have to remember, time moves slower for an immortal, especially one who's his age."

"Hearing from him might not be a good thing, anyway."

Kieran squeezed my hand. "As to that, I have no idea. No matter how much I think on his actions, some of the pieces don't fit. My best guess is that he's conflicted. My mom once told me that biology is a funny thing. When you have a child, there is a primal part of you that is wired to protect that child. It's not something you can easily shrug off. My father had no problem killing people, including his closest elite, and he would've killed me at the end, but I don't think he would've taken any pride in it. He was conflicted about me a lot of his life, I think, because of my mother. Magnus might be wrestling with his own demons. He clearly wanted to help you. He wanted you to succeed. He could've kidnapped you and forced you to join his team...so many times I hate even thinking about it. But he didn't. When he easily could have, he didn't. The only effort he made was halfhearted, and it's possible he only acted to preempt Aaron. There is something to that."

I sighed and pushed the thought away. There was no use obsessing over it—Magnus hadn't reached out to me, and I couldn't exactly call him up to chat. I was vulnerable and gullible when it came to this part of my life, and I didn't want him to take advantage. He might be conflicted, but he was still one of the more ruthless Demigods. I had to remember Magnus was an old pro at kid killing.

"How much did Daisy pack away, did you ever ask?" Kieran asked as we walked over the little knoll.

"I don't know. Whenever I ask, she tells me to mind my business. Dylan said it was a small fortune, and that he's teaching her to invest it. Did he tell you what she tried to do for him?"

"Giving him part of her savings? Yeah. That's a..." Kieran shook his head then squeezed my hand again, and we ambled on. "She's a damn good kid. She's hard, but her heart is in the right place. She's learned from you to help people in a tight spot."

"I think it's good for Dylan to have younger people around. People that still need looking after. He's got some serious scars. He's taking pains with Mordecai's training, as well, teaching him to react to the magic of Zeus. He hasn't said anything, but it seems like he feels more comfortable with them anchoring our crew."

"We *all* like having the kids around. They remind us that strategy and politics is a job, and family and a community is a life. A good life."

I opened my mouth to reply, and then stopped dead.

The concrete bench that used to perch on the cliff's edge had been replaced. In fact, the whole cliff face had been replaced.

Stone steps had been carved into the rock, leading down to a stone seat, carved directly into the cliff side with the polished surface Jerry was known for. The viewing platform was protected by a decorative rock banister.

"Shall we?" Kieran put out his hand to help me down.

The sand gathered in the creases on the soles of his shiny black dress shoes. His white trousers and open white jacket blew in the breeze, his light blue dress shirt, nearly the same color as my dress, pressing against his cut chest. His stormy eyes were subdued, sparkling with the love I felt blazing through our soul link, and the sun bathed his heart-throbbingly handsome face.

Tears in my eyes, I stepped back to snap a picture with my phone. I showed him the image with a smile. "For when I make a creepy fountain of you. It'll be this picture, right here."

He laughed, his smile boosting his handsomeness, and his Selkie magic stroked me in a way that made me gasp. He brought up his phone. "I'd better do a creepy fountain, too. I don't want to be out-creeped."

I took his hand and let him lead me down to the viewing area cut into the side of the cliff. A wave crashed far below, sending a sheet of mist up into the air. A rainbow sparkled within the haze.

"I've used my position for evil and rezoned this area," Kieran said as we stood at the rock banister. "I bought the permission from the non-magical government and then bought the land. Money talks. It's just a little slice—this little slice—but this part of the cliff is ours."

I wrapped my arms around his middle. "Jerry did a wonderful job. It's beautiful. Thank you."

He turned to me, pulling back just a bit so I could see his face. "Since the moment we met, we've been on a hard road. We've faced incredible danger—constant, incredible danger. Through it, you've stayed by my side. You've supported me when most people would've walked away. You gave me a family when I'd just lost mine. Magnus said that my father could see potential in people and create something great out of them. He was right, in a way, but while my father shaped my skills, I would've become morally bankrupt under his guidance. I would've hurt more than I helped. You've shaped my heart. You've made me a better man. A better leader. I owe you my life. I owe you my everything."

He sank down to a knee before me, and tears instantly clouded my vision again.

"Without you, there would be no me, Alexis," he said, and love poured through our links. It pooled in his eyes. He reached into his pocket and took out a little black velvet box. He opened the lid, revealing a gorgeous diamond center stone accented with blue and black gems, symbolic of the merging of our magics. "I love you with all my heart. I would give you everything that is mine. All I want is you, for the rest of my days and beyond. I will love you forever. Alexis Price, will you marry me?"

Tears streamed down my face. Sobs bubbled up through my middle. I barely registered his guys and the others coming up the path toward the cliff.

"Yes," I said, putting out my hand. "Yes! I love you."

With a triumphant smile, he slipped the ring onto my finger and stood, capturing my lips with his. The rock shuddered under our feet, nothing more than a pleasing vibration, Jerry giving his congratulations. Red rose petals caught the sun as they fluttered out over the ocean and danced in the air, Donovan's touch. Lightning came down from a suddenly building storm, curving into the shape of a heart, over and over, Dylan's support. Large rainbows blossomed into light shows,

Boman's congrats. A dead body pitched over the side and gave a thumbs-up on the way down.

"Bria's magic doesn't really match this scene," I said, watching it like I might a car wreck.

"It would've been really embarrassing if you'd said no," Kieran said, then kissed me again. "I love you, Alexis. You've made me the happiest man alive."

I let our kiss linger, reveling in the feel of him, before everyone came down to join us, all smiles and congratulations. I hugged my kids and stood with Kieran as we looked out over the tranquil waters. It might've been a hard road, but sometimes the hardest roads took you to the best destinations. I'd found my happily ever after.

THE END.

About the Author

K.F. Breene is a Wall Street Journal, USA Today, Washington Post, Amazon Most Sold Charts and #1 Kindle Store bestselling author of paranormal romance, urban fantasy and fantasy novels. With over three million books sold, when she's not penning stories about magic and what goes bump in the night, she's sipping wine and planning shenanigans. She lives in Northern California with her husband, two children and out of work treadmill.

Sign up for her newsletter to hear about the latest news and receive free bonus content.

www.kfbreene.com

Lightning Source UK Ltd.
Milton Keynes UK
UKHW010642171122
412355UK00005B/393